MOTHERS & DAUGHTERS

MOTHERS & DAUGHTERS

AN anthology

ALBERTO MANGUEL

CHRONICLE BOOKS
SAN FRANCISCO

See page 354 for a continuation of the copyright page.

Library of Congress Cataloging-in-Publication Data:
    Mothers and daughters : an anthology / [edited by] Alberto Manguel.
        p. cm.
    ISBN 0-8118-1629-X
    1. Mothers and daughters—Fiction. 2. Short stories.
    I. Manguel, Alberto.
PN6120.95.M7M68 1998
808.83'1083520431—dc21   97-32273
                                                              CIP

Book designed by Carole Goodman
Book composition by Suzanne Scott

Printed in the United States of America.

Distributed in Canada by Raincoast Books
8680 Cambie Street
Vancouver, British Columbia V6P 6M9

10 9 8 7 6 5 4 3 2 1

Chronicle Books
85 Second Street
San Francisco, California 94105

Web Site: www.chronbooks.com

To Barbara and Celia Reynaud

TABLE OF contents

INTRODUCTION

alas, I come to the subject as a foreigner entering an alien culture. This is the country of women, mothers and daughters, from which I, as a male, am barred. My knowledge of the country comes from its literature, from translated experiences. My only passport is that of a reader.

Or perhaps that of a fellow traveller. I watched my mother assisting my ninety-year-old grandmother through the treacherous geography of old age, I see my daughters guiding their mother through their own uncharted brave new worlds, and I compare their explorations with my own, undertaken in similar but different places under other skies.

There is, however, a shared essential experience, the experience of reflection. We are like the brittle Venusians invented by Theodore Sturgeon, creatures made of mirrors. Men or women, we hold ourselves up to our children, like our parents held themselves up to us. Clear or distorted, cracked or whole, we reflect back as we were reflected, the shades of experience and the glimmers of identity. "Parents," wrote George Santayana in the early years of this century, "lend their children their experience and a vicarious memory; children endow their parents with a vicarious immortality."

Cosmogonies load these images with responsibilities of which we are seldom or vaguely aware. For each of her daughters, Eve is a differently monstrous mother, vast as the earth and as nurturing, but also as invidious and as ruthless; and these daughters hardly suspect that behind the breast that fed them looms an entire mythology of She, who gave birth to us all. In the Judeo-Christian tradition, in Buddhism, in Islam, she has been expelled from the Pantheon, relegated to intercessionary or charitable roles; the triumphant deity is male, and in His image, we are told, we are made. Saint Augustine conveniently pointed out that, because of this, no woman could claim to godliness. The mirrored line then, for women in our cultures, has been in the shadows, at night, under the moon, when societies can bring out the things they hide and stories are most often told.

Within the shuttered precincts to which society confines them, women have, over the ages, always told tales to one another. In eleventh-century Heian Japan, barred from the official court Chinese in which high literature was written and discussed, women invented for themselves private narrations that would crystalize in the world's first novel, Lady Murasaki's *Tale of Genji*. Stories were their source of learning, passed on from mothers to daughters, in which the landscapes and epic adventures and multifarious characters that populated their empire, and which they would rarely if ever see, would be brought to life in words. "Even shut away in the country," wrote the Heian Lady Sarashina, "I somehow came to hear that the world contained things known as tales, and from that moment my greatest desire was to read them for myself." But since she lived at some distance from the court, in a country town where books were not easily available, her sister and her stepmother became Lady Sarashina's doors to the ocean of stories. For Lady Sarashina, world and word became synonymous.

From this narrative chain came not only the experience of a woman's condition but a vocabulary that allowed a woman to translate her own learning. Saint Teresa of Avila, who from her earliest childhood had been a passionate reader, found in stories both faith and instruction. Lives of saints and novels of chivalry excited her with the ideas of adventure and martyrdom, and at the age of seven she ran away from her home with the intention of roaming the world and converting the infidel. Later, seeking to explain the mysteries of her religious visions in the *Interior Castle*,

9

she resorted not to the bombastic vocabulary of theology but to domestic metaphors, to the language of her mother and her aunts, comparing for instance the abundance of divine revelations in the soul's chambers to the hodgepodge richness of pots and pans, tastes and odors in her mother's kitchen. "Think in terms of the domestic arts," Angela Carter urged writers in our time, pointing to the need to rescue from their alotted drabness the so-called inferior tasks of woman, recognizing their creative value, and giving them a place in the story.

In spite of such achievements, again and again women have had their narrative world altered by the codes of their fathers. The critic Marina Warner has pointed out that most fairy tales, now part of the anonymous dream-wealth of the world, were in fact created by women and made to undergo, in male retellings, a sex-change: the queen or mother disappears or dies, and the man, the king or father, comes to the foreground. In a more general way, women's tellings have been equated with gossiping, which, though said pejoratively, is in fact one of the glories of fiction. Henry James called the novel "literate gossip."

Throughout literature, mothers and daughters speak to one another in varying, and seemingly contradictory, moods. Their relationship is ambiguous; it can be one of teaching and learning tactics of survival, laid out in stories both protective and instructive, or one of effecting revenge, in stories that depict either the mother seeking to punish her daughter (or step-daughter) for her own sufferings or the mother, a female Lear, suffering at the hands of her daughter merely for being a woman.

Queen Clytemnestra, in the Greek myth, is the classic example of both the good and the evil mother. Clytemnestra has two daughters, Iphigenia and Electra. Agamemnon, her husband, in order to pacify the gods, decides to sacrifice Iphigenia. To avenge her daughter, Clytemnestra murders Agamemnon, which makes her an evil monster in her daughter Electra's eyes. But Clytemnestra is bound by the inexorability of her society's decreed role for women. If she respects her husband's wishes, she betrays one daughter; if she rebels against her husband, she antagonizes her other daughter. Whatever she does, as a mother, she must fail somewhere, to someone; she must either fail Iphigenia or fail Electra. I am reminded of a friend comparing childhood memories with her sister and discovering that what she took to be a happy, encouraging relationship with their mother, her sister remembered as bleak and miserable and destructive. If parents are mirrors, they are mirrors that send back confusing and variable images.

I wonder what mothers my daughters will be to *their* daughters, and how they will one day translate women's ancient wisdom into new and useful questions. Questions, and sometimes the shadow of an answer, appear in these stories which explore, through links of memory and blood, the most ordinary and most mysterious of relationships between woman and woman.

11

Alberto Manguel
London
June 1997

Elizabeth Jolley

One of the supreme examples of loyalty in the Old Testament is that of Ruth, the Moabite woman who abandoned her family, country, and faith to accompany her mother-in-law, Naomi, to Bethlehem. Because of her loyalty, Ruth became dearer to Naomi than her own seven sons, and Ruth's name was chosen to appear among the elect in the genealogy Matthew compiled for Jesus. Apparently what mothers (or mothers-in-law) expect from daughters is not what they expect from sons. Sons belong to another race, but with daughters a complicity can sometimes be found, a shared struggle, a common point of arrival if not of departure.

Born in England, educated in a Quaker school, brought up in a German-speaking household, and trained as a nurse in London, Elizabeth Jolley began her career as a writer after moving to Australia in 1959. Her eye is on the absurdities of common lives, the great unmentionable divide between convention and reality. Many of her stories are about ordinary people attempting valiant escapes from what the mother in "The Last Crop" calls "terrible dull lives with nothing to look forward to and no tastes of the pleasures she felt sure we were on this earth to enjoy."

THE LAST CROP

elizabeth jolley

in home science I had to unpick my darts as Hot Legs said they were all wrong and then I scorched the collar of my dress because I had the iron too hot.

'It's the right side too!' Hot Legs kept moaning over the sink as she tried to wash out the scorch. And then the sewing-machine needle broke and there wasn't a spare, that made her really wild and Peril Page cut all the notches off her pattern by mistake and that finished everything.

'I'm not ever going back there.' I took some bread and spread the butter thick, Mother never minded how much butter we had even when we were short of things. Mother was sitting at the kitchen table when I got home, she was wondering what to get my brother for his tea and she didn't say anything, so I said again, 'I'm finished with that place. I'm not going back.' So that was the two of us, my brother and me both leaving school before we should have, and he kept leaving jobs, one after the other, sometimes not even waiting for his pay.

'Well I s'pose they would have asked you to leave before the exam,' was all she said, which was what my brother said once on another occasion and, at the time, she had nearly killed him for saying what he said about the school not wanting expected failures to stay on.

'Whatever shall I get for him?' she said.

'What about a bit of lamb's fry and bacon,' I suggested and I spread more bread, leaving school so suddenly had made me hungry. She brightened up then and, as she was leaving to go up the terrace for her shopping, she said, 'You can come with me tomorrow and help me to get through quicker.'

So the next day I went to South Heights with her to clean these very posh apartments. Luxury all the way through, one place even has a fur-lined toilet. Mother doesn't like it as it clogs up the vacuum cleaner.

'Let's weigh ourselves,' I said when mother had had a quick look to see how much washing up there was.

'Just look at the mess,' she said. 'I really must get into the stove and the fridge today somehow I've been slipping lately.' She preferred them to eat out, which they did mostly.

'It's bringing the girls in that makes the mess,' she complained. 'Hair everywhere and panty hose dripping all over and grease on the stove. Why they want to cook beats me!'

'Let's weigh ourselves,' I got on the little pink scales.

'I'm bursting,' Mother said.

'Well weigh yourself before and after.'

'Whatever for!'

'Just for the interest,' I said and when I got off the scales I banged my head on the edge of the bathroom cupboard which is made all of looking glass.

'Really these expensive places!' Mother rubbed my head. 'All inconvenience not even a back door! Mind you, if there was a back door you'd step out and fall twenty-four floors to your death. And another thing, the washing machines drain into the bath. For all the money these places cost you can smell rubbish as soon as you enter the building and all day you can hear all the toilets flushing.'

Funnily enough her weight was no different after she'd been to the toilet and we worked like mad as Mother had some people coming into number eleven for a few hours.

'I want to get it nice for them,' she gave me the key to

go down ahead of her. 'I'll be finished here directly and I'll come down.' As I left she called me, 'Put some sheets in the freezer, the black ones, and see the bathroom's all nice and lay those photography magazines and the scent spray out on the bedside table.' She felt people had a better time in cold sheets. 'There's nothing worse than being all boiled up in bed,' she said.

Mother's idea came to her first when she was in jail the second time, it was after she had borrowed Mrs Lady's car to take my brother on a little holiday for his health. It was in the jail, she told me afterward, she had been struck forcibly by the fact that people had terrible dull lives with nothing to look forward to and no tastes of the pleasures she felt sure we were on this earth to enjoy.

'They don't ever get no pleasure,' she said to me. 'Perhaps the pictures now and then but that's only looking at other people's lives.' So she made it her business to get places in South Heights and quite soon she was cleaning several of the luxury apartments there.

She had her own keys and came and went as her work demanded and as she pleased.

'It's really gas in there,' she used one of my words to try and describe the place. And then bit by bit she began to let people from down our street, and other people too as the word spread, taste the pleasures rich people took for granted in their way of living. While the apartments were empty, you know, I mean while the people who lived there were away to their offices or to the hairdressers or to golf or horseriding or on business trips and the things rich people are busy with, she let other people in.

First, it was the old man who lived on the back verandah of our corner grocery store and then the shop keeper himself.

'They've been very deprived,' Mother said. She let them into Mr Baker's ground floor flat for an hour once a week while she brushed and folded Mr Baker's interesting clothes and washed his dishes. She admired Mr Baker though she had never seen him and she cherished his possessions for him. She once said she couldn't work for people if she didn't love them.

15

'How can you love anyone you never seen?' I asked.

'Oh I can see all about them all I need to know, even their shirt sizes and the colours of their socks tells you a lot,' she said. And then she said love meant a whole lot of things like noticing what people spent their money on and what efforts they made in their lives like buying bread and vegetables or books or records. All these things touched her she said. 'Even their pills are interesting,' she said. 'You can learn a lot about people just by looking in their bathroom cupboards.'

The first time I went with her I broke an ash tray, I felt terrible and showed her the pieces just when we were leaving. She wrote a note for Mr Baker, she enjoyed using his green biro and scrawled all over a piece of South Heights note paper.

'Very sorry about the ash tray, will try to find suitable replacement.' She put the broken pieces in an honest little heap by the note.

'Don't worry,' she said to me. 'Old Baldpate up in the penthouse has a whole cupboard of things she never uses, she's even got a twenty-four-piece dinner service; you don't see many of those these days. We'll find something there. Easy. She owes Mr Baker polish and an hour of his electric clothes drier so it'll all come straight.' She was forever borrowing things from one person for another and then paying them back from one to the other all without any of them knowing a thing about it.

As I was saying the old men came in once a week and had coffee served them on a tray with a thimble of French brandy and they sat in the bedroom, which was papered all over with nude arms and legs and bodies, they sat in armchairs in there as this had the best view of the swimming pool and they could watch the girls. There were always a lot of pretty girls around at South Heights with nothing to do except lie around and sunbake.

One of Mother's troubles was her own liking for expensive things, she didn't know why she had expensive tastes. She often sat at our kitchen table with a white dinner napkin on her lap.

'Always remember, they are napkins, only common people

16

call them serviettes,' she said and she would show me how to hold a knife with the palm of the hand over the handle. 'It's very important,' she said. Anyway there she sat, dinner napkin and all, and she would eat an avocado pear before bawling at me to go down the road to get our chips.

'I just hope they had a nice time,' Mother said when we cleaned up in number eleven that afternoon. 'It's terrible to be young and newly married living in her big family the way they have to. I'll bet they haven't got a bed to themselves in that house let alone a room. All that great family around them the whole time! A young couple need to be on their own. They'll have had a bit of peace and quiet in here.' Mother looked with approval at the carpeted secluded comfort of the apartment she'd let this young couple have for a morning.

'There's no need for young people to get babies now unless they really want to so I hope they've used their common sense and modern science,' Mother went on, she always talked a lot when she was working. She said when I wasn't with her she pulled faces at herself in all the mirrors and told herself off most of the time.

'Babies,' she said. 'Is all wind and wetting and crying for food and then sicking it up all over everything and no sooner does a baby grow up it's all wanting. Wanting and wanting this and that, hair and clothes and records and shoes and money and more money. And, after one baby there's always another and more wetting and sicking. Don't you ever tell me you haven't been warned!'

She washed out the black sheets and stuck them in the drier.

'Open the windows a bit,' she said to me. 'There's a smell of burned toast and scented groins in here. Young people always burn their toast, they forget about it with all that kissing. We'll get the place well aired before the Blacksons come home or they'll wonder what's been going on.'

On the way home Mother kept wondering whatever she could get for my brother's tea and she stood in the supermarket thinking and thinking and all she could come up with was fish fingers and a packet of jelly beans.

Somehow my brother looked so tall in the kitchen.

'You know I always chunder fish!' He was in a terrible mood. 'And I haven't eaten sweets in years!' He lit a cigarette and went out without any tea.

'If only he'd eat,' Mother sighed. She worried too much about my brother, the door slamming after him upset her and she said she wasn't hungry.

'If only he'd eat and get a job and live,' she said. 'That's all I ask.'

Sometimes at the weekends I went with Mother to look at Grandpa's valley. It was quite a long bus ride, we had to get off at the twenty-nine-mile peg, cross the Medulla Brook and walk up a country road with scrub and bush on either side till we came to some cleared acres of pasture which was the beginning of her father's land. She struggled through the wire fence hating the mud and the raw country air. She cursed out loud the old man for hanging on to the land and she cursed the money that was buried in the sodden meadows of cape weed and stuck fast in the outcrops of granite high up on the slopes where dead trees held up their gaunt arms, pitiful as if begging for something from the sky, she cursed the place because nothing could grow among their exposed gnarled boots as the topsoil had washed away. She cursed the pig styes built so solidly years ago of corrugated iron and old railway sleepers of jarrah, useful for nothing now but so indestructible they could not be removed.

She couldn't sell the land because Grandpa was still alive in a Home for the Aged and he wanted to keep the farm though he couldn't do anything with it. Even sheep died there. They either starved or got drowned depending on the time of year. It was either drought or flood, never anything happily between the two extremes.

There was a house there, weatherboard, with a wide wooden verandah all round it high off the ground. It could have been pretty and nice.

'Why don't we live there?' I asked her once.

'How could any of us get to work,' Mother said. 'It's too far from anywhere.'

And my brother said to her, 'It's only you as has to get to work,' and I thought Mother would kill him, she called him a good for nothing lazy slob.

'You're just nothing but a son of a bitch!' she screamed. He turned his eyes up till just the white showed.

'Well Dear Lady,' he said making his voice all furry and thick as if he'd been drinking. 'Dear Lady,' he said, 'if I'm the son of a bitch then you must be a bitch!' and he looked so like an idiot standing there we had to see the funny side and we roared our heads off.

The house was falling apart. The tenants were feckless, Mother suspected the man was working at some other job really. The young woman was mottled all over from standing too close to the stove and her little boys were always in wetted pants. They, the whole family, all had eczema. When a calf was born there it could never get up; that was the kind of place it was.

Every weekend Mother almost wept with the vexation of the land which was not hers and she plodded round the fences hating the scrub and the rocks where they invaded.

When we went to see Grandpa he wanted to know about the farm as he called it, and Mother tried to think of things to tell him to please him. She didn't say that the fence posts were crumbling away and that the castor-oil plants had taken over the yard so you couldn't get through to the barn.

There was an old apricot tree in the middle of the meadow, it was as big as a house and a terrible burden to us to get the fruit at the right time.

'Don't take that branch!' Mother screamed. 'I want it for the Atkinsons.' Grandpa owed those people some money and it made Mother feel better to give them apricots as a present. She liked to take fruit to the hospital too so that Grandpa could keep up his pride and self respect a bit.

In the full heat of the day I had to pick with an apron tied round me, it had big deep pockets for the fruit. I grabbed at the green fruit when I thought Mother wasn't looking and pulled it off, whole branches whenever I could, so it wouldn't be there to be picked later.

'Not them!' Mother screamed from the ground. 'Them's not ready yet. We'll have to come back tomorrow for them.'

I lost my temper and pulled off the apron full of fruit and hurled it down but it caught on a dumb branch and hung there laden and quite out of reach either from up the tree where I was or from the ground.

'Wait! Just you wait till I get hold of you!' Mother roared and pranced round the tree and I didn't come down till she had calmed down and by that time we had missed our bus and had to thumb a lift which is not so easy now as it used to be. On the edge of the little township the road seemed so long and desolate and seemed to lead nowhere and, when it got dark, all the dogs barked as if they were insane and a terrible loneliness came over me then.

'I wish we were home,' I said as cars went by without stopping.

'Wait a minute,' Mother said and in the dark she stole a piece of rosemary off someone's hedge. 'This has such a lovely fragrance,' she crushed it in her rough fingers and gave it to me to smell. 'Someone'll pick us up soon, you'll see,' she comforted.

One Sunday in the winter it was very cold but Mother thought we should go all the same. I had such a cold and she said, 'The country air will do you good,' and then she said, 'if it don't kill you first.' The cuckoo was calling and calling.

'Listen!' Mother said. 'That bird really sings up the scale,' and she tried to whistle like the cuckoo but she kept laughing and of course you can't whistle if you're laughing.

We passed some sheep huddled in a natural fold of furze and long withered grass, all frost-sparkled, the blackened trunk of a burnt and fallen tree made a kind of gateway to the sheep.

'Quick!' Mother said. 'We'll grab a sheep and take a bit of wool back to Grandpa.'

'But they're not our sheep.'

'Never mind!' And she was over the burnt tree in among the sheep before I could stop her. The noise was terrible. In all the commotion she managed to grab some wool.

'It's terrible dirty and shabby,' she complained, pulling at the shreds with her cold fingers. 'I don't think I've ever seen such miserable wool,' she said.

All that evening she was busy with the wool. She put it on the kitchen table.

'How will Modom have her hair done this week?' she addressed it. She tried to wash and comb it to make it look better. She put it on the table again and kept walking round and talking to it and looking at it from all sides of the table. Talk about laugh, she had me in fits, I was laughing till I ached.

'Let me put it round one of your curlers,' she said at last.

But even after being on a roller all night it still didn't look anything at all.

'I'm really ashamed of the wool,' Mother said.

'But it isn't ours.'

'I know but I'm ashamed all the same,' she said.

So at Mr Baker's she went in the toilet and cut a tiny bit off the white carpet, from the back part where it wouldn't show. It was so soft and silky, she wrapped it carefully in a piece of foil and in the evening we went to visit Grandpa. He was sitting with his poor paralysed legs under his tartan rug and the draughts board was set up beside him, he always had the black ones, but the other old men in the room had fallen asleep so he had no one to play a game with.

'Here's a bit of the wool clip Dad,' Mother said bending over and giving him a kiss. His whole face lit up.

'That's nice of you to bring it, really nice,' and he took the little corner of nylon carpet out of its wrapping.

'It's very good, deep and soft,' his old fingers stroked the smooth silkiness, he smiled at Mother as she searched his face for traces of disapproval or disappointment.

21

'They do wonderful things with sheep these days Dad,' she said.

'They do indeed,' he said, and all the time his fingers were feeling the bit of carpet.

'Are you pleased Dad?' she asked him anxiously. 'You are pleased aren't you?'

'Oh yes I am,' he assured her.

I thought I saw a moment of disappointment in his eyes, but the eyes of old people often look full of tears.

Mother was so tired, she was half asleep by the bed but she played three games of draughts and let him win them all and I watched the telly in the dinette with the night nurse. And then we really had to go as Mother had a full day ahead of her at the Heights, not so much work but a lot of arrangements and she would need every bit of her wits about her she said as we hurried home.

On the steps I tripped and fell against her.

'Ugh! I felt your bones!' Really she was so thin it hurt to bang into her.

'Well what d'you expect me to be, a boneless wonder? However could I walk if I didn't have bones to hold me up!'

The situation was terrible, really it was. Mother had such a hard life, for one thing, she was a good quick worker and she could never refuse people and so had too many jobs to get through as well as the other things she did. And the place where we lived was so ugly and cramped and squalid. She longed for a nice home with better things and she longed, more than anything, for my brother to get rid of what she called his deep unhappiness, she didn't know how he had got it but it was the reason for all his growling and his dislike of good food, she longed too for him to have some ambition or some aim in his life, she was always on about it to me.

Why wouldn't the old man agree to selling his land, it couldn't do him any good to keep it. His obstinacy really forced her to wishing he would die. She never said that to me but I could feel what she must be wishing because I found myself wishing him to die, every night I wished it, and whoever really wanted to wish someone to death!

It was only that it would sort things out a bit for us.

Next day we had to be really early as, though she had only one apartment to clean, she'd arranged a little wedding reception, with a caterer, in the penthouse. The lady who owned it, Baldpate Mother called her, had gone away on a trip for three months and during this time Mother had been able to make very good use of the place.

'They're a really splendid little set of rooms,' Mother said every time we went there. Once she tried on one of Baldpate's wigs it was one of those blue grey really piled-up styles and she looked awful. She kept making faces at herself in the mirror.

'I'm just a big hairy eagle in this,' she said. And when she put on a bathing cap later, you know, one of those meant to look like the petals of a flower she looked so mad I nearly died!

Baldpate was so rich she'd had a special lift put up the side of the building to have a swimming pool made after the South Heights had been built. Right up there on top of everything she had her own swimming pool.

'It makes me dizzy up here,' Mother said. 'Is my back hair all right?' I said it was, she was always asking about her back hair, it was awful but I never said so because what good would it have done. She never had time for her hair.

'Some day I'm going to write a book,' Mother said. We were setting out the glasses and silver forks carefully on the table by the window. Far below was the blue river and the main road with cars, like little coloured beetles, aimlessly crawling to and fro.

'Yes, I'm going to write this book,' she said. 'I want it brought out in paperjacks.'

'Paperbacks you mean.'

'Yes, like I said, paperjacks, with a picture on the front of a girl with her dress ripped off and her tied to a post in the desert and all the stories will have expensive wines in them and countries in Europe and the names of famous pictures and buildings and there will be wealthy people with expensive clothes and lovely jewels very elegant you know but doing and saying terrible things, the public will snap it up. I'll have scenes with people eating and making love at the same time. Maybe they'll want to make a film of it, it's what people want. It's called supply and demand.'

'That's a good title.'

She thought a moment. 'I hadn't thought of a title.' She had to interrupt her dream as the caterer arrived with his wooden trays of curried eggs and meat balls, and the guests who had got away quickly from the wedding were beginning to come in. Mother scattered frangipani blossoms made of plastic all over the rooms and, as soon as the bridal couple and their folks came in, we began serving.

'People really eat on these occasions,' Mother whispered to me. She really liked to see them enjoying themselves. 'Where else could they have such a pretty reception in such a nice place for the price.' She had even put out Baldpate's thick towels and she sent a quiet word round that any guest who would like to avail themselves of the facilities was welcome to have a shower, they were welcome to really enjoy the bathroom and there was unlimited hot water.

'Show them how to work those posh taps,' she whispered to me. 'They probably have never seen a bathroom like this one.' And smiling all over her face, she was a wonderful hostess everyone said so, she went on handing drinks and food to the happy guests.

In the middle of it all when Mother was whispering to me, 'It takes all the cheapness out of their lives to have an occasion like this and it's not hurting anybody at all. Even sordid things are all right if you have the right surroundings and don't hurt anyone—' she was interrupted by the doorbell ringing and ringing.

'Oh my Gawd!' Mother's one fear, the fear of being discovered, gripped. 'Open the balcony!' she pushed me to the double doors. 'This way to see the lovely view,' her voice rose over the noise of talking and laughing and eating. 'Bring your ice-cream and jelly out here and see the world.' She flung her arm towards the sky and came back in and hustled them all out onto the narrow space around the penthouse pool.

'No diving in,' she joked. 'Not in your clothes, anyhow.' She left me with the bewildered wedding and dashed to the door. I strained to listen trying to look unconcerned but I was that nervous. Baldpate could have come home sooner than she was expected and however would we explain about all these people in her penthouse. I couldn't hear a thing and my heart was thumping so I thought I would drop dead in front of everyone.

In a little while though Mother was back.

'A surprise guest brings luck to a wedding feast!' she announced and she drew all the people back inside for the champagne.

The surprise guest enjoyed herself very much. Mother had quite forgotten that she had told old Mrs Myer from down the bottom of our street that she could come any time to soak her feet and do her washing in the penthouse and she had chosen this day for both these things. One or two of the guests washed a few of their clothes as well to try out the machines.

'There's nothing so nice as clean clothes,' Mother said and then she proposed a special toast.

'Absent friend!' She was thinking lovingly of Baldpate she said to me. 'Absent friend!' And soon all the champagne was gone.

'Is my nose red?' she whispered to me anxiously during the speeches. Her nose was always red and got more so after wine of any sort or if she was shouting at my brother. She would really go for him and then ask him if her nose was red as if he cared. We could never see why she bothered so much.

'No,' I said.

'Oh! That's such a relief!' she said.

We were ages clearing up. Mother was terribly tired but so pleased with the success of the day. She seemed to fly round the penthouse singing and talking.

'Get this straight,' she said to me, 'one human being can't make another human being do anything. But if you are a mother this is the one thing you've got to do. Babies eat and sick and wet and sit up and crawl and walk and talk but after that you just got to make your children do the things they have to do in this world and that's why I got to keep shouting the way I do and, believe me, it's really hard!'

'Yes,' I said to her and then for some reason I began to cry. I really howled out loud. I knew I sounded awful bawling like that but I couldn't help it.

'Oh! I've made you work too hard!' Mother was so kind she made me sit down on the couch and she switched on the telly and made us both a cup of cocoa before we went home.

Grandpa was an old man and though his death was expected it was unexpected really and of course everything was suddenly changed. Death is like that. Mother said it just seemed like in five minutes, all at once, she had eighty-seven acres to sell. And there was the house too. Mother had a lot to do, she didn't want to let down the people at the South Heights so she turned up for work as usual and we raced through the apartments.

As it was winter there wasn't anything for old Fred and the Grocer to watch at the pool so Mother put on Mr Baker's record player for them and she let them wear the headphones. Luckily there were two sets, and you know how it is when you have these headphones on you really feel you are singing with the music, it's like your head is in beautiful cushions of voices and the music is right in your brain.

'Come and listen to them, the old crabs!' Mother beckoned to me, we nearly died of laughing hearing them bleating and moaning thinking they were really with those songs, they sounded like two old lost sheep.

'They're enjoying themselves, just listen!' I thought Mother would burst out crying she laughed herself silly behind the lounge room door.

'I'm so glad I thought of it,' she said. 'Whatever you do don't let them see you laughing like that!'

Mother decided she would sell the property by herself as she didn't want any agent to get his greasy hands on any percent

26

of that land. There was a man interested to buy it, Mother had kept him up her sleeve for years. I think he was an eye surgeon, Oscar Harvey, Mother said he should have a dance band with a name like that. Well Doctor Harvey wanted the valley he had said so ages ago and Mother was giving him first refusal.

We all three, Mother and myself and my brother, went out at the weekend to tidy things up a bit and to make sure those tenants didn't go off with things which had been Grandpa's and were now Mother's.

I don't think I ever noticed the country as being so lovely before, always I complained and wanted to go home as soon as I got there, but this time it was different. The birds were making a lot of noise.

'It's really like music,' Mother said. The magpies seemed to stroke the morning with their voices and we went slowly along the top end of the wet meadow.

'Summer land it's called,' Mother explained. And then suddenly we heard this strange noise behind us. And there was my brother running and running higher up on the slope, running like he was mad! And he was shouting and that was the noise we had heard. We didn't recognize his voice, it was like a man's, this voice shouting filling the valley. We hadn't ever seen him run like that before either, his thin arms and legs were flying in all directions and his voice lifted up in the wind.

'I do believe he's laughing!' Mother stood still sinking into the mud without noticing it. Tears suddenly came out of her eyes as she watched him. 'I think he's happy!' she said. 'He's happy!' she couldn't believe it. And I don't think I've ever seen her look so happy in her life before. We walked on up to the house. The tenant was at the side of the shed and he had just got the big tractor going and it had only crawled to the doorway, like a sick animal, and there it had stopped and he was supposed to get a firebreak made before the sale could go through.

My brother was nowhere to be seen but then I saw his thin white fingers poking through the castor oil plants in the yard.

'Halp!' and his fingers clutched the leaves and the air and then disappeared again. 'Halp! Halp!'

'He's stuck!' Mother was laughing, she pushed through the overgrown yard and my brother kept partly appearing and disappearing pretending he was really caught and she pulled at him and lost her balance and fell, both of them laughing like idiots. Funny I tell you it was a scream and for once I didn't feel cold there.

Mother and I started at once on the house sweeping and cleaning. They had repaired a few things and it was not as bad as she expected, there were three small rooms and quite a big kitchen. Grandpa had never lived there, he had only been able to buy the land late in life and had gone there weekends. He had always longed for the country.

'He was always on about a farm,' Mother said, she explained how he wanted to live here and was putting it all in order bit by bit when he had the stroke and after that of course he couldn't be there as it needed three people to move him around and whatever could he do out there paralysed like he was and then all those sad years in the hospital.

'It's not bad in here,' Mother said. 'It's nice whichever way you look out from these little windows and that verandah all round is really something! We'll sit there a bit later when we've finished.'

My brother came in, he was really keen about getting new fencing posts and wire and paint, he kept asking her, 'How about I paint the house?'

'Oh the new owner can do that,' Mother said, her head in the wood stove, she was trying to figure out the flues and how to clean them.

'Well, what if I paint the sheds then?' He seemed really interested. As she was busy she took no notice so he went off outside again.

Then we heard the tractor start up rattling and scraping over the rocks as it started up the slope to get into the scrub part which needed clearing to keep in with the regulations. Mother went out on to the verandah to shake the mats.

'Come and look!' she called me. And there was my brother
driving the tractor looking proud and as if he knew exactly what to do.

'He's like a prince on that machine!' Mother was pleased.
Of course he clowned a bit as he turned, pretending to fall off,
once he stopped and got off as if he had to push the great thing.
He hit the rocks and made a terrible noise and the tenant just
stood there staring at him.

'It's been years since the tractor got up there,' he said to
Mother.

We really had a wonderful day and, on the bus going
back, my brother fell asleep he was so unused to the fresh air his
nose and ears were bright red and Mother kept looking at him and
she was very quiet and I knew she was thinking and thinking.

Next day my brother went out there by himself to try to
get all the firebreaks finished, the agreement couldn't be signed
till they were done also the fencing posts. Before he left he told
Mother what to order and have sent out there, he suddenly
seemed to know all about everything. The change in him was like a
miracle, he was even quite nice to me.

As well as seeing to the sale there was Grandpa's funeral
and Mother said he had to have a headstone and she came up
with an inscription at the stone mason's.

'"It is in vain that ye rise thus early and eat the bread of
care, for He giveth his Beloved Sleep."'

I stared at her.

'I didn't know you knew the Bible.'

'I don't,' Mother said. 'It was in this morning's paper in
that little square "text for today" or something like it and I think
it's really beautiful and it's so suitable. I wouldn't mind having it
for myself but as I'm still after the bread of care and not as yet the
"Beloved" I'm putting it for Grandpa.'

There was no trouble about the price of the property.
This Dr Harvey really wanted it, he had asked about the valley
years ago, once when we were there, stopping his car just too
late to prevent it from getting bogged at the bottom end of the

29

track, and Mother had to say it wasn't for sale though, at the time, she said she would have given her right arm to be able to sell it but she promised him she'd let him know at once if she could ever put it on the market. We had to leave then for our bus and so were not able to help him get his car out of the mud. As he wasn't there by the next weekend we knew he must have got himself out somehow.

'You might as well come with me,' Mother said to me on the day the papers had to be signed. 'It won't do you any harm to learn how business is carried out, the best way to understand these things is to see for yourself.'

My brother had already gone by the early bus to the valley. Now that the property was ours in the true sense it seemed he couldn't be there enough even though it was about to belong to someone else. Mother watched him run off down our mean little street and she looked so thoughtful.

The weatherboard house at the top of the sunlit meadow kept coming into my mind too and I found I was comparing it all the time with the terrible back landing where our room and kitchen was. Having looked out of the windows of the cottage I realized how we had nothing to look at at home except the dustbins and people going by talking and shouting and coughing and spitting and hurrying all the time, having the same rushed hard life Mother had. Of course the money from the sale would make all the difference to Mother's life so I said nothing, she didn't say much except she seemed to argue with herself.

'Course the place means nothing, none of us ever came from there or lived there even.' I could hear her muttering as we walked.

No one can do anything with property, it doesn't matter how many acres it is, if you haven't any money, of course Mother needed the money so I didn't say out loud, 'Wouldn't it be lovely to live out there for a bit.' I guessed my brother was feeling the same though he never said anything but I saw him reading a bit of an old poultry magazine he must have picked up at the barber's place. As a little boy he never played much, Mother always said he stopped playing too soon. But he would often bring in a stray cat and beg to keep it and play with it and stroke it with a fondness we never saw him show any other way and he would walk several streets to a place where a woman had some fowls in her backyard and he would stand ages looking at them through a broken fence picket, perhaps some of Grandpa's farming blood was in him. I wondered if Mother was thinking the same things as I was but the next thing was we were in the lawyer's office. The doctor was there too, very nicely dressed. I could see Mother look at his well-laundered shirt with approval. The room was brown and warm and comfortable, all polished wood and leather and a window high up in the wall let in the sunshine so it came in a kind of dust-dancing spotlight on the corner of the great big desk.

I feel I will never forget that room for what happened there changed our lives in a way I could never even have dreamed of.

Well, we all sat down and I tried to listen as the lawyer spoke and read. It all sounded foreign to me. Acres I knew and roods and perches that was Hot Legs all over again, same with the hundreds and thousands of dollars, it was a bit like school and I began to think of clothes I would like and how I would have my hair. The lawyer was sorting pages. I gave up trying to follow things like 'searching the title', 'encumbered and unencumbered land', instead I thought about some kneeboots and a black coat with white lapels, fur I thought it was, and there was a little white round hat to go with it.

They were writing their names in turn on different papers, all of them busy writing.

'Here,' said the lawyer, Mr Rusk his name was, 'and here,' he pointed with his white finger for Mother to know where to put her name.

Mother suddenly leaned forward. 'I'm a little bit faint,' she said. She had a very strange look on her face.

'Don't you faint here in front of them,' I was that embarrassed.

31

Mr Rusk asked the secretary to fetch a glass of water.

'Thank you my dear,' Mother sipped the water. I was a bit afraid I can tell you as I don't think ever in my life had I seen Mother drink cold water straight like that.

'All right now?' Dr Harvey, the owner of so much money and now the owner of the lovely valley, looked at Mother gently. He really was a gentleman and a kind one too, I could see that.

'You see,' Mother said suddenly and her nose flushed up very red the way it does when she is full of wine or angry with my brother or, as it turned out in this case, when she had an idea. 'You see,' she said to the doctor, 'Dad longed to live in that house and to be in the valley. All his life he wished for nothing but having his farm, it was something in his blood and it meant everything to him and as it so happened he was never able to have his wish. Having waited so long for the valley yourself,' she went on to the doctor, 'You will understand and, loving the land as you do, you will understand how I feel now. I feel,' she said, 'I feel if I could be in the valley and live in the house and plant one crop there and just be there till it matures I feel Dad, your Grandpa,' she turned to me, 'I feel he would rest easier in his last resting place.' They looked at Mother and she looked back at them.

The doctor smiled kindly. 'Well,' he said, oh he was a generous man all right, he had just paid the whole price Mother asked. 'I don't see any harm in that.'

'It's not in the agreement,' Mr Rusk was quite annoyed but the doctor waved his hand to quieten old Rusk's indignation.

'It's a gentlemen's agreement,' and he came over and shook hands with Mother.

'That's the best sort,' Mother smiled up at him under her shabby brown hat.

Then the lawyer and the doctor had a bit of an argument and in the end the lawyer agreed to add in writing for them to sign that we could live in the house and be in the valley till the maturity of just one last crop.

'I wish your crop well,' the doctor came round the desk and shook hands with Mother again.

'Thank you,' Mother said.

* * *

'It's all settled and signed,' Mother told my brother in the evening. The few days of working in the country seemed to have changed him, he looked strong and sun tanned and, for once, his eyes had a bit of expression in them, usually he never revealed anything of himself by a look or a word except to be disagreeable. Mother always excused him saying the world wasn't the right place for him and his terrible mood was because he couldn't explain this to himself or to anyone and because he couldn't explain it he didn't know what to do about it. I thought he looked sad in his eyes even though we had had a bit of a spend for our tea we had ham off the bone and vanilla slices.

She told him how we could be there for one last crop.

'I'll paint the house then.'

'Good idea!' Mother said. 'We'll get the paint but we needn't rush, we can take our time getting things. We'll need a vehicle of some kind.'

'You haven't got your licence,' I said to my brother. Any other time he would have knocked me into next week for saying that.

'I'll get my test,' he said quietly.

'There's no rush,' Mother said.

'But one crop isn't very long.'

'It's long enough,' Mother said, she spent the evening studying catalogues she had picked up on the way home and she wrote a letter which she took out to post herself.

Mother was sorry to let down the people at the South Heights so badly but after the gentlemen's agreement everything seemed to happen differently and it was a bit of a rush for her. Already in her mind she was planning.

'We'll have the whole street out to a barbecue once the weather changes,' she said. They can come out on the eleven o'clock bus and walk up through the bottom paddocks. It'll be a

33

little taste of pleasure, a bit different, there's nothing like a change for people even for one day, it's as good as a holiday.'

The first night at the cottage seemed very quiet.

'I expect we'll get used to it,' Mother said. I meant to wake up and see the place as the sun came through the bush but I slept in and missed the lot.

Bit by bit Mother got things, oh it was lovely going out to spend, choosing new things like a teapot and some little wooden chairs which Mother wanted because they were so simple.

And then her crop came. The carter set down the boxes, they were like baskets only made of wood with wooden handles, he set them down along the edge of the verandah. They were all sewn up in sacking and every one was labelled with our name, and inside these boxes were a whole lot of tiny little seedlings, hundreds of them. When the carter had gone my brother lifted out one of the little plastic containers; I had never seen him doing anything so gently.

'What are they?'

'They're our crop. The last crop.'

'Yes I know but what are they?'

'Them? Oh they're a jarrah forest,' Mother said.

We looked at her.

'But that will take years and years to mature,' my brother said.

'I know,' she seemed unconcerned but the way her nose was going red I knew she was as excited about the little tiny seedling trees as we were. She of course had the idea already, it had to come upon us, the surprise of it I mean and we had to get over it.

'But what about Dr Harvey?' Somehow I could picture him pale and patient beside his car out on the lonely road which went through his valley looking longingly at his house and his meadows and his paddocks and at his slopes of scrub and bush.

'Well there's nothing in the gentlemen's agreement to say he can't come on his land whenever he wants to and have a look at us,' Mother said. 'We'll start planting tomorrow,' she said.

'We'll pick the best places and then clear the scrub and the dead stuff away as we go along. I've got full instructions as to how it's done.' She looked at her new watch. 'It's getting a bit late, I'll go for chips,' she said. 'I suppose I'll have to go miles for them from here.' She followed us into the cottage to get her purse. 'You'll be able to do your schooling by correspondence,' she said. 'I might even take a course myself!' It was getting dark quickly. 'Get a good fire going,' she said.

    We heard her drive down the track and, as she turned onto the road, we heard her crash the gears. My brother winced, he couldn't bear machinery to be abused but he agreed with me that she probably couldn't help it as it's been quite a while since she had anything to drive.

Sara Jeannette Duncan

In the late eighteenth century, as the French Revolution seemingly set out to question every social assumption, Donatien Alphonse, the Marquis de Sade, offered for consideration the basic notions of family on which society stood. "It is false to suppose," he argued in *Juliette,* "that you owe any feeling to the one issued from you; absurd to imagine that you owe it to your brothers, sisters, nephews, nieces. By what reason should blood establish obligations?" De Sade died in 1814, his question unanswered.

Born in Canada a mere forty-seven years later, of a Scottish father and an Irish mother who would not have countenanced, let alone read, the oeuvre of the scandalous Marquis, Sara Jeannette Duncan unknowingly grappled in her fiction with the question of the debt of blood. A novelist and a journalist, in her late twenties she travelled to India, where she met her husband and lived for the next three decades. Her last few years were spent in England. "A Mother in India," perhaps her clearest exploration of the subject, offers an answer that, in view of the social expectations of her time, is both uncompromisingly defiant and utterly compassionate.

A MOTHER IN INDIA

sara jeannette duncan

CHAPTER I

there were times when we had to go without
puddings to pay John's uniform bills, and always I did the facings
myself with a cloth-ball to save getting new ones. I would have
polished his sword, too, if I had been allowed; I adored his sword.
And once, I remember, we painted and varnished our own dog-
cart, and very smart it looked, to save fifty rupees. We had nothing
but our pay—John had his company when we were married, but
what is that?—and life was made up of small knowing economies,
much more amusing in recollection than in practise. We were
sodden poor, and that is a fact, poor and conscientious, which was
worse. A big fat spider of a money-lender came one day into the
veranda and tempted us—we lived in a hut, but it had a veranda—
and John threatened to report him to the police. Poor when everybody else had enough to live in the open-handed Indian fashion,
that was what made it so hard; we were alone in our sordid little
ways. When the expectation of Cecily came to us we made out to
be delighted, knowing that the whole station pitied us, and when
Cecily came herself, with a swamping burst of expense, we kept
up the pretense splendidly. She was peevish, poor little thing, and
she threatened convulsions from the beginning, but we both knew
that it was abnormal not to love her a great deal, more than life,

immediately and increasingly; and we applied ourselves honestly to do it, with the thermometer at a hundred and two, and the nurse leaving at the end of a fortnight because she discovered that I had only six of everything for the table. To find out a husband's virtues, you must marry a poor man. The regiment was under-officered as usual, and John had to take parade at daylight quite three times a week; but he walked up and down the veranda with Cecily constantly till two in the morning when a little cool-ness came. I usually lay awake the rest of the night in fear that a scorpion would drop from the ceiling on her. Nevertheless, we were of excellent mind towards Cecily; we were in such terror, not so much of failing in our duty towards her as towards the ideal standard of mankind. We were very anxious indeed not to come short. To be found too small for one's place in nature would have been odious. We would talk about her for an hour at a time, even when John's charger was threatening glanders and I could see his mind perpetually wandering to the stable. I would say to John that she had brought a new element into our lives—she had indeed!—and John would reply, "I know what you mean," and go on to prophesy that she would "bind us together." We didn't need binding together; we were more to each other, there in the desola-tion of that arid frontier outpost, than most husbands and wives; but it seemed a proper and hopeful thing to believe, so we believed it. Of course the real experience would have come, we weren't monsters; but fate curtailed the opportunity. She was just five weeks old when the doctor told us that we must either pack her home immediately or lose her, and the very next day John went down with enteric. So Cecily was sent to England with a sergeant's wife who had lost her twins, and I settled down under the direction of a native doctor, to fight for my husband's life, without ice or proper food, or sickroom comforts of any sort. Ah! Fort Samila, with the sun glaring up from the sand!—however, it is a long time ago now. I trusted the baby willingly to Mrs Berry and to Providence, and did not fret; my capacity for worry, I suppose, was completely absorbed. Mrs Berry's letter, describing the child's improvement on the voyage and safe arrival came, I remember, the day on which John was allowed his first solid mouthful; it had been a long siege. "Poor little wretch!" he said when I read it aloud; and after that Cecily became an episode.

She had gone to my husband's people; it was the best arrangement. We were lucky that it was possible; so many children had to be sent to strangers and hirelings. Since an unfortunate infant must be brought into the world and set adrift, the haven of its grandmother and its Aunt Emma and its Aunt Alice certainly seemed providential. I had absolutely no cause for anxiety, as I often told people, wondering that I did not feel a little all the same. Nothing, I knew, could exceed the conscientious devotion of all three Farnham ladies to the child. She would appear upon their somewhat barren horizon as a new and interesting duty, and the small additional income she also represented would be almost nominal compensation for the care she would receive. They were excellent persons of the kind that talk about matins and vespers, and attend both. They helped little charities and gave little teas, and wrote little notes, and made deprecating allowance for the eccentricities of their titled or moneyed acquaintances. They were the subdued, smiling, unimaginatively dressed women on a small definite income that you meet at every rectory garden-party in the country, a little snobbish, a little priggish, wholly conventional, but apart from these weaknesses, sound and simple and dignified, managing their two small servants with a display of the most exact traditions, and keeping a somewhat vague and belated but constant eye upon the doings of their country as chronicled in a bi-weekly paper. They were all immensely interested in royalty, and would read paragraphs aloud to each other about how the Princess Beatrice or the Princess Maud had opened a fancy bazaar, looking remarkably well in plain grey poplin trimmed with Irish lace—an industry which, as is well known, the Royal Family has set its heart on rehabilitating. Upon which Mrs Farnham's comment invariably would be, "How thoughtful of them, dear!" and Alice would usually say, "Well, if I were a princess, I should like something nicer than

39

plain grey poplin." Alice, being the youngest, was not always expected to think before she spoke. Alice painted in water-colours, but Emma was supposed to have the most common sense.

They took turns in writing to us with the greatest regularity about Cecily; only once, I think, did they miss the weekly mail, and that was when she threatened diphtheria and they thought we had better be kept in ignorance. The kind and affectionate terms of these letters never altered except with the facts they described—teething, creeping, measles, cheeks growing round and rosy, all were conveyed in the same smooth, pat, and proper phrases, so absolutely empty of any glimpse of the child's personality that after the first few months it was like reading about a somewhat uninteresting infant in a book. I was sure Cecily was not uninteresting, but her chroniclers were. We used to wade through the long, thin sheets and saw how much more satisfactory it would be when Cecily could write to us herself. Meanwhile we noted her weekly progress with much the feeling one would have about a far-away little bit of property that was giving no trouble and coming on exceedingly well. We would take possession of Cecily at our convenience; till then, it was gratifying to hear of our unearned increment in dear little dimples and sweet little curls.

She was nearly four when I saw her again. We were home on three months' leave; John had just got his first brevet for doing something which he does not allow me to talk about in the Black Mountain country; and we were fearfully pleased with ourselves. I remember that excitement lasted well up to Port Said. As far as the Canal, Cecily was only one of the pleasures and interests we were going home to: John's majority was the thing that really gave savour to life. But the first faint line of Europe brought my child to my horizon; and all the rest of the way she kept her place, holding out her little arms to me, beckoning me on. Her four motherless years brought compunction to my heart and tears to my eyes; she should have all the compensation that could be. I suddenly realized how ready I was—how ready!—to have her back. I rebelled fiercely against John's decision that we must not take her with us on our return to the frontier; privately, I resolved to dispute it, and, if necessary, I saw myself abducting the child— my own child. My days and nights as the ship crept on were full of a long ache to possess her; the defrauded tenderness of the last four years rose up in me and sometimes caught at my throat. I could think and talk and dream of nothing else. John indulged me as much as was reasonable, and only once betrayed by a yawn that the subject was not for him endlessly absorbing. Then I cried and he apologized. "You know," he said, "it isn't exactly the same thing. I'm not her mother." At which I dried my tears and expanded, proud and pacified. I was her mother!

Then the rainy little station and Alice, all-embracing in a damp waterproof, and the drive in the fly, and John's mother at the gate and a necessary pause while I kissed John's mother. Dear thing, she wanted to hold our hands and look into our faces and tell us how little we had changed for all our hardships; and on the way to the house she actually stopped to point out some alterations in the flower-borders. At last the drawing-room door and the smiling housemaid turning the handle and the unforgettable picture of a little girl, a little girl unlike anything we had imagined, starting bravely to trot across the room with the little speech that had been taught her. Half-way she came; I suppose our regards were too fixed, too absorbed, for there she stopped with a wail of terror at the strange faces, and ran straight back to the outstretched arms of her Aunt Emma. The most natural thing in the world, no doubt. I walked over to a chair opposite with my hand-bag and umbrella and sat down—a spectator, aloof and silent. Aunt Emma fondled and quieted the child, apologizing for her to me, coaxing her to look up, but the little figure still shook with sobs, hiding its face in the bosom that it knew. I smiled politely, like any other stranger, at Emma's deprecations, and sat impassive, looking at my alleged baby breaking her heart at the sight of her mother. It is not amusing even now to remember the anger that I felt. I did not touch her or speak to her; I simply sat observing my alien possession, in the frock I had not made and the sash I had not chosen, being coaxed and kissed and protected and petted by its Aunt Emma. Presently I asked to be taken to my room, and there I locked myself in for two atrocious hours. Just once my heart beat high, when a tiny knock came and a timid, docile little voice said that tea was ready. But I heard the rustle of a skirt, and guessed the directing angel in Aunt Emma, and responded, "Thank you, dear, run away and say that I am coming," with a pleasant visitor's inflection which I was able to sustain for the rest of the afternoon.

"She goes to bed at seven," said Emma.

"Oh, does she?" said I. "A very good hour, I should think."

"She sleeps in my room," said Mrs Farnham.

"We give her mutton broth very often, but seldom stock soup," said Aunt Emma. "Mamma thinks it is too stimulating."

"Indeed?" said I, to all of it.

They took me up to see her in her crib, and pointed out, as she lay asleep, that though she had "a general look" of me, her features were distinctively Farnham.

"Won't you kiss her?" asked Alice. "You haven't kissed her yet, and she is used to so much affection."

"I don't think I could take such an advantage of her," I said.

They looked at each other, and Mrs Farnham said that I was plainly worn out. I mustn't sit up to prayers.

If I had been given anything like reasonable time I might have made a fight for it, but four weeks—it took a month each way in those days—was too absurdly little; I could do nothing. But I would not stay at mamma's. It was more than I would ask of myself, that daily disappointment under the mask of gratified discovery, for long.

I spent an approving, unnatural week, in my farcical character, bridling my resentment and hiding my mortification with pretty phrases; and then I went up to town and drowned my sorrows in the summer sales. I took John with me. I may have been Cecily's mother in theory, but I was John's wife in fact.

We went back to the frontier, and the regiment saw a lot of service. That meant medals and fun for my husband, but economy and anxiety for me, though I managed to be allowed as close to the firing line as any woman.

Once the Colonel's wife and I, sitting in Fort Samila, actually heard the rifles of a punitive expedition cracking on the other side of the river—that was a bad moment. My man came in after fifteen hours' fighting, and went sound asleep, sitting before his food with his knife and fork in his hands. But service makes heavy demands besides those on your wife's nerves. We had saved two thousand rupees, I remember, against another run home, and it all went like powder, in the Mirzai expedition; and the run home diminished to a month in a boarding-house in the hills.

Meanwhile, however, we had begun to correspond with our daughter, in large round words of one syllable, behind which, of course, was plain the patient guiding hand of Aunt Emma. One could hear Aunt Emma suggesting what would be nice to say, trying to instil a little pale affection for the far-off papa and mamma. There was so little Cecily and so much Emma—of course, it could not be otherwise—that I used to take, I fear, but perfunctory joy in these letters. When we went home again I stipulated absolutely that she was to write to us without any sort of supervision—the child was ten.

"But the spelling!" cried Aunt Emma, with lifted eyebrows.

"Her letter aren't exercises," I was obliged to retort; "she will do the best she can."

We found her a docile little girl, with nice manners, a thoroughly unobjectionable child. I saw quite clearly that I could not have brought her up so well; indeed, there were moments when I fancied that Cecily, contrasting me with her aunt, wondered a little what my bringing up could have been like. With this reserve of criticism on Cecily's part, however, we got on very tolerably, largely because I found it impossible to assume any responsibility towards her, and in moments of doubt or discipline referred her to her aunts. We spent a pleasant summer with a little girl in the house whose interest in us was amusing, and whose outings it was gratifying to arrange; but when we went back, I had no desire to take her with us. I thought her very much better where she was.

Then came the period which is filled, in a subordinate degree, with Cecily's letters. I do not wish to claim more than I ought; they were not my only or even my principal interest in life. It was a long period; it lasted till she was twenty-one. John had had promotion in the meantime, and there was rather more money, but he had earned his second brevet with a bullet through one lung, and the doctors ordered our leave to be spent in South Africa. We had photographs, we knew she had grown tall and athletic and comely, and the letters were always very creditable. I had the unusual and qualified privilege of watching my daughter's development from ten to twenty-one, at a distance of four thousand miles, by means of the written word. I wrote myself as provocatively as possible; I sought for every string, but the vibration that came back across the seas to me was always other than the one I looked for, and sometimes there was none. Nevertheless, Mrs Farnham wrote me that Cecily very much valued my communications. Once when I had described an unusual excursion in a native state, I learned that she had read my letter aloud to the sewing circle. After that I abandoned description, and confined myself to such intimate personal details as no sewing circle could find amusing. The child's own letters were simply a mirror of the ideas of the Farnham ladies; that must have been so, it was not altogether my jaundiced eye. Alice and Emma and grandmamma paraded the pages in turn. I very early gave up hope of discoveries in my daughter, though as much of the original as I could detect was satisfactorily simple and sturdy. I found little things to criticize, of course, tendencies to correct; and by return post I criticized and corrected, but the distance and the deliberation seemed to touch my maxims with a kind of arid frivolity, and sometimes I tore them up. One quick, warm-blooded scolding would have been worth a sheaf of them. My studied little phrases could only inoculate her with a dislike for me without protecting her from anything under the sun.

However, I found she didn't dislike me, when John and I went home at last to bring her out. She received me with just a hint of kindness, perhaps, but on the whole very well.

CHAPTER II

John was recalled, of course, before the end of our furlough, which knocked various things on the head; but that is the sort of thing one learned to take with philosophy in any lengthened term of Her Majesty's service. Besides, there is usually sugar for the pill; and in this case it was a Staff command bigger than anything we expected for at least five years to come. The excitement of it when it was explained to her gave Cecily a charming color. She took a good deal of interest in the General, her papa; I think she had an idea that his distinction would alleviate the situation in India, however it might present itself. She accepted that prospective situation calmly; it had been placed before her all her life. There would always be a time when she should go and live with papa and mamma in India, and so long as she was of an age to receive the idea with rebel tears she was assured that papa and mamma would give her a pony. The pony was no longer added to the prospect; it was absorbed no doubt in the general list of attractions calculated to reconcile a young lady to a parental roof with which she had no practical acquaintance. At all events, when I feared the embarrassment and dismay of a pathetic parting with darling grandmamma and the aunties, and the sweet cat and the dear vicar and all the other objects of affection, I found an agreeable unexpected philosophy.

I may add that while I anticipated such broken-hearted farewells I was quite prepared to take them easily. Time, I imagined, had brought philosophy to me also, equally agreeable and equally unexpected.

It was a Bombay ship, full of returning Anglo-Indians. I looked up and down the long saloon tables with a sense of relief and of solace; I was again among my own people. They belonged to Bengal and to Burma, to Madras and to the Punjab, but they

45

were all my people. I could pick out a score that I knew in fact, and there were none that in imagination I didn't know. The look of wider seas and skies, the casual experienced glance, the touch of irony and of tolerance, how well I knew it and how well I liked it! Dear old England, sitting in our wake, seemed to hold by comparison a great many soft, unsophisticated people, immensely occupied about very particular trifles. How difficult it had been, all the summer, to be interested! These of my long acquaintance belonged to my country's Executive, acute, alert, with the marks of travail on them. Gladly I went in and out of the women's cabins and listened to the argot of the men; my own ruling, administering, soldiering little lot.

Cecily looked at them askance. To her the atmosphere was alien, and I perceived that gently and privately she registered objections. She cast a disapproving eye upon the wife of a Conservator of Forests, who scanned with interest a distant funnel and laid a small wager that it belonged to the *Messageries Maritimes.* She looked with a straightened lip at the crisply stepping women who walked the deck in short and rather shabby skirts with their hands in their jacket-pockets talking transfers and promotions; and having got up at six to make a water-colour sketch of the sunrise, she came to me in profound indignation to say that she had met a man in his pyjamas; no doubt, poor wretch, on his way to be shaved. I was unable to convince her that he was not expected to visit the barber in all his clothes.

At the end of the third day she told me that she wished these people wouldn't talk to her; she didn't like them. I had turned in the hour we left the Channel and had not left my berth since, so possibly I was not in the most amiable mood to receive a douche of cold water. "I must try to remember, dear," I said, "that you have been brought up altogether in the society of pussies and vicars and elderly ladies, and of course you miss them. But you must have a little patience. I shall be up tomorrow, if this beastly sea continues to go down; and then we will try to find somebody suitable to introduce to you."

"Thank you, mamma," said my daughter, without a ray of suspicion. Then she added consideringly, "Aunt Emma and Aunt Alice do seem quite elderly ladies beside you, and yet you are older than either of them, aren't you? I wonder how that is."

It was so innocent, so admirable, that I laughed at my own expense; while Cecily, doing her hair, considered me gravely. "I wish you would tell me why you laugh, mamma," quoth she; "you laugh so often."

We had not to wait after all for my good offices of the next morning. Cecily came down at ten o'clock that night quite happy and excited; she had been talking to a bishop, such a dear bishop. The bishop had been showing her his collection of photographs, and she had promised to play the harmonium for him at the eleven-o'clock service in the morning. "Bless me!" said I. "Is it Sunday?" It seemed she had got on very well indeed with the bishop, who knew the married sister, at Tunbridge, of her very greatest friend. Cecily herself did not know the married sister, but that didn't matter—it was a link. The bishop was charming. "Well, my love," said I—I was teaching myself to use these forms of address for fear she would feel an unkind lack of them, but it was difficult—"I am glad that somebody from my part of the world has impressed you favourably at last. I wish we had more bishops."

"Oh, but my bishop doesn't belong to your part of the world," responded my daughter sleepily. "He is travelling for his health."

It was the most unexpected and delightful thing to be packed into one's chair next morning by Dacres Tottenham. As I emerged from the music saloon after breakfast—Cecily had stayed below to look over her hymns and consider with her bishop the possibility of an anthem—Dacres's face was the first I saw; it simply illuminated, for me, that portion of the deck. I noticed with pleasure the quick toss of the cigar overboard as he recognized and bore down upon me. We were immense friends; John liked him too. He was one of those people who make a tremendous difference; in all our three hundred passengers there could be no one like him, certainly no one whom I could be more glad to see. We plunged at once into immediate personal affairs, we would get at the heart of them later. He gave his vivid word to everything he had seen and done; we laughed and exclaimed and were silent in a concert of admirable understanding. We were still unravelling, still demanding and explaining when the ship's bell began to ring for church, and almost simultaneously Cecily advanced towards us. She had a proper Sunday hat on, with flowers under the brim, and a church-going frock; she wore gloves and clasped a prayer-book. Most of the women who filed past to the summons of the bell were going down as they were, in cotton blouses and serge skirts, in tweed caps or anything, as to a kind of family prayers. I knew exactly how they would lean against the pillars of the saloon during the psalms. This young lady would be little less than a rebuke to them. I surveyed her approach; she positively walked as if it were Sunday.

"My dear," I said, "how *endimanchée* you look! The bishop will be very pleased with you. This gentleman is Mr Tottenham, who administers Her Majesty's pleasure in parts of India about Allahabad. My daughter, Dacres." She was certainly looking very fresh, and her calm grey eyes had the repose in them that has never known itself to be disturbed about anything. I wondered whether she bowed so distantly also because it was Sunday, and then I remembered that Dacres was a young man, and that the Farnham ladies had probably taught her that it was right to be very distant with young men.

"It is almost eleven, mamma."

"Yes, dear. I see you are going to church."

"Are you not coming, mamma?"

I was well wrapped up in an extremely comfortable corner. I had *La Duchesse Bleue* uncut in my lap, and an agreeable person to talk to. I fear that in any case I should not have been inclined to attend the service, but there was something in my daughter's intonation that made me distinctly hostile to the idea. I am putting things down as they were, extenuating nothing.

"I think not, dear."

"I've turned up two such nice seats."

"Stay, Miss Farnham, and keep us in countenance," said Dacres, with his charming smile. The smile displaced a look of discreet and amused observation. Dacres had an eye always for a situation, and this one was even newer to him than to me.

"No, no. She must run away and not bully her mamma," I said. "When she comes back we will see how much she remembers of the sermon," and as the flat tinkle from the companion began to show signs of diminishing, Cecily, with one grieved glance, hastened down.

"You amazing lady!" said Dacres. "A daughter—and such a tall daughter! I somehow never—"

"You knew we had one?"

"There was theory of that kind, I remember, about ten years ago. Since then—excuse me—I don't think you've mentioned her."

"You talk as if she were a skeleton in the closet!"

"You *didn't* talk—as if she were."

"I think she was, in a way, poor child. But the resurrection day hasn't confounded me as I deserved. She's a very good girl."

"If you had asked me to pick out your daughter—"

"She would have been the last you would indicate! Quite so," I said. "She is like her father's people. I can't help that."

"I shouldn't think you would if you could," Dacres remarked absently; but the sea air, perhaps, enabled me to digest his thoughtlessness with a smile.

"No," I said, "I am just as well pleased. I think a resemblance to me would confuse me, often."

There was a trace of scrutiny in Dacres's glance. "Don't you find yourself in sympathy with her?" he asked.

"My dear boy, I have seen her just twice in twenty-one years! You see, I've always stuck to John."

"But between mother and daughter—I may be old-fashioned, but I had an idea that there was an instinct that might be depended on."

"I am depending on it," I said, and let my eyes follow the little blue waves that chased past the hand-rail. "We are making very good speed, aren't we? Thirty-five knots since last night at ten. Are you in the sweep?"

"I never bet on the way out—can't afford it. Am I old-fashioned?" he insisted.

"Probably. Men are very slow in changing their philosophy about women. I fancy their idea of the maternal relation is firmest fixed of all."

"We see it a beatitude!" he cried.

"I know," I said wearily, "and you never modify the view."

Dacres contemplated the portion of the deck that lay between us. His eyes were discreetly lowered, but I saw embarrassment and speculation and a hint of criticism in them.

"Tell me more about it," said he.

"Oh, for heaven's sake don't be sympathetic!" I exclaimed. "Lend me a little philosophy instead. There is nothing to tell. There she is and there I am, in the most intimate relation in the world, constituted when she is twenty-one and I am forty." Dacres started slightly at the ominous word; so little do men realize that the women they like can ever pass out of the constated years of attraction. "I find the young lady very tolerable, very creditable, very nice. I find the relation atrocious. There you have it. I would like to break the relation into pieces," I went on recklessly, "and throw it into the sea. Such things should be tempered to one. I should feel it much less if she occupied another cabin, and would consent to call me Elizabeth or Jane. It is not as if I had been her mother always. One grows fastidious at forty—new intimacies are only possible then on a basis of temperament—"

I paused; it seemed to me that I was making excuses, and I had not the least desire in the world to do that.

"How awfully rough on the girl!" said Dacres Tottenham.

"That consideration has also occurred to me," I said candidly, "though I have perhaps been even more struck by its converse."

"You had no earthly business to be her mother," said my friend, with irritation.

I shrugged my shoulders—what would you have done?—and opened *La Duchesse Bleue.*

CHAPTER III

Mrs Morgan, wife of a judge of the High Court of Bombay, and I sat amidships on the cool side in the Suez Canal. She was outlining "Soiled Linen" in chain-stitch on a green canvas bag; I was admiring the Egyptian sands. "How charming," said I, "is this solitary desert in the endless oasis we are compelled to cross!"

"Oasis in the desert, you mean," said Mrs Morgan; "I haven't noticed any, but I happened to look up this morning as I was putting on my stockings, and I saw through my port-hole the most lovely mirage."

I had been at school with Mrs Morgan more than twenty years agone, but she had come to the special enjoyment of the dignities of life while I still liked doing things. Mrs Morgan was the kind of person to make one realize how distressing a medium is middle age. Contemplating her precipitous lap, to which conventional attitudes were certainly more becoming, I crossed my own knees with energy, and once more resolved to be young until I was old.

"How perfectly delightful for you to be taking Cecily out!" said Mrs Morgan placidly.

"Isn't it?" I responded, watching the gliding sands.

"But she was born in sixty-nine—that makes her twenty-one. Quite time, I should say."

"Oh, we couldn't put it off any longer. I mean—her father has such a horror of early débuts. He simply would not hear of her coming before."

"Doesn't want her to marry in India, I dare say—the only one," purred Mrs Morgan.

"Oh, I don't know. It isn't such a bad place. I was brought out there to marry and I married. I've found it very satisfactory."

"You always did say exactly what you thought, Helena," said Mrs Morgan excusingly.

"I haven't much patience with people who bring their daughters out to give them the chance they never would have in England, and then go about devoutly hoping they won't marry in India," I said. "I shall be very pleased if Cecily does as well as your girls have done."

"Mary in the Indian Civil and Jessie in the Imperial Service Troops," sighed Mrs Morgan complacently. "And both, my dear, within a year. It *was* a blow."

"Oh, it must have been!" I said civilly.

There was no use in bandying words with Emily Morgan.

"There is nothing in the world like the satisfaction and pleasure one takes in one's daughters," Mrs Morgan went on limpidly. "And one can be in such *close* sympathy with one's girls. I have never regretted having no sons."

"Dear me, yes. To watch oneself growing up again—call back the lovely April of one's prime, etcetera—to read every thought and anticipate every wish—there is no more golden privilege in life, dear Emily. Such a direct and natural avenue for affection, such a wide field for interest!"

I paused, lost in the volume of my admirable sentiments.

"How beautifully you talk, Helena! I wish I had the gift."

"It doesn't mean very much," I said truthfully.

"Oh, I think it's everything! And how companionable a girl is! I quite envy you, this season, having Cecily constantly with you and taking her about everywhere. Something quite new for you, isn't it?"

"Absolutely," said I; "I am looking forward to it immensely, but it is likely she will make her own friends, don't you think?" I added anxiously.

"Hardly the first season. My girls didn't. I was practically their only intimate for months. Don't be afraid; you won't be obliged to go shares in Cecily with anybody for a good long while," added Mrs Morgan kindly. "I know just how you feel about *that*."

The muddy water of the Ditch chafed up from under us against its banks with a smell that enabled me to hide the emotions Mrs Morgan evoked behind my handkerchief. The pale desert was pictorial with the drifting, deepening purple shadows of clouds, and in the midst a blue glimmer of the Bitter Lakes, with a white sail on them. A little frantic Arab boy ran alongside keeping pace with the ship. Except for the smell, it was like a dream, we moved so quietly; on, gently on and on between the ridgy clay banks and the rows of piles. Peace was on the ship; you could hear what the Fourth in his white ducks said to the quartermaster in his blue denims; you could count the strokes of the electric bell in the wheel-house; peace was on the ship as she pushed on, an ever-venturing, double-funneled impertinence, through the sands of the ages. My eyes wandered along a plank-line in the deck till they were arrested by a petticoat I knew, when they returned of their own accord. I seemed to be always seeing that petticoat.

"I think," resumed Mrs Morgan, whose glance had wandered in the same direction, "that Cecily is a very fine type of our English girls. With those dark grey eyes, a *little* prominent possibly, and that good colour—it's rather high now perhaps, but she will lose quite enough of it in India   and those regular features, she would make a splendid Britannia. Do you know, I fancy she must have a great deal of character. Has she?"

"Any amount. And all of it good," I responded, with private dejection.

"No faults at all?" chaffed Mrs Morgan.

I shook my head. "Nothing," I said sadly, "that I can put my finger on. But I hope to discover a few later. The sun may bring them out."

"Like freckles. Well, you are a lucky woman. Mine had plenty, I assure you. Untidiness was no name for Jessie, and Mary—I'm *sorry* to say that Mary sometimes fibbed."

"How lovable of her! Cecily's neatness is a painful example to me, and I don't believe she would tell a fib to save my life."

"Tell me," said Mrs Morgan, as the lunch-bell rang and she gathered her occupation into her work-basket, "who is that talking to her?"

"Oh, an old friend," I replied easily; "Dacres Tottenham, a dear fellow, and most benevolent. He is trying on my behalf to reconcile her to the life she'll have to lead in India."

"She won't need much reconciling, if she's like most girls," observed Mrs Morgan, "but he seems to be trying very hard."

That was quite the way I took it—on my behalf—for several days. When people have understood you very adequately for ten years you do not expect them to boggle at any problem you may present at the end of the decade. I thought Dacres was moved by a fine sense of compassion. I thought that with his admirable perception he had put a finger on the little comedy of fruitfulness in my life that laughed so bitterly at the tragedy of the barren woman, and was attempting, by delicate manipulation, to make it easier. I really thought so. Then I observed that myself had preposterously deceived me, that it wasn't like that at all. When Mr Tottenham joined us, Cecily and me, I saw that he listened more than he talked, with an ear specially cocked to register any small irony which might appear in my remarks to my daughter. Naturally he registered more than there were, to make up perhaps for dear Cecily's obviously not registering any. I could see, too, that he was suspicious of any flavour of kindness; finally, to avoid the strictures of his upper lip, which really, dear fellow, began to bore me, I talked exclusively about the distant sails and the Red Sea littoral. When he no longer joined us as we sat or walked together, I perceived that his hostility was fixed and his *parti pris*. He was brimful of compassion, but it was all for Cecily, none for the situation or for me. (She would have marvelled, placidly, why he pitied her. I am glad I can say that.) The primitive man in him rose up as Pope of nature and excommunicated me as a creature recusant to her functions. Then deliberately Dacres undertook an office of consolation; and I fell to wondering, while Mrs Morgan spoke her convictions plainly out, how far an impulse of reparation for a misfortune with which he had nothing to do might carry a man.

I began to watch the affair with an interest which even to me seemed queer. It was not detached, but it was semi-detached, and, of course, on the side for which I seem, in this history, to be perpetually apologizing. With certain limitation it didn't matter an atom whom Cecily married. So that he was sound and decent, with reasonable prospects, her simple requirements and ours for her would be quite met. There was the ghost of a consolation in that; one needn't be anxious or exacting.

I could predict with a certain amount of confidence that in her first season she would probably receive three or four proposals, any one of which she might accept with as much propriety and satisfaction as any other one. For Cecily it was so simple; prearranged by nature like her digestion, one could not see any logical basis for difficulties. A nice upstanding sapper, a dashing Bengal Lancer—oh, I could think of half a dozen types that would answer excellently. She was the kind of young person, and that was the summing up of it, to marry a type and be typically happy. I hoped and expected that she would. But Dacres!

Dacres should exercise the greatest possible discretion. He was not a person who could throw the dice indifferently with fate. He could respond to so much, and he would inevitably, sooner or later, demand so much response! He was governed by a preposterously exacting temperament, and he wore his nerves outside. And what vision he had! How he explored the world he lived in and drew out of it all there was, all there was! I could see him in the years to come ranging alone the fields that were sweet and the horizons that lifted for him, and ever returning to pace the common dusty mortal road by the side of a purblind wife. On general principle, as a case to point at, it would be a conspicuous pity. Nor would it lack the aspect of a particular, a personal misfortune. Dacres was occupied in quite the natural normal degree with his charming self; he would pass his misery on, and who would deserve to escape it less than his mother-in-law?

I listened to Emily Morgan, who gleaned in the ship more information about Dacres Tottenham's people, pay, and prospects than I had ever acquired, and I kept an eye upon the pair which was, I flattered myself, quite maternal. I watched them without acute anxiety, deploring the threatening destiny, but hardly nearer to it than one is in the stalls to the stage. My moments of real concern for Dacres were mingled more with anger than with sorrow—it seemed inexcusable that he, with his infallible divin-ing-rod for temperament, should be on the point of making such an ass of himself. Though I talk of the stage there was nothing at all dramatic to reward my attention, mine and Emily Morgan's. To my imagination, excited by its idea of what Dacres Tottenham's courtship ought to be, the attentions he paid to Cecily were most humdrum. He threw rings into buckets with her—she was good at that—and quoits upon the "bull" board; he found her chair after the decks were swabbed in the morning and established her in it; he paced the deck with her at convenient times and seasons. They were humdrum, but they were constant and cumulative. Cecily took them with an even breath that perfectly matched. There was hardly anything, on her part, to note—a little discreet observation of his comings and goings, eyes scarcely lifted from her book, and later just a hint of proprietorship, as the evening she came up to me on deck, our first night in the Indian Ocean. I was lying on my long chair looking at the thick, low stars and thinking it was a long time since I had see John.

"Dearest mamma, out here and nothing over your shoul-ders! You *are* imprudent. Where is your wrap? Mr Tottenham, will you please fetch mamma's wrap for her?"

"If mamma so instructs me," he said audaciously.

"Do as Cecily tells you," I laughed, and he went and did it, while I by the light of a quartermaster's lantern distinctly saw my daughter blush.

Another time, when Cecily came down to undress, she bent over me as I lay in the lower berth with unusual solicitude. I had been dozing, and I jumped.

"What is it, child?" I said. "Is the ship on fire?"

"No, mamma, the ship is not on fire. There is nothing wrong. I'm so sorry I startled you. But Mr Tottenham has been telling me all about what you did for the soldiers the time plague broke out in the lines at Mian-Mir. I think it was splendid, mamma, and so does he."

"Oh, *Lord!*" I groaned. "Good night."

CHAPTER IV

It remained in my mind, that little thing that Dacres had taken the trouble to tell my daughter; I thought about it a good deal. It seemed to me the most serious and convincing circumstance that had yet offered itself to my consideration. Dacres was no longer content to bring solace to the more appealing figure of the situation; he must set to work, bless him! to improve the situation itself. He must try to induce Miss Farnham, by telling her everything he could remember to my credit, to think as well of her mother as possible, in spite of the strange and secret blows which that mother might be supposed to sit up at night to deliver to her. Cecily thought very well of me already; indeed, with private reservations as to my manners and—no, *not* my morals, I believe I exceeded her expectations of what a perfectly new and untrained mother would be likely to prove. It was my theory that she found me all she could understand me to be. The maternal virtues of the outside were certainly mine; I put them on with care every morning and wore them with patience all day. Dacres, I assured myself, must have allowed his preconception to lead him absurdly by the nose not to see that the girl was satisfied, that my impatience, my impotence, did not at all make her miserable. Evidently, however, he had created our relations differently; evidently he had set himself to their amelioration. There was portent in it; things seemed to be closing in. I bit off a quarter of an inch of wooden penhandle in considering whether or not I should mention it in my letter to John, and decided that it would be better just perhaps to drop a hint. Though I could not expect John to receive it with any

57

sort of perturbation. Men are different; he would probably think Tottenham well enough able to look after himself.

I had embarked on my letter, there at the end of a corner-table of the saloon, when I saw Dacres saunter through. He wore a very conscious and elaborately purposeless air; and it jumped with my mood that he had nothing less than the crisis of his life in his pocket, and was looking for me. As he advanced towards me between the long tables doubt left me and alarm assailed me. "I'm glad to find you in a quiet corner," said he, seating himself, and confirmed my worst anticipations.

"I'm writing to John," I said, and again applied myself to my pen-handle. It is a trick Cecily has since done her best in vain to cure me of.

"I am going to interrupt you," he said. "I have not had an opportunity of talking to you for some time."

"I like that!" I exclaimed derisively.

"And I want to tell you that I am very much charmed with Cecily."

"Well," I said, "I am not going to gratify you by saying anything against her."

"You don't deserve her, you know."

"I won't dispute that. But, if you don't mind—I'm not sure that I'll stand being abused, dear boy."

"I quite see it isn't any use. Though one spoke with the tongues of men and of angels—"

"And had not charity," I continued for him. "Precisely. I won't go on, but your quotation is very apt."

"I so bow down before her simplicity. It makes a wide and beautiful margin for the rest of her character. She is a girl Ruskin would have loved."

"I wonder," said I. "He did seem fond of the simple type, didn't he?"

"Her mind is so clear, so transparent. The motive spring of everything she says and does is so direct. Don't you find you can most completely depend upon her?"

"Oh yes," I said, "certainly. I nearly always know what she is going to say before she says it, and under given circumstances I can tell precisely what she will do."

"I fancy her sense of duty is very beautifully developed."

"It is," I said. "There is hardly a day when I do not come in contact with it."

"Well, that is surely a good thing. And I find that calm poise of hers very restful."

"I would not have believed that so many virtues could reside in one young lady," I said, taking refuge in flippancy, "and to think that she should be my daughter!"

"As I believe you know, that seems to me rather a cruel stroke of destiny, Mrs Farnham."

"Oh yes, I know! You have a constructive imagination, Dacres. You don't seem to see that the girl is protected by her limitations, like a tortoise. She lives within them quite secure and happy and content. How determined you are to be sorry for her!"

Mr Tottenham looked at the end of this lively exchange as though he sought for a polite way of conveying to me that I rather was the limited person. He looked as if he wished he could say things. The first of them would be, I saw, that he had quite a different conception of Cecily, that it was illuminated by many trifles, nuances of feeling and expression, which he had noticed in his talks with her whenever they had skirted the subject of her adoption by her mother. He knew her, he was longing to say, better than I did; when it would have been natural to reply that one could not hope to compete in such a direction with an intelligent young man, and we should at once have been upon delicate and difficult ground. So it was as well perhaps that he kept silence until he said, as he had come prepared to say, "Well, I want to put that beyond a doubt—her happiness—if I'm good enough. I want her, please, and I only hope that she will be half as willing to come as you are likely to be to let her go."

It was a shock when it came, plump, like that; and I was horrified to feel how completely every other consideration was lost for the instant in the immense relief that it prefigured. To be my whole complete self again, without the feeling that a fraction of me was masquerading about in Cecily! To be freed at once, or almost, from an exacting condition and an impossible ideal! "Oh!" I exclaimed, and my eyes positively filled. "You *are* good, Dacres, but I couldn't let you do that."

His undisguised stare brought me back to a sense of the proportion of things. I saw that in the combination of influences that had brought Mr Tottenham to the point of proposing to marry my daughter consideration for me, if it had a place, would be fantastic. Inwardly I laughed at the egotism of raw nerves that had conjured it up, even for an instant, as a reason for gratitude. The situation was not so peculiar, not so interesting, as that. But I answered his stare with a smile; what I had said might very well stand.

"Do you imagine," he said, seeing that I did not mean to amplify it, "that I want to marry her out of any sort of *goodness?*"

"Benevolence is your weakness, Dacres."

"I see. You think one's motive is to withdraw her from a relation which ought to be the most natural in the world, but which is, in her particular and painful case, the most equivocal."

"Well, come," I remonstrated. "You have dropped one or two things, you know, in the heat of your indignation, not badly calculated to give one that idea. The eloquent statement you have just made, for instance—it carries all the patness of old conviction. How often have you rehearsed it?"

I am a fairly long-suffering person, but I began to feel a little annoyed with my would-be son-in-law. If the relation were achieved it would give him no prescriptive right to bully me; and we were still in very early anticipation of that.

"Ah!" he said disarmingly. "Don't let us quarrel. I'm sorry you think that; because it isn't likely to bring your favour to my project, and I want you friendly and helpful. Oh, confound it!" he exclaimed, with sudden temper. "You ought to be. I don't understand this aloofness. I half suspect it's pose. You undervalue Cecily—well, you have no business to undervalue me. You know me better than anybody in the world. Now are you going to help me to marry your daughter?"

"I don't think so," I said slowly, after a moment's silence, which he sat through like a mutinous schoolboy. "I might tell you that I don't care a button whom you marry, but that would not be true. I do care more or less. As you say, I know you pretty well. I'd a little rather you didn't make a mess of it; and if you must I should distinctly prefer not to have the spectacle under my nose for the rest of my life. I can't hinder you, but I won't help you."

"And what possesses you to imagine that in marrying Cecily I should make a mess of it? Shouldn't your first considera-tion be whether *she* would?"

"Perhaps it should, but, you see, it isn't. Cecily would be happy with anybody who made her comfortable. You would ask a good deal more than that, you know."

Dacres, at this, took me up promptly. Life, he said, the heart of life, had particularly little to say to temperament. By the heart of life I suppose he meant married love. He explained that its roots asked other sustenance, and that it throve best of all on simple elemental goodness. So long as a man sought in women mere casual companionship, perhaps the most exquisite thing to be experienced was the stimulus of some spiritual feminine counter-part; but when he desired of one woman that she should be always and intimately with him, the background of his life, the mother of his children, he was better advised to avoid nerves and sensibilities, and try for the repose of the common—the uncommon—domestic virtues. Ah, he said, they were sweet, like lavender. (Already, I told him, he smelled the housekeeper's linen chest.) But I did not inter-rupt him much; I couldn't, he was too absorbed. To temperamental pairing, he declared, the century owed its breed of decadents. I asked him if he had ever really recognized one; and he retorted that if he hadn't he didn't wish to make a beginning in his own family. In a quarter of an hour he repudiated the theories of a life-time, a gratifying triumph for simple elemental goodness. Having denied the value of the subtler pretensions to charm in woman as you marry her, he went artlessly on to endow Cecily with as many of them as could possibly be desirable. He actually persuaded himself to say that it was lovely to see the reflections of life in her tranquil spirit; and when I looked at him incredulously he grew angry, and hinted that Cecily's sensitiveness to reflections and other things might be a trifle beyond her mother's ken. "She responds instantly, intimately, to the beautiful everywhere," he declared.

"Aren't the opportunities of life on board ship rather limited to demonstrate that?" I inquired. "I know—you mean sunsets. Cecily is very fond of sunsets. She is always asking me to come and look at them."

"I was thinking of last night's sunset," he confessed. "We looked at it together."

"What did she say?" I asked idly.

"Nothing very much. That's just the point. Another girl would have raved and gushed."

"Oh, well, Cecily never does that," I responded. "Nevertheless she is a very ordinary human instrument. I hope I shall have no temptation ten years hence to remind you that I warned you of her quality."

"I wish, not in the least for my own profit, for I am well convinced already, but simply to win your cordiality and your approval—never did an unexceptional wooer receive such niggard encouragement!—I wish there were some sort of test for her quality. I would be proud to stand by it, and you would be convinced. I can't find words to describe my objection to your state of mind."

The thing seemed to me to be a foregone conclusion. I saw it accomplished with all its possibilities of disastrous commonplace. I saw all that I have here taken the trouble to foreshadow. So far as I was concerned, Dacres's burden would add itself to my philosophies, *voilà tout*. I should always be a little uncomfortable about it, because it had been taken from my back; but it would not be a matter for the wringing of hands. And yet—the hatefulness of the mistake! Dacres's bold talk of a test made no suggestion. Should my invention be more fertile? I thought of something.

"You have said nothing to her yet?" I asked.

"Nothing. I don't think she suspects for a moment. She treats me as if no such fell design were possible. I'm none too confident, you know," he added, with longer face.

"We go straight to Agra. Could you come to Agra?"

"Ideal!" he cried. "The memory of Mumtaz! The garden of the Taj! I've always wanted to love under the same moon as Shah Jehan. How thoughtful of you!"

"You must spend a few days with us in Agra," I continued. "And as you say, it is the very place to shrine your happiness, if it comes to pass there."

"Well, I am glad to have extracted a word of kindness from you at last," said Dacres, as the stewards came to lay the table. "But I wish," he added regretfully, "you could have thought of a test."

63

CHAPTER V

Four days later we were in Agra. A time there was when the name would have been the key of dreams to me; now it stood for John's headquarters. I was rejoiced to think I would look again upon the Taj; and the prospect of living with it was a real enchantment; but I pondered most the kind of house that would be provided for the General Commanding the District, how many the dining-room would seat, and whether it would have a roof of thatch or of corrugated iron—I prayed against corrugated iron. I confess these my preoccupations. I was forty, and at forty the practical considerations of life hold their own even against domes of marble, world-renowned, and set about with gardens where the bulbul sings to the rose. I smiled across the years at the raptures of my first vision of the place at twenty-one, just Cecily's age. Would I now sit under Arjamand's cypresses till two o'clock in the morning to see the wonder of her tomb at a particular angle of the moon? Would I climb one of her tall white ministering minarets to see anything whatever? I very greatly feared that I would not. Alas for the aging of sentiment, of interest! Keep your touch with life

and your seat in the saddle as long as you will, the world is no new
toy at forty. But Cecily was twenty-one, Cecily who sat stolidly
finishing her lunch while Dacres Tottenham talked about Akbar
and his philosophy. "The sort of man," he said, "that Carlyle might
have smoked a pipe with."

"But surely," said Cecily reflectively, "tobacco was not
discovered in England then. Akbar came to the throne in 1526."

"Nor Carlyle either for that matter," I hastened to observe.
"Nevertheless, I think Mr Tottenham's proposition must stand."

"Thanks, Mrs Farnham," said Dacres. "But imagine Miss
Farnham's remembering Akbar's date! I'm sure you didn't!"

"Let us hope she doesn't know too much about him," I
cried gaily, "or there will be nothing to tell!"

"Oh, really and truly very little!" said Cecily, "but as
soon as we heard papa would be stationed here Aunt Emma made
me read up about those old Moguls and people. I think I remember
the dynasty. Baber, wasn't he the first? and then Humayon, and
after him Akbar, and then Jehangir, and then Shah Jehan. But I've
forgotten every date but Akbar's."

She smiled her smile of brilliant health and even spirits as
she made the damaging admission, and she was so good to look at,
sitting there simple and wholesome and fresh, peeling her banana
with her well-shaped fingers, that we swallowed the dynasty as it
were whole, and smiled back upon her. John, I may say, was
extremely pleased with Cecily; he said she was a very satisfactory
human accomplishment. One would have thought, positively, the
way he plumed himself over his handsome daughter, that he alone
was responsible for her. But John, having received his family,
straightway set off with his Staff on a tour of inspection, and
thereby takes himself out of this history. I sometimes think that if
he had stayed—but there has never been the slightest recrimina-
tion between us about it, and I am not going to hint one now.

"Did you read," asked Dacres, "what he and the Court
poet wrote over the entrance gate to the big mosque at Fattehpur-
Sikri? It's rather nice. 'The world is a looking glass, wherein the

image has come and is gone—take as thine own nothing more than what thou lookest upon.'"

My daughter's thoughtful gaze was, of course, fixed upon the speaker, and in his own glance I saw a sudden ray of consciousness; but Cecily transferred her eyes to the opposite wall, deeply considering, and while Dacres and I smiled across the table, I saw that she had perceived no reason for blushing. It was a singularly narrow escape.

"No," she said, "I didn't; what a curious proverb for an emperor to make! He couldn't possibly have been able to see all his possessions at once."

"If you have finished," Dacres addressed her, "do let me show you what your plain and immediate duty is to the garden. The garden waits for you—all the roses expectant—"

"Why, there isn't one!" cried Cecily, pinning on her hat. It was pleasing, and just a trifle pathetic, the way he hurried her out of the scope of any little dart; he would not have her even within range of amused observation. Would he continue, I wondered vaguely, as, with my elbows on the table, I tore into strips the lemon-leaf that floated in my finger-bowl—would he continue, through life, to shelter her from his other clever friends as now he attempted to shelter her from her mother? In that case he would have to domicile her, poor dear, behind the curtain, like the native ladies—a good price to pay for a protection of which, bless her heart! she would be all unaware. I had quite stopped bemoaning the affair; perhaps the comments of my husband, who treated it with broad approval and satisfaction, did something to soothe my sensibilities. At all events, I had gradually come to occupy a high fatalistic ground towards the pair. If it was written upon their foreheads that they should marry, the inscription was none of mine; and, of course, it was true, as John had indignantly stated, that Dacres might do very much worse. One's interest in Dacres Tottenham's problematical future had in no way diminished; but the young man was so positive, so full of intention, so disinclined to discussion—he had not reopened the subject since that morning in the saloon of the *Caledonia*—that one's feeling about it rather took the attenuated form of a shrug. I am afraid, too, that the pleasurable excitement of such an impending event had a little supervened; even at forty there is no disallowing the natural interests of one's sex. As I sat there pulling my lemon-leaf to pieces, I should not have been surprised or in the least put out if the two had returned radiant from the lawn to demand my blessing. As to the test of quality that I had obligingly invented for Dacres on the spur of the moment without his knowledge or connivance, it had some time ago faded into what he apprehended it to be—a mere idyllic opportunity, a charming background, a frame for his project, of prettier sentiment than the funnels and the hand-rails of a ship.

Mr Tottenham had ten days to spend with us. He knew the place well; it belonged to the province to whose service he was dedicated, and he claimed with impressive authority the privilege of showing it to Cecily by degrees—the Hall of Audience to-day, the Jessamine Tower to-morrow, the tomb of Akbar another, and the Deserted City yet another day. We arranged the expeditions in conference, Dacres insisting only upon the order of them, which I saw was to be cumulative, with the Taj at the very end, on the night precisely of the full of the moon, with a better chance of roses. I had no special views, but Cecily contributed some; that we should do the Hall of Audience in the morning, so as not to interfere with the club tennis in the afternoon, that we should bicycle to Akbar's tomb and take a cold luncheon—if we were sure there would be no snakes—to the Deserted City, to all of which Dacres gave loyal assent. I endorsed everything; I was the encouraging chorus, only stipulating that my number should be swelled from day to day by the addition of such persons as I should approve. Cecily, for instance, wanted to invite the Bakewells because we had come out in the same ship with them; but I could not endure the Bakewells, and it seemed to me that our having made the voyage with them was the best possible reason for declining to lay eyes on them for the rest of our natural lives. "Mamma has such strong prejudices," Cecily remarked, as she reluctantly gave up the idea; and I waited to see whether the graceless Tottenham would unmurmuringly take down the Bakewells. How strong must be the sentiment that turns a man into a boa-constrictor without a pang of transmigration! But no, this time he was faithful to the principles of his pre-Cecilian existence. "They are rather Boojums," he declared. "You would think so, too, if you knew them better. It is that kind of excellent person that makes the real burden of India." I could have patted him on the back.

Thanks to the rest of the chorus, which proved abundantly available, I was no immediate witness to Cecily's introduction to the glorious fragments which sustain in Agra the memory of the Moguls. I may as well say that I arranged with care that if anybody must be standing by when Dacres disclosed them, it should not be I. If Cecily had squinted, I should have been sorry, but I would have found in it no personal humiliation. There were other imperfections of vision, however, for which I felt responsible and ashamed; and with Dacres, though the situation, Heaven knows, was none of my seeking, I had a little the feeling of a dealer who offers a defective *bibelot* to a connoisseur. My charming daughter—I was fifty times congratulated upon her appearance and her manners—had many excellent qualities and capacities which she never inherited from me; but she could see no more than the bulk, no further than the perspective; she could register exactly as much as a camera.

This was a curious thing, perhaps, to displease my maternal vanity, but it did; I had really rather she squinted; and when there was anything to look at I kept out of the way. I can not tell precisely, therefore, what the incidents were that contributed to make Mr Tottenham, on our return from these expeditions, so thoughtful, with a thoughtfulness which increased, towards the end of them, to a positive gravity. This would disappear during dinner under the influence of food and drink. He would talk nightly with new enthusiasm and fresh hope—or did I imagine it?—of the loveliness he had arranged to reveal on the following day. If again my imagination did not lead me astray, I fancied this occurred later and later in the course of the meal as the week went on; as if his state required more stimulus as time progressed. One evening, when I expected it to flag altogether, I had a whim to order champagne and observe the effect; but I am glad to say that I reproved myself, and refrained.

Cecily, meanwhile, was conducting herself in a manner which left nothing to be desired. If, as I sometimes thought, she took Dacres very much for granted, she took him calmly for granted; she seemed a prey to none of those fluttering uncertainties, those suspended judgements and elaborate indifferences which translate themselves so plainly in a young lady receiving addresses. She turned herself out very freshly and very well; she was always ready for everything, and I am sure that no glance of Dacres Tottenham's found aught but direct and decorous response. His society on these occasions gave her solid pleasure; so did the drive and the lunch; the satisfactions were apparently upon the same plane. She was aware of the plum, if I may be permitted a brusque but irresistible simile; and with her mouth open, her eyes modestly closed, and her head in a convenient position, she waited, placidly, until it should fall in. The Farnham ladies would have been delighted with the result of their labours in the sweet reason and eminent propriety of this attitude. Thinking of my idiotic sufferings when John began to fix himself upon my horizon, I pondered profoundly the power of nature in differentiation.

One evening, the last, I think, but one, I had occasion to go to my daughter's room, and found her writing in her commonplace-book. She had a commonplace-book, as well as a Where is It?, an engagement-book, an account-book, a diary, a Daily Sunshine, and others with purposes too various to remember. "Dearest mamma," she said, as I was departing, "there is only one 'p' in 'opulence,' isn't there?"

"Yes," I replied, with my hand on the door-handle, and added curiously, for it was an odd word in Cecily's mouth, "Why?"

She hardly hesitated. "Oh," she said, "I am just writing down one or two things Mr Tottenham said about Agra before I forget them. They seemed so true."

"He has a descriptive touch," I remarked.

"I think he describes beautifully. Would you like to hear what he said to-day?"

"I would," I replied, sincerely.

"'Agra,'" read this astonishing young lady, "'is India's one pure idyll. Elsewhere she offers other things, foolish opulence, tawdry pageant, treachery of eunuchs and jealousies of harems, thefts of kings' jewels and barbaric retributions; but they are all actual, visualized, or part of a past that shows to the backward glance hardly more relief and vitality than a Persian painting'— I should like to see a Persian painting—'but here the immortal tombs and pleasure-houses rise out of color delicate and subtle; the vision holds across three hundred years; the print of the court is still in the dust of the city.'"

"Did you really let him go on like that?" I exclaimed. "It has the license of a lecture!"

"I encouraged him to. Of course he didn't say it straight off. He said it naturally; he stopped now and then to cough. I didn't understand it all; but I think I have remembered every word."

"You have a remarkable memory. I'm glad he stopped to cough. Is there any more?"

"One little bit. 'Here the Moguls wrought their passions into marble, and held them up with great refrains from their religion, and set them about with gardens; and here they stand in the twilight of the glory of those kings and the noonday splendour of their own.'"

"How clever of you!" I exclaimed. "How wonderfully clever of you to remember!"

"I had to ask him to repeat one or two sentences. He didn't like that. But this is nothing. I used to learn pages letter-perfect for Aunt Emma. She was very particular. I think it is worth preserving, don't you?"

"Dear Cecily," I responded, "you have a frugal mind."

There was nothing else to respond. I could not tell her just how practical I thought her, or how pathetic her little book.

CHAPTER VI

We drove together, after dinner, to the Taj. The moonlight lay in an empty splendor over the broad sandy road, with the acacias pricking up on each side of it and the gardens of the station bungalows stretching back into clusters of crisp shadows. It was an exquisite February night, very still. Nothing seemed abroad but two or three pariah dogs, upon vague and errant business, and the Executive Engineer going swiftly home from the club on his bicycle. Even the little shops of the bazaar were dark and empty; only here and there a light showed barred behind the carved balconies of the upper rooms, and there was hardly any tom-tomming. The last long slope of the road showed us the river curving to the left, through a silent white waste that stretched indefinitely into the moonlight on one side, and was crowned by Akbar's fort on the other. His long high line of turrets and battlements still guarded a hint of their evening rose, and dim and exquisite above them hovered the three dome-bubbles of the Pearl Mosque. It was a night of perfect illusion, and the illusion was mysterious, delicate, and faint. I sat silent as we rolled along, twenty years nearer to the original joy of things when John and I drove through the same old dream.

Dacres, too, seemed preoccupied; only Cecily was, as they say, herself. Cecily was really more than herself, she exhibited an unusual flow of spirits. She talked continually, she pointed out this and that, she asked who lived here and who lived there. At regular intervals of about four minutes she demanded if it wasn't simply too lovely. She sat straight up with her vigorous profile and her smart hat; and the silhouette of her personality sharply refused to mingle with the dust of any dynasty. She was a contrast, a protest; positively she was an indignity. "Do lean back, dear child," I exclaimed at last. "You interfere with the landscape."

She leaned back, but she went on interfering with it in terms of sincerest enthusiasm.

When we stopped at the great archway of entrance I begged to be left in the carriage. What else could one do, when the

golden moment had come, but sit in the carriage and measure it?
They climbed the broad stone steps together and passed under the
lofty gravures into the garden, and I waited. I waited and remembered. I am not, as perhaps by this time is evident, a person of over-
whelming sentiment, but I think the smile upon my lips was gentle.
So plainly I could see, beyond the massive archway and across
a score of years, all that they saw at that moment—Arjamand's
garden, and the long straight tank of marble cleaving it full of
sleeping water and the shadows of the marshaling cypresses; her
wide dark garden of roses and of pomegranates, and at the end the
Vision, marvellous, aerial, the soul of something—is it beauty? is
it sorrow?—that great white pride of love in mourning such as
only here in all the round of our little world lifts itself to the stars,
the unpaintable, indescribable Taj Mahal. A gentle breath stole
out with a scent of jessamine and such a memory! I closed my
eyes and felt the warm luxury of a tear.

      Thinking of the two in the garden, my mood was very
kind, very conniving. How foolish after all were my cherry-stone
theories of taste and temperament before that uncalculating thing
which sways a world and builds a Taj Mahal! Was it probable that
Arjamand and her Emperor had loved fastidiously, and yet how
they had loved! I wandered away into consideration of the blind
forces which move the world, in which comely young persons like
my daughter Cecily had such a place; I speculated vaguely upon
the value of the subtler gifts of sympathy and insight which
seemed indeed, at that enveloping moment, to be mere flowers
strewn upon the tide of deeper emotions. The garden sent me a
fragrance of roses; the moon sailed higher and picked out the little
kiosks set along the wall. It was a charming, charming thing to
wait, there at the portal of the silvered, scented garden, for an
idyll to come forth.

      When they reappeared, Dacres and my daughter, they
came with casual steps and cheerful voices. They might have been
a couple of tourists. The moonlight fell full upon them on the
platform under the arch. It showed Dacres measuring with his

stick the length of the Sanskrit letters which declared the stately texts, and Cecily's expression of polite, perfunctory interest. They looked up at the height above them; they looked back at the vision behind. Then they sauntered towards the carriage, he offering a formal hand to help her down the uncertain steps, she gracefully accepting it.

"You—you have not been long," said I. "I hope you didn't hurry on my account."

"Miss Farnham found the marble a little cold under foot," replied Dacres, putting Miss Farnham in.

"You see," explained Cecily, "I stupidly forgot to change into thicker soles. I have only my slippers. But, mamma, how lovely it is! Do let us come again in the daytime. I am dying to make a sketch of it."

Mr Tottenham was to leave us on the following day. In the morning, after "little breakfast," as we say in India, he sought me in the room I had set aside to be particularly my own.

Again I was writing to John, but this time I waited for precisely his interruption. I had got no further than "My dearest husband," and my pen-handle was a fringe.

"Another fine day," I said, as if the old, old Indian joke could give him ease, poor man!

"Yes," said he, "we are having lovely weather."

He had forgotten that it was a joke. Then he lapsed into silence while I renewed my attentions to my pen.

"I say," he said at last, with so strained a look about his mouth that it was almost a contortion. "I haven't done it, you know."

"No," I responded, cheerfully, "and you're not going to. Is that it? Well!"

"Frankly—" said he.

"Dear me, yes! Anything else between you and me would be grotesque," I interrupted, "after all these years."

"I don't think it would be a success," he said, looking at me resolutely with his clear blue eyes, in which still lay, alas! the possibility of many delusions.

"No," I said, "I never did, you know. But the prospect had begun to impose upon me."

"To say how right you were would seem, under the circumstances, the most hateful form of flattery."

"Yes," I said, "I think I can dispense with your verbal endorsement." I felt a little bitter. It was, of course, better that the connoisseur should have discovered the flaw before concluding the transaction; but although I had pointed it out myself I was not entirely pleased to have the article returned.

"I am infinitely ashamed that it should have taken me all these days—day after day and each contributory—to discover what you saw so easily and so completely."

"You forget that I am her mother," I could not resist the temptation of saying.

"Oh, for God's sake don't jeer! Please be absolutely direct, and tell me if you have reason to believe that to the extent of a thought, of a breath—to any extent at all—she cares."

He was, I could see, very deeply moved; he had not arrived at this point without trouble and disorder not lightly to be put on or off. Yet I did not hurry to his relief, I was still possessed by a vague feeling of offense. I reflected that any mother would be, and I quite plumed myself upon my annoyance. It was so satisfactory, when one had a daughter, to know the sensations of even any mother. Nor was it soothing to remember that the young man's whole attitude towards Cecily had been based upon criticism of me, even though he sat before me whipped with his own lash. His temerity had been stupid and obstinate; I could not regret his punishment.

I kept him waiting long enough to think all this, and then I replied, "I have not the least means of knowing."

I can not say what he expected, but he squared his shoulders as if he had received a blow and might receive another. Then he looked at me with a flash of the old indignation. "You are not near enough to her for that!" he exclaimed.

"I am not near enough to her for that."

Silence fell between us. A crow perched upon an opened venetian and cawed lustily. For years afterward I never heard a crow caw without a sense of vain, distressing experiment. Dacres got up and began to walk about the room. I very soon put a stop to that. "I can't talk to a pendulum," I said, but I could not persuade him to sit down again.

"Candidly," he said at length, "do you think she would have me?"

"I regret to say that I think she would. But you would not dream of asking her."

"Why not? She is a dear girl," he responded inconsequently.

"You could not possibly stand it."

Then Mr Tottenham delivered himself of this remarkable phrase: "I could stand it," he said, "as well as you can."

There was far from being any joy in the irony with which I regarded him and under which I saw him gather up his resolution to go; nevertheless I did nothing to make it easy for him. I refrained from imparting my private conviction the Cecily would accept the first presentable substitute that appeared, although it was strong. I made no reference to my daughter's large fund of philosophy and small balance of sentiment. I did not even—though this was reprehensible—confess the test, the test of quality in these ten days with the marble archives of the Moguls, which I had almost wantonly suggested, which he had so unconsciously accepted, so disastrously applied. I gave him quite fifteen minutes of his bad quarter of an hour, and when it was over I wrote truthfully but furiously to John. . . .

That was ten years ago. We have since attained the shades of retirement, and our daughter is still with us when she is not with Aunt Emma and Aunt Alice—grandmamma has passed away. Mr Tottenham's dumb departure that day in February—it was the year John got his C.B.—was followed, I am thankful to say, by none of the symptoms of unrequited affection on Cecily's part. Not for ten minutes, so far as I was aware, was she the maid forlorn.

I think her self-respect was of too robust a character, thanks to the Misses Farnham. Still less, of course, had she any reproaches to serve upon her mother, although for a long time I thought I detected—or was it my guilty conscience?—a spark of shrewdness in the glance she bent upon me when the talk was of Mr Tottenham and the probabilities of his return to Agra. So well did she sustain her experience, or so little did she feel it, that I believe the impression went abroad that Dacres had been sent disconsolate away. One astonishing conversation I had with her some six months later, which turned upon the point of a particularly desirable offer. She told me something then, without any sort of embarrassment, but quite lucidly and directly, that edified me much to hear. She said that while she was quite sure that Mr Tottenham thought of her only as a friend—she had never had the least reason for any other impression—he had done her a service for which she could not thank him enough—in showing her what a husband might be. He had given her a standard; it might be high, but it was unalterable. She didn't know whether she could describe it, but Mr Tottenham was different from the kind of man you seemed to meet in India. He had his own ways of looking at things, and he talked so well. He had given her an ideal, and she intended to profit by it. To know that men like Mr Tottenham existed, and to marry any other kind would be an act of folly which she did not intend to commit. No, Major the Hon. Hugh Taverel did not come near it—very far short, indeed! He had talked to her during the whole of dinner the night before about jackal-hunting with a bobbery pack—not at all an elevated mind. Yes, he might be a very good fellow, but as a companion for life she was sure he would not be at all suitable. She would wait.

75

And she has waited. I never thought she would, but she has. From time to time men have wished to take her from us, but the standard has been inexorable, and none of them have reached it. When Dacres married the charming American whom he caught like a butterfly upon her Eastern tour, Cecily sent them as a wedding present an alabaster model of the Taj, and I let her do it—the gift was so exquisitely appropriate. I suppose he never looks at it without being reminded that he didn't marry Miss Farnham, and I hope that he remembers that he owes it to Miss Farnham's mother. So much I think I might claim; it is really very little considering what it stands for. Cecily is permanently with us—I believe she considers herself an intimate. I am very reasonable about lending her to her aunts, but she takes no sort of advantage of my liberality; she says she knows her duty is at home. She is growing into a firm and solid English maiden lady, with a good colour and great decision of character. That she always had.

I point out to John, when she takes our crumpets away from us, that she gets it from him. I could never take away any-body's crumpets, merely because they were indigestible, least of all my own parents'. She has acquired a distinct affection for us, by some means best known to herself; but I should have objection to that if she would not rearrange my bonnet-strings. That is fond liberty to which I take exception; but it is one thing to take exception and another to express it.

Our daughter is with us, permanently with us. She declares that she intends to be the prop of our declining years; she makes the statement often, and always as if it were humorous. Nevertheless I sometimes notice a spirit of inquiry, a note of investigation in her encounters with the opposite sex that suggests an expectation not yet extinct that another and perhaps more appreciative Dacres Tottenham may flash across her field of vision—alas, how improbable! Myself I can not imagine why she should wish it; I have grown in my old age into a perfect horror of cultivated young men; but if such a person should by a miracle at any time appear, I think it is extremely improbable that I will interfere on his behalf.

❁

Dorothy Parker

Dorothy Parker lived in a small flat on Fifty-seventh Street in New York where, she said, she had all she needed: "space to lay a hat—and a few friends." There she wrote her poison-pen verse, her acerbic short stories, and her acid reviews, inventing in the process a new style of humor that became associated with her name. She wasn't, she said, "particularly interested in money" though, in her golden years, she earned a fair amount. To a prospective employer, she said, "Salary is no object; I want only enough to keep body and soul apart." Her only possessions were a portable typewriter and a canary she called Onan because he spilled his seed on the ground.

Her friend, the writer Alexander Woollcott, defined her as "a combination of Little Nell and Lady Macbeth." Once, at a party, she saw a group of people gathered around a washtub and asked her host what in the world they were doing.

"They're ducking for apples," he explained.

"There," she sighed, "but for one typographical error, is the story of my life."

The epitaph she chose for herself was "Excuse my dust."

LOLITA

dorothy parker

mrs. Ewing was a short woman who accepted the obligation borne by so many short women to make up in vivacity what they lack in number of inches from the ground. She was a creature of little pats and prods, little crinklings of the eyes and wrinklings of the nose, little runs and ripples of speech and movement, little spirals of laughter. Whenever Mrs. Ewing entered a place, all stillness left it.

Her age was a matter of guesswork, save for those who had been at school with her. For herself, she declared that she paid no attention to her birthdays—didn't give a hoot about them; and it is true that when you have amassed several dozen of the same sort of thing, it loses that rarity which is the excitement of collectors. In the summertime, she wore little cotton play suits, though her only game was bridge, and short socks, revealing the veins along the backs of her legs. For winter, she chose frocks of audible taffeta, frilled and frilled again, and jackets made of the skins of the less-sought-after lower animals. Often, of an evening, she tied a pale ribbon in her hair. Through shimmering heat or stabbing wind Mrs. Ewing trudged to her hairdresser's; her locks had been so frequently and so drastically brightened and curled that to caress them, one felt, would be rather like running one's fingers through julienne potatoes. She decorated her small, square face in a manner not unusual among ladies of the South and the Southwest, powdering the nose and chin sharp white and applying circles of rouge to the cheeks. Seen from an end of a long, softly lighted room, Mrs. Ewing was a pretty woman.

She had long been a widowed lady. Even before her widowhood, she and Mr. Ewing had lived separately, while the sympathy of the town dwelt with her. She had dallied with the notion of divorce, for it is well known that the thought, much less the presence, of a merry divorcee sets gentlemen to pawing the ground and snorting. But before her plans took form, Mr. Ewing, always a devout believer in the doctrine of one more for the road, was killed in an automobile accident. Still, a widow, too, a soft little widow, has repute the world over for causing the hearts of gentlemen to beat warm and fast. Mrs. Ewing and her friends felt sure that she would marry again. Time slid on, and this did not happen.

Mrs. Ewing never vaunted her lorn condition, never shut herself within the shaded chambers of bereavement. She went right along, skipping and tinkling through all the social events of the town, and no week went by without her presiding in her own house over cheerful little dinners or evenings of passionate bridge. She was always the same, and always the same to everyone, although she reached her heights when there were men present. She coquetted with the solid husbands of her friends, and with the two or three bachelors of the town, tremulous antiques pouring pills into their palms at the dinner table, she was sprightly to the verge of naughtiness. To a stranger observing her might have come the thought that Mrs. Ewing was not a woman who easily abandoned hope.

Mrs. Ewing had a daughter: Lolita. It is, of course, the right of parents to name their offspring what they please, yet it would sometimes be easier if they could glimpse the future and see what the little one was going to look like later on. Lolita was of no color at all; she was thin, with insistent knobs at the ends of her bones, and her hair, so fine that it seemed sparse, grew straight.

There was a time when Mrs. Ewing, probably hostess to fantasies about a curly-headed tot, took to setting the child's hair severely and rolling it up on strips of rags when she went to bed. But when the strips were untied in the morning, down fell the hair again, straight as ever. All that came of the project was a series of white nights for Lolita, trying to rest her head on the hard knots of the rags. So the whole thing was given up, and her hair hung as it must thereafter. In her early days at school, the little boys would chase her around the schoolyard at recess, snatching at the limp strands and crying, "Oh, Lolita, give us a curl, willya? Ah, Lolita, give us one of your pretty curls!" The little girls, her little friends, would gather in a group to watch and say, "Oo, aren't they terrible?" and press their hands against their mouths to control their giggles.

Mrs. Ewing was always her own sparkling self with her daughter, but her friends, mothers of born belles, tried to imagine themselves in her place and their hearts ached for her. Gallant in their own way, they found cases to relate to her, cases of girls who went through periods of being plain and then turned suddenly into dazzling beauties; some of the more scholarly brought up references to the story of the ugly duckling. But Lolita passed through young girlhood and came of age and the only difference in her was that she was taller.

The friends did not dislike Lolita. They spoke sweetly to her and when she was not present always inquired of her mother about her, although knowing there would be no news. Their exasperation was not with her but with the Fates, who had foisted upon Mrs. Ewing that pale gawk—one, moreover, with no spirit, with never a word to say for herself. For Lolita was quiet, so quiet that often you would not realize she was in the room, until the light shone on her glasses. There was nothing to do about it; there were no hopeful anecdotes to cover the condition. The friends, thinking of their own winging, twittering young, sighed again for Mrs. Ewing.

There were no beaux draped along the railing of the Ewing porch in the evening; no young male voices asked for Lolita over the telephone. At first seldom, then not at all, did the other girls ask her to their parties. This was no mark of dislike; it was only that it was difficult to bear her in mind, since school was done with for all of them and they no longer saw her daily. Mrs. Ewing always had her present at her own little soirees, though the Lord knew she added nothing to them, and, dauntless, took her along to the public events attended by both old and young, festivals for the benefit of church or charity or civic embellishment. Even when brought into such festivities, Lolita would find a corner and stay there in her quiet. Her mother would call to her across the big public room, carolling high and clear above the social clatter: "Well, come on there, little old Miss Stick-in-the-Mud! Get up on your feet and start mixing around with people!" Lolita would only smile and stay where she was, quiet as she was. There was nothing morose about her stillness. Her face, if you remembered to see it, had a look of shy welcoming, and her smile might have been set high in the tiny list of her attractions. But such attributes are valuable only when they can be quickly recognized; who has time to go searching?

It often happens in the instance of an unsought maiden daughter and a gay little mother that the girl takes over the running of the house, lifting the burden from the mother's plump shoulders. But not Lolita. She had no domestic talents. Sewing was a dark mystery to her, and if she ventured into the kitchen to attempt some simple dish, the results would be, at best, ludicrous. Nor could she set a room in pretty order. Lamps shivered, ornaments shattered, water slopped out of flower vases before her touch. Mrs. Ewing never chided the girl for her clumsiness; she made jokes about it. Lolita's hands shook under railleries, and there would be only more spilled water and more splintered shepherdesses.

She could not even do the marketing successfully, although armed with a resume of the needs of the day in her mother's curly handwriting. She would arrive at the market at the proper hour, the time it was filled with women, and then seem to be unable to push her way through them. She stood aside until later arrivals had been served before she could go to the counter and murmur her wants; and so Mrs. Ewing's lunch would be late. The household would have tottered if it had not been for the maid Mrs. Ewing had had for years—Mardy, the super-cook, the demon cleaner. The other ladies lived uneasily with their servants, ridden with fears that they might either leave or become spoiled, but Mrs. Ewing was cozy with Mardy. She was as vigorously winsome with the maid as with the better-born. They enjoyed laughing together, and right at hand was the subject of Lolita's incompetences.

Experiments palled, and finally Lolita was relieved of domestic offices. She stayed still and silent; and time went on and Mrs. Ewing went on and on, bright as a bubble in the air.

Then there bloomed a certain spring, not gradually but all in a day, a season long to be referred to as the time John Marble came. The town had not before seen the like of John Marble. He looked as if he had just alighted from the chariot of the sun. He was tall and fair, and he could make no awkward move or utter no stumbling phrase. The girls lost all consciousness of the local young men, for they were nowhere as against John Marble. He was older than they—he had crossed thirty—and he must have been rich, for he had the best room at the Wade Hampton Inn and he drove a low, narrow car with a foreign name, a thing of grace and power. More, there was about him the magic of the transitory. There were the local young men, day after day, year in, year out. But John Marble had come on some real-estate dealings for his firm, some matters of properties outside the town limits, and when his business was done, he would go back to the great, glittering city where he lived. Time pressed; excitement heightened.

Through his business John Marble met important men of the town, the fathers of daughters, and there was eager entertaining for the brilliant stranger. The girls put on the fluffiest white, and tucked bunches of pink roses in their pale-blue sashes; their curls shone and swung like bells. In the twilight they sang little songs for John Marble, and one of them had a guitar. The local young men, whose evenings hung like wet seaweed around their necks, could only go in glum groups to the bowling alley or the moving-picture theater. Though the parties in John Marble's honor slackened, for he explained that because of the demands of his business he must regret invitations, still the girls impatiently refused appointments to the local young men, and stayed at home alone on the chance of a telephone call from John Marble. They beguiled the time of waiting by sketching his profile on the telephone pad. Sometimes they threw away their training and telephoned him, even as late as ten o'clock at night. When he answered, he was softly courteous, charmingly distressed that his work kept him from being with them. Then, more and more frequently, there was no answer to their calls. The switchboard operator at the inn merely reported that Mr. Marble was out.

Somehow, the difficulties in the way of coming nearer to John Marble seemed to stimulate the girls. They tossed their fragrant curls and let their laughter soar, and when they passed the Wade Hampton Inn, they less walked than sashayed. Their elders said that never in their memories had the young girls been so pretty and so spirited as they were that spring.

And with the whole townful of bright blossoms bended for his plucking, John Marble chose Lolita Ewing.

It was a courtship curiously without detail. John Marble would appear at the Ewing house in the evening, with no preliminary telephoning, and he and Lolita would sit on the porch while Mrs. Ewing went out among her friends. When she returned, she shut the gate behind her with a clang, and as she started up the brick path she uttered a loud, arch "A-hem," as if to warn the young people of her coming, so that they might wrench themselves one from the other. But there was never a squeal of the porch swing, never a creak of a floor board—those noises that tell tales of scurryings to new positions. The only sound was of John Marble's voice, flowing easily along; and when Mrs. Ewing came up on the porch, John Marble would be lying in the swing and Lolita would be sitting in a wicker chair some five feet away from him, with her hands in her lap, and, of course, not a peep out of her. Mrs. Ewing's conscience would smite her at the knowledge of John Marble's one-sided evening, and so she would sit down and toss the ball of conversation in the air and keep it there with reports of the plot of the moving picture she had seen or the hands of the bridge game in which she had taken part. When she, even she, came to a pause, John Marble would rise and explain that the next day was to be a hard one for him and so he must go. Mrs. Ewing would stand at the porch steps and as he went down the path would call after him roguish instructions that he was not to do anything that she would not do.

When she and Lolita came in from the dark porch to the lighted hall, Mrs. Ewing would look at her daughter in an entirely new way. Her eyes narrowed, her lips pressed together, and her mouth turned down at the corners. In silence she surveyed the girl, and still in silence not broken by even a good night, she would mount to her bedroom, and the sound of her closing door would fill the house.

The pattern of the evenings changed. John Marble no longer came to sit on the porch. He arrived in his beautiful car and took Lolita driving through the gentle dark. Mrs. Ewing's thoughts followed them. They would drive out in the country, they would turn off the road to a smooth dell with thick trees to keep it secret from passersby, and there the car would stop. And what would happen then? Did they—Would they—But Mrs. Ewing's thoughts could go no farther. There would come before her a picture of Lolita, and so the thoughts would be finished by her laughter.

All the days, now, she continued to regard the girl under lowered lids, and the downturn of her mouth became a habit with her, though not among her prettier ones. She seldom spoke to Lolita directly, but she still made jokes. When a wider audience was wanting, she called upon Mardy. "Hi, Mardy!" she would cry. "Come on in here, will you? Come in and look at her, sitting there like a queen. Little Miss High-and-Mighty, now she thinks she's caught her a beau!"

There was no announcement of engagement. It was not necessary, for the town sizzled with the news of John Marble and Lolita Ewing. There were two schools of thought as to the match: one blessed Heaven that Lolita had gained a man and the other mourned the callousness of a girl who could go away and leave her mother alone. But miracles were scarce in the annals of the town, and the first school had the more adherents. There was no time for engagement rites. John Marble's business was concluded, and he must go back. There were scarcely hours enough to make ready for the wedding.

It was a big wedding. John Marble first suggested, then stated, that his own plan would be for Lolita and him to go off alone, be married, and then start at once for New York; but Mrs. Ewing paid him no heed. "No, *sir*," she said. "Nobody's going to do *me* out of a great big lovely wedding!" And so nobody did.

Lolita in her bridal attire answered her mother's description of looking like nothing at all. The shiny white fabric of her gown was hostile to her colorless skin, and there was no way to pin the veil becomingly on her hair. But Mrs. Ewing more than made up for her. All in pink ruffles caught up with clusters of false forget-me-nots, Mrs. Ewing was at once bold sunlight and new moonlight, she was budding boughs and opening petals and little, willful breezes. She tripped through the throngs in the smilax garlanded house, and everywhere was heard her laughter. She patted the bridegroom on arm and cheek, and cried out, to guest after guest, that for two cents she would marry him herself. When the time came to throw rice after the departing couple, she was positively devil-may-care. Indeed, so extravagant was her pitching that one hard-packed handful of the sharp little grains hit the bride squarely in the face.

But when the car was driven off, she stood still looking after it, and there came from her downturned mouth a laugh not at all like her usual trill. "Well," she said, "we'll see." Then she was Mrs. Ewing again, running and chirping and urging more punch on her guests.

Lolita wrote to her mother every week without fail, telling of her apartment and the buying and placing of furniture and the always new adventure of shopping; each letter concluded with the information that John hoped Mrs. Ewing was well and sent her his love. The friends eagerly inquired about the bride, wanting to know above all if she was happy. Mrs. Ewing replied that well, yes, she said she was. "That's what I tell her every time I write to her," she said. "I say, 'That's right, honey, you go ahead and be happy just as long as you can.'"

It cannot be said in full truth that Lolita was missed in the town; but there was something lacking in the Ewing house, something lacking in Mrs. Ewing herself. Her friends could not actually define what it was, for she went on as always, flirting the skirts of her little dresses and trying on her little hair ribbons, and there was no slowing of her movements. Still, the glister was not quite so golden. The dinners and the bridge games continued, but somehow they were not as they had been.

Yet the friends must realize she had taken a stunning blow, for Mardy left her; left her, if you please, for the preposterous project of getting married; Mardy, after all the years and all Mrs. Ewing's goodness to her. The friends shook their heads, but Mrs. Ewing, after the first shock, could be gay about it. "I declare," she said, and her laugh spiralled out, "everybody around me goes off and gets married. I'm just a regular little old Mrs. Cupid." In the long line of new maids there were no Mardys; the once cheerful little dinners were gloomy with grease.

Mrs. Ewing made several journeys to see her daughter and son-in-law, bearing gifts of black-eyed peas and tins of herring roe, for New Yorkers do not know how to live and such delicacies are not easily obtained up North. Her visits were widely spaced; there was a stretch of nearly a year between two of them, while Lolita and John Marble travelled in Europe and then went to Mexico. ("Like hens on hot griddles," Mrs. Ewing said. "People ought to stay put.")

Each time she came back from New York, her friends gathered about her, clamoring for reports. Naturally, they quivered for news of oncoming babies. There was none to tell them. There was never any issue of those golden loins and that plank of a body. "Oh, it's just as well," Mrs. Ewing said comfortably, and left the subject there.

John Marble and Lolita were just the same, the friends were told.

John Marble was as devastating as he had been when he first came to the town, and Lolita still had not a word to say for herself. Though her tenth wedding anniversary was coming close, she could not yet give shape to her dresses. She had closets of expensive clothes—when Mrs. Ewing quoted the prices of some of the garments, the friends sucked in their breath sharply—but when she put on a new dress it might as well have been the old one. They had friends, and they entertained quite nicely, and they sometimes went out. Well, yes, they did seem so; they really did seem happy.

"It's just like I tell Lolita," Mrs. Ewing said. "Just like I always say to her when I write: 'You go ahead and be happy as long as you can.' Because—Well, you know. A man like John Marble married to a girl like Lolita! But she knows she can always come here. This house is her home. She can always come back to her mother."

For Mrs. Ewing was not a woman who easily abandoned hope.

Janet Frame

In 1947, Janet Frame, deeply affected by the drowning of two of her sisters in separate accidents, was committed to a psychiatric hospital. There, in her vivid words, the doctors appeared to have forgotten that the inmates too "possessed a prized humanity which needed care and love, that a tiny poetic essence could be distilled from their overflowing squalid truth." After one of her nervous breakdowns, it was suggested that a lobotomy might help her reduce "the tension in her head" and her mother was asked to sign the necessary papers. In her autobiography, Frame describes the moment in which, trapped between her mother and the doctors, she feels she has lost her place in the world. "'I want to go home,' I said. I did not mean to where my parents were living or to any other house of wood, stone or brick. I felt no longer human. I knew I would have to seek shelter now in a hole in the earth or a web in the corner of a high ceiling or a safe nest between two rocks on an exposed coast mauled by the sea. In the rush of loneliness that overcame me, at the doctor's words, I found no place to stay, nowhere to cling like a bat from a branch or spin a milk-white web about a thistle stalk."

"The Pictures," in which the child, though in another world from that of her mother, still has a place to call her own, comes from Frame's first collection, *The Lagoon and Other Stories*, published when she was twenty-one.

THE PICTURES

janet frame

she took her little girl to the pictures. She dressed her in a red pixie-cap and a woolly grey coat, and then she put on her own black coat that it was so hard to get the fluff off, and they got a number four tram to the pictures.

They stood outside the theatre, the woman in the black coat and the little girl in the red pixie-cap and they looked at the advertisements.

It was a wonderful picture. It was the greatest love story ever told. It was Life and Love and Laughter, and Tenderness and Tears.

They walked into the vestibule and over to the box where the ticket-girl waited.

One and a half in the stalls, please, said the woman.

The ticket-girl reached up to the hanging roll of blue tickets and pulled off one and a half, and then looked in the money-box for sixpence change.

Thank you, said the woman in the black coat.

And very soon they were sitting in the dark of the theatre, with people all around them, and they could hear the sound of lollies being unwrapped and papers being screwed up, and people half standing in their seats for other people to pass them, and voices saying can you see are you quite sure.

And then the lights went down further and they stood up for God Save the King. The woman would have liked to sing it, she would have liked to be singing instead of being quiet and just watching the screen with the photo of the King's face and the Union Jack waving through his face.

She had been in a concert once and sung God Save the King and How'd you like to be a baby girl. She had worn a long white nightie that Auntie Kit had run up for her on the machine, and she carried a lighted candle in her hand. Mother and Father were in the audience, and although she had been told not to look, she couldn't help seeing Mother and Father.

But she didn't sing this time. And soon everybody was sitting down and getting comfortable and the Pictures had begun.

The lion growling and then looking over his left shoulder, the kangaroo leaping from a height. That was Australian. The man winding the camera after it was all over. The Eyes and Ears of the World, The End.

There was a cartoon, too, about a cat and a mouse. The little girl laughed. She clapped her hands and giggled and the woman laughed with her. They were the happiest people in the world. They were at the pictures seeing a mouse being shot out of a cannon by a cat, away up the sky the mouse went and then landed whizz-thump behind the cat. And then it was the cat's turn to be shot into the sky whizz-thump and down again.

It was certainly a good picture. Everybody was laughing, and the children down the front were clapping their hands.

There was a fat man quite close to the woman and the little girl. The fat man was laughing haw-haw-haw.

And when the end came and the cat and mouse were both sitting on a cloud, the lights were turned up for Interval, and the lolly and ice-cream boys were walking up to the front of the theatre, ready to be signalled to, well then they were all wiping their eyes and saying, how funny how funny.

The woman and the little girl had sixpence worth of paper lollies to eat then. There were pretty colours on the screen, and pictures of how you ought to furnish your home and where to spend your winter holiday, and the best salon to have your hair curled at, and the clothes you ought to wear if you were a discriminating woman, everything was planned for you.

The woman leaned back in her seat and sighed a long sigh.

She remembered that it was such a nice day outside with all the spring flowers coming into the shops, and the blue sky over the city. Spring was the nicest of all. And in the boarding-house where the woman and the little girl lived there was a daffodil in the window-box.

It was awful living alone with a little girl in a boarding-house.

But there was the daffodil in the window-box, and there were the pictures to go to with the little girl.

And now the pictures had started again. It was the big picture, Errol Flynn and Olivia de Havilland.

Seven thousand feet, the woman said to herself. She liked to remember the length of the picture, it was something to be sure of.

She knew she could see the greatest love story in the world till after four o'clock. It was nice to come to the pictures like that and know how long the story would last.

And to know that in the end he would take her out in the moonlight and a band would play and he would kiss her and everything would be all right again.

So it didn't really matter if he left her, no it didn't matter a bit, even if she cried and then went into a convent and scrubbed stone cells all day and nearly all night . . .

It was sad here. Some of the people took out their handkerchiefs and sniffed in them. And the woman in the black coat hoped it wasn't too near the end for the lights to go up and everybody to see.

But it was all right again because she escaped from the convent and he was waiting for her in the shelter of the trees and they crossed the border into France.

Everything is so exciting and nice, thought the woman with the little girl. She wanted the story to last for ever.

And it was the most wonderful love story in the world. You could tell that. He kissed her so many times. He called her beloved and angel, and he said he would lay down his life for her, and in the end they kissed again, and they sailed on the lake, the beautiful lake with the foreign name. It was midnight and in the background you could see their home that had a white telephone in every room, and ferns in pots and marble pillars against the sky, it was lovely.

And on the lake there was music playing, and moonlight, and the water lapping very softly.

It is a wonderful ending, thought the woman. The full moon up there and the lights and music, it is a wonderful ending.

So the woman and the little girl got up from their seats because they knew it was the end, and they walked into the vestibule, and they blinked their eyes in the hard yellow daylight. There was a big crowd. Some had shiny noses where the tears had rolled.

The woman looked again at the advertisement. The world's greatest love story. Love and Laughter, Tenderness and Tears. It's true, thought the woman, with a happy feeling of remembering.

Together they walked to the tram-stop, the little girl in the red pixie-cap and the woman in the black coat. They stood waiting for a number three car. They would be home just in time for tea at the boarding-house. There were lots of other people waiting for a number three car. Some had gone to the pictures too, and they were talking about it, I like the bit where he, where she.

And although it was long after four o'clock the sun seemed still to be shining hard and bright. The light from it was clean and yellow and warm. The woman looked about her at the sun and the people and the tram-cars, and the sun, the sun sending a warm glow over everything.

There was a little pomeranian being taken along on a lead, and a man with a bunch of spring flowers done up in pink paper from the Floriana at the corner, and an old man standing smoking a pipe and a school-boy yelling *Sta-a-r, Sta-a-r*.

The world was full of people and little dogs and sun.

The woman stood looking, and thinking about going for tea, and the landlady saying, with one hand resting on the table and the other over her face, bless those in need and feed the hungry, and the fat boarder with his soup-spoon halfway up to his mouth, the Government will go out, and the other boarder who was a tram-conductor answering as he reached for the bread, the Government will stay in. And the woman thought of going upstairs and putting the little girl to bed and then touching and looking at the daffodil in the window-box, it was a lovely daffodil. And looking about her and thinking the woman felt sad.

But the little girl in the pixie-cap didn't feel sad, she was eating a paper lolly, it was greeny-blue and it tasted like peppermints.

93

❁

Daphne du Maurier

Daphne du Maurier's genius lay in her plots, which she spun with astounding originality and ease. Her novel *Rebecca,* her short stories "The Birds," "Don't Look Now," "The Blue Lenses," and dozens more have an effectiveness that makes them seem almost traditional, belonging not to any one author but to the imagination of the world. Apparently, she was not as good a stylist as she was a storyteller; her editors worked hard at refining her prose for publication.

"Split Second" is a mother-and-daughter variation on an ancient theme, that of the disturbance of time. According to a Spanish legend, a monk was once distracted from his prayers by the song of a bird in a rosebush. He went out into the garden and listened to the bird for what he thought was just a few minutes, and then returned to his prayers. Inside his abbey, everything had changed and no one knew who he was. To his astonishment (or horror), the monk discovered that a hundred years had passed between the beginning of the song and its end. In America, the legend took on the name of Rip Van Winkle and became the stuff of dreams; in England, in Daphne du Maurier's retelling, it acquired an almost unbearable reality.

SPLIT SECOND

daphne du maurier

m̃rs Ellis was methodical and tidy. She disliked disorder. Unanswered letters, unpaid bills, the litter and rummage of a slovenly writing desk were things that she abhorred.

Today, more than usual, she was in what her late husband used to call her 'clearing' mood.

She had wakened to this mood, it remained with her throughout breakfast and lasted the whole morning.

Besides, it was the first of the month, and as she ripped off the page of her daily calendar and saw the bright clean 1 staring at her, it seemed to symbolize a new start to her day.

The hours ahead of her must somehow seem untarnished like the date; she must let nothing slide.

First she checked the linen. The smooth white sheets lying in rows upon their shelves, pillow slips beside, and one set still in its pristine newness from the shop, tied with blue ribbon, waiting for a guest that never came.

Next, the store cupboard. The stock of homemade jam pleased her, the labels, and the date in her own handwriting.

There were also bottled fruit, and tomatoes, and chutney to her own recipe. She was sparing of these, keeping them in reserve for the holidays when Susan should be home, and even then, when she brought them down and put them proudly on the table, the luxury of the treat was spoilt by a little stab of disappointment; it would mean a gap upon the store-cupboard shelf.

When she had closed the store cupboard and hidden the key (she could never be quite certain of Grace, her cook), Mrs Ellis went into the drawing-room and settled herself at her desk.

She was determined to be ruthless. The pigeonholes were searched, and those old envelopes that she had kept because they were not torn and could be used again (to tradesmen, not to friends) were thrown away. She would buy fresh buff envelopes of a cheap quality instead.

Here were some receipts of two years back. Unnecessary to keep them now. Those of a year ago were filed, and tied with tape.

A little drawer, stiff to open, she found crammed with old counterfoils from her chequebook. This was wasting space.

Instead she wrote in her clear handwriting, 'Letters to Keep'. In the future, the drawer would be used for this purpose.

She permitted herself the luxury of filling her blotter with new sheets of paper. The pen tray was dusted. A new pencil sharpened. And steeling her heart, she threw the stub of the little old one, with worn rubber at the base, into the waste-paper basket.

She straightened the magazines on the side table, pulled the books to the front on the shelf beside the fire—Grace had an infuriating habit of pushing them all to the back—and filled the flower vases with clean water. Then with a bare ten minutes before Grace popped her head round the door and said, 'Lunch is in,' Mrs Ellis sat down, a little breathless, before the fire, and smiled in satisfaction. Her morning had been very full indeed. Happy, well-spent.

She looked about her drawing-room (Grace insisted on calling it the lounge and Mrs Ellis was forever correcting her) and thought how comfortable it was, and bright, and how wise they had been not to move when poor Wilfred suggested it a few months before he died. They had so nearly taken the house in the country, because of his health, and his fad that vegetables should be picked fresh every morning and brought to the table, and then luckily—well, hardly luckily, it was most terribly sad and a fearful shock to her—but before they had signed the lease, Wilfred had a heart attack and died. Mrs Ellis was able to stay on in the home she knew and loved, and where she had first gone as a bride ten years before.

People were inclined to say the locality was going downhill, that it had become worse than suburban. Nonsense. The blocks of flats that were going up at the top end of the road could not be seen from her windows, and the houses, solid like her own, standing in a little circle of front garden, were quite unspoilt.

Besides, she liked the life. Her mornings, shopping in the town, her basket over her arm. The tradesmen knew her, treated her well.

Morning coffee at eleven, at the Cosy Café opposite the bookshop, was a small pleasure she allowed herself on cold mornings—she could not get Grace to make good coffee—and in the summer, the Cosy Café sold ice cream.

Childishly, she would hurry back with this in a paper bag and eat it for lunch; it saved thinking of a sweet.

She believed in a brisk walk in the afternoons, and the heath was so close to hand, it was just as good as the country; and in the evenings she read, or sewed, or wrote to Susan.

Life, if she thought deeply about it, which she did not because to think deeply made her uncomfortable, was really built round Susan. Susan was nine years old, and her only child.

Because of Wilfred's ill-health and, it must be confessed, his irritability, Susan had been sent to boarding school at an early age. Mrs Ellis had passed many sleepless nights before making this decision, but in the end she knew it would be for Susan's good. The child was healthy and high-spirited, and it was impossible to keep her quiet and subdued in one room, with Wilfred fractious in another. It meant sending her down to the kitchen with Grace, and that, Mrs Ellis decided, did not do.

Reluctantly, the school was chosen, some thirty miles away. It was easily reached within an hour and a half by a Green

Line bus; the children seemed happy and well cared for, the principal was grey-haired and sympathetic, and as the prospectus described it, the place was a 'home from home'.

Mrs Ellis left Susan, on the opening day of her first term, in agony of mind, but constant telephone calls between herself and the headmistress during the first week reassured her that Susan had settled placidly to her new existence.

When her husband died, Mrs Ellis thought Susan would want to return home and go to a day school, but to her surprise and disappointment the suggestion was received with dismay, and even tears.

'But I love my school,' said the child; 'we have such fun, and I have lots of friends.'

'You would make other friends at a day school,' said her mother, 'and think, we would be together in the evenings.'

'Yes,' answered Susan doubtfully, 'but what would we do?'

Mrs Ellis was hurt, but she did not permit Susan to see this.

'Perhaps you are right,' she said. 'You are contented and happy where you are. Anyway, we shall always have the holidays.'

The holidays were like brightly coloured beads on a frame and stood out with significance in Mrs Ellis' engagement diary, throwing the weeks between into obscurity.

How leaden was February, in spite of twenty-eight days; how blue and interminable was March, for all that morning coffee at the Cosy Café, the choosing of library books, the visit with friends to the local cinema, or sometimes, more dashing, a matinee 'in town'.

Then April came, and danced its flowery way across the calendar. Easter, and daffodils, and Susan with glowing cheeks whipped by a spring wind, hugging her once again; honey for tea, scones baked by Grace ('You've been and grown again'), those afternoon walks across the heath, sunny and gay because of the figure running on ahead. May was quiet, and June pleasant because of wide-flung windows, and the snapdragons in the front garden; June was leisurely.

Besides, there was the school play on Parents' Day, and Susan, with bright eyes, surely much the best of the pixies, and although she did not speak, her actions were so good.

July dragged until the twenty-fourth, and then the weeks spun themselves into a sequence of glory until the last week in September. Susan at the sea . . . Susan on a farm . . . Susan on Dartmoor . . . Susan just at home, licking an ice cream, leaning out of a window.

'She swims quite well for her age,' thus casually, to a neighbour on the beach; 'she insists on going in, even when it's cold.'

'I don't mind saying,' this to Grace, 'that I hated going through that field of bullocks, but Susan did not mind a scrap. She has a way with animals.'

Bare scratched legs in sandals, summer frocks out-grown, a sun hat, faded, lying on the floor. October did not bear thinking about . . . But, after all, there was always plenty to do about the house. Forget November, and the rain, and the fogs that turned white upon the heath. Draw the curtains, poke the fire, settle to something. The *Weekly Home Companion. Fashions for Young Folk.* Not that pink, but the green with the smocked top, and a wide sash would be just the thing for Susan at parties in the Christmas holidays December . . . Christmas . . .

This was the best, this was the height of home enjoyment.

As soon as Mrs Ellis saw the first small tree standing outside the florist's and those orange boxes of dates in the grocer's window, her heart would give a little leap of excitement.

Susan would be home in three weeks now. Then the laughter and the chatter. The nods between herself and Grace. The smiles of mystery. The furtiveness of wrappings.

All over in one day like the bursting of a swollen balloon; paper ribbon, cracker novelties, even presents, chosen with care, thrown aside. But no matter. It was worth it.

Mrs Ellis, looking down upon a sleeping Susan tucked in with a doll in her arms, turned down the light and crept off to her own bed, sapped, exhausted.

99

The egg cosy, Susan's handiwork at school, hastily stitched, stood on her bedside table.

Mrs Ellis never ate boiled eggs, but, as she said to Grace, there is such gleam in the hen's eye; it's very cleverly done.

The fever, the pace of the New Year. The Circus, the Pantomime. Mrs Ellis watched Susan, never the performers.

'You should have seen her laugh when the seal blew the trumpet; I have never known a child with such a gift for enjoyment.'

And how she stood out at parties, in the green frock, with her fair hair and blue eyes. Other children were so stumpy. Ill-made little bodies, or big shapeless mouths.

'She said, "Thank you for a lovely time," when we left, which was more than most of them did. And she won at Musical Chairs.'

There were bad moments, too, of course. The restless night, the high spot of colour, the sore throat, the temperature of 102.

Shaking hands on the telephone. The doctor's reassuring voice. And his very footsteps on the stairs, a steady, reliable man.

'We had better take a swab, in case.'

A swab? That meant diphtheria, scarlet fever?

A little figure being carried down in blankets, an ambulance, hospital . . . ?

Thank God, it proved to be a relaxed throat. Lots of them about.

Too many parties, keep her quiet for a few days. Yes, Doctor, yes.

The relief from dread anxiety, and on and on without a stop, the reading to Susan from her *Playbook Annual*, story after story, terrible and trite, 'and so Nicky Nod *did* lose his treasure after all, which just served him right, didn't it, children?'

'All things pass,' thought Mrs Ellis, 'pleasure and pain, and happiness and suffering, and I suppose my friends would say my life is a dull one, rather uneventful, but I am grateful for it, and contented, and although sometimes I feel I did not do my utmost for poor Wilfred—his was a difficult nature, luckily Susan has not inherited it—at least I believe I have succeeded in making a happy home for Susan.' She looked about her, that first day of the month, and noticed with affection and appreciation those bits and pieces of furniture, the pictures on the walls, the ornaments on the mantelpiece, all the things she had gathered about her during ten years of marriage, and which meant herself, her home.

The sofa and two chairs, part of an original suite, were worn but comfortable. The pouf by the fire, she had covered it herself. The fire irons, not quite so polished as they should be, she must speak to Grace. The rather melancholy portrait of Wilfred in that dark corner behind the bookshelf, he looked at least distinguished. And was, thought Mrs Ellis to herself, hastily. The flower picture showed more to advantage over the mantelpiece; the green foliage harmonized so well with the green coat of the Staffordshire figure who stood with his lady beside the clock.

'I could do with new covers,' thought Mrs Ellis, 'and curtains too, but they must wait. Susan has grown so enormously the last few months. Her clothes are more important. The child is tall for her age.'

Grace looked round the door. 'Lunch is in,' she said.

'If she would open the door outright,' thought Mrs Ellis, 'and come right into the room, I have mentioned it a hundred times. It's the sudden thrust of the head that is so disconcerting, and if I have anyone to lunch . . .'

She sat down to guinea fowl and apple charlotte, and she wondered if they were remembering to give Susan extra milk at school this term, and the Minidex tonic; the matron was inclined to be forgetful.

Suddenly, for no reason, she laid her spoon down on the plate, swept with a wave of such intense melancholy as to be almost unbearable. Her heart was heavy. Her throat tightened. She could not continue her lunch.

'Something is wrong with Susan,' she thought; 'this is a warning that she wants me.'

She rang for coffee and went into the drawing-room. She crossed to the window and stood looking at the back of the house opposite. From an open window sagged an ugly red curtain, and a lavatory brush hung from a nail.

'The district *is* losing class,' thought Mrs Ellis. 'I shall have lodginghouses for neighbours soon.'

She drank her coffee, but the feeling of uneasiness, of apprehension, did not leave her. At last she went to the telephone and rang up the school.

The secretary answered. Surprised, and a little impatient, surely. Susan was perfectly all right. She had just eaten a good lunch. No, she had no sign of a cold. No one was ill in the school. Did Mrs Ellis want to speak to Susan? The child was outside with the others, playing, but could be called in if necessary.

'No,' said Mrs Ellis, 'it was just a foolish notion on my part that Susan might not be well. I am so sorry to have bothered you.'

She hung up the receiver, and then went to her bedroom to put on her outdoor clothes. A good walk would do her good.

She gazed in satisfaction upon the photograph of Susan on the dressing table. The photographer had caught the expression in her eyes to perfection. Such a lovely light on the hair too.

Mrs Ellis hesitated. Was it really a walk she needed? Or was this vague feeling of distress a sign that she was over-tired, that she had better rest?

She looked with inclination at the downy quilt upon her bed. Her hot-water bottle, hanging by the washstand, would take only a moment to fill.

She could loosen her girdle, throw off her shoes, and lie down for an hour on the bed, warm with the bottle under the downy quilt. No. She decided to be firm with herself. She went to the wardrobe and got out her camel coat, wound a scarf round her head, pulled on a pair of gauntlet gloves, and walked downstairs.

She went into the drawing-room and made up the fire, and put the guard in front of it. Grace was apt to be forgetful of the fire. She opened the window at the top so that the room should not strike stuffy when she came back.

She folded the daily papers ready to read when she returned, and replaced the marker in her library book.

'I'm going out for a little while. I shan't be long,' she called down to the basement to Grace.

'All right ma'am,' came the answer.

Mrs Ellis caught the whiff of cigarette, and frowned. Grace could do as she liked in the basement, but there was something not quite right about a maidservant smoking.

She shut the front door behind her, and went down the steps, and into the road, and turned left towards the heath.

It was a dull, grey day. Mild for the time of year, almost to oppression. Later, there would be fog, perhaps rolling up from London the way it did, in a great wall, stifling the clean air.

Mrs Ellis made her 'short round', as she always called it. Eastward, to the Viaduct ponds, and then back, circling to the Vale of Health.

It was not an inviting afternoon, and she did not enjoy her walk. She kept wishing she was home again, in bed with a hot-water bottle, or sitting in the drawing-room beside the fire, soon to shut out the muggy, murky sky, and draw the curtains.

She walked swiftly past nurses pushing prams, two or three of them in groups chatting together, their charges running ahead. Dogs barked beside the ponds. Solitary men in mackintoshes stared into vacancy. An old woman on a seat threw crumbs to chirping sparrows. The sky took on a darker, olive tone. Mrs Ellis quickened her steps. The fairground by the Vale of Health looked sombre, the merry-go-round shrouded in its winter wrappings of canvas, and two lean cats stalked each other in and out of the palings.

A milkman, whistling, clanked his tray of bottles and, lifting them to his cart, urged the pony to a trot.

'I must,' thought Mrs Ellis inconsequently, 'get Susan a bicycle for her birthday. Nine is a good age for a first bicycle.'

She saw herself choosing one, asking advice, feeling the handle bars, the colour red perhaps. Or a good blue. A little basket on the front and a leather bag, for tools, strapped to the back of the seat. The brakes must be good, but not too gripping, otherwise Susan would topple headfirst over the handle bars and graze her face.

Hoops were out of fashion, which was a pity. When she had been a child there had been no fun like a good springy hoop, struck smartly with a little stick, bowling its way ahead of you. Quite an art to it too. Susan would have been good with a hoop.

Mrs Ellis came to the junction of two roads, and crossed to the opposite side; the second road was her own, and her house the last one on the corner.

As she did so she saw the laundry van swinging down towards her, much too fast. She saw it swerve, heard the screech of its brakes. She saw the look of surprise on the face of the laundry boy.

'I shall speak to the driver next time he calls,' she said to herself. 'One of these days there will be an accident.'

She thought of Susan on the bicycle, and shuddered.

Perhaps a note to the manager of the laundry would do more good.

'If you could possibly give a word of warning to your driver, I should be grateful. He takes his corners much too fast.'

And she would ask to remain anonymous. Otherwise the man might complain about carrying the heavy basket down the steps each time.

She had arrived at her own gate. She pushed it open, and noticed with annoyance that it was nearly off its hinges. The men calling for the laundry must have wrenched at it in some way and done the damage. The note to the manager would be stronger still. She would write immediately after tea. While it was on her mind.

She took out her key and put it in the Yale lock of the front door. It stuck. She could not turn it. How very irritating.

She rang the bell. That would mean bringing Grace up from the basement, which she did not like.

Better to call down, perhaps, and explain the situation.

She leant over the steps and called down to the kitchen.

'Grace, it's only me,' she said, 'my key has jammed in the door; could you come up and let me in?'

She paused. There was no sound from below. Grace must have gone out. This was sheer deceit. It was an agreed bargain between them that when Mrs Ellis was out Grace must stay in. The house must not be left. But sometimes Mrs Ellis suspected that Grace did not keep to the bargain. Here was proof.

She called once again, rather more sharply this time. 'Grace?'

There was a sound of a window opening below, and a man thrust his head out of the kitchen. He was in his shirt sleeves. And he had not shaved.

'What are you bawling your head off about?' he said.

Mrs Ellis was too stunned to answer. So this was what happened when her back was turned. Grace, respectable, well over thirty, had a man in the house. Mrs Ellis swallowed, but kept her temper.

'Perhaps you will have the goodness to ask Grace to come upstairs and let me in,' she said.

The sarcasm was wasted, of course. The man blinked at her, bewildered.

'Who's Grace?' he said.

This was too much. So Grace had the nerve to pass under another name. Something fanciful, no doubt, Shirley, or Marlene.

She was pretty sure now what must have happened. Grace had slipped out to the public house down the road to buy this man beer. The man was left to loll in the kitchen. He might even have been poking his fingers in the larder. Now she knew why there was so little left on the joint two days ago.

'If Grace is out,' said Mrs Ellis, and her voice was icy, 'kindly let me in yourself. I prefer not to use the back entrance.'

That would put him in his place. Mrs Ellis trembled with rage. She was angry seldom; she was a mild, even-tempered woman. But this reception, from a lout in shirt sleeves, at her own kitchen window, was rather more than she could bear.

It was going to be unpleasant, the interview with Grace. Grace would give notice in all probability. But some things could not be allowed to slide, and this was one of them.

She heard shuffling footsteps coming along the hall. The man had mounted from the basement. He opened the front door and stood there, staring at her.

'Who is it you want?' he said.

Mrs Ellis heard the furious yapping of a little dog from the drawing-room. Callers . . . This was the end. How perfectly frightful, how really overwhelmingly embarrassing. Someone had called, and Grace had let them in, or, worse still, this man in his shirt sleeves had done so. What would people think?

'Who is in the drawing-room, do you know?' she murmured swiftly.

'I think Mr and Mrs Bolton are in, but I'm not sure,' he said. 'I can hear the dog yapping. Was it them you wanted to see?'

Mrs Ellis did not know a Mr and Mrs Bolton. She turned impatiently towards the drawing-room, first slipping off her coat and putting her gloves in her pocket.

'You had better go down to the basement again,' she said to the man, who was still staring at her; 'tell Grace not to bring tea until I ring. These people may not stay.'

The man appeared bewildered.

'All right,' he said, 'I'm going down. But if you want Mr and Mrs Bolton again, ring twice.'

He shuffled off down the basement stairs. He was drunk, no doubt. He meant to be insulting. If he proved difficult, later in the evening, after dark, it would mean ringing for the police.

Mrs Ellis slipped into the lobby to hang up her coat. No time to go upstairs if callers were in the drawing-room. She fumbled for the switch and turned it, but the bulb had gone. Another pinprick. Now she could not see herself in the mirror.

She stumbled over something, and bent to see what it was. It was a man's boot. And here was another, and a pair of shoes, and beside them a suitcase and an old rug. If Grace had allowed that man to put his things in her lobby, then Grace would go tonight. Crisis had come. High crisis.

Mrs Ellis opened the drawing-room door, forcing a smile of welcome, not too warm, upon her lips. A little dog rushed towards her, barking furiously.

'Quiet Judy,' said a man, grey-haired, with horn spectacles, sitting before the fire. He was clicking a typewriter.

Something had happened to the room. It was covered with books and papers; odds and ends of junk littered the floor. A parrot, in a cage, hopped on its perch and screeched a welcome.

Mrs Ellis tried to speak, but her voice would not come. Grace had gone raving mad. She had let that man into the house, and this one too, and they had brought the most terrible disorder; they had turned the room upside down; they had deliberately, maliciously, set themselves to destroy her things.

No. Worse! It was part of a great thieving plot. She had heard of such things. Gangs went about breaking into houses. Grace, perhaps, was not at fault. She was lying in the basement, gagged and bound. Mrs Ellis felt her heart beating much too fast. She also felt a little faint.

'I must keep calm,' she said to herself, 'whatever happens, I must keep calm. If I can get to the telephone, to the police, it is the only hope. This man must not see that I am planning what to do.'

The little dog kept sniffing at her heels.

'Excuse me,' said the intruder, pushing his horn spectacles on to his forehead, 'but do you want anything? My wife is upstairs.'

The diabolic cunning of the plot. The cool bluff of his sitting here, the typewriter on his knees. They must have brought all this stuff in through the door to the back garden; the French window was ajar. Mrs Ellis glanced swiftly at the mantelpiece. It was as she feared. The Staffordshire figures had been removed, and the flower picture too. There must be a car, a van, waiting down the road . . . Her mind worked quickly. It might be that the man had not guessed her identity. Two could play at bluff. Memories of amateur theatricals flashed through her mind. Somehow she must detain these people until the police arrived. How fast they had worked. Her desk was gone, the bookshelves too, nor could she see her armchair.

But she kept her eyes steadily on the stranger. He must not notice her brief glance around the room.

'Your wife is upstairs?' said Mrs Ellis, her voice strained, yet calm.

'Yes,' said the man, 'if you've come for an appointment, she always makes them. You'll find her in the studio. Room in the front.'

Steadily, softly, Mrs Ellis left the drawing-room, but the wretched little dog had followed her, sniffing at her heels.

One thing was certain. The man had not realized who she was. They believed the householder out of the way for the afternoon, and that she, standing now in the hall, listening, her heart beating, was some caller to be fobbed off with a lie about appointments.

She stood silently by the drawing-room door. The man had resumed typing on his machine. She marveled at the coolness of it, the drawn-out continuity of the bluff.

There had been nothing in the papers very recently about large-scale house robberies. This was something new, something outstanding. It was extraordinary that they should pick on her house. But they must know she was a widow, on her own, with one maidservant. The telephone had already been removed from the stand in the hall. There was a loaf of bread on it instead, and something that looked like meat wrapped up in newspaper. So they had brought provisions . . . There was a chance that the telephone in her bedroom had not yet been taken away, nor the wires cut. The man had said his wife was upstairs. It may have been part of his bluff, or it might be true that he worked with a woman accomplice. This woman, even now, was probably turning out Mrs Ellis' wardrobe, seizing her fur coat, ramming the single string of cultured pearls into a pocket.

Mrs Ellis thought she could hear footsteps in her bedroom.

Her anger overcame her fear. She had not the strength to do battle with the man, but she could face the woman. And if the worst came to the worst, she would run to the window, put her head out, and scream. The people next door would hear. Or some-one might be passing in the street.

Stealthily, Mrs Ellis crept upstairs. The little dog led the way with confidence. She paused outside her bedroom door. There was certainly movement from within. The little dog waited, his eyes fixed upon her with intelligence.

At that moment the door of Susan's small bedroom opened, and a fat elderly woman looked out, blowsy, and red in the face. She had a tabby cat under her arm. As soon as the dog saw the cat it started a furious yapping.

'Now that's torn it,' said the woman. 'What do you want to bring the dog upstairs for? They always fight when they meet. Do you know if the post's been yet? Oh, sorry. I thought you were Mrs Bolton.'

She brought an empty milk bottle from under her other arm and put it down on the landing.

'I'm blowed if I can manage the stairs today,' she said, 'somebody else will have to take it down for me. Is it foggy out?'

'No,' said Mrs Ellis, shocked into a natural answer, and then, feeling the woman's eyes upon her, hesitated between enter-ing her bedroom door and withdrawing down the stairs. This evil-looking old woman was part of the gang and might call the man from below.

'Got an appointment?' said the other. 'She won't see you if you haven't booked an appointment.'

A tremor of a smile appeared on Mrs Ellis' lips.

'Thank you,' she said, 'yes, I have an appointment.'

She was amazed at her own steadiness, and that she could carry off the situation with such aplomb. An actress on the London stage could not have played her part better.

The elderly woman winked and, drawing nearer, plucked Mrs Ellis by the sleeve.

'Is she going to do you straight or fancy?' she whispered. 'It's the fancy ones that get the men. You know what I mean!'

She nudged Mrs Ellis and winked again.

'I see by your ring you're married,' she said. 'You'd be surprised even the quietest husbands like their pictures fancy. Take a tip from an old pro. Get her to do you fancy.'

She lurched back into Susan's room, the cat under her arm, and shut the door.

'It's possible,' thought Mrs Ellis, the faint feeling coming over her again, 'that a group of lunatics have escaped from an asylum, and in their terrible, insane fashion, they have broken into my house not to thieve, not to destroy my belongings, but because in some crazed, deluded fashion they believe themselves to be at home.'

The publicity would be frightful once it became known. Headlines in the paper. Her photograph taken. So bad for Susan. Susan . . . That horrible, disgusting old woman in Susan's bedroom.

Emboldened, fortified, Mrs Ellis opened her own bedroom door. One glance revealed the worst. The room was bare, was stripped. There were several lights at various points of the room, flexes attached, and a camera on a tripod. A divan was pushed against the wall. A young woman, with a crop of thick fuzzy hair, was kneeling on the floor, sorting papers.

'Who is it?' she said. 'I don't see anyone without an appointment. You've no right to come in here.'

Mrs Ellis, calm, resolute, did not answer. She had made certain that the telephone, though it had been moved like the rest of her things, was still in the room.

She went to it and lifted the receiver.

'Leave my telephone alone,' cried the shock-haired girl, and she began to struggle to her knees.

'I want them to come at once to 17 Elmhurst Road. I am in great danger. Please report this message to the police at once.'

The girl was beside her now, taking the receiver from her. 'Who's sent you here?' said the girl, her face sallow, colourless, against the fuzzy hair. 'If you think you can come in snooping, you're mistaken. You won't find anything. Nor the police, neither. I have a trade licence for the work I do.'

Her voice had risen, and the dog, alarmed, joined her with high-pitched barks. The girl opened the door and called down the stairs.

'Harry?' she shouted. 'Come here and throw this woman out.'

Mrs Ellis remained quite calm. She stood with her back to the wall, her hands folded. The exchange had taken her message. It would not be long now before the police arrived.

She heard the drawing-room door open from below, and the man's voice called up, petulant, irritated.

'What's the matter?' he shouted. 'You know I'm busy. Can't you deal with the woman? She probably wants a special pose.'

The girl's eyes narrowed. She looked closely at Mrs Ellis.

'What did my husband say to you?' she said.

'Ah!' thought Mrs Ellis triumphantly. 'They are getting frightened. It's not such an easy game as they think.'

'I had no conversation with your husband,' said Mrs Ellis quietly; 'he merely told me I should find you upstairs. In this room. Don't try any bluff with me. It's too late. I can see what you have been doing.'

She gestured at the room. The girl stared at her.

'You can't put any phony business over on me,' she said; 'this studio is decent, respectable, everyone knows that I take camera studies of children. Plenty of clients can testify to that. You've got no proof of anything else. Show me a negative, and then I might believe you.'

Mrs Ellis wondered how long it would be before the police came. She must continue to play for time. Later, she might even feel sorry, perhaps, for this wretched, deluded girl who had wrought such havoc in the bedroom, believing herself to be a photographer; but this moment, now, she must be calm, calm.

'Well?' said the girl. 'What are you going to say when the police come? What's your story?'

It did not do to antagonize lunatics. Mrs Ellis knew that. They must be humoured. She must humour this girl until the

111

police came.

'I shall tell them that I live here,' she said gently; 'that is all they will need to know. Nothing further.'

The girl looked at her, puzzled, and lit a cigarette.

'Then it is a pose you want?' she said. 'That call was just a bluff? Why don't you come clean and say why you're here?'

The sound of their voices had attracted the attention of the old woman in Susan's room. She tapped on the door, which was already open, and stood on the threshold.

'Anything wrong, dear?' she said slyly to the girl.

'Push on out of it,' said the girl impatiently, 'this is none of your business. I don't interfere with you, and you don't interfere with me.'

'I'm not interfering, dear,' said the woman, 'I only wanted to know if I could help. Difficult client, eh? Wants something outsize?'

'Oh, shut your mouth,' said the girl.

The girl's husband, Bolton or whatever his name was, the spectacled man from the drawing-room, came upstairs and into the bedroom.

'Just what's going on?' he said.

The girl shrugged her shoulders and glanced at Mrs Ellis.

'I don't know,' she said, 'but I think it's blackmail.'

'Has she got any negatives?' said the man swiftly.

'Not that I know of. Never seen her before.'

'She might have got them from another client,' said the elderly woman, watching.

The three of them stared at Mrs Ellis. She was not afraid. She had the situation well in hand.

'I think we've all become a little overwrought,' she said, 'and much the best thing to do would be to go downstairs, sit quietly by the fire, and have a little chat, and you can talk to me about your work. Tell me, are you all three photographers?'

As she spoke, half of her mind was wondering where they had managed to hide her things. They must have bundled her bed into Susan's room; the wardrobe was in two parts, of course, and could be taken to pieces very soon; but her clothes . . . her ornaments . . . these must have been concealed in a lorry. Somewhere, there was a lorry filled with all her things. It might have been driven off already by yet another accomplice. The police were good at tracing stolen goods, she knew that, and everything was insured; but such a mess had been made of the house; insurance would never cover that, nor would her fire policy, unless there was some clause, some proviso against damage by lunatics; surely the insurance people would not call that an act of God . . . Her mind ran on and on, taking in the mess, the disorder, these people had created, and how many days and weeks would it take for her and Grace to get everything straight again?

Poor Grace. She had forgotten Grace. Grace must be shut up somewhere in the basement with that dreadful man in shirt sleeves, another of the gang, not a follower at all.

'Well,' said Mrs Ellis with the other half of her mind, the half that was acting so famously, 'shall we do as I suggest and go downstairs?'

She turned, and led the way, and to her surprise they followed her, the man and his wife, not the horrible old woman. She remained above, leaning over the banisters.

'Call me if you want me,' she said.

Mrs Ellis could not bear to think of her fingering Susan's things in the little bedroom.

'Won't you join us?' she said, steeling herself to courtesy. 'It's far more cheerful down below.'

The old woman smirked. 'That's for Mr and Mrs Bolton to say,' she said, 'I don't push myself.'

'If I can get all three of them pinned into the drawing-room,' thought Mrs Ellis, 'and somehow lock the door, and make a tremendous effort at conversation, I might possibly keep their attention until the police arrive. There is, of course, the door into the garden, but they will have to climb the fence, fall over that potting shed next door. The old woman, at least, would never do it.'

'Now,' said Mrs Ellis, her heart turning over inside at the havoc of the drawing-room, 'shall we sit down and recover ourselves, and you shall tell me all about this photography.'

But she had scarcely finished speaking before there was a ring at the front door, and a knock, authoritative, loud.

The relief sent her dizzy. She steadied herself against the door. It was the police. The man looked at the girl, a question in his eye.

'Better have 'em in,' he said, 'she's got no proof.'

He crossed the hall and opened the front door.

'Come in, officer,' he said. 'There's two of you, I see.'

'We had a telephone call,' Mrs Ellis heard the constable say, 'some trouble going on, I understand.'

'I think there must be some mistake,' said Bolton. 'The fact is, we've had a caller and I think she got hysterical.'

Mrs Ellis walked out into the hall. She did not recognize the constable, nor the young policeman from the beat. It was unfortunate, but it did not really matter. Both were stout, well-built men.

'I am not hysterical,' she said firmly, 'I am perfectly all right. I put the telephone call through to the exchange.'

The constable took out a notebook and a pencil.

'What's the trouble?' he said. 'But give me first your name and address.'

Mrs Ellis smiled patiently. She hoped he was not going to be a stupid man.

'It's hardly necessary,' she said, 'but my name is Mrs Wilfred Ellis of this address.'

'Lodge here?' asked the constable.

Mrs Ellis frowned. 'No,' she said, 'this is my house, I live here.' And then because she saw the look flash from Bolton to his wife, she knew the time had come to be explicit. 'I must speak to you alone, Constable,' she said, 'the matter is terribly urgent; I don't think you quite understand.'

'If you have any charge to bring, Mrs Ellis,' said the officer, 'you can bring it at the police station at the proper time. We were informed that somebody lodging here at Number 17 was in danger. Are you, or are you not, the person who gave that information to the exchange?'

Mrs Ellis began to lose control.

'Of course I am that person,' she said. 'I returned home
to find that my house had been broken into by thieves, these people
here, dangerous thieves, lunatics, I don't know what they are, and
my things carried away, the whole of my house turned upside
down, the most terrible disorder everywhere.'

She talked so rapidly, her words fell over themselves.

The man from the basement had now joined them in
the hall. He stared at the two policemen, his eyes goggling.

'I saw her come to the door,' he said; 'I thought she was
barmy. Wouldn't have let her in if I had known.'

The constable, a little nettled, turned to the interruption.

'Who are you?' he said.

'Name of Upshaw,' said the man, 'William Upshaw. Me
and my missus has the basement flat here.'

'That man is lying,' said Mrs Ellis, 'he does not live
here, he belongs to this gang of thieves. Nobody lives in the basement except my maid—perhaps I should say cook-general—Grace
Jackson, and if you will search the premises you will probably find
her gagged and bound somewhere, and by that ruffian.'

She had now lost all restraint. She could hear her voice,
usually low and quiet, rising to a hysterical pitch.

'Barmy,' said the man from the basement, 'you can see
the straw in her hair.'

'Quiet, please,' said the constable, and turned an ear to
the young policeman, who murmured something in his ear.

'Yes, yes,' he said, 'I've got the directory here. It's all
in order.'

He consulted another book. Mrs Ellis watched him
feverishly. Never had she seen such a stupid man. Why had they
sent out such a slow-witted fool from the police station?

The constable now turned to the man in the horn
spectacles.

'Are you Henry Bolton?' he asked.

'Yes, officer,' replied the man eagerly, 'and this is my wife. We have the ground floor here. This is my wife. She uses an upstairs room for a studio. Camera portraits, you know.'

There was a shuffle down the stairs, and the old evil woman came to the foot of the banister.

'My name's Baxter,' she said, 'Billie Baxter they used to call me in my old stage days. Used to be in the profession, you know. I have the first-floor back here at Number 17. I can witness this woman came as a sort of Paul Pry, and up to no good. I saw her looking through the keyhole of Mrs Bolton's studio.'

'Then she doesn't lodge here?' asked the constable. 'I didn't think she did: the name isn't in the directory.'

'We have never seen her before, officer,' said Bolton. 'Mr. Upshaw let her into the house through some error; she walked into our living-room, and then forced her way into my wife's studio, threatened her, and in hysterical fashion rang for the police.'

The constable looked at Mrs Ellis.

'Anything to say?' he said.

Mrs Ellis swallowed. If only she could keep calm, if only her heart would not beat so dreadfully fast, and the terrible desire to cry would not rise in her throat.

'Constable,' she said, 'there has been some terrible mistake. You are new to the district, perhaps, and the young policeman too—I don't seem to recognize him—but if you would kindly get through to your headquarters, they must know all about me; I have lived here for years. My maid Grace has been with me a very long time; I am a widow; my husband, Wilfred Ellis, has been dead two years; I have a little girl of nine at school. I went out for a walk on the heath this afternoon, and during my absence these people have broken into my house, seized or destroyed my belongings—I don't know which—the whole place is upside down; if you would please get through immediately to your headquarters . . .'

'There, there,' said the constable, putting his notebook away, 'that's all right; we can go into all that quietly down at the station. Now, do any of you want to charge Mrs Ellis with trespassing?'

There was silence. Nobody said anything.

'We don't wish to be unkind,' said Bolton diffidently; 'I think my wife and myself are quite willing to let the matter pass.'

'I think it should be clearly understood,' interposed the shock-haired girl, 'that anything this woman says about us at the police station is completely untrue.'

'Quite,' said the officer. 'You will both be called, if needed, but I very much doubt the necessity. Now, Mrs Ellis'—he turned to her, not harshly in any way, but with authority—'we have a car outside, and we can run you down to the station, and you can tell your story there. Have you a coat?'

Mrs Ellis turned blindly to the lobby. She knew the police station well; it was barely five minutes away. It was best to go there direct. See someone in authority, not this fool, this hopeless, useless fool. But in the meantime, these people were getting away with their criminal story. By the time she and an additional police force returned, they would have fled. She groped for her coat in the dark lobby, stumbling again over the boots, the suitcases.

'Constable,' she said softly, 'here, one minute.'

He moved towards her.

'Yes?' he said.

'They've taken away the electric bulb,' she said rapidly in a low whisper; 'it was perfectly all right this afternoon, and these boots, and this pile of suitcases, all these have been brought in, and thrown here; the suitcases are probably filled with my ornaments. I must ask you most urgently to leave the policeman in charge here until we return, to see that these people don't escape.'

'That's all right, Mrs Ellis,' said the officer. 'Now, are you ready to come along?'

She saw a look pass between the constable and the young policeman. The young policeman was trying to hide his smile.

Mrs Ellis felt certain that the constable was *not* going to remain in the house. And a new suspicion flashed into her mind. Could this officer and his subordinate be genuine members of the

117

police force? Or were they, after all, members of the gang? This would explain their strange faces, their obvious mishandling of the situation. In which case they were now going to take her away to some lair, drug her, kill her possibly.

'I'm not going with you,' she said, swiftly.

'Now, Mrs Ellis,' said the constable, 'don't give any trouble. You shall have a cup of tea down at the station, and no one is going to hurt you.'

He seized her arm. She tried to shake it off. The young policeman moved closer.

'Help,' she shouted, 'help . . . help . . .'

There must be someone. Those people from next door, she barely knew them, but no matter, if she raised her voice loud enough . . .

'Poor thing,' said the man in shirt sleeves, 'seems sad, don't it? I wonder how she got like it.'

Mrs Ellis saw his bulbous eyes fixed on her with pity, and she nearly choked.

'You rogue,' she said, 'how dare you, how dare you?' But she was being bundled down the steps, and through the front garden, and into the car, and there was another policeman at the wheel of the car; and she was thrust at the back, the constable keeping a steady hold upon her arm.

The car turned downhill, past the stretch of heath; she tried to see out of the windows the direction, but the bulk of the constable prevented her.

After twisting and turning, the car stopped, to her great surprise, in front of the police station.

Then these men were genuine, after all. They were not members of the gang. Stupefied for a moment, but relieved, thankful, Mrs Ellis stumbled from the car. The constable, still holding her arm, led her inside.

The hall was not unfamiliar; she remembered coming once before, years ago, when the ginger cat was lost; there was somebody in charge always, sitting at a sort of desk, everything very official, very brisk. She supposed she would stop here in the hall, but the constable led her on to an inner room, and here was another officer seated at a large desk, a more superior type altogether, thank heaven, and he looked intelligent.

She was determined to get her word in before the constable spoke.

'There has been great confusion,' she began. 'I am Mrs Ellis, of 17 Elmhurst Road, and my house has been broken into, robbery is going on at this moment on a huge scale; I believe the thieves to be very desperate and extraordinarily cunning; they have completely taken in the constable here, and the other policeman . . .'

To her indignation this superior officer did not look at her. He raised his eyebrows at the constable, and the constable, who had taken off his hat, coughed and approached the desk. A policewoman, appearing from nowhere, stood beside Mrs Ellis and held her arm.

The constable and the superior officer were talking together in low tones. Mrs Ellis could not hear what they were saying. Her legs trembled with emotion. She felt her head swim.

Thankfully, she accepted the chair dragged forward by the policewoman, and in a few moments, too, she was given a cup of tea. She did not want it though. Precious time was being lost.

'I must insist that you hear what I have to say,' she said, and the policewoman tightened her grip on Mrs Ellis' arm. The superior officer behind the desk motioned Mrs Ellis forward, and she was assisted to another chair, the policewoman remaining beside her all the while.

'Now,' he said, 'what is it you want to tell me?'

Mrs Ellis gripped her hands together. She had a premonition that this man, in spite of his superior face, was going to prove as great a fool as the constable.

'My name is Ellis,' she said, 'Mrs Wilfred Ellis of 17 Elmhurst Road. I am in the telephone book. I am in the directory. I am very well known in the district, and have lived at Elmhurst Road for ten years. I am a widow, and I have one little girl of nine

years at present at school. I employ one maidservant, Grace
Jackson, who cooks for me and does general work. This afternoon
I went for a short walk on the heath, round by the Viaduct and the
Vale of Health ponds, and when I returned home I found my
house had been broken into; my maid had disappeared; the rooms
were already stripped of my belongings, and the thieves were in possession of my home, putting up a stupendous act of bluff that
deceived even the constable here. I put the call through to the
exchange, which frightened the thieves, and I endeavoured to
keep them pinned in my drawing-room until help arrived.'

Mrs Ellis paused for breath. She saw that the officer
was paying attention to her story, and kept his eyes fixed upon her.

'Thank you,' he said, 'that is very helpful, Mrs Ellis.
Now, have you anything you can show me to prove your identity?'

She stared at him. Prove her identity? Well, of course.
But not here, not actually on her person. She had come away
without her handbag, and her calling cards were in the writing
desk, and her passport—she and Wilfred had been to Dieppe
once—was, if she remembered rightly, in the left-hand pigeonhole
of the small writing desk in her bedroom.

But she suddenly remembered the havoc of the house.
Nothing would be found . . .

'It's very unfortunate,' she said to the officer, 'but I did not
take my handbag with me when I went out for my walk this afternoon. I left it in the chest of drawers in the bedroom. My calling
cards are in the desk in the drawing-room, and there is a passport—
rather out of date; my husband and I did not travel much—in a
pigeonhole in a small desk in my bedroom. But everything has
been upset, taken by these thieves. The house is in utter chaos.'

The officer made a note on a pad beside him.

'You can't produce your identity card or your ration
book?' he asked.

'I have explained,' said Mrs Ellis, governing her temper,
'my calling cards are in my writing desk. I don't know what you
mean by ration book.'

The officer went on writing in his pad. He glanced at the policewoman, who began feeling Mrs Ellis' pockets, touching her in a familiar way. Mrs Ellis tried to think which of her friends could be telephoned to, who could vouch for her, who could come at once by car and make these idiots, these stone-witted fools, see sense.

'I must keep calm,' she told herself again, 'I must keep calm.'

The Collinses were abroad; they would have been the best, but Netta Draycott should be; she was usually at home about this time because of the children.

'I have asked you,' said Mrs Ellis, 'to verify my name and address in the telephone book, or the district directory. If you refuse to do that, ask the postmaster, or the manager of my bank, a branch of which is in the High Street, and where I cashed a cheque on Saturday. Finally, would you care to ring up Mrs Draycott, a friend of mine, 21 Charlton Court, the block of flats in Charlton Avenue, who will vouch for me?'

She sat back in the chair, exhausted. No nightmare, she told herself, could ever have the horror, the frustrated hopelessness, of her present plight. Little incident piled on little incident. If she had only remembered to bring her handbag, there was a calling-card case in her handbag. And all the while those thieves, those devils, breaking up her home, getting away with her precious things, her belongings . . .

'Now, Mrs Ellis,' said the officer, 'we have checked up on your statements, you know, and they won't do. You are not in the telephone book, nor in the directory.'

'I assure you I am,' said Mrs Ellis with indignation; 'give me the books and I'll show you.'

The constable, still standing, placed the books before her. She ran her finger down the name of Ellis to the position on the left-hand page where she knew it would be. The name Ellis was repeated, but not hers. And none with her address or number. She looked in the directory and saw that beside 17 Elmhurst Road were the names of Bolton, of Upshaw, of Baxter . . . She pushed both books away from her. She stared at the officer.

'There is something wrong with these books,' she said, 'they are not up to date, they are false, they are not the books I have at home.'

The officer did not answer. He closed the books.

'Now, Mrs Ellis,' he said, 'I can see you are tired, and a rest would do you good. We will try to find your friends for you. If you will go along now, we will get in touch with them as soon as possible. I will send a doctor along to you, and he may chat with you a little and give you a sedative, and then, after some rest, you will feel better in the morning and we may have news for you.'

The policewoman helped Mrs Ellis to her feet.

'Come along now,' she said.

'But my house?' said Mrs Ellis. 'Those thieves, and my maid Grace, Grace may be lying in the basement; surely you are going to do something about the house; you won't permit them to get away with this monstrous crime; even now we have wasted a precious half hour—'

'That's all right, Mrs Ellis,' said the officer, 'you can leave everything in our hands.'

The policewoman led her away, still talking, still protesting, and now she was being taken down a corridor, and the policewoman kept saying:

'Now, don't fuss, take it calmly; no one's going to hurt you,' and she was in a little room with a bed; heavens . . . it was a cell, a cell where they put the prisoners, and the policewoman was helping her off with her coat, unpinning the scarf that was still tied round her hair, and because Mrs Ellis felt so faint the policewoman made her lie down on the bed, covered her with the coarse grey blanket, placed the little hard pillow under her head.

Mrs Ellis seized the woman's hands. Her face, after all, was not unkind.

'I beg of you,' she said, 'ring up Hampstead 4072, the number of my friend Mrs Draycott, at Charlton Court, and ask her to come here. The officer won't listen to me. He won't hear my story.'

'Yes, yes, that will be all right,' said the policewoman.

Now somebody else was coming into the room, the cell. Clean-shaven, alert, he carried a case in his hands. He said good evening to the policewoman, and opened his case. He took out a stethoscope and a thermometer. He smiled at Mrs Ellis.

'Feeling a little upset, I hear,' he said, 'Well, we'll soon put that to rights. Now, will you give me your wrist?'

Mrs Ellis sat up on the narrow bed, pulling the blanket close.

'Doctor,' she said, 'there is nothing whatever the matter with me. I admit I have been through a terrible experience, quite enough to unnerve anyone; my house has been broken into; no one here will listen to my story, but I am Mrs Ellis, Mrs Wilfred Ellis, of 17 Elmhurst Road; if you can possibly persuade the authorities here . . .'

He was not listening to her. With the assistance of the policewoman he was taking her temperature, under her arm, not in the mouth, treating her like a child; and now he was feeling her pulse, dragging down the pupils of her eyes, listening to her chest. Mrs Ellis went on talking.

'I realize this is a matter of routine. You are obliged to do this. But I want to warn you that my whole treatment, since I have been brought here, since the police came to my house before that, has been infamous, scandalous. I don't personally know our MP; but I sincerely believe that when he hears my story he will take the matter up, and someone is going to answer for the consequences. Unfortunately I am a widow, no immediate relatives, my little daughter is away at school; my closest friends, a Mr and Mrs Collins, are abroad, but my bank manager . . .'

He was dabbing her arm with spirit; he was inserting a needle, and with a whimper of pain Mrs Ellis fell back on to the hard pillow. The doctor went on holding her arm, her wrist, and Mrs Ellis, her head going round and round, felt a strange numb

123

sensation as the injection worked into her bloodstream. Tears ran
down her cheeks, she could not fight. She was too weak.

'How is that?' said the doctor. 'Better, eh?'

Her throat was parched, her mouth without saliva. It
was one of those drugs that paralysed you, made you helpless.

But the emotion bubbling within her was eased, was
still. The anger, the fear and frustration that had keyed her nerves
to a point of contraction, seemed to die away.

She had explained things badly. The folly of coming out
without her handbag had caused half the trouble. And the terrible,
wicked cunning of those thieves. 'Be still,' she said to her mind,
'be still. Rest now.'

'Now,' said the doctor, letting go her wrist, 'supposing
you tell me your story again. You say your name is Mrs Ellis?'

Mrs Ellis sighed and closed her eyes. Must she go into
it all again? Had not they got the whole thing written down in
their notebooks? What was the use, when the inefficiency of the
whole establishment was so palpable? Those telephone books,
directories, with wrong names, wrong addresses. Small wonder
there were burglaries, murders, every sort of crime, with a police
force that was obviously rotten to the core. What was the name of
the Member? It was on the tip of her tongue. A nice man, sandy-
haired, always looked so trustworthy on a poster. Hampstead was
a safe seat, of course, he would take up her case . . .

'Mrs Ellis,' said the doctor, 'do you think you can
remember now your real address?'

Mrs Ellis opened her eyes. Wearily, patiently, she fixed
them upon the doctor.

'I live at 17 Elmhurst Road,' she said mechanically. 'I
am a widow, my husband has been dead two years. I have a little
girl of nine at school. I went for a short walk on the heath this
afternoon after lunch, and when I returned—'

He interrupted her.

'Yes,' he said, 'we know that. We know what happened after
your walk. What we want you to tell us is what happened before.'

'I had lunch,' said Mrs Ellis; 'I remember perfectly well what I ate. Guinea fowl and apple charlotte, followed by coffee. Then I nearly decided to take a nap upstairs on my bed, because I was not feeling very well, but decided the air would do me good.'

As soon as she said this, she regretted it. The doctor looked at her keenly.

'Ah!' he said. 'You weren't feeling very well. Can you tell me what the trouble was?'

Mrs Ellis knew what he was after. He and the rest of the police force at the station wanted to certify her as insane. They would make out she had suffered from some brain storm, that her whole story was fabrication.

'There was nothing much the matter,' she said quickly. 'I was rather tired from sorting things during the morning. I tidied the linen, cleared out my desk in the drawing-room—all that took time.'

'Can you describe your house, Mrs Ellis?' he said. 'The furniture, for instance, of your bedroom, your drawing-room?'

'Very easily,' she answered, 'but you must remember that the thieves who broke into the house this afternoon have done what I begin to fear is irreparable damage. Everything had been seized, hidden away. The rooms were strewn with rubbish, and there was a young woman upstairs in my bedroom pretending to be a photographer.'

'Yes,' he said, 'don't worry about that. Just tell me about your furniture, how the various things were placed, and so on.'

He was more sympathetic than she had thought. Mrs Ellis launched into a description of every room in her house. She named the ornaments, the pictures, the position of the chairs and tables.

'And you say your cook is called Grace Jackson?'

'Yes, Doctor, she has been with me several years. She was in the kitchen when I left this afternoon; I remember most distinctly calling down to the basement and saying that I was going for a short walk and would not be long. I am extremely worried about her, Doctor. Those thieves will have got hold of her, perhaps kidnapped her.'

'We'll see to that,' said the doctor. 'Now, Mrs Ellis, you have been very helpful, and you have given such a clear account of your home that I think we shan't be long in tracing it, and your relations. You must stay here tonight, and I hope in the morning we shall have news for you. Now, you say your small daughter is at school? Can you remember the address?'

'Of course,' said Mrs Ellis, 'and the telephone number too. The school is High Close, Bishop's Lane, Hatchworth, and the telephone number is Hatchworth 202. But I don't understand what you mean about tracing my home. I have told you, I come from 17 Elmhurst Road.'

'There is nothing to worry about,' said the doctor; 'you are not ill, and you are not lying. I quite realize that. You are suffering from a temporary loss of memory that often happens to all sorts of people, and it quickly passes. We've had many cases before.'

He smiled. He stood up, his case in his hand.

'But it isn't true,' said Mrs Ellis, trying to raise herself from the pillow. 'My memory is perfectly all right. I have given you every detail I can think of; I have told you my name, where I live, a description of my home, the address of my daughter at school . . .'

'All right,' he said, 'now, don't worry. Just try to relax and have a little sleep. We shall find your friends for you.'

He murmured something to the policewoman and left the cell. The policewoman came over to the bed and tucked in the blanket.

'Now cheer up,' she said, 'do as the doctor said. Get a little rest. Everything will be all right, you'll see.'

Rest . . . But how? Relax . . . But to what purpose? Even now her house was being looted, sacked, every room stripped. The thieves getting clear away with their booty, leaving no trace behind them. They would take Grace with them; poor Grace could not come down to the police station to give witness to her identity. But the people next door, the Furbers, surely they would be good enough; it would not be too much trouble . . . Mrs Ellis supposed she should have called, been more friendly, had them to tea, but after all, people did not expect that unless they lived in the country, it was out of date; if the police officer had not got hold of Netta Draycott then the Furbers must be got in touch with at once . . .

Mrs Ellis plucked at the policewoman's sleeve.

'The Furbers,' she said, 'next door, at number 19, they know me well by sight. We have been neighbours for quite six years. The Furbers.'

'Yes,' said the policewoman, 'try to get some sleep.'

Oh, Susan, my Susan, if this had happened in the holidays, how much more fearful; what would we have done? Coming back from an afternoon walk to find those devils in the house, and then, who knows, that dreadful photographer woman and her husband taking a fancy to Susan, so pretty, so fair, and wanting to kidnap her. Then what fear, what terror . . . At least the child was safe, knew nothing of what was happening, and if only the story could be kept out of the newspapers, she need never know. So shameful, so degrading, a night spent in a prison cell through such crass stupidity, through such appalling blunders . . .

'You've had a good sleep then,' said the policewoman, handing her a cup of tea.

'I don't know what you mean,' said Mrs Ellis, 'I haven't slept at all.'

'Oh yes, you have.' The woman smiled. 'They all say that.'

Mrs Ellis blinked, sat up on the narrow bed. She had been speaking to the policewoman only a moment before. Her head ached abominably. She sipped at the tea, tasteless, unrefreshing. She yearned for her bed at home, for Grace coming in noiselessly, drawing the curtains.

'You're to have a wash,' said the policewoman, 'and I'll give you a comb through, and then you are to see the doctor again.'

Mrs Ellis suffered the indignity of washing under supervision, of having her hair combed; then her scarf and coat and gloves were given to her again, and she was taken out of the cell, along the corridor, back through the hall to the room where they had questioned her the night before. This time a different

127

officer sat at the desk, but she recognized the police constable, and the doctor too.

The last came towards her with that same bland smile on his face.

'How are you feeling today?' he said. 'A little more like your true self?'

'On the contrary,' said Mrs Ellis, 'I am feeling very unwell indeed, and shall continue to do so until I know what has happened at home. Is anyone here prepared to tell me what has happened at 17 Elmhurst Road since last night? Has anything at all been done to safeguard my property?'

The doctor did not answer, but guided her towards the chair at the desk.

'Now,' he said, 'the officer here wants to show you a picture in a newspaper.'

Mrs Ellis sat down in the chair. The officer handed her a copy of *The News of the World*—a paper Grace took on Sundays; Mrs Ellis never looked at it—and there was a photograph of a woman with a scarf round her head, and chubby cheeks, wearing some sort of light-coloured coat. The photograph had a red circle round it, and underneath was written:

'Missing from Home, Ada Lewis, aged 36, widow, of 105 Albert Buildings, Kentish Town.'

Mrs Ellis handed the paper back across the desk.

'I'm afraid I can't help you,' she said. 'I don't know this woman.'

'The name Ada Lewis conveys nothing to you?' said the officer. 'Nor Albert Buildings?'

'No,' said Mrs Ellis, 'certainly not.'

Suddenly she knew the purpose of the interrogation. The police thought that she was the missing woman, this Ada Lewis from Albert Buildings. Simply because she wore a light-coloured coat and had a scarf round her hair. She rose from the chair.

'This is absolutely preposterous,' she said. 'I have told you my name is Ellis, Mrs Wilfred Ellis, of 17 Elmhurst Road, and you persist in disbelieving me. My detention here is an outrage; I demand to see a lawyer, my own lawyer . . .' But wait, she hadn't needed the services of a lawyer since Wilfred died, and the firm had moved or been taken over by somebody else; better not give the name; they would think she was lying once again; it was safer to give the name of the bank manager . . .

'One moment,' said the officer, and she was interrupted once again, because somebody else came into the room, a seedy, common-looking man in a checked shabby suit, holding his trilby hat in his hand.

'Can you identify this woman as your sister, Ada Lewis?' asked the officer.

A flush of fury swept Mrs Ellis as the man stepped forward and peered into her face.

'No, sir,' he said, 'this isn't Ada. Ada isn't so stout, and this woman's teeth seem to be her own. Ada wore dentures. Never seen this woman before.'

'Thank you,' said the officer, 'that's all. You can go. We will let you know if we find your sister.'

The seedy-looking man left the room. Mrs Ellis turned in triumph to the officer behind the desk.

'Now,' she said, 'perhaps you will believe me?'

The officer considered her a moment, and then, glancing at the doctor, looked down at some notes on his desk.

'Much as I would like to believe you,' he said, 'it would save us all a great deal of trouble if I could; unfortunately I can't. Your facts have been proved wrong in every particular. So far.'

'What do you mean?' said Mrs Ellis.

'First, your address. You do not live at 17 Elmhurst Road because the house is occupied by various tenants who have lived there for some time and who are known to us. Number 17 is an apartment house, and the floors are let separately. You are not one of the tenants.'

Mrs Ellis gripped the sides of her chair. The obstinate, proud, and completely unmoved face of the officer stared back at her.

'You are mistaken,' said Mrs Ellis quietly. 'Number 17 is not a lodginghouse. It is a private house. My own.'

The officer glanced down again at his notes.

'There are no people called Furber living at number 19,' he went on. 'Number 18 is also a lodginghouse. You are not in the directory under the name of Ellis, nor in the telephone book. There is no Ellis on the register of the branch of the bank you mentioned to us last night. Nor can we trace anyone of the name of Grace Jackson in the district.'

Mrs Ellis looked up at the doctor, at the police constable, at the policewoman, who was still standing by her side.

'Is there some conspiracy?' she said. 'Why are you all against me? I don't understand what I have done . . .'

Her voice faltered. She must not break down. She must be firm with them, be brave, for Susan's sake.

'You rang up my friend at Charlton Court?' she asked. 'Mrs Draycott, that big block of flats?'

'Mrs Draycott is not living at Charlton Court, Mrs Ellis,' said the police officer, 'for the simple reason that Charlton Court no longer exists. It was destroyed by a fire bomb.'

Mrs Ellis stared at him in horror. A fire bomb? But how perfectly terrible! When? How? In the night? Disaster upon disaster . . . Who could have done it, anarchists, strikers, unemployed, gangs of people, possibly those who had broken into her house? Poor Netta and her husband and children; Mrs Ellis felt her head reeling . . .

'Forgive me,' she said, summoning her strength, her dignity, 'I had no idea there had been such a fearful outrage. No doubt part of the same plot, those people in my house . . .'

Then she stopped, because she realized they were lying to her; everything was lies; they were not policemen; they had seized the building; they were spies; the government was to be overthrown; but then why bother with her, with a simple harmless individual like herself; why were they not getting on with the civil war, bringing machine guns into the street, marching to Buckingham Palace; why sit here, pretending to her?

A policeman came into the room and clicked his heels and stood before the desk.

'Checked up on all the nursing homes,' he said, 'and the mental homes, sir, in the district, and within a radius of five miles. Nobody missing.'

'Thank you,' said the officer. Ignoring Mrs Ellis, he looked across at the doctor.

'We can't keep her here,' he said; 'you'll have to persuade them to take her at Moreton Hill. The matron *must* find a room. Say it's a temporary measure. Case of amnesia.'

'I'll do what I can,' said the doctor.

Moreton Hill? Mrs Ellis knew at once what they meant by Moreton Hill. It was a well-known mental home somewhere near Highgate, very badly run, she always heard, a dreadful place.

'Moreton Hill?' she said. 'You can't possibly take me there. It has a shocking reputation. The nurses are always leaving. I refuse to go to Moreton Hill. I demand to see a lawyer—no, my doctor, Dr. Godber; he lives in Parkwell Gardens.'

The officer stared at her thoughtfully.

'She must be a local woman,' he said; 'she gets the names right every time. But Godber went to Portsmouth, didn't he? I remember Godber.'

'If he's at Portsmouth,' said Mrs Ellis, 'he would only have gone for a few days. He's most conscientious. But his secretary knows me. I took Susan there last holidays.'

Nobody listened to her though, and the officer was consulting his notes again.

'By the way,' he said, 'you gave me the name of that school correctly. Wrong telephone number, but right school. Co-educational. We got through to them last night.'

'I'm afraid then,' said Mrs Ellis, 'that you got the wrong school. High Close is most certainly not co-educational, and I should never have sent Susan there if it had been.'

'High Close,' repeated the officer, reading from his notes, 'is a co-educational school, run by a Mr Foster and his wife.'

131

'It is run by a Miss Slater,' said Mrs Ellis, 'a Miss Hilda Slater.'

'You mean it *was* run by a Miss Slater,' said the officer; 'a Miss Slater had the school and then retired, and it was taken over by Mr and Mrs Foster. They have no pupil there of the name of Susan Ellis.'

Mrs Ellis sat very still in her chair. She looked at each face in turn. None was harsh. None was unfriendly. And the policewoman smiled encouragement. They all watched her steadily. At last she said:

'You are not deliberately trying to mislead me? You do realize that I am anxious, most desperately anxious, to know what has happened? If all that you are saying is some kind of a game, some kind of torture, would you tell me so that I know, so that I can understand?'

The doctor took her hand, and the officer leant forward in his chair.

'We are trying to help you,' he said; 'we are doing everything we can to find your friends.'

Mrs Ellis held tight to the doctor's hand. It had suddenly become a refuge.

'I don't understand,' she said, 'what has happened. If I am suffering from loss of memory, why do I remember everything so clearly? My address, my name, people, the school . . . Where is Susan; where is my little girl?'

She looked round her in blind panic. She tried to rise from the chair.

'If Susan is not at High Close, where is she?' said Mrs Ellis.

Someone was patting her on the shoulder. Someone was giving her a glass of water.

'If Miss Slater had retired to give place to a Mr and Mrs Foster, I should have heard, they would have told me,' she kept repeating; 'I only telephoned the school yesterday. Susan was quite well, and playing in the grounds.'

'Are you suggesting that Miss Slater answered you herself?' enquired the officer.

'No, the secretary answered. I telephoned because I had . . . what seemed to me a premonition that Susan might not be well. The secretary assured me that the child had eaten a good lunch and was playing. I am not making this up. It happened yesterday. I tell you, the secretary would have told me if Miss Slater was making changes in the school.'

Mrs Ellis searched the doubtful faces fixed upon her. And momentarily her attention was caught by the large 2 on the calendar standing on the desk.

'I *know* it was yesterday,' she said, 'because today is the second of the month, isn't it? And I distinctly remember tearing off the page in my calendar, and because it was the first of the month I decided to tidy my desk, sort out my papers, during the morning.'

The police officer relaxed and smiled.

'You are certainly very convincing,' he said, 'and we can all tell from your appearance, the fact that you have no money on you, that your shoes are polished, and other little signs, that you definitely belong somewhere in this district; you have not wandered from any great distance. But you do not come from 17 Elmhurst Road, Mrs Ellis, that is quite certain. For some reason, which we hope to discover, that address has become fixed in your mind, and other addresses too. I promise you everything will be done to clear your mind and to get you well again and you need have no fear about going to Moreton Hill; I know it well, and they will look after you there.'

Mrs Ellis saw herself shut up behind those grey forbidding walls, grimly situated, frowning down upon the further ponds the far side of the heath. She had skirted those walls many times, pitying the inmates within.

The man who came with the groceries had a wife who became insane. Mrs Ellis remembered Grace coming to her one morning full of the story, 'and he says they've taken her to Moreton Hill.'

Once inside, she would never get out. These men at the

133

police station would not bother with her any more.

And now there was this new, hideous misunderstanding about Susan, and the talk of a Mr and Mrs Foster taking over the school.

Mrs Ellis leant forward, clasping her hands together.

'I do assure you,' she said, 'that I don't want to make trouble. I have always been a very quiet, peaceable sort of person, not easily excited, never quarrelsome, and if I have really lost my memory I will do what the doctor tells me, take any drugs or medicines that will help. But I am worried, desperately worried, about my little girl and what you have told me about the school and Miss Slater's having retired. Would you do just one thing for me? Telephone the school and ask where you can get in touch with Miss Slater. It is just possible that she has taken the house down the road and removed there with some of the children, Susan amongst them; and whoever answered the telephone was new to the work and gave you vague information.'

She spoke clearly, without any sort of hysteria or emotion; they must see that she was in deadly earnest, and this request of hers was not wild fancy.

The police officer glanced at the doctor, then he seemed to make up his mind.

'Very well,' he said, 'we will do that. We will try to contact this Miss Slater, but it may take time. Meanwhile, I think it is best if you wait in another room while we put through the enquiry.'

Mrs Ellis stood up, this time without the help of the policewoman. She was determined to show that she was well, mentally and bodily, and quite capable of managing her affairs without the assistance of anybody, if it could be permitted.

She wished she had a hat instead of the scarf, which she knew instinctively was unbecoming, and her hands were lost without her handbag. At least she had gloves. But gloves were not enough.

She nodded briskly to the police officer and the doctor— at all costs she must show civility—and followed the policewoman to a waiting room. This time she was spared the indignity of a cell.

Another cup of tea was brought to her.

'It's all they think about,' she said to herself, 'cups of tea. Instead of getting on with their job.'

Suddenly she remembered poor Netta Draycott and the terrible tragedy of the fire bomb. Possibly she and her family had escaped and were now with friends, but there was no immediate means of finding out.

'Is it all in the morning papers about the disaster?' she asked the policewoman.

'What disaster?' said the woman.

'The fire at Charlton Court the officer spoke to me about.'

The policewoman stared at her with a puzzled expression.

'I don't remember him saying anything about a fire,' she said.

'Oh yes, he did,' said Mrs Ellis. 'He told me that Charlton Court had been destroyed by fire, by some bomb. I was aghast to hear it because I have friends living there. It must surely be in all the morning papers.'

The woman's face cleared.

'Oh, that,' she said. 'I think the officer was referring to some fire bomb during the war.'

'No, no,' said Mrs Ellis impatiently 'Charlton Court was built a long time after the war. I remember the block being built when my husband and I first came to Hampstead. No, this accident apparently happened last night, the most dreadful thing.'

The policewoman shrugged her shoulders.

'I think you're mistaken,' she said; 'there's been no talk of any accident or disaster here.'

An ignorant, silly sort of girl, thought Mrs Ellis. It was a wonder she had passed her test into the force. She thought they only employed very intelligent women.

She sipped her tea in silence. No use carrying on any sort of conversation with her.

It seemed a long while before the door opened, but when it did it was to reveal the doctor, who stood on the threshold

135

with a smile on his face.

'Well,' he said, 'I think we're a little nearer home. We were able to contact Miss Slater.'

Mrs Ellis rose to her feet, her eyes shining.

'Oh, Doctor, thank heaven . . . Have you news of my daughter?'

'Steady a moment now. You mustn't get excited or we shall have all last night's trouble over again, and that would never do. I take it, when you refer to your daughter, you mean someone who is called, or was called, Susan Ellis?'

'Yes, yes, of course,' said Mrs Ellis swiftly. 'Is she all right, is she with Miss Slater?'

'No, she is not with Miss Slater, but she is perfectly well, and I have spoken to her on the telephone myself, and I have her present address here in my notebook.'

The doctor patted his breast pocket and smiled again.

'Not with Miss Slater?' Mrs Ellis stared in bewilderment. 'Then the school *has* been handed over; you spoke to these people called Foster. Is it next door? Have they moved far? What has happened?'

The doctor took her hand and led her to the seat once more.

'Now,' he said, 'I want you to think quite calmly and quite clearly and not be agitated in any way, and your trouble will be cleared up, and your mind will be free again. You remember last night you gave us the name of your maid, Jackson?'

'Yes, Doctor.'

'Now, take your time. Tell us a little about Grace Jackson.'

'Have you found her? Is she at home? Is she all right?'

'Never mind for the moment. Describe Grace Jackson.'

Mrs Ellis was horribly afraid poor Grace had been found murdered, and they were going to ask her to identify the body.

'She is a big girl,' she said, 'at least not really a girl, about my own age, but you know how one is inclined to talk of a servant as a girl; she has a large bust, rather thick ankles, brownish hair, grey eyes, and she would be wearing, let me see, I think she may not have changed into her cap and apron when those thieves arrived; she was still probably in her overalls; she is inclined to change rather late in the afternoon; I have often spoken about it; it looks so bad to open the front door in overalls, slovenly, like a boarding-house; Grace has good teeth and a pleasant expression, though of course if anything has happened to her she would hardly—'

Mrs Ellis broke off. Murdered, battered. Grace would not be smiling.

The doctor did not seem to notice this. He was looking closely at Mrs Ellis.

'You know,' he said, 'you have given a very accurate description of yourself.'

'Myself?' said Mrs Ellis.

'Yes. Figure, colouring, and so on. We think, you know, it is just possible that your amnesia has taken the form of mistaken identity and that you are really Grace Jackson, believing yourself to be a Mrs Ellis, and now we are doing our best to trace the relatives of Grace Jackson.'

This was too much. Mrs Ellis swallowed. Outraged pride rose in her.

'Doctor,' she said rapidly, 'you have gone a little too far. I bear no sort of resemblance to my maid, Grace Jackson, and if and when you ever find trace of the unfortunate girl, she would be the first to agree with me. Grace has been in my employment seven years; she came originally from Scotland; her parents were Scottish, I believe—in fact, I know it, because she used to go for her holiday to Aberdeen. Grace is a good, hard-working, and I like to think honest girl; we have had our little ups and downs, but nothing serious; she is inclined to be obstinate; I am obstinate myself—who is not?—but . . . '

If only the doctor would not look at her in that smiling, patronizing way.

'You see,' he said, 'you do know a very great deal about Grace Jackson.'

Mrs Ellis could have hit him. He was so self-assured, so

137

confident.

'I must keep my temper,' she told herself. 'I must, I must . . .'

Aloud she said: 'Doctor, I know about Grace Jackson because, as I have told you, she has been in my employment for seven years. If she is found ill or in any way hurt, I shall hold the police force here responsible, because in spite of my entreaties, I do not believe they kept a watch on my house last night. Now perhaps you will be good enough to tell me where I can find my child. She, at least, will recognize me.'

Mrs Ellis considered she had been very restrained, very calm. In spite of terrible provocation she had not lost control of herself.

'You insist that your age is thirty-five?' said the doctor, switching the subject. 'And that Grace Jackson was approximately the same?'

'I was thirty-five in August last,' said Mrs Ellis; 'I believe Grace to be a year younger, I am not sure.'

'You certainly don't look more,' said the doctor, smiling.

Surely, at such a moment, he was not going to attempt to appease her by gallantry?

'But,' he continued, 'following the telephone conversation I have just had, Grace Jackson should be, today, at least fifty-five or fifty-six.'

'There are probably,' said Mrs Ellis icily, 'several persons of the name of Grace Jackson employed as domestic servants. If you propose tracing every one of them it will take you and the police force a considerable time. I am sorry to insist, but I must know the whereabouts of my daughter Susan before anything else.'

He was relenting; she could see it in his eye.

'As a matter of fact,' he said, 'it happens, very conveniently, that Miss Slater was able to put us in touch with the lady; we have spoken to her on the telephone, and she is only a short distance away, in St John's Wood. She is not sure, but she thinks she would remember Grace Jackson if she saw her.'

For a moment Mrs Ellis was speechless. What in the world was Susan doing in St John's Wood? And how monstrous to drag the child to the telephone and question her about Grace. Of course she would be bewildered and say she 'thought' she would remember Grace, though goodness only knows it was only two months since Grace was waving her goodbye from the doorstep when she left for school.

Then she suddenly remembered the Zoo. Perhaps, if these changes at school were all being decided upon in a great hurry, one of the junior mistresses had taken a party of children up to London to the Zoo, to be out of the way. The Zoo or Madame Tussaud's.

'Do you know where she spoke from?' asked Mrs Ellis sharply. 'I mean, somebody was in charge, somebody was looking after her?'

'She spoke from 2a Halifax Avenue,' said the doctor, 'and I don't think you will find she needs any looking after. She sounded very capable, and I heard her turn from the telephone and call to a little boy named Keith to keep quiet and not to make so much noise, because she couldn't hear herself speak.'

A tremor of a smile appeared on Mrs Ellis' lips. How clever of Susan to have shown herself so quick and lively. It was just like her, though. She was so advanced for her age. Such a little companion. But Keith . . . It sounded very much as though the school *had* suddenly become co-educational; this was a mixed party being taken to the Zoo or Madame Tussaud's. They were all having lunch, perhaps, at Halifax Avenue, relations of Miss Slater's, or these Fosters, but really the whole thing was most inexcusable, that changes should come about like this, and the children be taken backwards and forwards from High Close to London without any attempt to notify the parents. Mrs Ellis would write very strongly to Miss Slater about it, and if the school had changed hands and was to be co-educational, she would remove Susan at the end of the term.

'Doctor,' she said, 'I am ready to go to Halifax Avenue at once, if the authorities here will only permit me to do so.'

'Very well,' said the doctor. 'I am afraid I can't accompany you, but we have arranged for that, and Sister Henderson, who knows all about the matter, will go with you.'

He nodded to the policewoman, who opened the door of the waiting room and admitted a severe middle-aged woman in nurse's uniform. Mrs Ellis said nothing, but her mouth tightened. She was very sure that Sister Henderson had been summoned from Moreton Hill.

'Now, Sister,' said the doctor cheerfully, 'this is the lady, and you know where to take her and what to do; and I think you will only be a few minutes at Halifax Avenue, and then we hope things will be straightened out.'

'Yes, Doctor,' said the nurse.

She looked across at Mrs Ellis with a quick professional eye.

'If only I had a hat,' thought Mrs Ellis, 'if only I had not come out with nothing but this wretched scarf, and I can feel bits and pieces of hair straggling at the back of my neck. No powder compact on me, no comb, nothing. Of course I must look terrible to them, ungroomed, common . . .'

She straightened her shoulders, resisted an impulse to put her hands in her pockets. She walked stiffly towards the open door. The doctor, the Sister, and the policewoman conducted her down the steps of the police station to a waiting car.

A uniformed chauffeur was to drive, she was thankful to see, and she climbed into the car, followed by the Sister.

The awful thought flashed through her mind that there might be some charge for the night's lodging in the cell and for the cups of tea; also, should she have tipped the policewoman? But anyway, she had no money. It was impossible. She nodded brightly to the policewoman as a sort of sop, to show she had no ill feeling. She felt rather different towards the doctor. She bowed rather formally, coldly. The car drove away.

Mrs Ellis wondered if she was expected to make conversation with the Sister, who sat stalwart and forbidding at her side. Better not, perhaps. Anything she said might be taken as evidence of mental disturbance. She stared straight in front of her, her gloved hands primly folded on her lap.

The traffic jams were very bad, worse than she had ever known. There must be a Motor Exhibition on. So many American cars on the road. A rally, perhaps . . .

She did not think much of Halifax Avenue when they came to it. Houses very shabby, and quite a number with windows broken.

The car drew up at a small house that had 2a written on the pillar outside. Curious place to take a party of children for lunch. A good Lyons Café would have been so much better.

The Sister got out of the car and waited to help Mrs Ellis. 'We shan't be long,' she said to the chauffeur.

141

'That's what you think,' said Mrs Ellis to herself, 'but I shall certainly stay with Susan as long as I please.'

They walked through the piece of front garden to the front door. The Sister rang the bell. Mrs Ellis saw a face looking at them from the front window and then quickly dart behind a curtain. Good heavens . . . It was Dorothy, Wilfred's younger sister, who was a schoolteacher in Birmingham; of course it was, it must be . . . Everything became clearer; the Fosters must know Dorothy; people to do with education always knew each other, but how awkward, what a bore. Mrs Ellis had never cared for Dorothy, had stopped writing to her in fact; Dorothy had been so unpleasant when poor Wilfred died, and had insisted that the writing bureau was hers, and rather a nice piece of jewellery that Mrs Ellis had always understood had been given by Wilfred's mother to her, Mrs Ellis; and in fact the whole afternoon after the funeral had been spent in most unpleasant argument and discussion, that Mrs Ellis had been only too glad to send Dorothy away with the jewellery, and the bureau, and very nice rug to which she had no right at all.

Dorothy was the last person Mrs Ellis wanted to see,

and especially in these very trying circumstances, with this Sister at her side, and herself looking so untidy, without a hat or a bag.

There was not time to compose herself because the door opened. No . . . no, it was not Dorothy after all, but . . . how strange, so very like her. That same thin nose and rather peeved expression. A little taller, perhaps, and the hair was lighter. The resemblance, though, was really quite extraordinary.

'Are you Mrs Drew?' asked the Sister.

'Yes,' answered the young woman, and then because a child was calling from an inner room she called back over her shoulder impatiently, 'Oh, be quiet, Keith, do, for heaven's sake.'

A little boy of about five appeared along the hall dragging a toy on wheels. 'Dear little fellow,' thought Mrs Ellis, 'what a tiresome nagging mother. But where are all the children; where is Susan?'

'This is the person I have brought along for you to identify,' said the Sister.

'You had better come inside,' said Mrs Drew rather grudgingly. 'I'm afraid everything's in a fearful mess. I've got no help, and you know how it is.'

Mrs Ellis, whose temper was beginning to rise again, stepped neatly over a broken toy on the door mat and, followed by the Sister, went into what she supposed was this Mrs Drew's living room. It was certainly a mess. Remains of breakfast not cleared away—or was it lunch?—and toys everywhere, and some material for cutting out spread on a table by the window.

Mrs Drew laughed apologetically.

'What with Keith's toys and my material—I'm a dressmaker in my spare time—and trying to get a decent meal for my husband when he comes home in the evening, life isn't a bed of roses,' she said.

Her voice was *so* like Dorothy's. Mrs Ellis could hardly take her eyes off her. The same note of complaint.

'We don't want to take up your time,' said the Sister civilly, 'if you will just say whether this person is Grace Jackson or not.'

The young woman, Mrs Drew, stared at Mrs Ellis thoughtfully.

'No,' she said at length, 'I'm sure she is not. I haven't seen Grace for years, not since I married; I used to look her up in Hampstead occasionally before then; but she had quite a different appearance from this person. She was stouter, darker, older too.'

'Thank you,' said the Sister, 'then are you sure you have never seen this lady before?'

'No, never,' said Mrs Drew.

'Very well then,' said the Sister, 'we needn't detain you any longer.'

She turned, as though to go, but Mrs Ellis was not to be fobbed off with the nonsense that had just passed.

'Excuse me,' she said to Mrs Drew, 'there has been a most unfortunate misunderstanding all round, but I understand you spoke to the doctor at the police station at Hampstead this morning, or someone did from this house, and that you have a party of school children here from High Close, my child amongst them. Can you tell me if she is still here; is anyone from the school in charge?'

The Sister was about to intervene, but Mrs Drew did not notice this, because the little boy had come into the room, dragging his toy.

'Keith, I *told* you to stay outside,' she nagged.

Mrs Ellis smiled at the boy. She loved all children.

'What a pretty boy,' she said, and she held out her hand to him. He took it, holding it tight.

'He doesn't usually take to strangers,' said Mrs Drew, 'he's very shy. It makes me wild at times when he won't speak and hangs his head.'

'I was shy myself as a child, I understand it,' said Mrs Ellis.

Keith looked up at her with confidence and trust. Her heart warmed to him. But she was forgetting Susan . . .

'We were talking about the party from High Close,' she said.

'Yes,' said Mrs Drew, 'but the police officer was rather an

idiot, I'm afraid, and got everything wrong. My name was Susan Ellis before I married, and I used to go to school at High Close, and that's where the mistake came in. There are no children from the school here.'

'What a remarkable coincidence,' said Mrs Ellis, smiling, 'because my name is Ellis, and my daughter is called Susan, and an even stranger coincidence is that you are so like a sister of my late husband's.'

'Oh?' said Mrs Drew. 'Well, the name is common enough, isn't it? The butcher is Ellis, down the road.'

Mrs Ellis flushed. Not a very tactful remark. And she felt suddenly nervous, too, because the Sister was advancing and was leaning forward as though to take her by the arm and walk to the front door. Mrs Ellis was determined not to leave the house. Or at any rate, not to leave it with the Sister.

'I've always found High Close such a money sort of school,' she said rapidly, 'but I am rather distressed about the changes they are making there, and I am afraid it is going to be on rather a different tone in the future.'

'I don't think they've changed it much,' said Mrs Drew; 'most small children are horrible little beasts, anyway, and it does them good not to see too much of their parents and to be thoroughly well mixed up with every sort of type.'

'I'm afraid I don't agree with you on that,' said Mrs Ellis. So peculiar. The tone, the expression might have been Dorothy's.

'Of course,' said Mrs Drew, 'I can't help being grateful to old Salty. She's a funny old stick, but a heart of gold, and she did her best for me, I'll say that, and kept me in the holidays, even after my mother was killed in a street accident.'

'How good of her,' said Mrs Ellis, 'and what a dreadful thing for you.'

Mrs Drew laughed.

'I was pretty tough, I think,' she said. 'I don't remember much about it. But I do remember my mother was a very kind person, and pretty too. I think Keith takes after her.'

The little boy had not relinquished Mrs Ellis' hand.

'It's time we were getting along,' said the Sister. 'Come now, Mrs Drew has told us all we need to know.'

'I don't want to go,' said Mrs Ellis calmly, 'and you have no right to make me go.'

The Sister exchanged a glance with Mrs Drew.

'I'm sorry,' she said in a low tone, 'I shall have to get the chauffeur. I wanted them to send another nurse with me, but they said it wouldn't be necessary.'

'That's all right,' said Mrs Drew. 'So many people are bats these day, one extra doesn't make much difference. But perhaps I had better remove Keith to the kitchen, or she may kidnap him.'

Keith, protesting, was carried from the room.

Once again the Sister looked at Mrs Ellis.

'Come along now,' she said, 'be reasonable.'

145

'No,' said Mrs Ellis, and with a quickness that surprised herself she reached out to the table where Mrs Drew had been cutting out material, and seized the pair of scissors.

'If you come near me, I shall stab you,' she said.

The Sister turned and went quickly out of the room and down the steps, calling for the chauffeur. The next few moments passed quickly, but for all this Mrs Ellis had time to realize that her tactics were brilliant, rivalling the heroes of detective fiction.

She crossed the room, opened the long French windows that gave on to a back yard. The window of the bedroom was open; she could hear the chauffeur calling.

'Tradesmen's entrance is ajar,' he shouted; 'she must have gone this way.'

'Let them go on with their confusion,' thought Mrs Ellis, leaning against the bed. 'Let them. Good luck to them in their running about. This will take down some of that Sister's weight. Not much running about for her at Moreton Hill. Cups of tea at all hours, and sweet biscuits, while the patients were given bread and water.'

The movement went on for some time. Somebody used the telephone. There was more talk. And then, when Mrs Ellis was nearly dozing off against the bed valance, she heard the car drive away.

Everything was silent. Mrs Ellis listened. The only sound was the little boy playing in the hall below. She crept to the door and listened once more. The wheeled toy was being dragged backwards and forwards, up and down the hall.

And there was a new sound coming from the living-room. The sound of a sewing machine going at great speed. Mrs Drew was at work.

The Sister and the chauffeur had gone.

An hour, two hours must have passed since they had left. Mrs Ellis glanced at the clock on the mantelpiece. It was two o'clock. What an untidy, scattered sort of room, everything all over the place. Shoes in the middle of the floor, a coat flung down on a chair, and Keith's cot had not been made up; the blankets were rumpled, anyhow.

'Badly brought up,' thought Mrs Ellis, 'and such rough, casual manners. But poor girl, if she had no mother . . . '

She took a last glance round the room, and she saw with a shrug of her shoulder that even Mrs Drew's calendar had a printing error. It said 1952 instead of 1932. How careless . . .

She tiptoed to the head of the stairs. The door of the living-room was shut. The sound of the sewing machine came at breathless speed.

'They must be hard up,' thought Mrs Ellis, 'if she has to do dressmaking. I wonder what her husband does for a living.'

Softly she crept downstairs. She made no sound. And if she had, the sound of the sewing machine would have covered it.

As she passed the living-room door it opened. The boy stood there, staring at her. He said nothing. He smiled. Mrs Ellis smiled back at him. She could not help herself. She had a feeling that he would not give her away.

'Shut the door, Keith, *do*,' nagged his mother from within. The door slammed. The sound of the sewing machine became more distant, muffled. Mrs Ellis let herself out of the house and slipped away . . . She turned northward, like an animal scenting direction, because northward was her home.

She was soon swallowed up in traffic, the buses swinging past her in the Finchley Road, and her feet began to ache, and she was tired, but she could not take a bus or summon a taxi because she had no money.

No one looked at her; no one bothered with her; they were all intent upon their business, either going from home or returning, and it seemed to Mrs Ellis, as she toiled up the hill towards Hampstead, that for the first time in her life she was friendless and alone. She wanted her house, her home, the consolation of her own surroundings; she wanted to take up her normal, everyday life that had been interrupted in so brutal a fashion.

There was so much to straighten out, so much to do, and Mrs Ellis did not know where to begin or whom to ask for help.

'I want everything to be as it was before that walk yesterday,' thought Mrs Ellis, her back aching, her feet throbbing. 'I want my home. I want my little girl.'

And here was the heath once more. This was where she had stood before crossing the road. She even remembered what she had been thinking about. She had been planning to buy a red bicycle for Susan. Something light, but strong, a good make.

The memory of the bicycle made her forget her troubles, her fatigue. As soon as all this muddle and confusion were over, she would buy a red bicycle for Susan.

Why, though, for the second time, that screech of brakes when she crossed the road, and the vacant face of the laundry boy looking down at her?

❁

James Purdy

James Purdy's first books brought him extravagant praise from the likes of Edith Sitwell ("I think it undoubted that James Purdy will come to be recognized as one of the greatest writers of fiction in our language," she declared) but, in spite of critical acclaim, he never managed to establish himself among the best-selling authors in his native America. Tennessee Williams and Gore Vidal both shared a passion for Purdy's writing, but did little to secure him a vaster audience. As an explanation, Vidal suggested that "there's something in the American air that's so sectarian, censorious, narrow, dumb . . ." In any case, Purdy's intricate, tortured world of suffering and redemption, in which characters go to great lengths to free themselves from the misfortunes allotted to them by fate, does not make for easy or pleasant reading.

"You are sworn to tell the truth when you write," Purdy explains. "Writers write what they see, and what they hear people say. They're not testifying. But if you don't tell the truth, you are found guilty." And he adds, "I don't write for anyone. I write for the soul."

MRS. BENSON

james purdy

"*i* don't know why Mrs. Carlin entertained," Mrs.
Benson admitted. "She didn't like it, and she couldn't do it."

"I had to sit an entire hour under one of those potted palms
she had in her house," Mrs. Benson's daughter, Wanda, recalled.
"There was a certain odor about it—whether from the soil, or the
plant, or the paper about the container. I felt terribly uncomfortable."

The two women, Wanda Walters, unmarried and thirty,
from Philadelphia, and her mother, who lived in Europe, and had
been married many times, and who was now Mrs. Benson, had
nearly finished their tea, in an English tearoom within walking
distance from the American Express, in Paris.

Mrs. Benson had known the English tearoom for many
years, though she could never exactly remember its French name,
and so could not ever recommend it to her friends, and she and
her daughter, when they had their yearly reunions in Paris, always
came to it. Their meeting in Paris this year had been rather a
prolonged one, owing to Wanda's having failed to get a return
passage to the States, and it had been a summer that was hot,
humid, and gray—and not eventful for either of them.

This year, too, they found themselves going less and less
anywhere at all, and they were somewhat embarrassed—at least,

Mrs. Benson said *she* was—to find that they spent the better part of the day in the English tearoom, talking for the most part, about people they had both known in Philadelphia twenty-odd years ago, when Wanda had been "little," and when Mrs. Benson—well, as she said, had at least had a different name!

It was the first time in many years, perhaps *the* first, that Mrs. Benson had really talked with her daughter at length about anything (they had always *traveled* before, as the older woman said), and certainly the first time in Wanda's memory that they had talked at all about "back home," as Mrs. Benson now called it with a chilly, condescending affection. And if their French or American friends happened by now, Mrs. Benson, if not Wanda, expressed by a glance or word a certain disappointment that their "talk" must be interrupted.

Mrs. Benson had made it a fixed practice not to confide in her daughter (she had once said to a close friend of hers: "I don't know my daughter, and it's a bit too late to begin!"), but the name *Mrs. Carlin,* which had come into their conversation so haphazardly, as if dropped from the awning of the café, together with the gloominess of their Paris, had set Mrs. Benson off. *Mrs. Carlin* came to open up a mine of confidences and single isolated incidents.

This was interesting to Wanda because Mrs. Benson had always been loath to "tell," to reminisce. Mrs. Benson hated anecdotes, regarding them as evidence of senility in the old, and cretinism in the young, and though there were other people "back home," of course, Mrs. Carlin could easily carry them through for the rest of Paris, and the potted palms, which had so dismayed Wanda, seemingly set Mrs. Benson "right" at last.

"I don't suppose you remember when they were popular," Mrs. Benson referred to the palms. "But they were once nearly everywhere. I've always disliked them, and, I think, perhaps, I even vaguely *fear* them."

"I don't think Mrs. Carlin *liked* them," Wanda said abruptly, so abruptly that Mrs. Benson dropped a long ash from her cigarette into her tea, and then called the waiter.

"How on earth do you know Mrs. Carlin didn't like them?" Mrs. Benson flushed slightly and then paused while the waiter brought her a fresh cup.

Wanda paused also. She felt that her mother did not want to know that she knew anything about Mrs. Carlin, and Wanda, in any case, was not very much interested in explaining what she did mean.

"I simply meant this," Wanda felt she must explain, under the *look* her mother gave her. "The part of the house Mrs. Carlin used for *entertainment* could not have reflected *anybody's* taste."

Mrs. Benson opened her eyes wide, and brought her mouth into a kind of cupid's bow. Then, in a voice quieter than her expression, she said: "I'd have to say, Wanda, that you were right!

"But how on earth did you *know?*" Mrs. Benson suddenly brought out, and she looked at her daughter as if a fresh light had been thrown on the latter's character also.

"What I think I meant," Wanda began again, tearing apart one of the tiny envelopes of sugar that lay beside her spoon, "Mrs. Carlin was, as we both know, more than a *little* wealthy . . ."

Mrs. Benson cleared her throat, but then decided, evidently, not to speak, and her silence was as emphatic as she could make it.

"That is," Wanda went on slowly, "she could *afford* to entertain rather shabbily."

"Rather *shabbily?*" Mrs. Benson considered this. "That is a terribly queer word for *her.*"

"But you yourself . . ."

"I don't like potted palms," Mrs. Benson pushed through to what was, as her face showed, the important matter here, "and I don't like all those original early 19th-century landscapes with cattle," she became now as firm as if in court, "but as to her house being *shabby* . . ."

"*Depressing* then," Wanda said. "It was certainly depressing."

Mrs. Benson laughed, guardedly indulgent. "You're so hard on the poor dear," she said in a tone of voice unlike her own.

"But I thought you thought as I did," Wanda cried. "About *her,* at least!" Displeasure and boredom rang in her voice, but there was an even stronger expression there of confusion and doubt.

"I do, and I don't," Mrs. Benson put endearment and confidence now into her voice. Then, unaccountably, she looked at her rings. She had many. They were, without doubt, too genuine, if anything, and as they shone in the later afternoon light, they made her mother look, Wanda felt, both very rich and very old.

"I think you're right, though," Wanda heard Mrs. Benson's voice continuing, "right about Mrs. Carlin's not caring whether she impressed *people* or not."

"I don't know if I quite meant that," Wanda told her mother, but under her breath now. "I mean only she didn't care whether they *enjoyed* themselves or not at her house."

They were both silent for a moment, as if surprised at the difficulties which had suddenly sprung up from nowhere, difficulties that were so obscure in themselves, and yet which offered some kind of threat of importance.

"The potted palms were a fright, of course," Mrs. Benson seemed either conciliatory or marking time. "And even for potted palms, they were dreadful." She touched her daughter's arm lightly. "They looked *dead.*"

Going on, Mrs. Benson added: "I always thought of old-fashioned small-town Greek candy-kitchens when I saw those palm trees at Mrs. Carlin's. And her strange little painted-glass player piano, too!"

"I never saw *that,*" Wanda admitted. She looked away from her mother's expression.

"Oh, you've forgotten it, is all," Mrs. Benson said. "It played for *all* the guests, that player piano . . . at least once." She laughed. "Mrs. Carlin seldom invited anybody twice."

Mrs. Benson had a peculiar, oblique, faraway look in

her eyes, a look Wanda did not remember quite ever having seen on her mother's face before—indeed, on anybody's face.

Then, suddenly clearing her throat, Mrs. Benson coughed ceremoniously, struggling perhaps with a decision.

The one thing, Wanda remembered again, the thing that her mother disliked so much in others, was stories, *anecdotes*—indeed any narration which was prolonged beyond the length of a paragraph. But usually when Mrs. Benson cleared her throat *and* coughed, she was going to tell something which was important and necessary, if not long, or anecdotal.

But then, quickly, as if she had been given a reprieve of some kind, Mrs. Benson cried: "Oh, it's all so *nothing!*" and poured herself some tea.

"But what else was there?" Wanda cried, annoyance and curiosity both in her voice. Mrs. Benson shook her head.

"You did have something special, I believe," Wanda was positive.

"Oh, not actually," Mrs. Benson said. Then, with her faraway look again, she managed to say, "I *was* remembering an afternoon—oh, a long, long time ago at Mrs. Carlin's. . . . But in a *different* part of the house, you see."

Wanda waited, suddenly touched with something stronger than curiosity. But she knew that if she so much as moved now, Mrs. Benson might remember her own horror of anecdotes, and would close up tight.

"I dread to think how long ago that actually was," Mrs. Benson continued carefully, and her eyes then strayed out to the street, where a bus was slowing down to stop for a woman and a small child.

Mrs. Benson waited for the woman and child to board the bus, then commencing again: "I can't believe that it was so long ago as 1935, I mean, or along in there. . . . But, Mrs. Carlin had already begun to entertain her guests in one part of the house . . . and to *live* herself in another! She had begun dividing up her life in that way!"

153

She smiled at Wanda, almost in the manner of one who had finished her story there.

Wanda nodded only enough to let her mother know she was listening.

"I don't care much for this *tea,* today," Mrs. Benson said suddenly in an unexpectedly loud voice, and she looked up and about the room.

When Wanda said nothing, but showed that she was waiting, Mrs. Benson drank some more of the tea she did not like, and said: "Mrs. Carlin had never, I think, been particularly interested in *me,* as distinct from the others, until your father left me. . . . Evidently, *she* had never been too happy in her marriage, either . . . I gathered that from something she once let drop. . . .

"However," Mrs. Benson said, raising the empty tea cup, and looking up under at the bottom of it hurriedly, "however, she wanted me to see things. I knew that. She wanted me to see the things—the part of the house, you understand, that the *others* never saw."

Wanda nodded, a kind of fleeting awareness in her face.

"That was when she called me, well *aside,* I suppose one would have to say, and said something to me like, '*I want to really have you in some time, Rose.*'"

It came as a sort of shock to Wanda to hear her mother's Christian name. She had not only not heard it for many years— she had actually forgotten it, so separate had their two lives, and their very names, become.

But Mrs. Benson had gone right on now through her daughter's surprise, or shock: "At first I hadn't quite understood what Mrs. Carlin meant, you see. . . . She had taken hold of my arm, gently, and led me out of the room where she had always entertained the *others.* We got into a small gold elevator, and were gone in a minute. . . . When we got out, well—let me assure you, there wasn't a potted palm in the place!

"It was another house, another atmosphere, another place and time!"

A look of something like pain crossed Wanda's face, but her mother missed this in her final decision to "tell."

"It was a bit incredible to me then, and it's more so now," Mrs. Benson anticipated her daughter's possible incredulity, or indifference.

Pausing briefly, it was Mrs. Benson's turn now to study her daughter's face critically, but evidently, at the last, she found nothing on the younger woman's face to stop her.

Still, Mrs. Benson waited, looking at nothing in particular, while the waiter removed the empty cups, wiped the marble swiftly with a small cloth, bowed vaguely, and muttering part of a phrase, left.

Mrs. Benson commented perfunctorily on the indulgence of French waiters and French cafés, pointing out how wonderful it was to be able to stay *forever* when one wanted to.

Outside the light was beginning to fail, and a slight breeze came across to them from the darkening boulevard.

Wanda moved suddenly and unceremoniously in her chair, and Mrs. Benson fixed her with a new and indeterminate expression.

Raising her voice, almost as if to reach the street, Mrs. Benson said: "A week after Mrs. Carlin had showed me the 'real' part of the house, she invited me again, in an invitation she had written in her own hand, and which I must have somewhere, still. . . . I had never had a *written* invitation before from her, nobody had . . . always telephoned ones. . . . It was a dark January afternoon, I recall, and I was feeling, well, at that time, pretty low. . . . In the *new* part of the house—and I couldn't get over this time its *immensity*—tea was never mentioned, thank God, and we had some wonderful ancient Portuguese brandy. . . . But as we sat there talking, I kept hearing something soft but arresting. . . ."

Mrs. Benson stopped now in the guise of one who hears only what she is describing.

"Looking back away from Mrs. Carlin," Mrs. Benson said, "in the furthest part of the room, I was quite taken aback to see some actual *musicians*. Mrs. Carlin had an entire small string orchestra playing there for her. . . .You know I thought I was mistaken. I thought it was perhaps a large oil, a mural, or something. . . . But Mrs. Carlin touched my hand just then, and said, '*They're for you, Rose.*'"

Mrs. Benson pressed her daughter's hand lightly at that, as if to convey by some touch *part* of the reality of that afternoon.

"I think she wanted to *help* me," Mrs. Benson said in a flat plain voice now, and with a helpless admission of anticlimax. "Your father—as I've said, had just *gone,* and I think she knew how everything stood."

Mrs. Benson avoided her daughter's glance by looking at her hands, which she held before her again now, so that there was the sudden quick scintillation again, and then went on: "When Mrs. Carlin took me to the door that day, I knew she wanted to say something else, something still more *helpful,* if you will, and I was afraid she was going to say what in fact she did."

Wanda's open-eyed expression made her mother suddenly smile.

"It was nothing sensational, my dear, or alarming! Mrs. Carlin was never *that!*"

"Well, for heaven's sake, then," Wanda cried.

"I said it was nothing sensational." In Mrs. Benson's dread of the *anecdote*—the inevitable concomitant of old age—she had so often told people nothing at all, and safety still, of course, lay in being silent. But as Wanda watched Mrs. Benson struggle there, postponing the telling of what she would have liked so much to tell, she realized in part what the struggle meant: Mrs. Benson had invariably all her life told her daughter *nothing*.

But Mrs. Benson had gone on again: "Mrs. Carlin was still beautiful then, and as I see now, *young*. . . . And I rather imagine that when she was very young, and when there had been, after all, a Mr. Carlin . . ."

A look from Wanda sped Mrs. Benson on: "I don't know *why* I treasure what Mrs. Carlin said to me," she hurried faster now. "But it is one of the few things that any other human being ever said to me that I do hold on to."

Mrs. Benson looked at the *addition* which the waiter had left, and her lips moved slightly over what was written there.

"Mrs. Carlin said to me," she went on, still looking at the waiter's bill, although her eyes were closed, "'You're the only one who could *possibly* be asked in here with me, my dear. . . . I couldn't have the *others*, and I knew I couldn't have them. . . . They're not for *us* . . . And if you should ever feel you would like to *stay on*,' Mrs. Carlin said, *'why don't you, my dear?'*"

"She actually thought so well of you!" Wanda said, and then hearing the metallic hardness of her own voice, lowered her eyes in confusion.

"Of course, that was a long time ago," Mrs. Benson said vaguely, more of a cold edge now in her voice. "She wouldn't want *anyone* there now," she added.

157

"She is such a recluse then?" Wanda asked. Mrs. Benson did not answer. She had taken some francs out of her purse and was staring at them.

"Some of this money," she pointed out, "have you noticed? It comes to pieces in one's hands. I hardly know what to do with some of the smaller notes."

"These little reunions in Paris are such a pleasure, Mother," Wanda said in a rather loud, bright voice.

"Are they, my dear?" Mrs. Benson answered in her old firm manner. Then, in a sudden hard voice: "I'm so glad if they are."

The two women rose from the table at the same time, Mrs. Benson having deposited some of the notes on the marble-topped table, and they moved toward the front of the café, and into the street.

❁

Carson McCullers

When Christopher Isherwood met Carson McCullers in 1955 in Philadelphia, at the première of Tennessee Williams's *Cat on a Hot Tin Roof*, he was taken aback by what he described as "the most alarming kind of masochism." "She lost all her money when she came down here," he noted in his diary. "She wears a quite unnecessarily repulsive brace on her paralyzed arm. And she really ought to powder her nose."

McCullers's thoughts were on other things than powdering her nose; and, with few exceptions, she took little interest in male writers. Women writers, on the other hand, older women writers, were for Carson McCullers objects of idolatry, and none more than Katherine Anne Porter. Porter was everything McCullers wanted her own mother to be: intelligent, self-determined, and successful. When Porter visited the writers' colony of Yaddo, McCullers followed her around relentlessly until Porter was forced to lock herself up in her room. McCullers pounded on the door, crying: "Please, Katherine Anne, let me come in and talk with you, I do love you so very much!" Porter demanded that McCullers leave and refused to come out until the younger writer had done so. At last it was time for dinner. Thinking that McCullers had left, Porter cautiously opened the door. McCullers lay sprawled across the threshold. "But I'd had enough," said Porter. "I merely stepped over her and continued on my way to dinner. And that was the last time she ever bothered me."

BREATH FROM THE SKY

carson mccullers

her peaked, young face stared for a time, unsatis-
fied, at the softer blue of the sky that fringed the horizon. Then
with a quiver of her open mouth she rested her head again on the
pillow, tilted the panama hat over her eyes, and lay motionless in
the canvas striped chair. Chequered shade patterns jerked over
the blanket covering her thin body. Bee drones sounded from the
spirea bushes that sprayed out their white blossoms nearby.

Constance dozed for a moment. She awoke to the
smothering smell of hot straw—and Miss Whelan's voice.

"Come on now. Here's your milk."

Out of her sleepy haze a question came that she had
not intended to ask, that she had not even been consciously thinking about: "Where's Mother?"

Miss Whelan held the glistening bottle in her plump
hands. As she poured the milk it frothed white in the sunlight and
crystal frost wreathed the glass.

"Where—?" Constance repeated, letting the word slide
out with her shallow release of breath.

"Out somewhere with the other kids. Mick was raising a
fuss about bathing suits this morning. I guess they went to town
to buy those."

Such a loud voice. Loud enough to shatter the fragile sprays of the spirea so that the thousands of tiny blossoms would float down, down, down in a magic kaleidoscope of whiteness. Silent whiteness. Leaving only the stark, prickly twigs for her to see.

"I bet your mother will be surprised when she finds where you are this morning."

"No," whispered Constance, without knowing the reason for the denial.

"I should think she would be. Your first day out and all. I know *I* didn't think the doctor would let you talk him into coming out. Especially after the time you had last night."

She stared at the nurse's face, at her white clad bulging body, at her hands serenely folded over her stomach. And then at her face again—so pink and fat that why—why wasn't the weight and the bright color uncomfortable—why didn't it sometimes droop down tiredly toward her chest—?

Hatred made her lips tremble and her breath come more shallowly, quickly.

In a moment she said: "If I can go three hundred miles away next week—all the way to Mountain Heights—I guess it won't hurt to sit in my own side yard for a little while."

Miss Whelan moved a pudgy hand to brush back the girl's hair from her face. "Now, now," she said placidly. "The air up there'll do the trick. Don't be impatient. After pleurisy—you just have to take it easy and be careful."

Constance's teeth clamped rigidly. Don't let me cry, she thought. Don't, please, let her look at me ever again when I cry. Don't ever let her look at me or touch me again. Don't, please—Ever again.

When the nurse had moved off fatly across the lawn and gone back into the house, she forgot about crying. She watched a high breeze make the leaves of the oaks across the street flutter with a silver sheen in the sun. She let the glass of milk rest on her chest, bending her head slightly to sip now and then.

Out again. Under the blue sky. After breathing the yellow walls of her room for so many weeks in stingy hot breaths. After watching the heavy footboard of her bed, feeling it crush down on her chest. Blue sky. Cool blueness that could be sucked in until she was drenched in its color. She stared upward until a hot wetness welled in her eyes.

As soon as the car sounded from far off down the street she recognized the chugging of the engine and turned her head toward the strip of road visible from where she lay. The automobile seemed to tilt precariously as it swung into the driveway and jerked to a noisy stop. The glass of one of the rear windows had been cracked and plastered with dingy adhesive tape. Above this hung the head of a police dog, tongue palpitating, head cocked.

Mick jumped out first with the dog. "Looka there, Mother," she called in a lusty child's voice that rose up almost to a shriek. "She's *out.*"

Mrs. Lane stepped to the grass and looked at her daughter with a hollow, strained face. She drew deeply at her cigarette that she held in her nervous fingers, blew out airy grey ribbons of smoke that twisted in the sunshine.

"Well—" Constance prompted flatly.

"Hello, stranger," Mrs. Lane said with a brittle gaiety. "Who let you out?"

Mick clung to the straining dog. "See, Mother! King's trying to get to her. He hasn't forgotten Constance. See. He knows her good as anybody—don't you, boyoboyoboy—"

"Not so loud, Mick. Go lock that dog in the garage."

Lagging behind her mother and Mick was Howard—a sheepish expression on his pimply, fourteen year old face. "Hello, Sister," he mumbled after a gangling moment. "How do you feel?"

To look at the three of them, standing there in the shade from the oaks, somehow made her more tired than she had felt since she came out. Especially Mick—trying to straddle King with her muscular little legs, clinging to his flexed body that looked ready any moment to spring out at her.

"See, Mother! King—"

Mrs. Lane jerked one shoulder nervously. "Mick—Howard take that animal away this instant—now mind me—and lock him up somewhere." Her slender hands gestured without purpose. "This instant."

The children looked at Constance with sidelong gazes and moved off across the lawn toward the front porch.

"Well—" said Mrs. Lane when they were gone. "Did you just pick up and walk out?"

"The doctor said I could—finally—and he and Miss Whelan got that old rolling chair out from under the house and—helped me."

The words, so many of them at once, tired her. And when she gave a gentle gasp to catch her breath, the coughing started again. She leaned over the side of the chair, Kleenex in hand, and coughed until the stunted blade of grass on which she had fastened her stare had, like the cracks in the floor beside her bed, sunk ineffaceably into her memory. When she had finished she stuffed the Kleenex into a cardboard box beside the chair and looked at her mother—standing by the spirea bush, back turned, vacantly singeing the blossoms with the tip of her cigarette.

Constance stared from her mother to the blue sky. She felt that she must say something. "I wish I had a cigarette," she pronounced slowly, timing the syllables to her shallow breath.

Mrs. Lane turned. Her mouth, twitching slightly at the corners, stretched out in a too bright smile. "Now *that* would be pretty!" She dropped the cigarette to the grass and ground it out with the toe of her shoe. "I think maybe I'll cut them out for a while myself. My mouth feels all sore and furry—like a mangy little cat."

Constance laughed weakly. Each laugh was a huge burden that helped to sober her.

"Mother—"

"Yes."

"The doctor wanted to see you this morning. He wants you to call him."

Mrs. Lane broke off a sprig of the spirea blossoms and crushed it in her fingers. "I'll go in now and talk to him. Where's that Miss Whelan? Does she just set you out on the lawn by yourself when I'm gone—at the mercy of dogs and—"

"Hush, Mother. She's in the house. It's her afternoon off, you know, today."

"Is it? Well, it isn't afternoon."

The whisper slid out easily with her breath. "Mother—"

"Yes, Constance."

"Are—are you coming back out?" She looked away as she said it—looked at the sky that was a burning, fevered blue.

"If you want me to—I'll be out."

She watched her mother cross the lawn and turn into the gravel path that led to the front door. Her steps were as jerky as those of a little glass puppet. Each bony ankle stiffly pushing past the other, the thin bony arms rigidly swinging, the delicate neck held to one side.

She looked from the milk to the sky and back again. "Mother," her lips said, but the sound came out only in a tired exhalation.

The milk was hardly started. Two creamy stains drooped from the rim side by side. Four times, then, she had drunk. Twice on the bright cleanliness, twice with a shiver and eyes shut. Constance turned the glass half an inch and let her lips sink down on an unstained part. The milk crept cool and drowsy down her throat.

When Mrs. Lane returned she wore her white string garden gloves and carried rusty, clinking shears.

"Did you phone Doctor Reece?"

The woman's mouth moved infinitesimally at the corners as though she had just swallowed. "Yes."

"Well—"

"He thinks it best—not to put off going too long. This waiting around—The sooner you get settled the better it'll be."

"When, then?" She felt her pulse quiver at her finger tips like a bee on a flower—vibrate against the cool glass.

"How does the day after tomorrow strike you?"

She felt her breath shorten to hot, smothered gasps. She nodded.

From the house came the sound of Mick's and Howard's voices. They seemed to be arguing about the belts of their bathing suits. Mick's words merged into a scream. And then the sounds hushed.

That was why she was almost crying. She thought about water, looking down into great jade swirls of it, feeling the coolness of it on her hot limbs, splashing through it with long, effortless strokes. Cool water—the color of the sky.

"Oh, I do feel so dirty—"

Mrs. Lane held the shears poised. Her eyebrows quivered upward over the white sprays of blossoms she held. "Dirty?"

"Yes—yes. I haven't been in a bathtub for—for three months. I'm sick of being just sponged—stingily—"

Her mother crouched over to pick up a scrap of a candy wrapper from the grass, looked at it stupidly for a moment, and let it drop to the grass again.

"I want to go swimming—feel all the cool water. It isn't fair—isn't fair that I can't."

"Hush," said Mrs. Lane with testy sibilance. "Hush, Constance. You don't have to worry over nonsense."

"And my hair—" She lifted her hand to the oily knot that bumped out from the nape of her neck. "Not washed with water in—months—nasty awful hair that's going to run me wild. I can stand all the pleurisy and drains and t.b. but—"

Mrs. Lane was holding the flowers so tightly that they curled limply into each other as though ashamed. "Hush," she repeated hollowly. "This isn't necessary."

The sky burned brightly—blue jet flames. Choking and murderous to air.

"Maybe if it were just cut off short—"

The garden shears snipped shut slowly. "Here—if you want me to—I guess I could clip it. Do you really want it short?"

She turned her head to one side and feebly lifted one hand to tug at the bronze hairpins. "Yes—real short. Cut it all off."

Dank brown, the heavy hair hung several inches below the pillow. Hesitantly Mrs. Lane bent over and grasped a handful of it. The blades, blinding bright in the sun, began to shear through it slowly.

Mick appeared suddenly from behind the spirea bushes. Naked, except for her swimming trunks, her plump little chest gleamed silky white in the sun. Just above her round child's stomach were scolloped two soft lines of plumpness. "Mother! Are you giving *her* a haircut?"

Mrs. Lane held the dissevered hair gingerly, staring at it for a moment with her strained face. "Nice job," she said brightly. "No little fuzzes around your neck, I hope."

"No," said Constance, looking at her little sister.

The child held out an open hand. "Give it to me, Mother. I can stuff it into the cutest little pillow for King. I can—"

"Don't dare let her touch the filthy stuff," said Constance between her teeth. Her hand fingered the stiff, loose fringes around her neck, then sank tiredly to pluck at the grass.

Mrs. Lane crouched over and, moving the white flowers from the newspaper where she had laid them, wrapped up the hair and left the bundle lying on the ground behind the invalid's chair.

"I'll take it when I go in—"

The bees droned on in the hot stillness. The shade had grown blacker, and the little shadows that had fluttered by the side of the oak trees were still. Constance pushed the blanket down to her knees. "Have you told Papa about my going so soon?"

"Yes, I telephoned him."

"To Mountain Heights?" asked Mick, balancing herself on one bare leg and then the other.

"Yes, Mick."

"Mother, isn't that where you went to see Unca Charlie?"

165

"Yes."

"Is that where he sent us the cactus candy from—a long time ago?"

Lines, fine and grey as the web of a spider, cut through the pale skin around Mrs. Lane's mouth and between her eyes. "No, Mick. Mountain Heights is just the other side of Atlanta. That was Arizona."

"It was funny tasting," said Mick.

Mrs. Lane began cutting the flowers again with hurried snips. "I—I think I hear that dog of yours howling somewhere. Go tend to him—go—run along, Mick."

"You don't hear King, Mother. Howard's teaching him to shake hands out on the back porch. Please don't make me go." She laid her hand on her soft mound of stomach. "Look! You haven't said anything about my bathing suit. Aren't I nice in it, Constance?"

The sick girl looked at the flexed, eager muscles of the child before her, and then gazed back at the sky. Two words shaped themselves soundlessly on her lips.

"Gee! I wanna hurry up and get in. Did you know they're making people walk through a kind of ditch thing so you won't get sore toes this year—And they've got a new chute-ty-chute."

"Mind me this instant, Mick, and go on in the house."

The child looked at her mother and started off across the lawn. As she reached the path that led to the door she paused and, shading her eyes, looked back at them. "Can we go soon?" she asked, subdued.

"Yes, get your towels and be ready."

For several minutes the mother and daughter said nothing. Mrs. Lane moved jerkily from the spirea bushes to the fever-bright flowers that bordered the driveway, snipping hastily at the blooms, the dark shadow at her feet dogging her with noonday squatness. Constance watched her with eyes half closed against the glare, with her bony hands against the bubbling, thumping dynamo that was her chest. Finally she shaped the words on her lips and let them emerge. "Am I going up there by myself?"

"Of course, my dear. We'll just put you on a bicycle and give you a shove—"

She mashed a string of phlegm with her tongue so that she would not have to spit, and thought about repeating the question.

There were no more blooms ready for cutting. The woman looked sidewise at her daughter from over the flowers in her arm, her blue veined hand shifting its grasp on the stems. "Listen, Constance—The garden club's having some sort of a to-do today. They're all having lunch at the club—and then going to somebody's rock garden. As long as I'm taking the children over I thought I—you don't mind if I go, do you?"

"No," said Constance after a moment.

"Miss Whelan promised to stay on. Tomorrow maybe—"

She was still thinking about the question that she must repeat, but the words clung to her throat like gummy pellets of mucus and she felt that if she tried to expel them she would cry. She said instead, with no special reason: "Lovely—"

"Aren't they? Especially the spirea—so graceful and white."

"I didn't even know they'd started blooming until I got out."

"Didn't you? I brought you some in a vase last week."

"In a vase—" Constance murmured.

"At night, though. That's the time to look at them. Last night I stood by the window—and the moonlight was on them. You know how white flowers are in the moonlight—"

Suddenly she raised her bright eyes to those of her mother. "I heard you," she said half accusingly. "In the hall—tipping up and down. Late. In the living room. And I thought I heard the front door open and close. And when I was coughing once I looked at the window and I thought I saw a white dress up and down the grass like a ghost—like a—"

"Hush!" said her mother in a voice as jagged as splintered glass. "Hush. Talking is so—exhausting."

It was time for the question—as though her throat were

swollen with its matured syllables. "Am I going by myself to Mountain Heights, or with Miss Whelan, or—"

"I'm going with you. I'll take you up on the train. And stay a few days until you're settled."

Her mother stood against the sun, stopping some of the glare so that she could look into her eyes. They were the color of the sky in the cool morning. They were looking at her now with a strange stillness—a hollow restfulness. Blue as the sky before the sun had burned it to its gaseous brilliance. She stared with trembling, open lips, listening to the sound her breath made. "Mother—"

The end of the word was smothered by the first cough. She leaned over the side of the chair, feeling them beat at her chest like great blows risen from some unknown part inside her. They came, one after another with equal force. And when the last toneless one had wrenched itself clear she was so tired that she hung with unresisting limpness on the chair arm, wondering if the strength to raise her dizzy head would ever again be hers.

In the gasping minute that followed, the eyes that were still before her stretched to the vastness of the sky. She looked, and breathed, and struggled up to look again.

Mrs. Lane had turned away. But in a moment her voice rang out bitterly bright. "Goodbye, pet—I'll run along now. Miss Whelan'll be out in a minute and you'd better go right in. So long—"

As she crossed the lawn Constance thought she saw a delicate shudder shake her shoulders—a movement as perceptible as that of a crystal glass that had been thumped too soundly.

Miss Whelan stood placidly in her line of vision as they left. She only had a glimpse of Howard's and Mick's half naked bodies and the towels they flapped lustily at each other's rears. Of King thrusting his panting head above the broken window glass with its dingy tape. But she heard the overfed roar of the engine, the frantic stripping of the gears as the car backed from the driveway. And even after the last sound of the motor had trailed into silence, it was as though she could still see her mother's strained white face bent over the wheel—

"What's the matter?" asked Miss Whelan calmly. "Your side's not hurting you again, I hope."

She turned her head twice on the pillow.

"There now. Once you're in again you'll be all right."

Her hands, limp and colorless as tallow, sank over the hot wetness that streamed down her cheeks. And she swam without breath in a wide, ungiving blueness like the sky's.

Ai Bei

In 1989, Ai Bei arrived in the United States to attend a writers' conference. Outraged by the Tiananmen Square massacre in her native Beijing, Ai Bei spoke out against the Chinese government on both radio and television. As a result, the government suspended her grant money and ordered her to return to China to be disciplined. Ai Bei refused and, like so many of her countrypeople, became an exile.

"Earth Mother," wrote Ai Bei as an introduction to the following story, "is the central icon in the Potala Palace, a mythical, benevolent Buddhist saint. She is said to have seven eyes, with which She can see into people's hearts. Her right leg is stretched out in symbolic suppression of anger and realization of mercy. Earth Mothers come in five colors—white, red, blue, yellow, and green—of which green is the most basic. A powerful roc [a fabulous bird] with golden wings is perched atop the green Earth Mother's head; it is her protector."

GREEN EARTH MOTHER

ai bei

earth Mother is the central icon in the Potala
Palace, a mythical, benevolent Buddhist saint. She is said to have
seven eyes, with which She can see into people's hearts. Her right
leg is stretched out in symbolic suppression of anger and realiza-
tion of mercy. Earth Mothers come in five colors—white, red, blue,
yellow, and green—of which green is the most basic. A powerful
roc with golden wings is perched atop the green Earth Mother's
head; it is Her protector.

Night again deceived people's eyes. The wind relentlessly
toyed with the overripe berries. In the orange morning light, Mimi
pushed open the double cedar doors. The earth was blotted with the
reddish-brown juice of crushed berries—already rotten, they hid a
hope brighter than the eyes of birds in their hearts: now that winter
had passed, who could stop the multicolored seeds from sprouting green
buds? Mimi asked him about the ancient division of the seasons. Spring
is spring winter is winter flowers bloom in the summertime fruit ripens
on autumn days once you enter that time mountains rivers flowers
trees wind clouds thunder lightning snow rain frost fog all things fuse
or multiply even the excretions of men and women and boys and girls
increase or decrease. He said it all in one breath.

Why?

People are powerless against the mysteries of Heaven and Earth. He put on a pair of greasy blue shorts and walked toward the inner room, his skin a snowy white. Mimi's heart floated softly along on two hairless, spindly legs. For days Mimi had been longing for a snowfall that would cover the land, freezing Heaven and Earth, solidifying the people in their places to keep their corrupt souls from fluttering all over the streets, even if her own heart was also frozen into a lump of ice. Mimi wanted to stick out her scalding tongue—I'll kiss you, kiss every pore on your body, suck in all the hidden flavors. Her tongue was already frozen. Ice and snow fused Heaven and Earth, embracing withered branches and dead leaves, wastelands and abandoned slopes, the bare stems of shriveled petals and the ancient forest far from the bustling city, its ruined, rust-blotched trees, and those aged, green-skinned people hobbling all over the world. The aged people wore an overcoat of snow as they seduced the young by singing the praises of parental love. Spring came, the snow slunk away to reveal the ravaged land in all its ugliness. Beneath the sun's rays, it shed tears as it related a tale of short-lived purity and a false love it should never have known.

Kiss me. Why are you afraid of Her?

It just isn't right.

It's not fair. Just look at Her wrinkled old mouth that has been stamped by hundreds, thousands of full-blooded lips, a once rosy color that has peeled away completely from countless scrapings. A kiss, you have to kiss me in front of Her.

It's as out of place as wearing a bathing suit on the street. The sound of his voice shriveled into a lump; the words ran together.

It's as ridiculous as wearing a mandarin gown in a swimming pool.

Blasphemous, sacred motherly love!

I want what's mine, it's got nothing to do with Her!

Okay, tonight we'll go to some deserted spot . . .

No, I don't want any more stolen kisses in the dark.

Mimi got up out of the bathtub, every pore on her bright pink body spreading open willfully, steam obscuring the reflection of her tender fresh naked female body in the dressing mirror. She pressed her face against the cold silvery surface. Not a single wrinkle anywhere, especially on her pink forehead. In twenty-five years, nine thousand days and nights, those delicate lips had never tasted a bright shining kiss! What appeared to be an invisible dark hand in the mirror was thrust into Mimi's small narrow chest, where it stroked a weakly beating heart that was covered by a thick, heavy layer of dust. Two streams of hot tears gouged out two pale scars. In the darkness Mimi was hopelessly entwined by pity.

If She opened her eyes, a lover's kiss would immediately become a sinful intrigue.

If, in a world of respect for one's elders, there's no room for a kiss in broad daylight, I'd rather have languished in my mother's womb and never have opened my eyes.

Not so loud. Mother will hear. He was breathing hard, his every word chiseled on Mimi's heart.

Mimi composed herself and gazed at the pale tiny tightly closed mouth in the dressing mirror. Her pink body was cooling off, turning as pale as wax. A delicate hand glided down it from top to bottom as she mused, Maybe this doesn't belong to me. No . . . but maybe . . . Love knotted in her heart, spun a thread that circled the earth three times, maybe more. Mimi was sure that sooner or later the world would be destroyed—by love.

Are you crying? Are you . . . The words stuck in his throat and simply wouldn't come out. He put a towel printed with cats' eyes—red, yellow, blue, white—over Mimi's shoulders. She shook her head, raining tears onto the back of his hand. When Mimi was little, Mama had said she was born under a crying star, that she had come into this world with tears in her eyes. Grannie believed she was an unlucky child, so on snowy days she secretly fed her snowballs. Mimi's mouth was frozen open like a trumpet as she sang and sang and sang, never stopping. All Mama could do was buy a set of imported earplugs.

Are you crying again? His hand was lily white and supple, so soft it seemed boneless. He wiped away the tears on her cheeks, then carried her back to the bathtub and the hot water. He rubbed her back, massaged her shoulders, then let his supple hands rest on her trembling breasts. Beads of water dripped through his fingers. Ribbons of orange light filtered in through a dark green bamboo grove. The ribbons, like spirit threads, tied up her tender little heart as they swayed back and forth. Pricked by sharp leaves, her heart settled like a fine powder over her childhood dream world, with all its colored lamps. The colored lamps congealed into a swarm of moths. The moths greedily sucked up the orange-colored light, which shone through their transparent wings. Mimi had been afraid of the moon's orange rays ever since she was little.

174

Knock-knock. She was at the door.

I'm taking a bath. What do you want?

Is he in there?

He . . . Before she could get it out, he covered Mimi's lips with his boneless hand.

Say I'm not here. His mouth was boring into Mimi's ear.

Why?

I shouldn't be here while you're taking a bath.

I'm your wife, I share your bed. What's wrong with a bath?

Blasphemous . . . blasphemous, sacred motherly love.

Ptui! Pettiness is the true blasphemous love! Mimi kicked the tub over. A pair of purple slippers floated toward the door on the spilled water.

Ai! A heavy sigh from the other side of the door splintered Mimi's heart. She hadn't left. Instead She cupped a brilliant excuse in her hands. I bought you a *Moonlight Sonata* tape. Come out here and we'll listen to it together.

Ma—he was embarrassed beyond belief. A snow white back slipped through the cedar doors.

It's my chest, the same old problem. The moans of a sick cat outside the door.

Ma—I'll massage it for you.

Mimi stood barefoot next to the window. She tumbled into a sea of mist, floated off toward a deep canyon—compressed into a breathless speck of dust, her bloodless lips parted, she gazed up at the creases squirming in the sky. A ruined face like a piece of rotting wood appeared in the tattered vault of heaven. Mimi rubbed her wildly beating heart. What is it I still want? she asked herself. Why hasn't my heart ossified? In spite of herself Mimi looked down into the courtyard. That knifelike face spread out across a hairless, snow white chest. Mimi was thinking, The flowers in Her eyes are blooming at an angle, the clouds are drifting at an angle, people are walking at an angle. Her happiness spilled out of Her crisscrossing creases. Like the new bloom of a withered flower, Her face came back to life. Four spindly legs intertwined; two bodies folded together As though she were watching a centipede, Mimi hid, trembling, behind the curtain. Soap bubbles kept popping; water spread silently in all directions . . . a pair of tiny feet, made plump by soap bubbles, stepped on the scarlet gravel. A shout—Mama—the orbs of her buttocks arched as she walked, arched and quivered as though restless animals were hiding in them. Arms thrust out in front of her, Mimi ran toward the churning white foam stretching out before her, leaving behind a trail of happy birds' nests with her feet. A pile of bubbles was created in a second; a drab blueness required countless millennia. She ran into it, a flesh red butterfly toying with a boundless expanse of waves. As she swam ahead, the fleshy red became white, the blue became a deep green.

Oh Mama, the ocean isn't blue! Mimi raised her pudgy arms, threw them around Mama's youthful long neck and floated lightly upward, the weight of twelve years seemingly as light as a feather. Mama scooped little Mimi out of the water, cupping her like a living heart. Watery eyes spread open, a rose. You're twelve years old today. Taking you swimming in the ocean is Mama's present to you, because you never enjoyed the love of a father . . .

Mama! Two wet faces pressed together; a childish heart grew suddenly solemn. A ferocious wave crashed over them. Mimi swallowed a mouthful of seawater, brackish and salty. Mama staggered back to the beach cradling Mimi in her arms. She looked at the stunned expression on Mama's face and felt resentment, sadness. She never swam in the ocean again.

The first time Mimi saw him was on her second trip to the seashore. She was sitting alone on the beach staring up at the moon, a sheet of red paper stuck onto the canopy of heaven above the sea. She was laden with sorrow. He walked up and sat down beside her. The beach was deserted, the sand unbearably cold and cheerless. He spoke to Mimi in a disbelieving voice. You look just like Her, the same sadness, the same purity. She loves the moon, the early morning sun, Beethoven, Spinoza . . .

A poet?

No, unemployed. Gets by by doing odd jobs. She published a story when She was eighteen; at twenty She had a solo vocal recital, as a coloratura. But like ordinary women, She gleaned scraps of coal and carried manure buckets, all for the sake of Her son . . . his voice quickly faded out. Mimi's heart leapt into her mouth. The sea was unbelievably calm; all she could hear were the softly lapping waves and the violent beating of her heart.

Do you love Her?

I adore Her. My only goal in life is to make Her happy.

Mimi's heart crawled; her narrow chest began to swell. The broad expanse of the beach was nearly unbearable. She headed over to a shaded path that led to the shore. The thick branches of the towering kola nut trees were intertwined, their thick shade forming a dark umbrella over Mimi's head. He followed quietly behind her, as still as a shadow.

Who is She?

My mother.

Thunder roared; the moon was gone. In the pitch darkness he grabbed Mimi's hand and drew up next to her, purring like a cat. Her suspended heart settled back down, dissolving into millions of pearls of tribute. The "motherhood" memorial arch screened out the last traces of jealousy. All the emotions in the world could be written with only the words affection or filiality; otherwise it would be blasphemy. A bolt of lightning flashed between them; two twisted faces drew together. In the space of a minute, countless driven raindrops crashed into two bodies and two hearts consumed by flames at the base of an ancient tree. They saw nothing, they heard nothing. There was only the driven rain and the mud and an inextinguishable fireball. Tens of thousands of years ago, the heavens had opened up angrily, just like tonight, and a pair of lovers had died for love beneath the branches of this ancient tree. After tens of thousands of springs, tens of thousands of summers, two carnal-colored seeds had formed deep beneath the roots of this gnarled, ancient tree. Maybe the vows would be answered on this rainy night, and the two love seeds would finally germinate and sprout forth. As the rain fell, they exchanged their burning hearts, which sizzled with each raindrop. A chill wind brushed past, whipping up flames of joy. Thunder roared angrily; the gigantic canopy of the tree rose into the air, then crashed to the ground. Their souls flew out of their bodies. The fire was out, but gray smoke continued to curl upward. The wind died down, the rain stopped, a cluster of rice-colored stars was set free to cleanse the canopy of heaven. They stared silently at one another like a pair of clay statues, gazing into each other's expression, all genuine feelings now lost.

Come to my place and change into some dry clothes.

No, Mother's waiting anxiously for me to come home.

They held hands tightly in the darkness, then let go. No words of comfort, no good-byes as they parted.

He knew it had been an extraordinary rainy night, and that he'd given her an even more extraordinary love. Mimi knew it had been a soul-stirring rainy night, and that she'd relinquished soul-stirring emotions to the rainy night. The rainy night had incurred a heavy debt. What they'd taken from the rainy night could never be easily abandoned. Love had turned their hearts into a scorched mass, but they remained fused together to avoid the pain of being ripped apart.

Mother wants to meet you.

Why?

She has to give Her permission for me to marry. I know She'll like you.

On Sunday he climbed the Great Wall, Mimi holding his left hand, Mother holding his right. He used up a roll of color film beside the North Sea, his left arm around Mimi's shoulder, his right hand gripping Mother's arm. Mimi let him hold the parasol, She handed him her feather-light handbag; Mimi took off her jacket and put it over his shoulders, She put her half-eaten popsicle up to his mouth; Mimi could see resentment in Her eyes. She could see superfluousness in Mimi's face. He tried to please Mimi by buying a popsicle, he tried to please Her by buying a soft drink, all the time panting like a cat in heat.

At dusk Mimi's first glance took in Her thick black hair, oppressive, impenetrable. Three pink moles at the corner of Her mouth were so close together they were almost one. From then on unlucky omens began to appear in Mimi's dreams. Bright red, meaty growths appeared. Countless pink eyes hidden in Her thick black hair, shedding tears like blood . . . Mimi often woke from her dreams in terror; in the surrounding blackness, she refreshed her image of him by looking through photographs.

How about this one?

No, you can't see Ma's disposition in it. This one's no good either. You can't see Mother's grace in it. Um-um, these are even worse . . .

This one's pretty good.

Her hair isn't dyed.

Gray hair's a sign of kindness.

No, She looks too old. Mimi, under no circumstances are you to let Mother see this photo!

Why?

If She sees Herself looking so old, She'll be upset. From now on you're not to call Her an old lady to Her face. His words were strings of water drops that seeped into Mimi's heart like poison. Mimi's nerves felt raw; she was trembling. She walked out of the house and wandered aimlessly. She walked up to a shop where people were selling all kinds of diapers; countless wrinkled chapped feet stepped over pudgy babies lying on the ground as they fought over the colorful diapers. Mimi reached out. Four huge cats' eyes bit down painfully. She pulled her hand back and realized that her face was still pressed up against the icy window. She stared at the orange moon as it scurried in and out of a jumbled mass of clouds. Another daydream! Mimi dragged her stiffened legs out the door. What was this, a blanket of stars in the sky above and on the ground below? Heaven and Earth, everything was all jumbled up! Her face was soaked; water filled her eyes. She stepped in a puddle, shattering it as an orange moon landed on her instep. She kicked it away and walked up to the room, stepping in one puddle after another. Mimi stood in the doorway, oblivious to the passage of time. His broad, heavy back blocked her view of the reclining chair. They couldn't see Mimi, but Mimi could see his limp, boneless hand massaging a mound of withered, yellowed wrinkles. Amid the wrinkles countless stringy mammary glands converged to form two dark purple nipples, like overripe squishy grapes.

The pain in my chest started when I was pregnant with you. Her voice seemed to float up from the depths of a dying well, then sank slowly back down. Mimi could see Her parted lips, Her half-closed eyes, the three pink moles quivering in a red tide.

Ma, it feels better when I massage you, doesn't it?

Much better. Your head was so big it was a very hard delivery. For two days and three nights, that wretched father of yours never showed his face at the delivery room door. I was so angry I couldn't eat. My stomach ached from hunger . . .

Ma. Grief and indignation caused the big pale boneless hands to dig in too hard. The overripe purple grapes oozed two drops of pus-colored liquid. They hung there on the verge of falling off, quivering drops of muddy yellow, like a secret mixture of splendor and decay fighting off death. Mimi suddenly saw in the glass her own ghostly image.

Ai, you're all grown up. But I still remember what you were like as a child. You nursed at my breast every night and listened to me read *Snow White*. You didn't blink. Remember? I spanked you once because you stole Leilei's hanky, and you curled up in my lap and cried half the night. Pretty soon I started crying, too. Ai . . . words gradually gave way to soft moans.

Ma—the two mounds of withered yellow wrinkled skin were getting hot from the rubbing, turning red. His hands hesitated; they began to tremble. Terrified, he stared at the overripe, oozing purple grapes . . .

180

Mimi threw the towel over her shoulders, burst into the room, and stood there ramrod straight, beads of water streaming down her body.

You! The big pale boneless hands froze above Her chest. All rubbing motions stopped for a full two minutes.

Reluctantly She opened her eyes. After a momentary fright She calmed Herself down.

What's wrong with you? He quickly picked up the sheet to cover up Mimi's naked body. As though awakened from a dream, Mimi cast a flustered look at her own dripping body, knocked his hand away, and recoiled to the side.

I told you long ago she's got emotional problems. Look at her, the poor thing. You stay here; I'll take her to the hospital. A look of great compassion on Her face.

No. Mimi huddled next to him and gripped his hand tightly.

Mimi, go to the hospital with Mother and let them see what's wrong, okay?

Mimi looked at him as though he were a stranger for a moment before jerking her hand free and throwing off the sheet that covered her. She ran to her own room, stepping on the rays of starlight. The bed was swirling, she buried her head in the fluffy pillow, her eyes were tightly shut. He held Mimi in his arms. He could feel her trembling, but couldn't hear the sobs stuck in her throat. His body was wracked by a cold shudder that stabbed into his heart. Her long damp hair gave off steam that encircled the two faces. A sharp pain in his heart as he dug his fingernails into Mimi's flesh. Mimi shrunk into his embrace; for a long, long time her terrified eyes were glued to those fleshy big pale boneless hands. He peeled the wet strands of hair off her cheeks, touched her full lips. His muscles tensed as he nervously reached for her hand. Two limpid drops of water oozed out from under her tightly shut eyelids. Don't open your eyes, hold my hand. Let's find our way out of this dark green grove together. Pointed leaves cradled strings of last night's dewdrops, emitting light yellow rays. Don't reach out. Every dewdrop knocked to the ground is one more shattered heart. Pressed tightly together, they walked forward, hand in hand. Stillness reigned, broken only by the even sounds of their labored breathing. As he raised his head, his face was imprinted with golden splotches of light filtering through cracks in the dark green canopy above. So was Mimi's snowy white blouse. Creeping forward cautiously, their shoulders bent, they made their way through the dark green grove, a pair of intertwining silk ribbons gliding back and forth like an empty emotion being poured into an empty heart

Kiss me. In the translucent light of the sun, a pair of feet like those of a tiny animal rose up on their tiptoes. The pointed leaves rustled interminably, sending light yellow dewdrops cascading to the ground, shattered. His back blocked out the sunlight; a wall of darkness suddenly spread out before Mimi's eyes, probably because the lamp at the head of the bed was smashed. In a flash two naked bodies formed a scarlet forest. Mimi's mouth opened wide, fingernails dug into his back. No, don't, stop . . . don't stop. Mimi wanted to push him away, but she dug her fingers deeply into flesh that could have been his or could have been hers. Two vibrant lives formed a bright rainbow. Four eyes were tightly shut, blood-filled lips fused together, Heaven and Earth were about to explode, the ark was capsizing . . . Don't move! I hear something. Footsteps on broken glass, hobbling back and forth beyond the door. A swarm of ants gently raised up a berry; several little stars silently leapt onto the wet window ledge. Rain dripping from the eaves turned into fine drops, falling freely to the ground in threads. The berries were completely smashed, oozing crimson earth. Already rotten, they hid a hope brighter than the eyes of birds in their hearts; now that winter had passed, who could stop the multicolored seeds from sprouting green buds? The scarlet forest began to fade, gradually becoming a gloomy violet. Mimi's verdant heart suddenly withered and cracked; springtime fled without a trace.

Is she better? Her voice was soft and supple, like a rope twisted out of rubber.

Much better, Ma—He was desperate to convince Her that nothing had happened a moment ago.

Is she asleep?

She fell asleep long ago, Ma. Still desperate to convince Her, he turned on the light and opened the door. An icy hand descended on Mimi's forehead. Oh! She's feverish. Mimi raised her eyelids, which were nearly stuck together. She saw a knifelike old face leaning over her, a glinting cold light like the dead grasses covering a winter pasture in whose roots were hidden the hope of rebirth for snakes and scorpions, ants and bugs. Mimi was like a spring that had been stretched too far, its tension completely lost. The channels in her heart slowed down, twisted; last night, so transparent, would decompose where it stuck. She tossed down a green stone. The echo from the bottom of her heart reverberated, was still reverberating. I'm not sick! I'm not. Mimi sensed that she was an emotional, kind-hearted sparrow silently keeping watch over a nonexistent snake track in the darkness of a vast forest. Deep autumn, when the birds fly south, and Mimi no longer had the strength to cross the single-file bridge of his heart. Profound sorrow wrapped itself around her. All Mimi could do was cry.

Mimi, you're sick.

There are yardsticks all over the world, but not a speck of land for me anywhere. Take my measure with Your yardstick, take Your measure with mine.

What nonsense is that? Mimi. You really are sick.

She has no husband, I have no father. None of us has a father.

Mimi, snap out of it. I love you, Mother loves you, too . . . She loves . . .

She loves acting high and mighty the foreign superstition of not going outside on Friday the thirteenth eating sausage sandwiches even if they taste funny drinking coffee without sugar destroying nerves that are already too fragile . . .

Why do you insist on making this relationship impossible!

The relationship is cruel enough already. At first I was confident in my youth and my good looks, confident that no one could replace the love of a wife. Heh-heh, I was wrong. You'll never have the courage to cut the umbilical cord, and, of course, that's what She's counting on. It's not enough just to be your wife . . .

God damn that Freud and his theories!

No, it's more than that. It's castration. Most Chinese men are swallowed up by maternal love. There's nothing left. I want nothing. I'm leaving.

What nonsense is that? You're sick. Where do you think you're going?

. . . Mimi walked into the gray, misty dusk empty-handed.

You can't leave. He reached out, but grabbed only the empty dusk air, like an infant who's lost the nipple and stares into a great void.

Let her go and walk it off. She's just tired. She walked over abruptly and stood in his way, Her face suffused with the innocence of an eighteen-year-old girl.

Ma—she's still got a fever. She's talking nonsense. Now that he'd found an excuse, he was as excited as a drowning man reaching out to grasp a straw, someone who'd found the hope to go on living.

Take it easy. Nothing will happen. Her voice was thinner than paper.

Ma—he felt like crying, but he didn't though his eyes were burning.

An ancient ugly dying forest way off in the corner of the dark green sky. Decrepit forked branches, so rusted they looked as if they'd never borne flowers or brought forth tender new buds—ancient trees forced to bear the stigma that they hadn't seen the color of green in thousands of years. Flocks of birds perching densely on the shaky forked branches were exchanging curses that birds have known since antiquity. Pair after pair of bulging eyes looked down on Mimi's life and her lives to come. Mimi was frightened out of her wits. She wouldn't choose this decaying den of spies as the place to end her life. She emerged from the forest and lay down on a desolate slope covered with years of loneliness. The grass around her was restless; the desolate slope lifted her up until she was floating in the air. Snakes and scorpions, bugs and ants lazily raised their heads, eyes heavy with sleep. Mimi was so tired she couldn't keep her eyes open. An icy softness kept brushing past her hands. There was a tautness in her belly, a weightiness, painful cramps. She undid her underwear and held her bulging belly with both hands, letting the first flakes of snow moisten the tiny new life. A momentary throbbing reminded her that the child would be born under the sign of the serpent. Why is there so much movement during a period of hibernation? A smile spread across Mimi's face, as tranquility settled upon her once again.

It's snowing hard now, and Mimi still isn't home. I'll find her and bring her back to talk some sense into her. His reproach was filled with anxiety.

I won't allow you to talk sense into her. Let her calm down first. Who knows, maybe she went to her mother's home. Mother held his arm. Her withered, yellowing body blocked the huge cedar doors.

Ma, let me bring her back and give her a good talking to. He tried to wrench his arm free from Her grip, but She held on for dear life.

I won't allow you to frighten her! She shouted anxiously.

Ma—he pushed Her hand away and burst through the door.

Stop right there! She ran out after him, stumbled, nearly fell. He had no choice but to rush back and steady Her. Her mouth was open wide; She was gasping. She couldn't speak.

Ma—

I won't allow you to be rough with Mimi. It's cold out there. I'll go with you to find her. Suddenly calm again, She looked at him tenderly. He lowered his head to avoid Her eyes. His voice was so low he seemed to be talking to himself. She's still got a fever.

Mimi raised her leg—it was stiff from the cold. She didn't have the heart to stamp a footprint onto the translucent surface, though maybe that was the way for her to experience the pleasure of destroying purity. White sky. White snow. White night. Tender snowflakes translucent in the boundless translucence. Not a breath of wind. The flakes seemed to be floating in their prescribed spots, a scene of chaos, nihilism. This was Mimi's cherished hope— Heaven and Earth a single color. As she stood in the snow, she could no longer see herself. Fossilized bones glistened so brightly they dazzled her eyes, her terrified, trembling heart had petrified, been transformed into a heart-shaped green agate tossed onto the boundless snow all by itself. Don't open the door, people, give the world a chance to hold on to this pale, powerless purity! Hide under the snowbound roof to cry alone over your own death. Look, the sky is responding to human misery by sending down its symbol of filial piety—snow that covers the ground. In the snow-covered wilderness, only the emerald green agate awaits rebirth—maybe the tragedy of these two legs will be replayed somewhere else in the universe. Mimi was overcome by sorrow, but she was at peace. Inadvertently, she discovered a long piece of light purple silk rolling back and forth across the earth's crust with a soft tearing sound, leaving behind an eternal silence. Mimi had no sense of her own being, not even as a tiny snowflake. As she slumped slowly to the snow-covered ground, she saw the bright, snowy red of the ancient grove with its rusted trees. Flowers in full bloom were like huge tongues stretching up into the vault of heaven, sucking dry all the blood vessels, turning the anemic Heaven and Earth paler than ever. The delicate and beautiful ancient forest trembled in the dazzling snow, sending skyward a cloud of red mist . . .

He picked Mimi up, his face as dark as the earth. He gazed in stupefaction at Mother's silvery new teeth. A confused look on his face, the twin expressions of laughter and crying.

✿

Dorothy Allison

In Greece and Rome, it was one of the signs of a well-educated person to know all of Sappho's poems by heart. Born sometime in the seventh or sixth century B.C., her poems, mostly addressed to her female lovers, earned her the title of "tenth muse." Until late in the eleventh century, her work was copied and translated; then, in 1075, Pope Gregory VIII condemned Sappho's poems as obscene and had all copies of her books burnt in Rome and Constantinople. Sappho survives today in a handful of fragments and in one word, "lesbian," coined from the name of her island of birth.

Because for the longest time lesbian readers found no identifiable images in fiction, much of the earliest lesbian fiction was didactic. Dorothy Allison never found it her mission to teach her audience. "I do not think that my purpose in life is to explain, particularly to explain to straight people, what lesbian lives are like." Instead, Allison explores in her fiction the many ways in which women learn about themselves—through love of other women, through their own reflected images, through their mothers, through their daughters—in order to find both freedom and healing. But, "to get to the healing," Allison argues, "you have to break your heart first. You have to crack the scar. That's what good writing is about."

MAMA

dorothy allison

above her left ankle my mother has an odd star-shaped scar. It blossoms like a violet above the arch, a purple pucker riding the muscle. When she was a little girl in South Carolina they still bled people in sickness, and they bled her there. I thought she was just telling a story, when she first told me, teasing me or covering up some embarrassing accident she didn't want me to know about. But my aunt supported her.

"It's a miracle she's alive, girl. She was such a sickly child, still a child when she had you, and then there was the way you were born."

"How's that?"

"Assbackward," Aunt Alma was proud to be the first to tell me, and it showed in the excitement in her voice. "Your mama was unconscious for three days after you were born. She'd been fast asleep in the back of your Uncle Lucius's car when they hit that Pontiac right outside the airbase. Your mama went right through the windshield and bounced off the other car. When she woke up three days later, you were already out and named, and all she had was a little scar on her forehead to show what had happened. It was a miracle like they talk about in Bible school, and I know there's something your mama's meant to do because of it."

"Oh yeah," Mama shrugged when I asked her about it. "An't no doubt I'm meant for greater things—bigger biscuits, thicker gravy. What else could God want for someone like me, huh?" She pulled her mouth so tight I could see her teeth pushing her upper lip, but then she looked into my face and let her air out slowly.

"Your aunt is always laying things to God's hand that he wouldn't have interest in doing anyway. What's true is that there was a car accident and you got named before I could say much about it. Ask your aunt why you're named after her, why don't you?"

On my stepfather's birthday I always think of my mother. She sits with her coffee and cigarettes, watches the sun come up before she must leave for work. My mama lives with my stepfather still, though she spent most of my childhood swearing that as soon as she had us up and grown she'd leave him flat. Instead, we left, my sister and I, and on my stepfather's birthday we neither send presents nor visit. The thing we do—as my sister has told me and as I have told her—is think about Mama. At any moment of the day we know what she will be doing, where she will be, and what she will probably be talking about. We know, not only because her days are as set and predictable as the schedule by which she does the laundry, we know in our bodies. Our mother's body is with us in its details. She is recreated in each of us, strength of bone and the skin curling over the thick flesh the women of our family have always worn.

When I visit Mama, I always look first to her hands and feet to reassure myself. The skin of her hands is transparent—large-veined, wrinkled and bruised—while her feet are soft with the lotions I rubbed into them every other night of my childhood. That was a special thing between my mother and me, the way she'd give herself the care of my hands, lying across the daybed, telling me stories of what she'd served down at the truckstop, who had complained and who tipped specially well, and most important, who had said what and what she'd said back. I would sit at her feet, laughing and nodding and stroking away the tightness in her muscles, watching the way her mouth would pull taut while under her pale eyelids the pulse of her eyes moved like kittens behind a blanket. Sometimes my love for her would choke me, and I would ache to have her open her eyes and see me there, to see how much I loved her. But mostly I kept my eyes on her skin, the fine traceries of the veins and the knotted cords of ligaments, seeing where she was not beautiful and hiding how scared it made me to see her close up, looking so fragile, and too often, so old.

190

When my mama was twenty-five she already had an old woman's hands, and I feared them. I did not know then what it was that scared me so. I've come to understand since it was the thought of her growing old, of her dying and leaving me alone. I feared those brown spots, those wrinkles and cracks that lined her wrists, ankles, and the soft-shadowed sides of her eyes. I was too young to imagine my own death with anything but an adolescent's high romantic enjoyment; I pretended often enough that I was dying of a wasting disease that would give lots of time for my aunts, uncles, and stepfather to mourn me. But the idea that anything could touch my mother, that anything would dare to hurt her was impossible to bear, and I woke up screaming the one night I dreamed of her death—a dream in which I tried bodily to climb to the throne of a Baptist god and demand her return to me. I thought of my mama like a mountain or a cave, a force of nature, a woman who had saved her own life and mine, and would surely save us both over and over again. The wrinkles in her hands made me think of earthquakes and the lines under her eyes hummed of tidal waves in the night. If she was fragile, if she was human, then so was I, and anything might happen. If she was not the backbone of creation itself, then fear would overtake me. I could not allow that, would not. My child's solution was to try to cure my mother of wrinkles in the hope of saving her from death itself.

Once, when I was about eight and there was no Jergens lotion to be had, I spooned some mayonnaise out to use instead. Mama leaned forward, sniffed, lay back and laughed into her hand.

"If that worked," she told me, still grinning, "I wouldn't have dried up to begin with—all the mayonnaise I've eaten in my life."

"All the mayonnaise you've spread—like the butter of your smile, out there for everybody," my stepfather grumbled. He wanted his evening glass of tea, wanted his feet put up, and maybe his neck rubbed. At a look from Mama, I'd run one errand after another until he was settled with nothing left to complain about. Then I'd go back to Mama. But by that time we'd have to start on dinner, and I wouldn't have any more quiet time with her till a day or two later when I'd rub her feet again.

I never hated my stepfather half as much for the beatings he gave me as for those stolen moments when I could have been holding Mama's feet in my hands. Pulled away from Mama's side to run get him a pillow or change the television channel and forced to stand and wait until he was sure there was nothing else he wanted me to do, I entertained myself with visions of his sudden death. Motorcycle outlaws would come to the door, mistaking him for a Drug Enforcement Officer, and blow his head off with a sawed-off shotgun just like the one my Uncle Bo kept under the front seat in his truck. The lawn mower would explode, cutting him into scattered separate pieces the emergency squad would have to collect in plastic bags. Standing and waiting for his orders while staring at the thin black hairs on his balding head, I would imagine his scalp seen through blood-stained plastic, and smile wide and happy while I thought out how I would tell that one to my sister in our dark room at night, when she would whisper back to me her own version of our private morality play.

When my stepfather beat me I did not think, did not imagine stories of either escape or revenge. When my stepfather beat me I pulled so deeply into myself I lived only in my eyes, my eyes that watched the shower sweat on the bathroom walls, the pipes under the sink, my blood on the porcelain toilet seat, and the buckle of his belt as it moved through the air. My ears were disconnected so I could understand nothing—neither his shouts, my own hoarse shameful strangled pleas, nor my mother's screams from the other side of the door he locked. I would not come back to myself until the beating was ended and the door was opened and I saw my mother's face, her hands shaking as she reached for me. Even then, I would not be able to understand what she was yelling at him, or he was yelling at both of us. Mama would take me into the bedroom and wash my face with a cold rag, wipe my legs and, using the same lotion I had rubbed into her feet, try to soothe my pain. Only when she had stopped crying would my hearing come back, and I would lie still and listen to her voice saying my name—soft and tender, like her hand on my back. There were no stories in my head then, no hatred, only an enormous gratitude to be lying still with her hand on me and, for once, the door locked against him.

192

Push it down. Don't show it. Don't tell anyone what is really going on. We are not safe, I learned from my mama. There are people in the world who are, but they are not us. Don't show your stuff to anyone. Tell no one that your stepfather beats you. The things that would happen are too terrible to name.

Mama quit working honkytonks to try the mill as soon as she could after her marriage. But a year in the mill was all she could take; the dust in the air got to her too fast. After that there was no choice but to find work in a diner. The tips made all the difference, though she could have made more money if she'd stayed with the honkytonks or managed a slot as a cocktail waitress. There was always more money serving people beer and wine, more still in hard liquor, but she'd have had to go outside Greenville County to do that. Neither she nor her new husband could imagine going that far.

The diner was a good choice anyway, one of the few respectable ones downtown, a place where men took their families on Sunday afternoon. The work left her tired, but not sick to death like the mill, and she liked the people she met there, the tips and the conversation.

"You got a way about you," the manager told her.

"Oh yeah, I'm known for my ways," she laughed, and no one would have known she didn't mean it. Truckers or judges, they all liked my mama. And when they weren't slipping quarters in her pocket, they were bringing her things, souvenirs or friendship cards, once or twice a ring. Mama smiled, joked, slapped ass, and firmly passed back anything that looked like a down payment on something she didn't want to sell. She started taking me to work with her when I was still too short to see over the counter, letting me sit up there to watch her some, and tucking me away in the car when I got cold or sleepy.

"That's my girl," she'd brag. "Four years old and reads the funny papers to me every Sunday morning. She's something, an't she?"

"Something," the men would nod, mostly not even looking at me, but agreeing with anything just to win Mama's smile. I'd watch them closely, the wallets they pulled out of their back pockets, the rough patches on their forearms and scratches on their chins. Poor men, they didn't have much more than we did, but they could buy my mama's time with a cup of coffee and a nickel slipped under the saucer. I hated them, each and every one.

My stepfather was a truck driver—a little man with a big rig and a bigger rage. He kept losing jobs when he lost his temper. Somebody would say something, some joke, some little thing, and my little stepfather would pick up something half again his weight and try to murder whoever had dared to say that thing. "Don't make him angry," people always said about him. "Don't make him angry," my mama was always saying to us.

I tried not to make him angry. I ran his errands. I listened to him talk, standing still on one leg and then the other, keeping my face empty, impartial. He always wanted me to wait on him.

193

When we heard him yell, my sister's face would break like a pool of water struck with a handful of stones. Her glance would fly to mine. I would stare at her, hate her, hate myself. She would stare at me, hate me, hate herself. After a moment, I would sigh—five, six, seven, eight years old, sighing like an old lady—tell her to stay there, get up and go to him. Go to stand still for him, his hands, his big hands on his little body. I would imagine those hands cut off by marauders sweeping down on great black horses, swords like lightning bolts in the hands of armored women who wouldn't even know my name but would kill him anyway. Imagine boils and blisters and wasting diseases; sudden overturned cars and spreading gasoline. Imagine vengeance. Imagine justice. What is the difference anyway when both are only stories in your head? In the everyday reality you stand still. I stood still. Bent over. Laid down.

"Yes, Daddy."

"No, Daddy."

"I'm sorry, Daddy."

"Don't do that, Daddy."

"Please, Daddy."

Push it down. Don't show it. Don't tell anyone what is really going on. We are not safe. There are people in the world who are, but they are not us. Don't show your fear to anyone. The things that would happen are too terrible to name.

Sometimes I wake in the middle of the night to the call of my name shouted in my mama's voice, rising from silence like an echo caught in the folds of my brain. It is her hard voice I hear, not the soft one she used when she held me tight, the hard voice she used on bill collectors and process servers. Sometimes her laugh comes too, that sad laugh, thin and foreshadowing a cough, with her angry laugh following. I hate that laugh, hate the sound of it in the night following on my name like shame. When I hear myself laugh like that, I always start to curse, to echo what I know was the stronger force in my mama's life.

As I grew up my teachers warned me to clean up my language, and my lovers became impatient with the things I said. Sugar and honey, my teachers reminded me when I sprinkled my sentences with the vinegar of my mama's rage—as if I was supposed to want to draw flies. And, "Oh, honey," my girlfriends would whisper, "do you have to talk that way?" I did, I did indeed. I smiled them my mama's smile and played for them my mama's words while they tightened up and pulled back, seeing me for someone they had not imagined before. They didn't shout, they hissed; and even when they got angry, their language never quite rose up out of them the way my mama's rage would fly.

"Must you? Must you?" they begged me. And then, "For God's sake!"

"Sweet Jesus!" I'd shout back but they didn't know enough to laugh.

"Must you? Must you?"

Hiss, hiss.

"For God's sake, do you have to end everything with *ass?* An anal obsession, that's what you've got, a goddamn anal obsession!"

"I do, I do," I told them, "and you don't even know how to say *goddamn*. A woman who says *goddamn* as soft as you do isn't worth the price of a meal of shit!"

Coarse, crude, rude words and ruder gestures—Mama knew them all. You *assfucker, get out of my yard,* to the cop who came to take the furniture. *Shitsucking bastard!* to the man who put his hand under her skirt. *Jesus shit a brick,* every day of her life. Though she slapped me when I used them, my mama taught me the power of nasty words. Say *goddamn*. Say anything but begin it with *Jesus* and end it with *shit*. Add that laugh, the one that disguises your broken heart. Oh, never show your broken heart! Make them think you don't have one instead.

"If people are going to kick you, don't just lie there. Shout back at them."

"Yes, Mama."

Language then, and tone, and cadence. Make me mad, and I'll curse you to the seventh generation in my mama's voice. But you have to work to get me mad. I measure my anger against my mama's rages and her insistence that most people aren't even worth your time. "We are another people. Our like isn't seen on earth that often," my mama told me, and I knew what she meant. I know the value of the hard asses of this world. And I am my mama's daughter—tougher than kudzu, meaner than all the ass-kicking, bad-assed, cold-assed, saggy-assed fuckers I have ever known. But it's true that sometimes I talk that way just to remember my mother, the survivor, the endurer, but the one who could not always keep quiet about it.

We are just like her, my sister and I. That March when my sister called, I thought for a moment it was my mama's voice. The accent was right, and the language—the slow drag of matter-of-fact words and thoughts, but the beaten-down quality wasn't Mama, couldn't have been. For a moment I felt as if my hands were gripping old and tender flesh, the skin gone thin from age and wear, my granny's hands, perhaps, on the day she had stared out at her grandsons and laughed lightly, insisting I take a good look at them. "See, see how the blood thins out." She spit to the side and clamped a hand down on my shoulder. I turned and looked at her hand, that hand as strong as heavy cord rolled back on itself, my bare shoulder under her hand and the muscles there rising like bubbles in cold milk. I had felt thick and strong beside her, thick and strong and sure of myself in a way I have not felt since. That March when my sister called I felt old; my hands felt wiry and worn, and my blood seemed hot and thin as it rushed through my veins.

My sister's voice sounded hollow; her words vibrated over the phone as if they had iron edges. My tongue locked to my teeth, and I tasted the fear I thought I had put far behind me.

"They're doing everything they can—surgery again this morning and chemotherapy and radiation. He's a doctor, so he knows, but Jesus . . ."

"Jesus shit."

"Yeah."

Mama woke up alone with her rage, her grief. "Just what I'd always expected," she told me later. "You think you know what's going on, what to expect. You relax a minute and that's when it happens. Life turns around and kicks you in the butt."

Lying there, she knew they had finally gotten her, the they that had been dogging her all her life, waiting for the chance to rob her of all her tomorrows. Now they had her, her body pinned down under bandages and tubes and sheets that felt like molten lead. She had not really believed it possible. She tried to pull her hands up to her neck, but she couldn't move her arms. "I was so mad I wanted to kick holes in the sheets, but there wasn't no use in that." When my stepfather came in to sit and whistle his sobs beside the bed, she took long breaths and held her face tight and still. She became all eyes, watching everything from a place far off inside herself.

"Never want what you cannot have," she'd always told me. It was her rule for survival, and she grabbed hold of it again. She turned her head away from what she could not change and started adjusting herself to her new status. She was going to have to figure out how to sew herself up one of those breast forms so she could wear a bra. "Damn things probably cost a fortune," she told me when I came to sit beside her. I nodded slowly. I didn't let her see how afraid I was, or how uncertain, or even how angry. I showed her my pride in her courage and my faith in her strength. But underneath I wanted her to be angry, too. "I'll make do," she whispered, showing me nothing, and I just nodded.

"Everything's going to be all right," I told her.

"Everything's going to be all right," she told me. The pretense was sometimes the only thing we had to give each other.

When it's your mama and it's an accomplished fact, you can't talk politics into her bleeding. You can't quote from last month's article about how a partial mastectomy is just as effective. You can't talk about patriarchy or class or confrontation strategies.

I made jokes on the telephone, wrote letters full of healthy recipes and vitamin therapies. I pretended for her sake and my own that nothing was going to happen, that cancer is an everyday occurrence (and it is) and death is not part of the scenario.

Push it down. Don't show it. Don't tell anybody what is really going on. My mama makes do when the whole world cries out for things to stop, to fall apart, just once for all of us to let our anger show. My mama clamps her teeth, laughs her bitter laugh, and does whatever she thinks she has to do with no help, thank you, from people who only want to see her wanting something she can't have anyway.

Five, ten, twenty years—my mama has had cancer for twenty years. "That doctor, the one in Tampa in '71, the one told me I was gonna die, that sucker choked himself on a turkey bone. People that said what a sad thing it was—me having cancer, and surely meant to die—hell, those people been run over by pickups and dropped down dead with one thing and another, while me, I just go on. It's something, an't it?"

It's something. Piece by piece, my mother is being stolen from me. After the hysterectomy, the first mastectomy, another five years later, her teeth that were easier to give up than to keep, the little toes that calcified from too many years working waitress in bad shoes, hair and fingernails that drop off after every bout of chemotherapy, my mama is less and less the mountain, more and more the cave—the empty place from which things have been removed.

"With what they've taken off me, off Granny, and your Aunt Grace—shit, you could almost make another person."

A woman, a garbage creation, an assembly of parts. When I drink I see her rising like bats out of deep caverns, a gossamer woman—all black edges, with a chrome uterus and molded glass fingers, plastic wire rib cage and red unblinking eyes. My mama, my grandmother, my aunts, my sister and me—every part of us that can be taken has been.

"Flesh and blood needs flesh and blood," my mama sang for me once, and laughing added, "but we don't need as much of it as we used to, huh?"

When Mama talked, I listened. I believed it was the truth she was telling me. I watched her face as much as I listened to her words. She had a way of dropping her head and covering her bad teeth with her palm. I'd say, "Don't do that." And she'd laugh at how serious I was. When she laughed with me, that shadow, so grey under her eyes, lightened, and I felt for a moment—powerful, important, never so important as when I could make her laugh.

I wanted to grow up to do the poor-kid-done-good thing, the Elvis Presley/Ritchie Valens movie, to buy my mama her own house, put a key in her hand and say, "It's yours—from here to there and everything in between, these walls, that door, that gate, these locks. You don't ever have to let anyone in that you don't want. You can lay in the sun if you want to or walk out naked in the moonlight if you take the mood. And if you want to go into town to mess around, we can go do it together."

I did not want to be my mother's lover; I wanted more than that. I wanted to rescue her the way we had both wanted her to rescue me. *Do not want what you cannot have,* she told me. But I was not as good as she was. I wanted that dream. I've never stopped wanting it.

The day I left home my stepfather disappeared. I scoured him out of my life, exorcising every movement or phrase in which I recognized his touch. All he left behind was a voice on a telephone line, a voice that sometimes answered when I called home. But Mama grew into my body like an extra layer of warm protective fat, closing me around. My muscles hug my bones in just the way hers do, and when I turn my face, I have that same bulldog angry glare I was always ashamed to see on her. But my legs are strong, and I do not stoop the way she does; I did not work waitress for thirty years, and my first lover taught me the importance of buying good shoes. I've got Mama's habit of dropping my head, her quick angers, and that same belly-gutted scar she was so careful to hide. But nothing marks me so much her daughter as my hands—the way they are aging, the veins coming up through skin already thin. I tell myself they are beautiful as they recreate my mama's flesh in mine.

My lovers laugh at me and say, "Every tenth word with you is *mama*. Mama said. Mama used to say. My mama didn't raise no fool."

I widen my mouth around my drawl and show my mama's lost teeth in my smile.

200   Watching my mama I learned some lessons too well. Never show that you care, Mama taught me, and never want something you cannot have. Never give anyone the satisfaction of denying you something you need, and for that, what you have to do is learn to need nothing. Starve the wanting part of you. In time I understood my mama to be a kind of Zen Baptist—rooting desire out of her own heart as ruthlessly as any mountaintop ascetic. The lessons Mama taught me, like the lessons of Buddha, were not a matter of degree but of despair. My mama's philosophy was bitter and thin. She didn't give a damn if she was ever born again, she just didn't want to be born again poor and wanting.

I am my mama's daughter, her shadow on the earth, the blood thinned down a little so that I am not as powerful as she, as immune to want and desire. I am not a mountain or a cave, a force of nature or a power on the earth, but I have her talent for not seeing what I cannot stand to face. I make sure that I do not want what I do not think I can have, and I keep clearly in mind what it is I cannot have. I roll in the night all the stories I never told her, cannot tell her still—her voice in my brain echoing love and despair and grief and rage. When, in the night, she hears me call her name, it is not really me she hears, it is the me I constructed for her—the one who does not need her too much, the one whose heart is not too tender, whose insides are iron and silver, whose dreams are cold ice and slate—who needs nothing, nothing. I keep in mind the image of a closed door, Mama weeping on the other side. She could not rescue me. I cannot rescue her. Sometimes I cannot even reach across the wall that separates us.

On my stepfather's birthday I make coffee and bake bread pudding with bourbon sauce. I invite friends over, tell outrageous stories, and use horrible words. I scratch my scars and hug my lover, thinking about Mama twelve states away. My accent comes back and my weight settles down lower, until the ache in my spine is steady and hot. I remember Mama sitting at the kitchen table in the early morning, tears in her eyes, lying to me and my sister, promising us that the time would come when she would leave him—that as soon as we were older, as soon as there was a little more money put by and things were a little easier—she would go.

I think about her sitting there now, waiting for him to wake up and want his coffee, for the day to start moving around her, things to get so busy she won't have to think. Sometimes, I hate my mama. Sometimes, I hate myself. I see myself in her, and her in me. I see us too clearly sometimes, all the little betrayals that cannot be forgotten or changed.

When Mama calls, I wait a little before speaking.

"Mama," I say, "I knew you would call."

Anna Maria Ortese

Born in Rome in 1914, Anna Maria Ortese began writing short stories but became celebrated after the publication of her first novel, *Il mare non bagna Napoli* ("The sea does not surround Naples"), in 1953. Several of her books have a fantastic element— *L'iguana* ("The iguana"), *Il cardillo addolorato* ("The lament of the linnet") and *Il porto di Toledo* ("The port of Toledo")—closer to the Anglo-Saxon supernatural world than to French surrealism. Of Ortese's writing, Roberto Calasso has written, "Take any of Ortese's outstanding books and you'll find that there is a vast and varied monologue on the nature of reality, on all levels, to be glimpsed like a watermark under each page. You immediately sense how the author removes what we take for real from its usual frame or form of presentation, and quietly places it under a new sort of light, which alters it completely."

"A Pair of Glasses" is one of Ortese's more straight-forward stories, yet it still stands for what she defines as "the need to reinfuse reality with a meaningful sense of belonging to another, vaster, unknowable reality; it is against this other reality that we should measure ourselves at times if we wish to feel renewed."

A PAIR OF GLASSES

anna maria ortese

don Peppino Quaglia stood near the threshold of
the basement apartment, singing "Ce sta' o sole . . .'o sole!"

"Leave the sun to God," his wife Rosa answered, her
soft, vaguely cheerful voice rising from within where she was laid
up in bed with arthritic pain, complicated by heart disease; and
addressing her sister-in-law, who was in the bathroom, she added:
"You know what I'm going to do, Nunziata? I'll get up later and
take the soaking clothes out of the wash."

"Do as you please, but I think you're crazy," Nunziata
answered from the little cubbyhole, in her dry, sad voice. "With
the pains that you have, one more day in bed wouldn't hurt you!"
A silence. "We have to put down that other poison, I found a
cockroach in my sleeve this morning."

And then Eugenia's calm, quiet voice called from the
bed in the rear of the room, a veritable grotto with its low ceiling
vault strung with spider webs:

"Mama, today I get my glasses."

There was a kind of secret jubilation in the little girl's
subdued tone; she was Don Peppino's third-born (the first two,
Carmela and Luisella, were with the nuns, and would soon don the
veil, convinced as they were that this life is a punishment; and the

two small ones, Pasqualino and Teresella, still lay feet first, snoring in their mother's bed).

"And smash them too, I bet," her aunt insisted, even more irritated now, from behind the door. She made everybody pay for the displeasures of her life, most importantly the displeasure of being unmarried and of being subjected, as she saw it, to her sister-in-law's charity, although she never failed to mention that she offered this humiliation to God. She had put a little of her own savings aside, however, and since she was not really mean, she offered to buy glasses for Eugenia after the family had discovered that she couldn't see a thing. "And what they cost!" she added now. "Eight thousand lire in hard cash." Eugenia heard water running in the basin and pictured her washing her face, squinting, her eyes full of soap, and she didn't bother to answer.

Anyway, she was much too happy to bother.

A week ago she and her aunt had gone to an optometrist on Via Roma. There, in that elegant store full of shining tables and a marvelous green reflection that rained down from the curtains, the doctor had tested her eyes, making her read entire columns of letters printed on a card, some as big as boxes and others as tiny as pins, while he changed lenses. "This poor child is nearly blind," he finally said to her aunt, as if in commiseration. "She must never take these glasses off again." And then, while Eugenia sat waiting anxiously on a stool, he quickly placed another pair of lenses in a white wire frame on her face and said to her: "Now look at the street." Eugenia stood, her legs trembling with excitement, and could not hold back a little shout of joy. Well-dressed people, so many of them, passed before her on the sidewalk, and they were crystal clear even if smaller than usual: ladies in silk suits and powdered faces, young men with long hair and colorful sweaters, an old man with a white beard and reddened hands clasping a cane with a silver handle; and in the street, beautiful automobiles that looked like toys, painted shiny red or light green; and green trolleys as big as houses. Across the street, the elegant stores whose windows shone like mirrors (sales clerks in black smocks were polishing them) were so full of fine things that Eugenia's heart swelled. There was a cafe with red and yellow tables outside, and young girls with golden hair sitting cross-legged laughed as they drank from tall, colored glasses. Above the cafe, balcony doors stood ajar, as it was already spring; the embroidered curtains blew, revealing blue and gold paintings, heavy gold and crystal chandeliers that glittered. Amazing! Enthralled by all that splendor, she had not followed the conversation between her aunt and the doctor. Her aunt, standing at some distance from the glass counter in her brown Sunday dress, now broached the subject of the price with a timidity that was unnatural for her. "Doctor, don't forget to give us a good price, we're poor people . . ." And when she had heard "eight thousand lire," she nearly fainted.

"For two pieces of glass? What are you saying? Jesus Christ!"

"You see, when people are ignorant, they never reason things out. But if you give this child two pieces of glass, tell me, won't she see better? She has nine diopters in one eye, and ten in the other. And if you want to know the truth, she's nearly blind."

While the doctor wrote down the child's first and last name, "Eugenia Quaglia, vicolo della Cupa, Santa Maria in Portico," Nunziata walked over to Eugenia, who still stood in the doorway of the store, adjusting the glasses with her damp hands and looking about eagerly. "Look, look, my lovely girl. You see what this luxury is costing us! Eight thousand lire, did you hear? Eight thousand in hard cash!" She could barely breathe. Eugenia had turned completely red, not so much at this reproach, but at the gaze of the cashier who had been looking at them while her aunt announced the family's poverty. She took off the glasses.

"But how can she be so young and so myopic already?" the cashier asked as Nunziata signed the receipt, adding "and wrinkled too?"

"My good lady, there's not a pair of bad eyes in our house, this is just a stroke of bad luck that came . . . along with all the others. God rubs salt in our wounds. . . . "

"Come back in a week," the doctor said, "The glasses will be ready."

Eugenia tripped on the stairs as she was leaving.

"Thank you, Aunt Nunzia," she said after a while. "I'm always so rude to you and you're so nice to buy me glasses."

Her voice was trembling.

"Listen, my dear, it's better not to see the world than to see it," Nunziata answered with sudden melancholy.

Eugenia did not even answer her this time. Aunt Nunzia was often strange; she cried and shouted over nothing and said so many ugly words. On the other hand, she went to mass conscientiously; she was a good Christian, and whenever some wretch needed help, she was always there, with a full heart. Eugenia didn't have to worry.

From that day on, Eugenia lived in a sort of rapture, waiting for those blessed glasses that would allow her to see every single person, every little thing in its minutest detail. Until now, she had been enveloped in a fog: the room where she lived, the courtyard that was always hung with clothes, the *vicolo,* spilling over with colors and noises—all of that for her was covered by a thick veil: the only faces she knew well were those of her intimates— her mother especially, and her brothers and sister because they often slept together. Sometimes when she woke in the night, she would look at them in the gaslight. Her mother slept with her mouth open, and Eugenia could see her broken, yellowed teeth; and Pasqualino and Teresella were always dirty and covered with boils, their noses full of mucus: when they slept, they made a strange noise, as if they had beasts inside them. Once in a while, Eugenia caught herself staring without really knowing what she was thinking. She felt confusedly that beyond that room, forever filled with its dripping clothing, broken chairs and stinking toilet, there must be beautiful light, sounds, things; and the moment she had put the glasses on, the revelation struck her: the world outside was beautiful, quite beautiful.

"Respects, Marchesa. . . ."

It was her father speaking. She saw his tattered shirt, his back moving out of the doorframe.

"You must do me a favor, Don Peppino . . . ," the marchesa said now in a placid, indifferent voice.

"Whatever you want, tell me . . ."

Eugenia wriggled out of bed without a sound, slipped into a dress and went barefoot to the door. The sun, which entered the ugly courtyard early every morning through a fissure between the buildings, came towards her in all its purity and splendor, illuminating her little old woman's face, her strawlike, disheveled hair, her small, coarse wooden hands with their long, dirty fingernails. Oh, if only she had glasses now! The marchesa was standing there with that majestic and kindly air that so enchanted Eugenia, wearing a black silk suit, a little lace scarf, her white hands covered with jewels; but her face was not clear, it was an oval, a whitish stain. Two violet feathers quivered above it.

"Listen, you must do the child's mattress again . . . Can you come up at around ten-thirty?"

"Gladly, gladly, but I wouldn't be ready until this afternoon, Signora marchesa . . ."

"No, Don Peppino, it must be done in the morning. People are coming this afternoon. You can work out on the terrace. Don't make me beg you, do me this favor. They're ringing the bells for mass now. Call me at ten-thirty."

And without waiting for an answer, she walked away, carefully avoiding a yellow stream of water that was spilling down from one of the terraces into a puddle on the ground.

"Papa," Eugenia said, coming up behind her father as he headed back inside the basement apartment. "The marchesa is so good, isn't she! She treats you like a gentleman. God will reward her for it."

"A good Christian she certainly is," Don Peppino answered, implying another meaning beyond Eugenia's understanding. Exploiting the fact that she was the landlord, the Marchesa D'Avanzo made the people in the courtyard serve her continually; she would give Don Peppino a pittance for the mattress; and Rosa, who waited on the marchesa even when her bones burned, was always at her beck and call to bring clean sheets. It's true, the marchesa had cloistered the girls, saving two souls from the world's perils, which are numerous for the poor. But she charged three thousand lire, and not one less, for that basement space where everyone had gotten sick. She loved to repeat, with a certain cool tone, "I would do it with all my heart, I would, it's just the money that's missing. These days, Don Peppino, you're a gentleman, and you should be grateful that you have no worries, thankful that providence has given you such a situation, has saved you. . . ." Donna Rosa felt a sort of adoration for the marchesa and her religious sentiments: whenever they saw one another, they spoke continually of the other life. And though the marchesa didn't put much credence in it, she didn't say so; she exhorted the mother of the family to be patient and hope.

"Did you speak to her?" Donna Rosa asked anxiously from the bed.

"She wants me to make a bed for her nephew," said Don Peppino, annoyed. He had taken the tripod stove, a gift from the nuns, outside to heat some coffee and now came back in for water. "I won't do it for less than five hundred," he said.

"That's a fair price."

"And who's going to pick up Eugenia's glasses?" asked Aunt Nunzie, coming out of the bathroom. She was wearing a shirt, a skirt whose hem was down, and slippers. Her pointed shoulders, grey as rocks, poked through her shirt. She was drying her face with a napkin. "I can't go and Rosa is sick . . ."

Nobody noticed Eugenia's large, nearly blind eyes filling with tears. See, maybe she wouldn't have her glasses for another day now. She sidled up to her mother's bed and let her arms and forehead fall on the blanket with a pathetic gesture. Donna Rosa reached a hand out to caress her.

"I'll go, Nunzia, don't get worked up. In fact, it'll do me good to go out."

"Mama!" Eugenia kissed her hand.

At eight, there was a great commotion in the courtyard. Rosa had just stepped out; in the stained, too-short black coat without shoulder pads, she was a tall, gaunt figure whose legs stuck out like wooden sticks. She held a shopping bag on her arm for the bread she'd pick up on her way back from the optician. Don Peppino was sweeping the water out of the middle of the courtyard with a long broom, a useless effort because the tub leaked constantly, like a spring. The courtyard was hung with the clothes of the two families upstairs: the Greborio sisters on the first floor, and the cavaliere Amodio's wife, who'd had a baby two days early. In fact, the Greborio's maid, Lina Tarallo, was making a terrible racket as she shook out the carpets on the balcony. The dust, mixed with real filth, drifted down and gradually settled like a cloud over those poor people. But nobody paid it any attention. Then suddenly shrill screams, cries broke out: Aunt Nunzia was calling upon all the saints to be her witness: she was cursed, and all because Pasqualino was bawling and screeching like a devil to go with his mother. "Look at him, look at this demon!" screamed Aunt Nunzia. "*Madonna bella,* have mercy on me, let me die, let me die now if you can, because only thieves and bad women are fit for this life." Teresella, who was smaller than her brother because she was born the year the king fled, sat in the doorway smiling; every now and then she would lick a crust of bread that she found under a chair.

Eugenia was sitting on the steps of the doorkeeper Mariuccia's apartment, looking at a page from a children's magazine which had fallen from the third floor. She had her nose to it because that was the only way she could read the words under the colored figures: a little blue river in the middle of an endless meadow, and a boat going . . . going . . . who knows where? It was not in dialect but in Italian, so she didn't understand much. But now and then she would laugh for no reason.

"So, today you're going to get your glasses?" said Mariuccia, leaning over her shoulder. Everybody in the courtyard knew because Eugenia could not resist telling, and also because Aunt Nunziata had found it necessary to announce that she was the only one in the family who would spend her own money. . . .

"Your aunt is giving them to you, eh?" added Mariuccia, smiling good-naturedly. She was a small woman, almost a dwarf with a man's face, full of whiskers. Just then she was brushing the long black hair which reached her knees: one of the few attributes that attested to the fact that she was a woman too. She brushed slowly, her sly, kind, mousey eyes smiling.

"Mama went to Via Roma to get them," said Eugenia with a look of gratitude. "We paid eight thousand lire for them, you know, in hard cash. . . . My aunt is," she was adding, when Nunziata appeared in the doorway of the cubbyhole and screeched furiously: "Eugenia!"

Pasqualino stood behind her with a terrible grimace of disdain and surprise on his face, all red and dazed. "Go to the tobacconist and buy me two three-lire caramels from Don Vincenzo. And come back right away!"

"Yes, Aunt."

She took the money in her fist, without another thought of the magazine, and walked out of the courtyard swiftly.

As she entered the tobacconist's, she grazed by Rosaria Buonincontri's yellow basket. Rosaria, the Amodio's fat maid, was wearing black but her legs were white, and her face flushed, calm. "Tell your mama to come up for a moment today, Signora Amodio has a message for her."

Eugenia recognized the voice.

"She's not home. She went to Via Roma to pick up my glasses."

"I have to get a pair too, but my fiancee doesn't want me to."

Eugenia did not grasp the meaning of this prohibition. She answered ingenuously:

"They really cost a lot, you have to take care of them."

They entered the hole that was Don Vincenzo's store.

People were waiting and Eugenia was pushed backwards. "Move up . . . you really are blind," Amodio's maid commented, with a kindly smile.

"But now your Aunt Nunzia is giving you glasses," Don Vincenzo cut in, winking with a playful, complicitous air when he overheard. He wore glasses too.

"At your age," he said, handing her the candies, "I could see like a cat, my grandmother wanted me around all the time because I could thread needles at night . . . but now I'm old . . ."

Eugenia nodded vaguely.

"None of my friends wear glasses," she said. Then turning back to Buonincontri, but speaking for Don Vincenzo's benefit as well: "Only me . . . I have nine diopters in one eye and ten in the other . . . I'm practically blind!" she stressed gently.

"See how lucky you are," Don Vincenzo to her, laughing; and to Rosaria: "How much salt?"

"Poor thing!" said Amodio's maid after Eugenia had gone, all contented. "It's the damp that ruined her. It nails us down in that house. Now Donna Rosa has pains in her bones. Give me a kilo of coarse salt and a package of the fine type."

"You've got it."

"What a morning we have today, eh, Don Vincenzo? It seems like summer already."

Walking back more slowly than she had come, Eugenia began to unwrap one of the candies without thinking and stuck it in her mouth. It was lemon-flavored. "I'll tell Aunt Nunzia that I lost it on the street," she decided. She was happy, she didn't care if her nice aunt (who was so good to her) got angry.

What a great day! Maybe mama was returning now with the glasses all wrapped in a package. . . . Soon she would be wearing them, she would. . . . A fury of slaps pounded her head, a real avalanche. She felt as if she were crumbling; futilely, she raised her hands to defend herself. It was Aunt Nunzia—who else?— furious that she was late, and right behind her Pasqualino was throwing a tantrum because he didn't believe the line about the candies anymore. "I'm dying! Here, blind, ugly thing! . . . And I give you everything I have for this kind of gratitude! You'll end up a good-for-nothing, that's what you'll be! Eight thousand lire it cost me! These demons . . . they're killing me! . . ."

She let her hands drop to her sides only to burst out into tears. "Suffering virgin, Jesus, for the wounds you suffered, let me die."

Now Eugenia was crying hard too.

"Oh, Aunt, forgive me . . . Aunt . . ."

"Uh . . . uh . . . uh . . . ," Pasqualino grunted, his mouth gaping.

"Poor thing," said Donna Mariuccia walking over to Eugenia, who was trying to hide her blotched, tear-stained face from her aunt's anger. "She didn't do it on purpose, Nunzia . . . , calm down." And to Eugenia: "What did you do with the candies?"

Eugenia answered softly, hopelessly, holding out the remaining candy in a dirty hand. "I ate one. I was hungry."

Before her aunt could attack the child again, the marchesa's voice called down softly, calmly, from the third floor, where the sun was shining.

"Nunziata!"

Aunt Nunzia lifted her embittered face which resembled the one at the end of her bed, the Madonna of the seven afflictions.

"Today is the first Friday of the month. Offer your prayers to God."

"Marchesa, you are so kind! These children make me commit so many little sins, I am losing my soul, I . . . ," and her head collapsed into her pawlike hands, the skin brown and scaly as a laborer's.

"Your brother isn't home?"

"Your poor aunt, she buys you a pair of glasses and this is how you thank her . . . ," Mariuccia said to Eugenia who was still trembling.

"Yes, signora, here I am," answered Don Peppino, emerging from behind the apartment door that had half-concealed him; he'd been fanning the fire under his lunch with a piece of cardboard.

"Can you come up now?"

"My wife went to get Eugenia's glasses. . . . I'm watching the beans . . . would you mind waiting?"

"Then send up the little girl. I have a dress for Nunziata. I want to give it to her."

"God will reward you. We're ever so grateful," answered Don Peppino with a sigh of relief, because this was the one thing that would calm his sister. But looking over at Nunziata, he realized that she was not cheered at all. She went on crying her heart out, and her lament had so stunned Pasqualino that the child had fallen into a silence of fascination, a small sweet smile on his face; he was licking the mucus that dripped from his nose.

"Did you hear? Go up to the marchesa's, she wants to give you a dress," Don Peppino said to his daughter.

Eugenia's eyes were fixed on something in the air, seeing nothing; opened wide, they focused and focused. She started and got up quickly, obediently.

"Tell her, 'God will reward you,' and stay outside the door."

"Yes, Papa."

"Believe me, Mariuccia," Aunt Nunziata said when Eugenia was out of earshot, "I adore that child, and afterwards I regret slapping her, God only knows. But believe me, when I have to struggle with kids the blood goes right to my head. I'm not young anymore, as you can see . . . ," and she touched her sunken cheeks. "Sometimes I feel like a mad woman. . . ."

"On the other hand, they also have to let off steam," answered Donna Mariuccia, "they're just innocent souls. They'll have plenty of time for tears. When I look at them and think they'll become like us . . . " She went to fetch a broom and pushed a cabbage leaf over the threshold, "I really wonder what God is up to."

"You're giving it away brand new!" said Eugenia, pressing her nose to the green dress, spread across the kitchen sofa while the marchesa went to look for an old newspaper to wrap it in.

Signora D'Avanzo was thinking that the child could not see at all if she didn't realize the dress was ancient and darned all over (it was her dead sister's), but she said nothing. Only when she returned with the newspaper did she finally ask after several seconds:

"And the glasses your aunt gave you? Are they new?"

"They have gold wires. And they cost eight thousand lire," Eugenia answered in a breath, moved again at the thought of the privilege that had touched her. "Because I'm nearly blind," she added bluntly.

"In my opinion," said the marchesa, wrapping the dress in the newspaper gently and then opening the package again because a sleeve was sticking out, "your aunt could've spent less. I've seen the best eyeglasses for only two thousand lire at a store on Ascenzione."

Eugenia blushed. She realized that the marchesa was displeased. "Each in his own range, we must all limit ourselves. . . ." She had heard her say so many times when Donna Rosa brought up the clean wash and lingered to lament the family's financial straits.

"Maybe they weren't any good . . . . I have nine diopters," Eugenia answered timidly.

The marchesa raised an eyebrow, but fortunately Eugenia didn't see.

"I'm telling you, they were good," Signora D'Avanzo insisted, her voice hardening slightly. Then regretting it, she said more gently, "My dear child, I'm saying this because I know your family's troubles. With that six thousand lire, you could buy bread for ten days, you could buy . . . why, why should you need to see well? With what is around you! . . ." There was a silence. "To read? Do you read?"

"No, Signora."

"But I've seen you with your nose in a book sometimes. So, you're a liar too, my child. . . . That's no good. . . ."

Eugenia did not answer this time. Feeling utterly hopeless, she fixed her nearly white eyes on the dress.

"Is it silk?" she asked stupidly.

The marchesa looked at her pensively.

"You don't deserve it, but I want to give you a little something," she said suddenly, and she walked toward an armoire of white wood. Just at that moment, the telephone, which was in the hall, began to ring, and instead of opening the armoire Signora D'Avanzo went to answer it. Eugenia was so discouraged by those words she had barely heard the old woman's consoling hint; and as soon as she was alone, she began looking—as best as she could— all around her. There were so many beautiful, fine things, just like the store on Via Roma! And there, right before her eyes, was an open balcony covered with vases of flowers.

She went out on the balcony. So much space, so much blue! The houses seemed to be covered by a blue veil, and the vicolo below looked like a well with so many ants coming and going . . . like her family. . . . What were they doing, where were they going? They came out and went back inside little holes, carrying large crumbs of bread: that's what they were doing, they had done it yesterday, they would do it again tomorrow, and forever . . . forever. So many holes, so many ants. And all around, nearly invisible in the great light, was the world as God had made it, with wind and sun, and further away, the great, clear sea. . . . She stood there thoughtfully, resting her chin on the grating, with an expression of pain, of dismay that made her ugly. The marchesa's voice called out, calm, pious. In her hand, her smooth ivory hand, she held a little book covered with black pasteboard and gold letters.

"These are the saints' reflections, dear girl. You people today don't read anything, and that's why the world is changing. Take it, it's my gift. But you must promise me that you'll read a little every night. Now that you've got glasses."

"Yes, Signora," Eugenia replied quickly as she took the book, blushing once again because the marchesa had found her on the balcony. The signora gazed at her, pleased.

"The Lord wanted to save you, my child!" she said, going to get the package with the dress and handing it to her. "You're not pretty, quite the contrary, you already look like an old woman. The

Lord chose you above others, precisely so that you wouldn't get into trouble. He wants you to be saintly, like your sisters!"

Because Eugenia had been long prepared for a life lacking in joy, albeit unconsciously, she was not really wounded by these words, but she was disturbed nevertheless. And it seemed to her, if only for a moment, that the sun was less bright: even the thought of the glasses failed to cheer her. She stared vaguely, her eyes nearly dark, at the faded green of Posillipo that stretched into the sea like a lizard.

"Tell your papa," the marchesa went on, "that we won't be doing anything about the child's mattress today. My cousin called, and I have to be down at Posillipo all day."

"I was once there too," Eugenia began, coming alive again at the sound of that name and gazing out toward it with a look of enchantment.

"Oh, really?" Signora D'Avanzo was indifferent; to her the name meant nothing. Then, moving with all the majesty of her person, she walked to the front door with the child, who lingered, turning back to stare at that luminous point until the door closed gently behind her.

It was as she was stepping off the last step into the courtyard that the shadow which had momentarily darkened her forehead lifted, and her mouth opened in a cry of joy as she caught sight of her mother returning. Her familiar shabby figure was easily recognizable. She threw the dress down on a chair and ran toward her.

"Mama, my glasses!"

"Slow down, child. You'll knock me down!"

Immediately a small crowd gathered around them. Donna Mariuccia, Don Peppino, one of the Geborios who had stopped to rest on a chair before tackling the stairs, Amodio's maid who had just come in, and of course, Pasqualino and Teresella who were screeching to see too, their hands outstretched. Nunziata was observing the unwrapped dress with a crestfallen expression.

"See Mariuccia, this looks like pretty old stuff to me. . . .

It's all worn out under the arms," she said approaching the group. But nobody paid her any attention. Donna Rosa was taking the wrapped case from the collar of her dress, opening it with the utmost care. Like a sort of radiant insect with two big, big eyes and two curved antennae, it lay shining in a blurred ray of sunlight, as Donna Rosa extended her long, red hand into the circle of those poor admiring people.

"Eight thousand lire for a thing like this," said Donna Rosa, gazing religiously but with a sort of remorse at the glasses.

Then silently she placed them on Eugenia's face; ecstatic, the child raised her hands to push the antennae carefully behind her ears. "Well, do you see us?" she asked, nearly moved to tears.

Arranging them with her hands, as if she were afraid someone would grab them away, her eyes half-closed and her mouth half-open in an enraptured smile, Eugenia took two steps backward, stumbling into a chair.

"Congratulations," said Greborio's maid.

"Congratulations," said Signora Greborio.

"She looks like a teacher, doesn't she?" said Don Peppino, delighted.

"Not as much as a thank you," said Aunt Nunziata, looking bitterly at the dress. "Even after all this: Congratulations."

"She's afraid, my dear," murmured Donna Rosa, walking towards the door of the apartment to put down her things. "This is the first time she's ever worn glasses," she said, looking up at the first floor balcony where the other Greborio sister stood gazing down.

"Everybody looks so little," Eugenia said in a strange voice that sounded as if it were coming from under a chair. "And very, very black."

"Of course, it's a double lens. But do you see well?" asked Don Peppino. "That's the important thing. She's wearing her glasses for the first time," he repeated, turning to Sir Amodio who was passing by with an opened newspaper in his hand.

"I warn you," said Amodio, after having stared at Eugenia for a moment as if she were a cat, "the stairs have not been swept. . . . I found fish bones in front of the door!" And he walked off, all but hidden behind the newspaper, bent over an article about the proposed law for pensions that concerned him.

Eugenia walked to the front door to look out into the Vicolo della Cupa, her hands still on the glasses. Her legs were shaking, her head spinning, all the joy had gone out of her. She wanted to smile, but her whitened lips were turned down in an idiotic grimace. Suddenly, there were so many balconies—two thousand, one-hundred thousand; the vegetable carts rushed towards her, the voices filling the air, the cries, the sound of the whip, all filled her head at once as if she were sick. Staggering, she turned back towards the courtyard, and the terrible impression grew: the courtyard she saw now, a slimy funnel pointing up towards the sky, had leprous walls and decrepit balconies. There were black arches over the ground floor apartments and circles of bright bulbs around Our Lady of Sorrows; the pavement was white with soapy water and cauliflower leaves, scraps of paper, garbage; and in the middle of the courtyard, that group of tattered, deformed Christians, their faces pocked by poverty and resignation, turned their eyes toward her now, full of love. They began to twist, to blur, to grow. Through the two bewitched circles of her glasses, she saw them coming at her all at once. But it was Mariuccia who realized that the little girl was not well and pulled off her glasses. Whimpering, Eugenia had doubled over and vomited.

"They made her sick to her stomach!" yelled Mariuccia, feeling her forehead. "Go get a coffee bean, Nunziata!"

"Eight thousand lire in hard cash!" Aunt Nunziata cried with fury in her eyes, as she ran to the basement apartment to take a coffee bean from a bottle on the credenza; and she raised the new glasses into the air, as if to receive some explanation from God. "And now they're not even right!"

"It's always like this the first time," Amodio's maid said to Donna Rosa calmly. "You shouldn't be alarmed; she'll adjust to them with time."

"It's nothing, child, nothing, don't be afraid," but Donna Rosa's heart tightened at the thought of how unfortunate they were.

When Aunt Nunziata came back with the coffee, she was still screaming, "Eight thousand in hard cash!" while Eugenia, who had turned white as a ghost, gagged uselessly, for there was nothing left inside her. Her bulging eyes were nearly crossed from the strain, and her tear-stained, ancient face appeared stunned. She leaned against her mother and shook.

"Mama, where are we?"

"We're in the courtyard, that's where, child," Donna Rosa said patiently, and the flickering smile of pity and awe that shone in her eyes suddenly brightened the faces of all those wretched people.

"She's half-blind!"

"She's half-stupid is what she is!"

"Let her be, poor thing, she's just shocked," said Donna Mariuccia, her face grim with compassion as she walked back into her own apartment which looked darker than ever.

Only Aunt Nunziata was still wringing her hands:

"Eight thousand lire!"

※

Angela Carter

According to Marina Warner, one of the oldest versions of Cinderella (or Ashenputtle as she is sometimes called) was written down in the mid-ninth century in China. Almost a thousand years later, the story reached the elegant Parisian drawing rooms through the art of Charles Perrault. In most versions, the unfortunate Cinderella is helped by the spirit of her dead mother, who takes on the appearance of a familiar animal. In Grimm's version of the tale, the helpers are doves; in the Scottish version, "Rashin Coatie" (collected by Andrew Lang), the helper is a red calf. In a German variant of the story, "Falada," the helper is a talking horse who continues to advise the young woman even after its head has been cut off.

For Angela Carter, fairy tales are of the creative essence of the community of women. "Ours is a highly individualized culture," she explained, "with a great faith in the work of art as a unique one-off, and the artist as an original, a godlike and inspired creator of unique one-offs. But fairy tales are not like that, nor are their makers. Who first invented meatballs? In what country? Is there a definitive recipe for potato soup? Think in terms of the domestic arts." Carter's versions of the traditional fairy tales, as in "Ashputtle" here, begin at the end of this collective and immemorial telling. "We start from our conclusions," she once wrote.

ASHPUTTLE: OR,
THE MOTHER'S GHOST

angela carter

A) THE MUTILATED GIRLS

but although you can easily center the story not on Ashputtle but on the mutilated stepsisters, can think of it as a story about cutting bits off women so that they will *fit in,* nevertheless the story always begins with Ashputtle's mother, as though it is really always the story of her mother, even if, at the beginning of the story, she is already at death's door: "A rich man's wife fell sick, and, feeling that her end was near, she called her only daughter to her bedside."

Note the absence of the husband/father. Although the woman is defined by her relation to him ("a rich man's wife"), the daughter is unambiguously hers, as if hers alone, and the entire drama concerns only women, takes place almost exclusively among women, is a battle between two groups of women, on the one hand, Ashputtle and her mother, and, on the other, the stepmother and *her* daughters.

It is a drama between two female families in opposition to one another because of their rivalry over men (husband/father, husband/son), who seem no more than passive victims of their fancy and yet whose significance is absolute because it is ("a rich man," "a king's son") purely economic.

Ashputtle's father, the old man, is the first object of their desire and their dissension; the stepmother snatches him from the dead mother before her corpse is cold, as soon as her grip loosens. Then there is the young man, the potential bridegroom, the hypothetical son-in-law, for whose possession the mothers fight, using their daughters as instruments of war or as surrogates in the business of mating.

If the men, and the bank balances for which they stand, are the passive victims of the two grown women, then the girls, all three, are animated solely by the wills of their mothers. Even if Ashputtle's mother dies at the beginning of the story, her status as one of the dead only makes her position more authoritative; the mother's ghost dominates the narrative and is, in a real sense, the motive center, the event that makes all the other events happen.

The mother assures the daughter: "I shall always look after you and always be with you."

At this point, Ashputtle is nameless. She is her mother's daughter. That's all. It is the stepmother who names her Ashputtle, as a joke, and, in doing so, wipes out her real name, whatever that is, banishes her from the family, exiles her from the shared table to the lonely hearth, among the cinders, removes her contingent but honorable status as daughter and gives her, instead, the contingent but disreputable status of servant.

Her mother told Ashputtle she would always look after her but, untrustworthy, she died and the father married again, and gave Ashputtle an imitation mother with daughters of her own whom she loves with the same fierce passion as Ashputtle's mother did and still, posthumously, does, as we shall find out.

Now comes the vexed question: who shall be the daughters of the house? "Mine shall!" declares the stepmother and sets the freshly named nondaughter Ashputtle to sweep and scrub and sleep on the hearth while her own daughters lie between clean sheets in Ashputtle's bed. Ashputtle, no longer known as the daughter of her mother or of her father, either, goes by a dry, dirty, cindery nickname, for everything has turned to dust and ashes.

Meanwhile, the false mother sleeps in the bed where

the real mother died and is, presumably, pleasured by the husband/ father in that bed (unless there is no pleasure in it for her). We are not told what the father/husband does but we can make this assumption, that they share a bed.

And what can the real mother do? Burn as she might with love and anger, she is dead and buried.

The father, in this story, is a mystery to me. Is he so besotted with his new wife that he cannot see how his daughter is soiled with kitchen refuse and filthy from her ashy bed and always hard at work? If he sensed there was a drama at hand, he was content to leave the entire production to the women for, absent as he might be, always remember it is in *his* house that Ashputtle sleeps on the cinders, and he is the invisible link that binds both sets of mothers and daughters in their violent equation. He is the unmoved mover, the unseen organizing principle, like God, and, like God, up he pops in person, one fine day, to introduce an essential plot device.

Without the absent father, there would be no story because there would have been no conflict.

If they had been able to put aside these differences and discuss everything amicably, they'd have combined to expel the father. Then all the women could have slept in the one bed.

This is the essential plot device introduced by the father: he says, "I am about to take a business trip. What presents would my three girls like me to bring back for them?"

Note that: his *three* girls.

It occurs to me that perhaps the stepmother's daughters were really, all the time, his own daughters, just as much his own daughters as Ashputtle, his "natural" daughters, as they say, as though there is something inherently unnatural about legitimacy. *That* would realign the forces in the story. It would make his connivance with the ascendancy of the other girls more plausible. It would make the speedy marriage, the stepmother's hostility, more probable.

But it would also transform the story into something

223

else, because it would provide motivation, and so on; it would mean I'd have to provide a past for all these people, that I would have to equip them with three dimensions, with tastes and memories, and I would have to think of things for them to eat and wear and say. It would transform "Ashputtle" from the bare necessity of fairy tale, with its characteristic copula formula, "and then," to the emotional and technical complexity of bourgeois realism. They would have to learn to think. Everything would change.

I will stick with what I know.

What presents do his three girls want?

"Bring me a silk dress," said his eldest girl. "Bring me a string of pearls," said the middle one. What about the third one, the forgotten one, called out of the kitchen on a charitable impulse and drying her hands, raw with housework, on her apron, bringing with her the smell of old fire?

"Bring me the first branch that knocks against your hat on the way home," said Ashputtle.

Why did she ask for that? Did she make an informed guess at how little he valued her? Or had a dream told her to use this random formula of unacknowledged desire, to allow blind chance to choose her present for her? Unless it was her mother's ghost, awake and restlessly looking for a way home, that came into the girl's mouth and spoke the request for her.

He brought her back a hazel twig. She planted it on her mother's grave and watered it with tears. It grew into a hazel tree. When Ashputtle came out to weep upon her mother's grave, the turtledove crooned: "I'll never leave you, I'll always protect you."

Then Ashputtle knew that the turtledove was her mother's ghost and she herself was still her mother's daughter and although she had wept and wailed and longed to have her mother back again, now her heart sank a little to find out that her mother, though dead, was no longer gone and henceforward she must do her mother's bidding.

Came the time for that curious fair they used to hold in that country, when all the resident virgins went to dance in front of

224

the king's son so that he could pick out the girl he wanted to marry.

The turtledove was mad for that, for her daughter to marry the prince. You might think her own experience of marriage would have taught her to be wary but no, needs must, what else is a girl to do? The turtledove was mad for her daughter to marry so she flew in and picked up the new silk dress with her beak, dragged it to the open window, threw it down to Ashputtle. She did the same with the string of pearls. Ashputtle had a good wash under the pump in the yard, put on her stolen finery and crept out the back way, secretly, to the dancing grounds, but the stepsisters had to stay home and sulk because they had nothing to wear.

The turtledove stayed close to Ashputtle, pecking her ears to make her dance vivaciously, so that the prince would see her, so that the prince would love her, so that he would follow her and find the clue of the fallen slipper, for the story is not complete without the ritual humiliation of the other woman and the mutilation of her daughters.

The search for the foot that fits the slipper is essential to the enactment of this ritual humiliation.

The other woman wants that young man desperately. She would do anything to catch him. Not losing a daughter, but gaining a son. She wants a son so badly she is prepared to cripple her daughters. She takes up a carving knife and chops off her elder daughter's big toe, so that her foot will fit the little shoe.

Imagine.

Brandishing the carving knife, the woman bears down on her child, who is as distraught as if she had not been a girl but a boy and the old woman was after a more essential portion than a toe. No! she screams. Mother! No! Not the knife! No! But off it comes, all the same, and she throws it in the fire, among the ashes, where Ashputtle finds it, wonders at it, and feels both awe and fear at the phenomenon of mother love.

Mother love, which winds about these daughters like a shroud.

The prince saw nothing familiar in the face of the tearful young woman, one shoe off, one shoe on, displayed to him in triumph by her mother, but he said: "I promised I would marry whomever the shoe fitted so I will marry you," and they rode off together.

The turtledove came flying round and did not croon or coo to the bridal pair but sang a horrid song: "Look! look! there's blood in the shoe!"

The prince returned the ersatz ex-fiancée at once, angry at the trick, but the stepmother hastily lopped off her other daughter's heel and pushed that poor foot into the bloody shoe as soon as it was vacant so, nothing for it, a man of his word, the prince helped up the new girl and once again he rode away.

Back came the nagging turtledove: "look!" And, sure enough, the shoe was full of blood again.

(The shoe full of blood. Horrible. An open wound.)

"Let Ashputtle try," said the eager turtledove.

So now Ashputtle must put her foot into this hideous receptacle, still slick and warm and wet as it is, for nothing in any of the texts of this tale suggests the prince washed it out between the fittings. It was an ordeal in itself to put a naked foot into that bloody shoe but her mother, the turtledove, urged her to do so in a soft, cooing croon that could not be denied.

If she does not plunge without revulsion into this open wound, she won't be fit to marry. That is the song of the turtledove, while the other mad mother stood impotently by.

Ashputtle's foot, the size of the bound foot of a Chinese woman; a stump. Already an amputee, she put her foot in it.

"Look! look!" cried the turtledove in triumph, even as she betrayed the secret of her ghostly nature by becoming progressively more and more immaterial as Ashputtle stood up in the shoe and commenced to walk around, squelching but proud. "Her foot fits the shoe like a corpse fits a coffin!

"See how well I look after you, my darling!"

B) THE BURNED CHILD

A burned child lived in the ashes. No, not really burned, more charred, a little bit charred, like a stick half-burned and picked off the fire. She looked like charcoal and ashes because she lived in the ashes since her mother died and the hot ashes burned her so she was scabbed and scarred. The burned child lived on the hearth, covered in ashes, as if she were still mourning.

After her mother died and was buried, her father forgot the mother and forgot the child and married the woman who used to rake the ashes, and that was why the child lived in the unraked ashes, and there was nobody to brush her hair so it stuck out like a mat nor to wipe the dirt off her scabbed face and she had no heart to do it for herself but she raked the ashes and slept beside the little cat and got the burned bits from the bottom of the pot to eat, scraping them out, squatting on the floor, by herself in front of the fire, not as if she were human, because she was still in mourning.

Her mother was dead and buried but felt perfect exquisite pain of love when she looked up through the earth and saw the burned child covered in ashes.

"Milk the cow, burned child, and bring back all the milk," said the stepmother, who used to rake the ashes and milk the cow, once upon a time, but the burned child did all that, now.

The ghost of the mother went into the cow.

"Drink milk, grow fat," said the mother's ghost.

The burned child pulled on the udder and drank enough milk before she took the bucket back and nobody saw, and time passed, she drank milk every day, she grew fat, she grew breasts, she grew up.

There was a man the stepmother wanted and asked into the kitchen to get his dinner but she made the burned child cook it, although the stepmother did all the cooking before. After the burned child cooked the dinner the stepmother sent her off to milk the cow.

"I want that man for myself," said the burned child to the cow.

The cow let down more milk, and more, and more, enough for the girl to have a drink and wash her face and wash her hands. When she washed her face, she washed the scabs off and now she was not burned at all, but the cow was empty.

"Give your own milk, next time," said the ghost of the mother inside the cow. "You've milked me dry."

The little cat came by. The ghost of the mother went into the cat.

"Your hair wants doing," said the cat. "Lie down."

The little cat unpicked her raggy lugs with its clever paws until the burned child's hair hung down nicely but it had been so snagged and tangled that the cat's claws were all pulled out before it was finished.

"Comb your own hair next time," said the cat. "You've maimed me."

The burned child was clean and combed but stark naked.

There was a bird sitting in the apple tree. The ghost of the mother left the cat and went into the bird. The bird stuck its own breast with its beak. Blood poured down onto the burned child under the tree. It ran over her shoulders and covered her front and covered her back. When the bird had no more blood, the burned child got a red silk dress.

"Make your own dress, next time," said the bird. "I'm through with that bloody business."

The burned child went into the kitchen to show herself to the man. She was not burned any more, but lovely. The man left off looking at the stepmother and looked at the girl.

"Come home with me and let your stepmother stay and rake the ashes," he said to her and off they went. He gave her a house and money. She did all right.

"Now I can go to sleep," said the ghost of the mother. "Now everything is all right."

C) THE TRAVELLING COSTUME

The cruel stepmother burned the orphan's face with a poker because she did not rake the ashes. The girl went to her mother's grave. Deep in the earth her mother said:

"It must be raining. Or else it is snowing. Unless there is a heavy dew tonight."

"It isn't raining, it isn't snowing, it's too early for the dew. But my tears are falling on your grave, mother."

The dead woman waited until night came. Then she climbed out and went to the house. The stepmother slept on a feather bed but the burned child slept on the hearth among the ashes. When the dead woman kissed her, the scar vanished. The girl woke up. The dead woman gave her a red dress.

"I had it when I was your age, I used it for travelling."

The girl put the travelling costume on. The dead woman took worms out of her eye sockets; they turned to jewels. The girl put on a handful of rings.

"Sell them as you need to."

They went together to the grave.

"Step into my coffin."

She trusted her mother. She stepped into the coffin. At once it turned into a coach and horses. The horses stamped, eager to be gone.

"Now go and seek your fortune, darling."

❁

Frances Newman

The medieval commentary to the Old Testament known as the *Midrash* lists Rachel as one of history's twelve outstanding women and one of the four matriarchs. Of the two wives of Jacob in the Book of Genesis, Rachel is supposed to have been the favorite. Unable at first to bear children, she dutifully offered her handmaiden to her husband instead. In her old age, she gave birth to Joseph and Benjamin. The prophet Jeremiah saw her as the personification of Israel, weeping for her dead children; and she came to symbolize a mother's grief, echoed in the ancient Jewish curse, "May you outlive your children."

Frances Newman, a somewhat shadowy figure in American literature of the early years of this century, takes up the traditional figure of Rachel and turns it in an ironic twist. The grief of a mother weeping for her deceased daughter, a classic emblem in small-village society, becomes a lament for time past, for time wasted, and for a woman's own neglected life.

RACHEL AND HER CHILDREN

frances newman

everyone agreed that a perfect stranger 231
could not have seen Mrs. Foster's funeral without realizing that Mrs.
Foster had lived a well-rounded life. There was her husband in the
front pew, vainly struggling to conceal his grief so that he could
console Mrs. Foster's mother, old Mrs. Overton. There were her
two sons, vainly struggling to conceal their grief so that they could
console Mrs. Foster's daughters-in-law, their wives. There were her
four little grandchildren, as downcast as anyone could ask. There
were her six faithful servants, as heartbroken as her daughters-in-
law. The society of Colonial Dames was there, in a body, and the
Daughters of the Confederacy were there in a body. The Woman's
Club was there, in a body, and even the Chamber of Commerce
was there, in a body. There was all of the Social Register which
did not happen to be on its yachts, or in sanatoria, or abroad. And
there were the wreaths, and the harps, and the crescents, and the
sheaves of all those bodies and of all those personages.

The hearts of the community went out to every member
of Mrs. Foster's stricken family, so the rector told his audience
and his God. But in particular it went out to Mrs. Foster's mother,
for not a month before she had stood by her only son's open grave,
and now she was about to stand beside her only daughter's open

grave. She sat among them in the church—as the rector said, like Rachel weeping for her children. But she was veiled in English crêpe of excellent quality and so the most acute eyes of the community could not count the number of her tears. It was fortunate, indeed, that Mr. Foster could afford that excellent quality of crêpe, for old Mrs. Overton was not actually weeping like Rachel—in fact, she was not weeping at all.

Old Mrs. Overton had dreamed indirectly of Mrs. Foster's funeral on at least a hundred different nights. Thus she had now no difficulty in realizing that her brilliant daughter's mortal remains were reposing in that gray coffin which was so magnificently concealed by its blanket of lilies and pink roses. Old Mrs. Overton was seventy-four years old; she belonged to a generation which believed that dreaming of a funeral was a sign of a wedding, and that dreaming of a wedding was a sign of a funeral. She had never read the works of Dr. Siegmund Freud—she had, in fact, never heard of Dr. Freud—and so she had no idea what Dr. Freud's disciples would have entered on the card describing her case. Old Mrs. Overton sat comfortably in the best corner of the cushioned pew and, in the pleasant shelter of her well-draped veil, thought about things.

She thought of the time when she was sixteen, back in 1864. She thought of Captain Ashby, with his black plume and his black horse. They had stood in the box garden, and she had fairly ached with adoration of his six feet, his black hair, his black eyes, of the wound in some vaguely invisible spot that no Southern lady could even think about, of his gallant war record, not yet embalmed in the Confederate Museum. She was familiar with the works of Mr. Dickens and Mr. Thackeray and Sir Walter Scott, but she had never been allowed to read the story of Jane Eyre and Mr. Rochester. She flutteringly expected . . . she flutteringly hoped . . . that one night soon, perhaps that very night, Captain Ashby would drop on his gray-trousered knees, and implore her to do him the great honour of becoming his wife. She would accept the great honour, she would beg him not to kneel before one so unworthy, and Captain Ashby would rise. He would timidly bend down and kiss her respectfully on the forehead. And then Captain Ashby and his betrothed would walk in to his betrothed's father, and Captain Ashby would ask her hand in marriage. That was what Mr. Dickens and Mr. Thackeray led one to expect, and that was what her mother, who had been twice married and therefore twice engaged, led her to expect.

But that was not what happened. Captain Ashby stopped talking. Even eager questions about his recent heroic deeds were barely answered. The moment might be approaching. Sally had no desire to postpone it, and so she stopped asking the eager questions. Captain Ashby seized her in a passionate embrace, he covered her face with passionate kisses, he kissed her under her soft chin, and just below the brown curls on her neck. It was instantly obvious to Sally that Captain Ashby did not love her. Ivanhoe would never have kissed the fair Rowena like that; David Copperfield would never have kissed the angelic Agnes like that, or even Dora who could not keep her accounts straight. Sally's heart was broken. She tore herself from the embrace of this man who had proved that he did not love her by kissing her, she rushed into her father's house, and up the stairs to her own four-poster. She wept there until her mother came to find her, and to hear the tragic tale. And her mother, though she had been twice married and twice engaged, confirmed Sally's belief that she had been insulted. And Captain Ashby rode away on his black horse.

Mrs. Overton sighed a little under the crêpe veil. She had waited six months for the black horse to gallop back up the avenue between the magnolias, but it had been years before she discovered that a kiss before proposal did not necessarily insult a great love. Meanwhile, her mother had decided to marry her to a certain Colonel Overton, and had had no great difficulty in overcoming Colonel Overton's intention of being legally faithful to the memory of his Julia. Sally's heart, of course, was broken, but that was no reason for being a forlorn old maid, and she thought it would be rather pleasant to decide for herself what frock she would wear, and whether she would go to the Springs in the summer, and how she would do her hair. Elderly husbands were said to be tractable, and Sally had been very tired of talking only when Mama didn't want to talk, or only to people Mama didn't want to talk to, and of always sitting with her back to the horses like an inconsequential Prince Consort. She had been convinced that the dignity of marriage would offset its disadvantages, and, besides, she had no very clear idea of marriage except that it meant a change of name and of residence, and sitting at the head of one's own table, behind one's own silver tea service. People hardly talked then of the boredom of sitting at the other end of the table from the wrong man every morning: certainly they never talked of the occasions when there wasn't a table between one and the wrong man.

234   The choir was singing "Lead, Kindly Light," which had been Mrs. Foster's favourite hymn, and which, she always mentioned, was written by the late Cardinal Newman before he became a Catholic, much less a Cardinal. Old Mrs. Overton shivered a little under her veil when they came to

> And with the morn those angel faces smile
> That I have loved long since and lost awhile.

Mrs. Overton had no doubt that Mama, tulle cap, black bombazine, and all, and Colonel Overton, beard, temper, and all, would be smiling among those angels, and the idea was not cheering. She had been an old man's darling, but she had also been an old man's slave, a carefully treasured harem of one. Colonel Overton had been fond of saying, of declaiming, that he did not believe in the honour of any man, or the virtue of any woman. Sally had never thought of deceiving him even about the price of a new gown, but even if she had been the most abandoned creature she would have been saved in spite of herself. When she went to a dentist, Colonel Overton was beside her. When she bought a new hat, Colonel Overton was there to protect her from the shop's manager and also from an unbecoming bonnet. Sally had never danced even the Virginia Reel or the Lancers after the morning when Colonel Overton had confirmed her idea of respectful proposals by asking the honour of her hand in marriage and then kissing her chastely on the brow.

Now she looked at the lilies and pink roses that concealed Mrs. Foster's coffin under their expensive fragrance. She was thinking of the day Mrs. Foster was born—something less than a year after the respectful proposal. It was not a coincidence that the baby, now a corpse, had been christened Cornelia for the maternal grandmother whose capacity for being obeyed she had inherited. Mrs. Overton's mother had not waited to receive a namesake with that pleased surprise which ordinarily greets namesakes and proposals and legacies. She had taken the name for granted, quite audibly, on the day when a granddaughter's probable advent was announced to her. The younger Cornelia had justified her grandmother. She allowed her mother to sit in her own carriage facing her own horses, and she allowed her to continue filling her own cups with tea and coffee from her own silver urn. That was the correct thing, and Cornelia always did the correct thing, in all matters from sleeves and shoes to husbands and religions. But after Cornelia was four years old, her mother was never allowed to talk to the people she wanted to talk to about the things she wanted to talk about—not even when her husband permitted her the luxury of an unchaperoned feminine visit. And when Colonel Overton very unwillingly died, Cornelia had seen that her mother was faithful to his memory.

Cornelia was nineteen when that event took place, and just in the process of marrying herself to a rising young lawyer named Henry Foster. The marriage took place shortly afterward, with a simple elegance which the newspaper notices attributed to the recent bereavement in the bride's family. But the simplicity of the elegance at Cornelia's marriage was really due to the disappearance of the late colonel's prosperity rather than to the disappearance of the late colonel himself. His wife and his daughter and his son

knew that their acquaintances attributed part of this disappearance to the colonel's extraordinary gratitude to a prepossessing
coloured—just barely coloured—nurse, who had been the comfort
of his declining years. But Mrs. Overton had never been so indis-
creet as to mention this theory to her daughter, even on the most
tempting occasions.

Mrs. Overton had been as faithful to her husband as
her sex required in the days when a good woman had no history
except that recorded in the parish register. Her husband, she supposed, had been no more faithful to her than his sex will continue
to require until nature changes her ways. But her daughter was
inexpressibly shocked when she began to show signs of considering
a second alliance.

Mrs. Overton, at that time, was still sufficiently under
forty not to have begun comparing the corners of her eyes and the
line under her chin with those of her contemporaries. The aspiring
Mr. Robinson was not an Overton, but the war had been over long
enough for prosperous Robinsons and impoverished Overtons to
marry each other without scandal. Mrs. Overton would have liked
to sit behind her own silver tea service again, and in her own
drawing room, and Mr. Robinson would have been so honoured by
the gift of her hand in marriage that she would at last have been
able to talk to the people she wanted to talk to about the things
she wanted to talk about. But Cornelia disapproved of second mar-
riages so positively that people who did not know her might well
have thought she was sorry that she had been born. Cornelia was
then expecting the birth of that son who was now trying to conceal his own grief so that he could console her first daughter-in-
law. And Cornelia had been thrown into such a state by her
mother's announcement that Mrs. Overton had felt obliged to give
up the idea.

So she had continued to sit on the side of her daughter's
table for nine months of every year, and on the side of her son
William's table for three months of every year. Even when tea

services on breakfast tables went out, and round tables came in, tables continued to have a head and a side, and Mrs. Overton had continued to grieve for her own tea service and her own table. She had never ceased to long for a house where a ringing telephone would mean that someone in the world wanted to talk with her badly enough to go through the trouble of getting a telephone number; where a ringing door bell would mean that someone wanted to see her, if it were only a book agent, or the laundry man.

For thirty-four years Mrs. Overton had spoken to Daughters of the American Revolution and Daughters of the Confederacy and newspaper reporters and officers of those clubs which seem to exist chiefly to elect officers. But she had spoken only to tell them that Mrs. Foster was lunching or dining or pre-siding at some house or some club where she either could or could not be called to the telephone. She had talked to a great many callers, but she had talked to callers of no consequence, while Mrs. Foster talked to callers of great consequence—local, if not international. And then Mrs. Foster had fallen ill. And William Overton had fallen ill. And old Mrs. Overton began to be Rachel weeping for her children.

Mrs. Foster was ill, desperately ill, for six months. For their convenience, if not for hers, the doctors decreed that Mrs. Foster must be in a hospital, and that she must receive no visitors. Old Mrs. Overton suffered with her daughter, but she revived the pleasant old custom of pouring the breakfast coffee from her own silver urn, and Mr. Foster was delighted. She carried the pantry keys, and the silver-closet keys, and the linen-room keys; she went to market alone; she went shopping alone. All the ladies of high position, and all the officers of all Mrs. Foster's clubs came to call on Mrs. Overton—to ask about Mrs. Foster, of course, but even on such occasions other subjects are discussed, and Mrs. Overton must be cheered and strengthened for the ordeal she was under-going. Then William Overton was mercifully released from his sufferings. And then Mrs. Foster was mercifully released from her longer sufferings.

Old Mrs. Overton had received hundreds of notes. She had scores of callers, and she had felt herself able to receive them all—decorously, in her own bedroom, one or two at a time. Her fortitude was considered remarkable. She had ordered delicate lunches for the faithful friends who were downstairs receiving the wreaths and the sheaves of Mrs. Overton's other friends and of all her societies. And she had ordered her own veil of the best English crêpe.

The choir was singing "Asleep in Jesus," and Mrs. Foster's funeral was nearly over. Mrs. Overton began to look about a little, under the shadow of her veil. She was thinking of all the visitors she would have the next day and the next week; of the days the granddaughters-in-law and the great-grandchildren would spend with her, of the birthday party she would give for little Cornelia in the spring—Mrs. Foster would want her namesake to have the party she had promised her. She was thinking of all the people who would beg her and Mr. Foster to come and have dinner with them, very quietly—since they, too, had loved Mrs. Foster.

And then Mrs. Overton happened to look across the aisle at Mrs. Turner, and Mrs. Turner was looking beyond her at Mr. Foster. Mrs. Turner's look was only a decorous look of heart-felt sympathy, but Mrs. Overton suddenly felt cold and forlorn. She remembered how attentive Mrs. Turner had been to her and to Mr. Foster. And she remembered that Mrs. Turner had lost Mr. Turner three years before. And she remembered how many of the kind women who had come to cheer her for her great ordeal, who had received the flowers that were banked about the chancel, had lost their husbands three or four or five years before. She remembered the statistics of the number of widows in the state that she had read for one of Mrs. Foster's erudite club papers. The whole church, the whole world, seemed to be filled with widows—widows whose daughters would not discourage their mothers from taking names different from their own.

Mrs. Overton had no doubt that in a year she would go

back to the side of another Mrs. Foster's table, that she would receive telephone messages for another Mrs. Foster—and that this Mrs. Foster would not even be her daughter.

That last prayer was over. The eight eminent pallbearers were gathering. Mr. Foster rose and offered his arm to his mother-in-law. Mrs. Overton stood up, shaking with bitter sobs, and took the offered arm. She walked up the aisle behind the blanket of lilies and pink roses that covered Mrs. Foster's coffin. All the hearts of the community went out to old Mrs. Overton, weeping like Rachel for her children.

Hannes Meinkema

One evening in 1896, someone mentioned to Henry James the situation of "some luckless child of a divorced couple" affected "by the remarriage of one of its parents." The facts of the case disturbed James, who recalled later, "The light of an imagination touched by them couldn't help therefore projecting a further ray, thanks to which it became quaintly clear that, not less than the chance of misery and of a degraded state, the chance of happiness and of an improved state might be here involved for the child, round about whom the complexity of life would thus turn to fineness, to richness." In search of these happier possibilities, James wrote *What Maisie Knew*.

The protagonist of Hannes Meinkema's story is no longer a child, but the same situation—the divorce of her parents and the arrival of an outsider—offers identical possibilities of despair or contentment. One of Holland's best-known novelists, Meinkema published her first book, *The Mooneater,* in 1974. The following story first appeared in a collection aimed at portraying women's lives through the eyes of women writers from nine different countries.

MY MOTHER'S NAME
(DE NAAM VAN MIJN MOEDER)

hannes meinkema

Translated from the Dutch by James Brockway

why did I do it? Did I do it to revenge myself on her, or just to be closer to her? Am I crazy, am I sick?

After the divorce we were completely dependent on each other, but that didn't matter, I could already do quite a lot. I could go and lie at her side when she cried in bed, I could do the shopping. I told her what she should wear in the morning.

My father had been a man with a mustache who was away at sea for eight months in the year: so you'd say it didn't make all that difference whether she was married or divorced, but it made an awful lot of difference to her. My mother's a person who always knows the way everything ought to be done—after the divorce she'd become entirely unsure of herself. You could tell by little things. You could tell, for example, when the potatoes for our evening meal were ready long before the greens or the meat—and while I was sitting on a chair in the kitchen just as in the past, watching her, full of admiration for her timing, and to grind the nutmeg if need be, because I was so fond of the shape of the little nutmeg grater, with its rounded little tummy and its little box, complete with lid, to catch the grains in— while I was sitting there I was struck by the way she would often walk backwards and forwards, unnecessarily, and even drop things. My capable mother. And at night I'd hear the john flush four, five times: the worry had given her diarrhea. The next morning she'd laugh about that herself: I have to act so hard outwardly, she'd say, that I go all soft inside as a reaction—and I'd laugh with her, but when I heard the john flush three times in an hour, I didn't laugh at all.

I saw to it that I went straight home after school in case there was something I could do for her. I would make tea for the two of us and we would drink it in the kitchen while discussing how we'd tackle the problem of the evening meal. I, who was so fond of departing from the rules, insisted we have a hot meal every day—she ate so little, she was growing so thin. And if my girl friends asked me to come and play at their home I told them they'd have to come to mine. They did, too, in the beginning, but I don't know, I couldn't really show much interest in all that anymore, and after a while they stayed away and I didn't miss them.

Four years passed in this way, years in which, it's true, I did sit my entrance exam and passed, so changed schools and had to deal with a separate teacher for each subject and a class full of unfamiliar children—but what went on at school only acquired significance when I told about it at home and my mother said what she thought about it. My real life was at home, where we did everything together, my mother and I, where I knew who I was, and where I was needed too, even though my mother now only rarely had any trouble with her stomach.

When I was fourteen my mother acquired a friend. I say a friend, but I mean Gerrit. He fell in love with her and she probably with him, although she didn't tell me as much, but that's how it must have been, for after a period during which she let me share her feelings less and less and I grew more and more unhappy because she was drawing away from me, there came a day when she said he was coming to live with us.

Just like that.

I hated him, and I hated her too for bringing him into our house. I hated the bedroom, I hated the sound of the john at night telling me how unneeded I had become. I hated the meals when everything I told about school would be heard by him too.

I began to come home less. I stopped drinking tea in the kitchen. I began to keep my mouth shut at table. And if my mother sought my company and wanted to talk to me I was purposely as rude as I could be, I said things to her that I knew would hurt her (I said she was getting old, I said she looked so awful I was ashamed of her). And then I hated myself. But hated her too, her too, because I knew she would go and talk to him about what she was sure to call my "problems with adapting." I hated her because she had betrayed me. I hated her because she was no longer mine.

Yes, I was jealous, but it took me a few months to realize it. For a long time I thought that she alone was responsible for the estrangement between us. Her feelings for me must have changed. She was behaving differently, wasn't she? I don't know, the atmosphere at home was exactly like that in a television ad—all forced cheerfulness, with mommie, poppie and teenage daughter. For instance, my mother began calling me "my darling" too, a thing she had never done before.

I began to feel sorry for myself. I drew in bags under my eyes with a lead pencil to appear pitiable, and hoped there'd be someone who'd notice how bad I looked, so they'd pay attention to me . . .

I was jealous but didn't recognize my feelings. After all, I had never before felt I wanted her to belong to me: you don't feel things that are natural as anything extraordinary.

It was a few months before I understood what I felt, and I was ashamed. Hating him didn't matter, but her—I didn't want that.

A teacher at my school once told me I am the sort of person who is good at coming to decisions. I decided to get used to the situation, because I did realize I could only master my feelings if I learned to accept his presence in the house. So I tried to.

243

It wasn't easy and at night I'd cry in my bed because it was so difficult. But once I've started off on a thing, I go through with it, and I reminded myself why I was doing it. That helped. I didn't, after all, want to lose her love! And she could only love me if I liked him. So . . .

And so it came about that I didn't go upstairs that evening. My mother had a meeting, he and I were alone together in the house, and I stayed downstairs instead of going up and doing my homework, for I wanted there to be some contact between us.

I sat on the sofa, and he on one of the two chairs opposite. I was reading a pop magazine, he the *Weekly Post*. Minutes went by, then I slapped my magazine to and looked at him. Till he felt me looking at him.

"What are you reading about?" I asked.

"Oh," he said and laughed (actually it was that grown-ups' laugh I'd always disliked so much), "that wouldn't interest you."

"If it didn't interest me I wouldn't ask." I wasn't entirely honest—I wasn't really interested in what he was reading, but I did want to hear what he thought was interesting and how he'd talk about it.

As he was speaking (it was about trade unions and some agreement or other the Cabinet had come to with them and which some members of the government no longer wanted to keep to, something of that sort), I watched him and saw what attracted my mother in him. When he grew enthusiastic he had something attractive about him—I hadn't noticed it before, because he'd never been enthusiastic in my presence. So I tried to keep him talking by asking him questions (the difference between the two houses of Parliament, I'm always forgetting that), but there came a moment all the same when we had nothing left to talk about. So I just sat and smiled at him.

"Do you already have boy friends?" he then asked.

"At times," I said.

He looked at me for a moment, then stood up. "You'd like a drink, I bet," he said. "What shall I pour you?"

I didn't know. I never touch strong drink.

"I'm having a whisky," he said. "Care to join me?"

"All right," I said, and we drank whisky. I didn't enjoy the first glass, but he said you had to get used to the taste, so I took courage and went on drinking and, indeed, the second glass didn't taste so bad.

For a while we talked of other things, my school, his work (he does something in computers), and then he returned to the subject of my boy friends.

"What do you get up to with them?" he asked. He was really attractive when he smiled.

"Nothing special, a French kiss or two," I said, though it was none of his business.

He poured me a third glass of whisky. "Aren't you curious to know what happens after that?" he asked. I looked at his hand which was clasping the bottle and was reminded of those advertisements in magazines in which men are holding bottles, and I saw his hand and I thought that's a man's hand, man's hand, and he bent over toward me after he'd put the bottle aside and he put his fingers under my chin so that I was forced to look at him and he smelled of tobacco, and he asked me again if I wasn't curious and suddenly I *was*, although I'd never been before, so I nodded.

And then we went to bed.

Since he'd been living with us my mother made breakfast in the mornings, and the next morning I was scared to go downstairs. I hung around as long as I could so that I'd have to rush through breakfast to get to school on time. But all she asked was if I'd slept well. Nothing else was said.

That afternoon I stayed away till dinnertime and when I got home he was already there. We sat down to table. Nothing unusual. And there was no tension either, everything was the same as at other times. Even he acted toward me exactly as before. As if nothing had happened, as though that thing between us had never taken place.

I went upstairs immediately after the meal, I was all confused. I didn't understand a thing about it. My mother is the sort of person who always reacts if anything happens, so she couldn't know. He hadn't told her. The rotter. My mother still didn't know a thing!

I thought about it that night in bed. I couldn't sleep. It kept going through my head, the way it was: he hadn't said anything, she didn't know about it, what would happen now, how would it go on from here?

There was only one solution, of course. I had to tell. I couldn't very well let myself be maneuvered into a situation where he and I would know something she didn't; I had no wish to share a secret with him. What we already shared was bad enough.

So, home from school the following day, I told her. I didn't say much, I simply told her what had happened.

She hardly believed it at first, then she grew very quiet, tense, I don't know, it was terrible the way she looked, it hurt to see her face, but she did look at me. All she asked was whether he had used a preventative and I said, yes, a condom, and she said, "Thank God," but she didn't, of course, sound at all grateful, "and now you go and do your homework."

Later I heard the awful sounds of quarreling downstairs, I couldn't help but cry about it, it reminded me of the days when my father was still living with us and, that made me afraid, for now everything would change just as it had then.

I knew it, and this time it was my fault.

It did change: he packed his bags and left.

But after he'd gone, things weren't the same as they'd been before. My mother and I went on acting coolly to each other. She no longer talked with me. He'd left, but he was more present in her thoughts than I was. She didn't see me. We shared our meals, she even went on getting the breakfast, but she didn't speak. Except to ask how was school today. Nothing more. And she didn't mention that evening again and never uttered Gerrit's name.

I understood what she meant. It was my fault he'd left,

that's why she was no longer speaking. That I was still there had to be a punishment for her. She had had to choose between him and me and because I was still too young to look after myself, she'd had to choose me, and now she hated me because I had come between him and her and it was my fault he'd left.

So the other thing had to be my fault too. That drinking, I mean, and the sex with him.

Formerly, this was precisely what I would have liked to talk to her about, because it was this that I was always thinking about. About how it had all been—dizzy-making, and he'd made me curious, afterward it felt as though he'd tricked me into it, but she was punishing me, so it really was my fault.

Why did I do it? To revenge myself on her for having brought him into the house? Because I'd be closer to her if I went to bed with her lover? Am I crazy? Or sick?

After a week I was wishing she had sent *me* packing. I couldn't concentrate any longer at school, and being at home was even worse. But I didn't know how I could change it, I didn't know what I ought to do.

Until one day, during the meal, someone rang her up. It was so simple, yet it shocked me. It altered something. "Yes," she said into the receiver. "Lisbeth here." I'd heard her say it hundreds of times before. Her name. Her first name. "Lisbeth." I've known my mother's name was Lisbeth since I was a toddler. When I was little I even called her by that name for a while. Lisbeth.

But that evening all at once it was something very important, the way she said her name, so naturally over the telephone, as though to her it was completely a matter of course that she was called Lisbeth.

To me she was my mother, but to herself she was an individual. She was Lisbeth, a woman who had been divorced and had a daughter and who had had a lover. An individual who had lived for thirty-five years, twenty of them without me.

I couldn't sleep again that night, but more because I was excited rather than unhappy. And I understood what I had to do. I had to talk to her—to Lisbeth—even if I had to begin myself, because it was important to me to know what she thought of me and what she felt about that awful sex episode. And if she condemned me, if she condemned me, I had to know that too, for then, perhaps, she'd be able to show me why it was I'd done that with him and then I'd be able to change until I'd become someone she could respect again.

For I can't do without her. Not because she is my mother, but because of who she is.

I spoke her name. After school it was, I'd sat down at her side, I'd made tea just as in the old days, I poured her out a cup and gave it to her and spoke her name. She looked at me.

"I want to talk to you," I said. I was near to tears. "I want to know exactly what it is you are so angry with me about," I said. "Are you so sorry it's finished between you?"

She looked up then, at that question, then she looked at me *and she began to laugh.* And that took me by surprise again, it gave me such a shock that I suddenly began to cry very loudly, and then, and then she put her arms tightly around me and she said all sorts of things, poor child, she said, how could I know you were blaming yourself, no, of course I'm not sorry, she said, that blackguard, such a rotter to take advantage of your curiosity, no, she said, it isn't that, I am sorry, it's true, I'm sorry because something that could have been very special for you and that you could have found out about all on your own in your own time, that he should have robbed you of that, that's what I'm sorry about, she said, my baby, I didn't say anything because you said nothing, I thought let's forget this unpleasant episode as soon as possible, as soon as possible.

So now everything is just as it was before he came. Just as before. But I don't know whether I'm happy about it.

❁

Edith Wharton

Edith Wharton was vastly famous at the beginning of the century, a fame that seems to be rightly restored to her at the end. She was generous to her friends, and could afford to be. To Henry James, whom she loved and admired, she explained that she had just bought a new car with the proceeds of her latest novel. "With the proceeds of *my* last novel," said James meditatively, "I purchased a small go-cart, or hand-barrow, on which my guests' luggage is wheeled from the station to my house. It needs a coat of paint. With the proceeds of my next novel I shall have it painted." To help James, Wharton secretly arranged that their common publisher, Scribner's, should take eight thousand dollars out of Wharton's royalties and offer the sum to James as an advance on his new book. James accepted (his agent took ten percent) "with the greatest joy and without suspicion." With her characters (such as the mother and daughter in "Autre Temps . . ."), she was less generous and watched them implacably as they either lost themselves or (more rarely) survived.

AUTRES TEMPS . . .

edith wharton

Mrs. Lidcote, as the huge menacing mass of New York defined itself far off across the waters, shrank back into her corner of the deck and sat listening with a kind of unreasoning terror to the steady onward drive of the screws.

She had set out on the voyage quietly enough—in what she called her "reasonable" mood—but the week at sea had given her too much time to think of things and had left her too long alone with the past.

When she was alone, it was always the past that occupied her. She couldn't get away from it, and she didn't any longer care to. During her long years of exile she had made her terms with it, had learned to accept the fact that it would always be there, huge, obstructing, encumbering, bigger and more dominant than anything the future could ever conjure up. And, at any rate, she was sure of it, she understood it, knew how to reckon with it; she had learned to screen and manage and protect it as one does an afflicted member of one's family.

There had never been any danger of her being allowed to forget the past. It looked out at her from the face of every acquaintance, it appeared suddenly in the eyes of strangers when a word enlightened them: "Yes, *the* Mrs. Lidcote, don't you know?"

It had sprung at her the first day out, when, across the dining room, from the captain's table, she had seen Mrs. Lorin Boulger's revolving eyeglass pause and the eye behind it grow as blank as a dropped blind. The next day, of course, the captain had asked: "You know your ambassadress, Mrs. Boulger?" and she had replied that, No, she seldom left Florence, and hadn't been to Rome for more than a day since the Boulgers had been sent to Italy. She was so used to these phrases that it cost her no effort to repeat them. And the captain had promptly changed the subject.

No, she didn't, as a rule, mind the past, because she was used to it and understood it. It was a great concrete fact in her path that she had to walk around every time she moved in any direction. But now, in the light of the unhappy event that had summoned her from Italy,—the sudden unanticipated news of her daughter's divorce from Horace Pursh and remarriage with Wilbour Barkley—the past, her own poor miserable past, stared up at her with eyes of accusation, became, to her disordered fancy, like the afflicted relative suddenly breaking away from nurses and keepers and publicly parading the horror and misery she had, all the long years, so patiently screened and secluded.

Yes, there it had stood before her through the agitated weeks since the news had come—during her interminable journey from India, where Leila's letter had overtaken her, and the feverish halt in her apartment in Florence, where she had had to stop and gather up her possessions for a fresh start—there it had stood grinning at her with a new balefulness which seemed to say: "Oh, but you've got to look at me *now*, because I'm not only your own past but Leila's present."

Certainly it was a master stroke of those arch-ironists of the shears and spindle to duplicate her own story in her daughter's. Mrs. Lidcote had always somewhat grimly fancied that, having so signally failed to be of use to Leila in other ways, she would at least serve her as a warning. She had even abstained from defending herself, from making the best of her case, had stoically refused to plead extenuating circumstances, lest Leila's impulsive sympathy should lead to deductions that might react disastrously on her own life. And now that very thing had happened, and Mrs. Lidcote could hear the whole of New York saying with one voice: "Yes, Leila's done just what her mother did. With such an example what could you expect?"

Yet if she had been an example, poor woman, she had been an awful one; she had been, she would have supposed, of more use as a deterrent than a hundred blameless mothers as incentives. For how could anyone who had seen anything of her life in the last eighteen years have had the courage to repeat so disastrous an experiment?

Well, logic in such cases didn't count, example didn't count, nothing probably counted but having the same impulses in the blood; and that was the dark inheritance she had bestowed upon her daughter. Leila hadn't consciously copied her; she had simply "taken after" her, had been a projection of her own long-past rebellion.

Mrs. Lidcote had deplored, when she started, that the "Utopia" was a slow steamer, and would take eight full days to bring her to her unhappy daughter; but now, as the moment of reunion approached, she would willingly have turned the boat about and fled back to the high seas. It was not only because she felt still so unprepared to face what New York had in store for her, but because she needed more time to dispose of what the "Utopia" had already given her. The past was bad enough, but the present and future were worse, because they were less comprehensible, and because, as she grew older, surprises and inconsequences troubled her more than the worst certainties.

There was Mrs. Boulger, for instance. In the light, or rather the darkness, of new developments, it might really be that Mrs. Boulger had not meant to cut her, but had simply failed to recognize her. Mrs. Lidcote had arrived at this hypothesis simply by listening to the conversation of the persons sitting next to her on deck—two lively young women with the latest Paris hats on their heads and the latest New York ideas in them. These ladies, as to whom it would have been impossible for a person with Mrs. Lidcote's old-fashioned categories to determine whether they were married or unmarried, "nice" or "horrid," or any one or other of the definite things which young women, in her youth and her society, were conveniently assumed to be, had revealed a familiarity with the world of New York that, again according to Mrs. Lidcote's traditions, should have implied a recognized place in it. But in the present fluid state of manners what did anything imply except what their hats implied—that no one could tell what was coming next?

They seemed, at any rate, to frequent a group of idle and opulent people who executed the same gestures and revolved on the same pivots as Mrs. Lidcote's daughter and her friends: their Coras, Matties and Mabels seemed at any moment likely to reveal familiar patronymics, and once one of the speakers, summing up a discussion of which Mrs. Lidcote had missed the beginning, had affirmed with headlong confidence: "Leila? Oh, *Leila's* all right."

Could it be *her* Leila, the mother had wondered, with a sharp thrill of apprehension? If only they would mention surnames! But their talk leaped elliptically from allusion to allusion, their unfinished sentences dangled over bottomless pits of conjecture, and they gave their bewildered hearer the impression not so much of talking only of their intimates, as of being intimate with everyone alive.

Her old friend Franklin Ide could have told her, perhaps; but here was the last day of the voyage, and she hadn't yet found courage to ask him. Great as had been the joy of discovering his name on the passenger list and seeing his friendly bearded face in the throng against the taffrail at Cherbourg, she had as yet said nothing to him except, when they had met: "Of course I'm going out to Leila."

She had said nothing to Franklin Ide because she had always instinctively shrunk from taking him into her confidence. She was sure he felt sorry for her, sorrier perhaps than anyone had ever felt; but he had always paid her the supreme tribute of not showing it. His attitude allowed her to imagine that compassion was not the basis of his feeling for her, and it was part of her joy in his friendship that it was the one relation seemingly unconditioned by her state, the only one in which she could think and feel and behave like any other woman.

Now, however, as the problem of New York loomed nearer, she began to regret that she had not spoken, had not at least questioned him about the hints she had gathered on the way. He did not know the two ladies next to her, he did not even, as it chanced, know Mrs. Lorin Boulger; but he knew New York, and New York was the sphinx whose riddle she must read or perish.

Almost as the thought passed through her mind his stooping shoulders and grizzled head detached themselves against the blaze of light in the west, and he sauntered down the empty deck and dropped into the chair at her side.

"You're expecting the Barkleys to meet you, I suppose?" he asked.

It was the first time she had heard any one pronounce her daughter's new name, and it occurred to her that her friend, who was shy and inarticulate, had been trying to say it all the way over and had at last shot it out at her only because he felt it must be now or never.

"I don't know. I cabled, of course. But I believe she's at—they're at—his place somewhere."

"Oh, Barkley's; yes, near Lenox, isn't it? But she's sure to come to town to meet you."

He said it so easily and naturally that her own constraint was relieved, and suddenly, before she knew what she meant to do, she had burst out: "She may dislike the idea of seeing people."

Ide, whose absent shortsighted gaze had been fixed on the slowly gliding water, turned in his seat to stare at his companion.

"Who? Leila?" he said with an incredulous laugh.

Mrs. Lidcote flushed to her faded hair and grew pale again. "It took me a long time—to get used to it," she said.

His look grew gently commiserating. "I think you'll

find"—he paused for a word— "that things are different now—altogether easier."

"That's what I've been wondering—ever since we started." She was determined now to speak. She moved nearer, so that their arms touched, and she could drop her voice to a murmur. "You see, it all came on me in a flash. My going off to India and Siam on that long trip kept me away from letters for weeks at a time; and she didn't want to tell me beforehand—oh, I understand that, poor child! You know how good she's always been to me; how she's tried to spare me. And she knew, of course, what a state of horror I'd be in. She knew I'd rush off to her at once and try to stop it. So she never gave me a hint of anything, and she even managed to muzzle Susy Suffern—you know Susy is the one of the family who keeps me informed about things at home. I don't yet see how she prevented Susy's telling me; but she did. And her first letter, the one I got up at Bangkok, simply said the thing was over—the divorce, I mean—and that the very next day she'd—well, I suppose there was no use waiting; and *he* seems to have behaved as well as possible, to have wanted to marry her as much as—"

"Who? Barkley?" he helped her out. "I should say so! Why what do you suppose—" He interrupted himself: "He'll be devoted to her, I assure you."

"Oh, of course; I'm sure he will. He's written me—really beautifully. But it's a terrible strain on a man's devotion. I'm not sure that Leila realizes —"

Ide sounded again his little reassuring laugh. "I'm not sure that you realize. *They're* all right."

It was the very phrase that the young lady in the next seat had applied to the unknown "Leila," and its recurrence on Ide's lips flushed Mrs. Lidcote with fresh courage.

"I wish I knew just what you mean. The two young women next to me—the ones with the wonderful hats—have been talking in the same way."

"What? About Leila?"

"About *a* Leila; I fancied it might be mine. And about

society in general. All their friends seem to be divorced; some of them seem to announce their engagements before they get their decree. One of them—*her* name was Mabel—as far as I could make out, her husband found out that she meant to divorce him by noticing that she wore a new engagement ring."

"Well, you see Leila did everything 'regularly,' as the French say," Ide rejoined.

"Yes; but are these people in society? The people my neighbors talk about?"

He shrugged his shoulders. "It would take an arbitration commission a good many sittings to define the boundaries of society nowadays. But at any rate they're in New York; and I assure you you're *not*; you're farther and farther from it."

"But I've been back there several times to see Leila." She hesitated and looked away from him. Then she brought out slowly: "And I've never noticed—the least change—in—in my own case—"

"Oh," he sounded deprecatingly, and she trembled with the fear of having gone too far. But the hour was past when such scruples could restrain her. She must know where she was and where Leila was. "Mrs. Boulger still cuts me," she brought out with an embarrassed laugh.

"Are you sure? You've probably cut *her*; if not now, at least in the past. And in a cut if you're not first you're nowhere. That's what keeps up so many quarrels."

The word roused Mrs. Lidcote to a renewed sense of realities. "But the Purshes," she said—"The Purshes are so strong! There are so many of them, and they all back each other up, just as my husband's family did. I know what it means to have a clan against one. They're stronger than any number of separate friends. The Purshes will *never* forgive Leila for leaving Horace. Why, his mother opposed his marrying her because of—of me. She tried to get Leila to promise that she wouldn't see me when they went to Europe on their honeymoon. And now she'll say it was my example."

Her companion, vaguely stroking his beard, mused a

moment upon this; then he asked, with seeming irrelevance, "What did Leila say when you wrote that you were coming?"

"She said it wasn't the least necessary, but that I'd better come, because it was the only way to convince me that it wasn't."

"Well, then, that proves she's not afraid of the Purshes."

She breathed a long sigh of remembrance. "Oh, just at first, you know—one never is."

He laid his hand on hers with a gesture of intelligence and pity. "You'll see, you'll see," he said.

A shadow lengthened down the deck before them, and a steward stood there, proffering a Marconigram.

"Oh, now I shall know!" she exclaimed.

She tore the message open, and then let it fall on her knees, dropping her hands on it in silence.

Ide's inquiry roused her: "It's all right?"

"Oh, quite right. Perfectly. She can't come; but she's sending Susy Suffern. She says Susy will explain." After another silence she added, with a sudden gush of bitterness: "As if I needed any explanation!"

She felt Ide's hesitating glance upon her. "She's in the country?"

"Yes. 'Prevented last moment. Longing for you, expecting you. Love from both.' Don't you *see,* the poor darling, that she couldn't face it?"

"No, I don't." He waited. "Do you mean to go to her immediately?"

"It will be too late to catch a train this evening; but I shall take the first tomorrow morning." She considered a moment. "Perhaps it's better. I need a talk with Susy first. She's to meet me at the dock, and I'll take her straight back to the hotel with me."

As she developed this plan, she had the sense that Ide was still thoughtfully, even gravely, considering her. When she ceased, he remained silent a moment; then he said almost ceremoniously: "If your talk with Miss Suffern doesn't last too late, may I come and see you when it's over? I shall be dining at my club, and

I'll call you up at about ten, if I may. I'm off to Chicago on business tomorrow morning, and it would be a satisfaction to know, before I start, that your cousin's been able to reassure you, as I know she will."

He spoke with a shy deliberateness that, even to Mrs. Lidcote's troubled perceptions, sounded a long-silenced note of feeling. Perhaps the breaking down of the barrier of reticence between them had released unsuspected emotions in both. The tone of his appeal moved her curiously and loosened the tight strain of her fears.

"Oh, yes, come—do come," she said, rising. The huge threat of New York was imminent now, dwarfing, under long reaches of embattled masonry, the great deck she stood on and all the little specks of life it carried. One of them, drifting nearer, took the shape of her maid, followed by luggage-laden stewards, and signing to her that it was time to go below. As they descended to the main deck, the throng swept her against Mrs. Lorin Boulger's shoulder, and she heard the ambassadress call out to someone, over the vexed sea of hats: "So sorry! I should have been delighted, but I've promised to spend Sunday with some friends at Lenox."

II

Susy Suffern's explanation did not end till after ten o'clock, and she had just gone when Franklin Ide, who, complying with an old New York tradition, had caused himself to be preceded by a long white box of roses, was shown into Mrs. Lidcote's sitting room.

He came forward with his shy half-humorous smile and, taking her hand, looked at her for a moment without speaking.

"It's all right," he then pronounced.

Mrs. Lidcote returned his smile. "It's extraordinary. Everything's changed. Even Susy had changed; and you know the extent to which Susy used to represent the old New York. There's no old New York left, it seems. She talked in the most amazing way. She snaps her fingers at the Purshes. She told me—*me,* that every woman had a right to happiness and that self-expression was the highest duty. She accused me of misunderstanding Leila; she said my point of view was conventional! She was bursting with pride at having been in the secret, and wearing a brooch that Wilbour Barkley'd given her!"

Franklin Ide had seated himself in the armchair she had pushed forward for him under the electric chandelier. He threw back his head and laughed. "What did I tell you?"

"Yes; but I can't believe that Susy's not mistaken. Poor dear, she has the habit of lost causes; and she may feel that, having stuck to me, she can do no less than stick to Leila."

"But she didn't—did she—openly defy the world for you? She didn't snap her fingers at the Lidcotes?"

Mrs. Lidcote shook her head, still smiling. "No. It was enough to defy *my* family. It was doubtful at one time if they would tolerate her seeing me, and she almost had to disinfect herself after each visit. I believe that at first my sister-in-law wouldn't let the girls come down when Susy dined with her."

"Well, isn't your cousin's present attitude the best possible proof that times have changed?"

"Yes, yes; I know." She leaned forward from her sofa-corner, fixing her eyes on his thin kindly face, which gleamed on her indistinctly through her tears. "If it's true, it's—it's dazzling. She says Leila's perfectly happy. It's as if an angel had gone about lifting gravestones, and the buried people walked again, and the living didn't shrink from them."

"That's about it," he assented.

She drew a deep breath, and sat looking away from him down the long perspective of lamp-fringed streets over which her window hung.

"I can understand how happy you must be," he began at length.

She turned to him impetuously. "Yes, yes; I'm happy. But I'm lonely, too—lonelier than ever. I didn't take up much room in the world before; but now—where is there a corner for me? Oh, since I've begun to confess myself, why shouldn't I go on? Telling you this lifts a gravestone from *me*! You see, before this,

Leila needed me. She was unhappy, and I knew it, and though we hardly ever talked of it I felt that, in a way, the thought that I'd been through the same thing, and down to the dregs of it, helped her. And her needing me helped *me*. And when the news of her marriage came my first thought was that now she'd need me more than ever, that she'd have no one but me to turn to. Yes, under all my distress there was a fierce joy in that. It was so new and wonderful to feel again that there was one person who wouldn't be able to get on without me! And now what you and Susy tell me seems to have taken my child from me; and just at first that's all I can feel."

"Of course it's all you feel." He looked at her musingly. "Why didn't Leila come to meet you?"

"That was really my fault. You see, I'd cabled that I was not sure of being able to get off on the 'Utopia,' and apparently my second cable was delayed, and when she received it she'd already asked some people over Sunday—one or two of her old friends, Susy says. I'm so glad they should have wanted to go to her at once; but naturally I'd rather have been alone with her."

"You still mean to go, then?"

"Oh, I must. Susy wanted to drag me off to Ridgefield with her over Sunday, and Leila sent me word that of course I might go if I wanted to, and that I was not to think of her; but I know how disappointed she would be. Susy said she was afraid I might be upset at her having people to stay, and that, if I minded, she wouldn't urge me to come. But if *they* don't mind, why should I? And of course, if they're willing to go to Leila it must mean—"

"Of course. I'm glad you recognize that," Franklin Ide exclaimed abruptly. He stood up and went over to her, taking her hand with one of his quick gestures. "There's something I want to say to you," he began—

The next morning, in the train, through all the other contending thoughts in Mrs. Lidcote's mind there ran the warm undercurrent of what Franklin Ide had wanted to say to her.

He had wanted, she knew, to say it once before, when, nearly eight years earlier, the hazard of meeting at the end of a rainy autumn in a deserted Swiss hotel had thrown them for a fortnight into unwonted propinquity. They had walked and talked together, borrowed each other's books and newspapers, spent the long chill evenings over the fire in the dim lamplight of her little pitch-pine sitting room; and she had been wonderfully comforted by his presence, and hard frozen places in her had melted, and she had known that she would be desperately sorry when he went. And then, just at the end, in his odd indirect way, he had let her see that it rested with her to have him stay. She could still relive the sleepless night she had given to that discovery. It was preposterous, of course, to think of repaying his devotion by accepting such a sacrifice; but how to find reasons to convince him? She could not bear to let him think her less touched, less inclined to him than she was: the generosity of his love deserved that she should repay it with the truth. Yet how let him see what she felt, and yet refuse what he offered? How confess to him what had been on her lips when he made the offer: "I've seen what it did to one man; and there must never, never be another"? The tacit ignoring of her past had been the element in which their friendship lived, and she could not suddenly, to him of all men, begin to talk of herself like a guilty woman in a play. Somehow, in the end, she had managed it, had averted a direct explanation, had made him understand that her life was over, that she existed only for her daughter, and that a more definite word from him would have been almost a breach of delicacy. She was so used to behaving as if her life were over! And, at any rate, he had taken her hint, and she had been able to spare her sensitiveness and his. The next year, when he came to Florence to see her, they met again in the old friendly way; and that till now had continued to be the tenor of their intimacy.

And now, suddenly and unexpectedly, he had brought up the question again, directly this time, and in such a form that she could not evade it: putting the renewal of his plea, after so long an interval, on the ground that, on her own showing, her chief argument against it no longer existed.

"You tell me Leila's happy. If she's happy, she doesn't need you—need you, that is, in the same way as before. You wanted, I know, to be always in reach, always free and available if she should suddenly call you to her or take refuge with you. I understood that—I respected it. I didn't urge my case because I saw it was useless. You couldn't, I understand well enough, have felt free to take such happiness as life with me might give you while she was unhappy, and, as you imagined, with no hope of release. Even then I didn't feel as you did about it; I understood better the trend of things here. But ten years ago the change hadn't really come; and I had no way of convincing you that it was coming. Still, I always fancied that Leila might not think her case was closed, and so I chose to think that ours wasn't either. Let me go on thinking so, at any rate, till you've seen her, and confirmed with your own eyes what Susy Suffern tells you."

III

All through what Susy Suffern told and retold her during their four-hours' flight to the hills this plea of Ide's kept coming back to Mrs. Lidcote. She did not yet know what she felt as to its bearing on her own fate, but it was something on which her confused thoughts could stay themselves amid the welter of new impressions, and she was inexpressibly glad that he had said what he had, and said it at that particular moment. It helped her to hold fast to her identity in the rush of strange names and new categories that her cousin's talk poured out on her.

With the progress of the journey Miss Suffern's communications grew more and more amazing. She was like a cicerone preparing the mind of an inexperienced traveler for the marvels about to burst on it.

"You won't know Leila. She's had her pearls reset. Sargent's to paint her. Oh, and I was to tell you that she hopes you won't mind being the least bit squeezed over Sunday. The house was built by Wilbour's father, you know, and it's rather old-fashioned—only ten spare bedrooms. Of course that's small for what they mean to do, and she'll show you the new plans they've had made. Their idea is to keep the present house as a wing. She told me to explain—she's so dreadfully sorry not to be able to give you a sitting room just at first. They're thinking of Egypt for next winter, unless, of course, Wilbour gets his appointment. Oh, didn't she write you about that? Why, he wants Rome, you know—the second secretaryship. Or, rather, he wanted England; but Leila insisted that if they went abroad she must be near you. And of course what she says is law. Oh, they quite hope they'll get it. You see Horace's uncle is in the Cabinet—one of the assistant secretaries—and I believe he has a good deal of pull—"

"Horace's uncle? You mean Wilbour's, I suppose," Mrs. Lidcote interjected, with a gasp of which a fraction was given to Miss Suffern's flippant use of the language.

"Wilbour's? No, I don't. I mean Horace's. There's no bad feeling between them, I assure you. Since Horace's engagement was announced—you didn't know Horace was engaged? Why, he's marrying one of Bishop Thorbury's girls; the red-haired one who wrote the novel that everyone's talking about. *This Flesh of Mine.* They're to be married in the cathedral. Of course Horace *can*, because it was Leila who—but, as I say, there's not the *least* feeling, and Horace wrote himself to his uncle about Wilbour."

Mrs. Lidcote's thoughts fled back to what she had said to Ide the day before on the deck of the "Utopia." "I didn't take up much room before, but now where is there a corner for me?" Where indeed in this crowded, topsy-turvy world, with its headlong changes and helter-skelter readjustments, its new tolerances and indifferences and accommodations, was there room for a character fashioned by slower sterner processes and a life broken under their inexorable pressure? And then, in a flash, she viewed the chaos from a new angle, and order seemed to move upon the void. If the old processes were changed, her case was changed with them; she, too, was a part of the general readjustment, a tiny

fragment of the new pattern worked out in bolder freer harmonies.
Since her daughter had no penalty to pay, was not she herself
released by the same stroke? The rich arrears of youth and joy
were gone; but was there not time enough left to accumulate new
stores of happiness? That, of course, was what Franklin Ide had
felt and had meant her to feel. He had seen at once what the
change in her daughter's situation would make in her view of her
own. It was almost—wondrously enough!—as if Leila's folly has
been the means of vindicating hers.

Everything else for the moment faded for Mrs. Lidcote
in the glow of her daughter's embrace. It was unnatural, it was
almost terrifying, to find herself standing on a strange threshold,
under an unknown roof, in a big hall full of pictures, flowers,
firelight, and hurrying servants, and in this spacious unfamiliar
confusion to discover Leila, bareheaded, laughing, authoritative,
with a strange young man jovially echoing her welcome and trans-
mitting her orders; but once Mrs. Lidcote had her child on her
breast, and her child's "It's all right, you old darling!" in her ears,
every other feeling was lost in the deep sense of well-being that
only Leila's hug could give.

The sense was still with her, warming her veins and
pleasantly fluttering her heart, as she went up to her room after
luncheon. A little constrained by the presence of visitors, and not
altogether sorry to defer for a few hours the "long talk" with her
daughter for which she somehow felt herself tremulously unready,
she had withdrawn, on the plea of fatigue, to the bright luxurious
bedroom into which Leila had again and again apologized for having
been obliged to squeeze her. The room was bigger and finer than
any in her small apartment in Florence; but it was not the standard of affluence implied in her daughter's tone about it that
chiefly struck her, nor yet the finish and complexity of its appointments. It was the look it shared with the rest of the house, and
with the perspective of the gardens beneath its windows, of being
part of an "establishment"—of something solid, avowed, founded

on sacraments and precedents and principles. There was nothing about the place, or about Leila and Wilbour, that suggested either passion or peril: their relation seemed as comfortable as their furniture and as respectable as their balance at the bank.

This was, in the whole confusing experience, the thing that confused Mrs. Lidcote most, that gave her at once the deepest feeling of security for Leila and the strongest sense of apprehension for herself. Yes, there was something oppressive in the completeness and compactness of Leila's well-being. Ide had been right: her daughter did not need her. Leila, with her first embrace, had unconsciously attested the fact in the same phrase as Ide himself and as the two young women with the hats. "It's all right, you old darling!" she had said: and her mother sat alone, trying to fit herself into the new scheme of things which such a certainty betokened.

Her first distinct feeling was one of irrational resentment. If such a change was to come, why had it not come sooner? Here was she, a woman not yet old, who had paid with the best years of her life for the theft of the happiness that her daughter's contemporaries were taking as their due. There was no sense, no sequence, in it. She had had what she wanted, but she had had to pay too much for it. She had had to pay the last bitterest price of learning that love has a price; that it is worth so much and no more. She had known the anguish of watching the man she loved discover this first, and of reading the discovery in his eyes. It was a part of her history that she had not trusted herself to think of for a long time past: she always took a big turn about that haunted corner. But now, at the sight of the young man downstairs, so openly and jovially Leila's, she was overwhelmed at the senseless waste of her own adventure, and wrung with the irony of perceiving that the success or failure of the deepest human experiences may hang on a matter of chronology.

Then gradually the thought of Ide returned to her. "I chose to think that our case wasn't closed," he had said. She had been deeply touched by that. To everyone else her case had been closed so long! *Finis* was scrawled all over her. But here was one man who had believed and waited, and what if what he believed in and waited for were coming true? If Leila's "all right" should really foreshadow hers?

As yet, of course, it was impossible to tell. She had fancied, indeed, when she entered the drawing room before luncheon, that a too-sudden hush had fallen on the assembled group of Leila's friends, on the slender vociferous young women and the lounging golf-stockinged young men. They had all received her politely, with the kind of petrified politeness that may be either a tribute to age or a protest at laxity; but to them, of course, she must be an old woman because she was Leila's mother, and in a society so dominated by youth the mere presence of maturity was a constraint.

One of the young girls, however, had presently emerged from the group, and, attaching herself to Mrs. Lidcote, had listened to her with a blue gaze of admiration which gave the older woman a sudden happy consciousness of her long-forgotten social graces. It was agreeable to find herself attracting this young Charlotte Wynn, whose mother had been among her closest friends, and in whom something of the soberness and softness of the earlier manners had survived. But the little colloquy, broken up by the announcement of luncheon, could of course result in nothing more definite than this reminiscent emotion.

No, she could not yet tell how her own case was to be fitted into the new order of things; but there were more people—"older people" Leila had put it—arriving by the afternoon train, and that evening at dinner she would doubtless be able to judge. She began to wonder nervously who the newcomers might be. Probably she would be spared the embarrassment of finding old acquaintances among them; but it was odd that her daughter had mentioned no names.

Leila had proposed that, later in the afternoon, Wilbour should take her mother for a drive: she said she wanted them to have a "nice, quiet talk." But Mrs. Lidcote wished her talk with Leila to come first, and had, moreover, at luncheon, caught stray allusions to an impending tennis match in which her son-in-law was engaged. Her fatigue had been a sufficient pretext for declining the drive, and she had begged Leila to think of her as peacefully resting in her room till such time as they could snatch their quiet moment.

"Before tea, then, you duck!" Leila with a last kiss had decided; and presently Mrs. Lidcote, through her open window, had heard the fresh loud voices of her daughter's visitors chiming across the gardens from the tennis court.

I V

Leila had come and gone, and they had had their talk. It had not lasted as long as Mrs. Lidcote wished, for in the middle of it Leila had been summoned to the telephone to receive an important message from town, and had sent word to her mother that she couldn't come back just then, as one of the young ladies had been called away unexpectedly and arrangements had to be made for her departure. But the mother and daughter had had almost an hour together, and Mrs. Lidcote was happy. She had never seen Leila so tender, so solicitous. The only thing that troubled her was the very excess of this solicitude, the exaggerated expression of her daughter's annoyance that their first moments together should have been marred by the presence of strangers.

"Not strangers to me, darling, since they're friends of yours," her mother had assured her.

"Yes; but I know your feeling, you queer wild mother. I know how you've always hated people." (*Hated people!* Had Leila forgotten why?) "And that's why I told Susy that if you preferred to go with her to Ridgefield on Sunday I should perfectly understand, and patiently wait for our good hug. But you didn't really mind them at luncheon, did you, dearest?"

Mrs. Lidcote, at that, had suddenly thrown a startled look at her daughter. "I don't mind things of that kind any longer," she had simply answered.

"But that doesn't console me for having exposed you to the bother of it, for having let you come here when I ought to have *ordered* you off to Ridgefield with Susy. If Susy hadn't been stupid she'd have made you go there with her. I hate to think of you up here all alone."

Again Mrs. Lidcote tried to read something more than a rather obtuse devotion in her daughter's radiant gaze. "I'm glad to have had a rest this afternoon, dear; and later—"

"Oh, yes, later, when all this fuss is over, we'll more than make up for it, shan't we, you precious darling?" And at this point Leila had been summoned to the telephone, leaving Mrs. Lidcote to her conjectures.

These were still floating before her in cloudy uncertainty when Miss Suffern tapped at the door.

"You've come to take me down to tea? I'd forgotten how late it was," Mrs. Lidcote exclaimed.

Miss Suffern, a plump peering little woman, with prim hair and a conciliatory smile, nervously adjusted the pendent bugles of her elaborate black dress. Miss Suffern was always in mourning, and always commemorating the demise of distant relatives by wearing the discarded wardrobe of their next of kin. "It isn't *exactly* mourning," she would say; "but it's the only stitch of black poor Julia had—and of course George was only my mother's step-cousin."

As she came forward Mrs. Lidcote found herself humorously wondering whether she were mourning Horace Pursh's divorce in one of his mother's old black satins.

"Oh, *did* you mean to go down for tea?" Susy Suffern peered at her, a little fluttered. "Leila sent me up to keep you company. She thought it would be cozier for you to stay here. She was afraid you were feeling rather tired."

"I was; but I've had the whole afternoon to rest in. And this wonderful sofa to help me."

"Leila told me to tell you that she'd rush up for a minute before dinner, after everybody had arrived; but the train is always dreadfully late. She's in despair at not giving you a sitting room; she wanted to know if I thought you really minded."

"Of course I don't mind. It's not like Leila to think I should." Mrs. Lidcote drew aside to make way for the housemaid, who appeared in the doorway bearing a table spread with a bewildering variety of tea cakes.

"Leila saw to it herself," Miss Suffern murmured as the door closed. "Her one idea is that you should feel happy here."

It struck Mrs. Lidcote as one more mark of the subverted state of things that her daughter's solicitude should find expression in the multiplicity of sandwiches and the piping hotness of muffins; but then everything that had happened since her arrival seemed to increase her confusion.

The note of a motor horn down the drive gave another turn to her thoughts. "Are those the new arrivals already?" she asked.

"Oh, dear, no; they won't be here till after seven." Miss Suffern craned her head from the window to catch a glimpse of the motor. "It must be Charlotte leaving."

"Was it the little Wynn girl who was called away in a hurry? I hope it's not on account of illness."

"Oh, no; I believe there was some mistake about dates. Her mother telephoned her that she was expected at the Stepleys, at Fishkill, and she had to be rushed over to Albany to catch a train."

Mrs. Lidcote meditated. "I'm sorry. She's a charming young thing. I hoped I should have another talk with her this evening after dinner."

"Yes; it's too bad." Miss Suffern's gaze grew vague. "You *do* look tired, you know," she continued, seating herself at the tea table and preparing to dispense its delicacies. "You must go straight back to your sofa and let me wait on you. The excitement has told on you more than you think, and you mustn't fight against it any longer. Just stay quietly up here and let yourself go. You'll have Leila to yourself on Monday."

Mrs. Lidcote received the teacup which her cousin proffered, but showed no other disposition to obey her injunctions. For a moment she stirred her tea in silence; then she asked: "Is it your idea that I should stay quietly up here till Monday?"

Miss Suffern set down her cup with a gesture so sudden that it endangered an adjacent plate of scones. When she had assured herself of the safety of the scones she looked up with a fluttered laugh. "Perhaps, dear, by tomorrow you'll be feeling differently. The air here, you know—"

"Yes, I know." Mrs. Lidcote bent forward to help herself to a scone. "Who's arriving this evening?" she asked.

Miss Suffern frowned and peered. "You know my wretched head for names. Leila told me—but there are so many—"

"So many? She didn't tell me she expected a big party."

"Oh, not big: but rather outside of her little group. And of course, as it's the first time, she's a little excited at having the older set."

"The older set? Our contemporaries, you mean?"

"Why—yes." Miss Suffern paused as if to gather herself up for a leap. "The Ashton Gileses," she brought out.

"The Ashton Gileses? Really? I shall be glad to see Mary Giles again. It must be eighteen years," said Mrs. Lidcote steadily.

"Yes," Miss Suffern gasped, precipitately refilling her cup.

"The Ashton Gileses; and who else?"

"Well, the Sam Fresbies. But the most important person, of course, is Mrs. Lorin Boulger."

"Mrs. Boulger? Leila didn't tell me she was coming."

"Didn't she? I suppose she forgot everything when she saw you. But the party was got up for Mrs. Boulger. You see, it's very important that she should—well, take a fancy to Leila and Wilbour; his being appointed to Rome virtually depends on it. And you know Leila insists on Rome in order to be near you. So she asked Mary Giles, who's intimate with the Boulgers, if the visit couldn't possibly be arranged; and Mary's cable caught Mrs. Boulger at Cherbourg. She's to be only a fortnight in America; and getting her to come directly here was rather a triumph."

"Yes; I see it was," said Mrs. Lidcote.

"You know, she's rather—rather fussy; and Mary was a little doubtful if—"

"If she would, on account of Leila?" Mrs. Lidcote murmured.

"Well, yes. In her official position. But luckily she's a friend of the Barkleys. And finding the Gileses and Fresbies here will make it all right. The times have changed!" Susy Suffern indulgently summed up.

Mrs. Lidcote smiled. "Yes; a few years ago it would have seemed improbable that I should ever again be dining with Mary Giles and Harriet Fresbie and Mrs. Lorin Boulger."

Miss Suffern did not at the moment seem disposed to enlarge upon this theme; and after an interval of silence Mrs. Lidcote suddenly resumed: "Do they know I'm here, by the way?"

The effect of her question was to produce in Miss Suffern an exaggerated excess of peering and frowning. She twitched the tea things about, fingered her bugles, and, looking at the clock, exclaimed amazedly: "Mercy! Is it seven already?"

"Not that it can make any difference, I suppose," Mrs. Lidcote continued. "But did Leila tell them I was coming?"

Miss Suffern looked at her with pain. "Why, you don't suppose, dearest, that Leila would do anything—"

Mrs. Lidcote went on: "For, of course, it's of the first importance, as you say, that Mrs. Lorin Boulger should be favorably impressed, in order that Wilbour may have the best possible chance of getting Rome."

"I *told* Leila you'd feel that, dear. You see, it's actually on *your* account—so that they may get a post near you—that Leila invited Mrs. Boulger."

"Yes, I see that." Mrs. Lidcote, abruptly rising from her seat, turned her eyes to the clock. "But, as you say, it's getting late. Oughtn't we to dress for dinner?"

Miss Suffern, at the suggestion, stood up also, an agitated hand among her bugles. "I do wish I could persuade you to stay up here this evening. I'm sure Leila'd be happier if you would. Really, you're much too tired to come down."

"What nonsense, Susy!" Mrs. Lidcote spoke with a

sudden sharpness, her hand stretched to the bell. "When do we dine? At half-past eight? Then I must really send you packing. At my age it takes time to dress."

Miss Suffern, thus projected toward the threshold, lingered there to repeat: "Leila'll never forgive herself if you make an effort you're not up to." But Mrs. Lidcote smiled on her without answering, and the icy light-wave propelled her through the door.

V

Mrs. Lidcote, though she had made the gesture of ringing for her maid, had not done so.

When the door closed, she continued to stand motionless in the middle of her soft spacious room. The fire which had been kindled at twilight danced on the brightness of silver and mirrors and sober gilding; and the sofa toward which she had been urged by Miss Suffern heaped up its cushions in inviting proximity to a table laden with new books and papers. She could not recall having ever been more luxuriously housed, or having ever had so strange a sense of being out alone, under the night, in a wind-beaten plain. She sat down by the fire and thought.

A knock on the door made her lift her head, and she saw her daughter on the threshold. The intricate ordering of Leila's fair hair and the flying folds of her dressing gown showed that she had interrupted her dressing to hasten to her mother; but once in the room she paused a moment, smiling uncertainly, as though she had forgotten the object of her haste.

Mrs. Lidcote rose to her feet. "Time to dress, dearest? Don't scold! I shan't be late."

"To dress?" Leila stood before her with a puzzled look. "Why, I thought, dear—I mean, I hoped you'd decided just to stay here quietly and rest."

Her mother smiled. "But I've been resting all the afternoon!"

"Yes, but—you know you *do* look tired. And when Susy told me just now that you meant to make the effort—"

"You came to stop me?"

"I came to tell you that you needn't feel in the least obliged—"

"Of course. I understand that."

There was a pause during which Leila, vaguely averting herself from her mother's scrutiny, drifted toward the dressing table and began to disturb the symmetry of the brushes and bottles laid out on it. "Do your visitors know that I'm here?" Mrs. Lidcote suddenly went on.

"Do they—of course—why, naturally," Leila rejoined, absorbed in trying to turn the stopper of a salts bottle.

"Then won't they think it odd if I don't appear?"

"Oh, not in the least, dearest. I assure you they'll *all* understand." Leila laid down the bottle and turned back to her mother, her face alight with reassurance.

Mrs. Lidcote stood motionless, her head erect, her smiling eyes on her daughter's. "Will they think it odd if I *do*?"

Leila stopped short, her lips half parted to reply. As she paused, the color stole over her bare neck, swept up to her throat, and burst into flame in her cheeks. Thence it sent its devastating crimson up to her very temples, to the lobes of her ears, to the edges of her eyelids, beating all over her in fiery waves, as if fanned by some imperceptible wind.

Mrs. Lidcote silently watched the conflagration; then she turned away her eyes with a slight laugh. "I only meant that I was afraid it might upset the arrangement of your dinner table if I didn't come down. If you can assure me that it won't, I believe I'll take you at your word and go back to this irresistible sofa." She paused, as if waiting for her daughter to speak; then she held out her arms. "Run off and dress, dearest; and don't have me on your mind." She clasped Leila close, pressing a long kiss on the last afterglow of her subsiding blush. "I do feel the least bit overdone, and if it won't inconvenience you to have me drop out of things, I believe I'll basely take to my bed and stay there till your party scatters. And now run off, or you'll be late; and make my excuses to them all."

VI

The Barkleys' visitors had dispersed, and Mrs. Lidcote, completely restored by her two days' rest, found herself, on the following Monday, alone with her children and Miss Suffern.

There was a note of jubilation in the air, for the party had "gone off" so extraordinarily well, and so completely, as it appeared, to the satisfaction of Mrs. Lorin Boulger, that Wilbour's early appointment to Rome was almost to be counted on. So certain did this seem that the prospect of a prompt reunion mitigated the distress with which Leila learned of her mother's decision to return almost immediately to Italy. No one understood this decision; it seemed to Leila absolutely unintelligible that Mrs. Lidcote should not stay on with them till their own fate was fixed, and Wilbour echoed her astonishment.

"Why shouldn't you, as Leila says, wait here till we can all pack up and go together?"

Mrs. Lidcote smiled her gratitude with her refusal. "After all, it's not yet sure that you'll be packing up."

"Oh, you ought to have seen Wilbour with Mrs. Boulger," Leila triumphed.

"No, you ought to have seen Leila with her," Leila's husband exulted.

Miss Suffern enthusiastically appended: "I *do* think inviting Harriet Fresbie was a stroke of genius!"

"Oh, we'll be with you soon," Leila laughed. "So soon that it's really foolish to separate."

But Mrs. Lidcote held out with the quiet firmness which her daughter knew it was useless to oppose. After her long months in India, it was really imperative, she declared, that she should get back to Florence and see what was happening to her little place there; and she had been so comfortable on the "Utopia" that she had a fancy to return by the same ship. There was nothing for it, therefore, but to acquiesce in her decision and keep her with them till the afternoon before the day of the "Utopia's" sailing. This arrangement fitted in with certain projects which, during her two days' seclusion, Mrs. Lidcote had silently matured. It had become to her of the first importance to get away as soon as she could, and the little place in Florence, which held her past in every fold of its curtains and between every page of its books, seemed now to her the one spot where that past would be endurable to look upon.

She was not unhappy during the intervening days. The sight of Leila's well-being, the sense of Leila's tenderness, were, after all, what she had come for; and of these she had had full measure. Leila had never been happier or more tender; and the contemplation of her bliss, and the enjoyment of her affection, were an absorbing occupation for her mother. But they were also a sharp strain on certain overtightened chords, and Mrs. Lidcote, when at last she found herself alone in the New York hotel to which she had returned the night before embarking, had the feeling that she had just escaped with her life from the clutch of a giant hand.

She had refused to let her daughter come to town with her; she had even rejected Susy Suffern's company. She wanted no viaticum but that of her own thoughts; and she let these come to her without shrinking from them as she sat in the same high-hung sitting room in which, just a week before, she and Franklin Ide had had their memorable talk.

She had promised her friend to let him hear from her, but she had not kept her promise. She knew that he had probably come back from Chicago, and that if he learned of her sudden decision to return to Italy it would be impossible for her not to see him before sailing; and as she wished above all things not to see him she had kept silent, intending to send him a letter from the steamer.

There was no reason why she should wait till then to write it. The actual moment was more favorable, and the task, though not agreeable, would at least bridge over an hour of her lonely evening. She went up to the writing table, drew out a sheet of paper and began to write his name. And as she did so, the door opened and he came in.

The words she met him with were the last she could have imagined herself saying when they had parted. "How in the world did you know that I was here?"

He caught her meaning in a flash. "You didn't want me to, then?" He stood looking at her. "I suppose I ought to have taken your silence as meaning that. But I happened to meet Mrs. Wynn, who is stopping here, and she asked me to dine with her and Charlotte, and Charlotte's young man. They told me they'd seen you arriving this afternoon, and I couldn't help coming up."

There was a pause between them, which Mrs. Lidcote at last surprisingly broke with the exclamation: "Ah, she *did* recognize me, then!"

"Recognize you?" He stared. "Why—"

"Oh, I saw she did, though she never moved an eyelid. I saw it by Charlotte's blush. The child has the prettiest blush. I saw that her mother wouldn't let her speak to me."

Ide put down his hat with an impatient laugh. "Hasn't Leila cured you of your delusions?"

She looked at him intently. "Then you don't think Margaret Wynn meant to cut me?"

"I think your ideas are absurd."

She paused for a perceptible moment without taking this up; then she said, at a tangent: "I'm sailing tomorrow early. I meant to write to you—there's the letter I'd begun."

Ide followed her gesture, and then turned his eyes back to her face. "You didn't mean to see me, then, or even to let me know that you were going till you'd left?"

"I felt it would be easier to explain to you in a letter—"

"What in God's name is there to explain?" She made no reply, and he pressed on: "It can't be that you're worried about Leila, for Charlotte Wynn told me she'd been there last week, and there was a big party arriving when she left: Fresbies and Gileses, and Mrs. Lorin Boulger—all the board of examiners! If Leila has passed *that,* she's got her degree."

Mrs. Lidcote had dropped down into a corner of the sofa where she had sat during their talk of the week before. "I was stupid," she began abruptly. "I ought to have gone to Ridgefield with Susy. I didn't see till afterward that I was expected to."

"You were expected to?"

"Yes. Oh, it wasn't Leila's fault. She suffered—poor darling; she was distracted. But she'd asked her party before she knew I was arriving."

"Oh, as to that—" Ide drew a deep breath of relief. "I can understand that it must have been a disappointment not to have you to herself just at first. But, after all, you were among old friends or their children: the Gileses and Fresbies—and little Charlotte Wynn." He paused a moment before the last name, and scrutinized her hesitatingly. "Even if they came at the wrong time, you must have been glad to see them all at Leila's."

She gave him back his look with a faint smile. "I didn't see them."

"You didn't see them?"

"No. That is, excepting little Charlotte Wynn. That child is exquisite. We had a talk before luncheon the day I arrived. But when her mother found out that I was staying in the house she telephoned her to leave immediately, and so I didn't see her again."

The color rushed to Ide's sallow face. "I don't know where you get such ideas!"

She pursued, as if she had not heard him: "Oh, and I saw Mary Giles for a minute too. Susy Suffern brought her up to my room the last evening, after dinner, when all the others were at bridge. She meant it kindly—but it wasn't much use."

"But what were you doing in your room in the evening after dinner?"

"Why, you see, when I found out my mistake in coming,—how embarrassing it was for Leila, I mean—I simply told her I was very tired, and preferred to stay upstairs till the party was over."

Ide, with a groan, struck his hand against the arm of his chair. "I wonder how much of all this you simply imagined!"

"I didn't imagine the fact of Harriet Fresbie's not even asking if she might see me when she knew I was in the house. Nor of Mary Giles's getting Susy, at the eleventh hour, to smuggle her up to my room when the others wouldn't know where she'd gone;

nor poor Leila's ghastly fear lest Mrs. Lorin Boulger, for whom the party was given, should guess I was in the house, and prevent her husband's giving Wilbour the second secretaryship because she'd been obliged to spend a night under the same roof with his mother-in-law!"

Ide continued to drum on his chair arm with exasperated fingers. "You don't *know* that any of the acts you describe are due to the causes you suppose."

Mrs. Lidcote paused before replying, as if honestly trying to measure the weight of this argument. Then she said in a low tone: "I know that Leila was in an agony lest I should come down to dinner the first night. And it was for me she was afraid, not for herself. Leila is never afraid for herself."

"But the conclusions you draw are simply preposterous. There are narrow-minded women everywhere, but the women who were at Leila's knew perfectly well that their going there would give her a sort of social sanction, and if they were willing that she should have it, why on earth should they want to withhold it from you?"

"That's what I told myself a week ago, in this very room after my first talk with Susy Suffern." She lifted a misty smile to his anxious eyes. "That's why I listened to what you said to me the same evening, and why your arguments half-convinced me, and made me think that what had been possible for Leila might not be impossible for me. If the new dispensation had come, why not for me as well as for the others? I can't tell you the flight my imagination took!"

Franklin Ide rose from his seat and crossed the room to a chair near her sofa-corner. "All I cared about was that it seemed—for the moment—to be carrying you toward me," he said.

"I cared about that, too. That's why I meant to go away without seeing you." They gave each other grave look for look. "Because, you see, I was mistaken," she went on. "We were both mistaken. You say it's preposterous that the women who didn't object to accepting Leila's hospitality should have objected to meeting me under her roof. And so it is; but I begin to understand why. It's simply that society is much too busy to revise its own judgments. Probably no one in the house with me stopped to consider that my case and Leila's were identical. They only remembered that I'd done something which, at the time I did it, was condemned by society. My case had been passed on and classified: I'm the woman who has been cut for nearly twenty years. The older people have half-forgotten why, and the younger ones have never really known: it's simply become a tradition to cut me. And traditions that have lost their meaning are the hardest of all to destroy."

Ide sat motionless while she spoke. As she ended, he stood up with a short laugh and walked across the room to the window. Outside, the immense black prospect of New York, strung with its myriad lines of light, stretched away into the smoky edges of the night. He showed it to her with a gesture.

"What do you suppose such words as you've been using—'society,' 'tradition,' and the rest—mean to all the life out there?"

She came and stood by him in the window. "Less than nothing, of course. But you and I are not out there. We're shut up in a little tight round of habit and association, just as we're shut up in this room. Remember, I thought I'd got out of it once; but what really happened was that the other people went out, and left me in the same little room. The only difference was that I was there alone. Oh, I've made it habitable now, I'm used to it; but I've lost any illusions I may have had as to an angel's opening the door."

Ide again laughed impatiently. "Well, if the door won't open, why not let another prisoner in? At least it would be less of a solitude—"

She turned from the dark window back into the vividly lighted room.

"It would be more of a prison. You forget that I know all about that. We're all imprisoned, of course—all of us middling people, who don't carry our freedom in our brains. But we've accommodated ourselves to our different cells, and if we're moved suddenly into the new ones we're likely to find a stone wall where we thought there was thin air, and to knock ourselves senseless against it. I saw a man do that once."

Ide, leaning with folded arms against the window frame, watched her in silence as she moved restlessly about the room, gathering together some scattered books and tossing a handful of torn letters into the paper basket. When she ceased, he rejoined: "All you say is based on preconceived theories. Why didn't you put them to the test by coming down to meet your old friends? Don't you see the inference they would naturally draw from your hiding yourself when they arrived? It looked as though you were afraid of them—or as though you hadn't forgiven them. Either way, you put them in the wrong instead of waiting to let them put you in the right. If Leila had buried herself in a desert do you suppose society would have gone to fetch her out? You say you were afraid for Leila and that she was afraid for you. Don't you see what all these complications of feeling mean? Simply that you were too nervous at the moment to let things happen naturally, just as you're too nervous now to judge them rationally." He paused and turned his eyes to her face. "Don't try to just yet. Give yourself a little more time. Give *me* a little more time. I've always known it would take time."

He moved nearer, and she let him have her hand. With the grave kindness of his face so close above her she felt like a child roused out of frightened dreams and finding a light in the room.

"Perhaps you're right—" she heard herself begin; then something within her clutched her back, and her hand fell away from him.

"I know I'm right: trust me," he urged. "We'll talk of this in Florence soon."

She stood before him, feeling with despair his kindness, his patience and his unreality. Everything he said seemed like a painted gauze let down between herself and the real facts of life; and a sudden desire seized her to tear the gauze into shreds.

She drew back and looked at him with a smile of superficial reassurance. "You *are* right—about not talking any longer now. I'm nervous and tired, and it would do no good. I brood over things too much. As you say, I must try not to shrink from people." She turned away and glanced at the clock. "Why, it's only ten! If I send you off I shall begin to brood again; and if you stay we shall go on talking about the same thing. Why shouldn't we go down and see Margaret Wynn for half an hour?"

She spoke lightly and rapidly, her brilliant eyes on his face. As she watched him, she saw it change, as if her smile had thrown a too vivid light upon it.

"Oh, no—not tonight!" he exclaimed.

"Not tonight? Why, what other night have I, when I'm off at dawn? Besides, I want to show you at once that I mean to be more sensible—that I'm not going to be afraid of people any more. And I should really like another glimpse of little Charlotte." He stood before her, his hand in his beard, with the gesture he had in moments of perplexity. "Come!" she ordered him gaily, turning to the door.

He followed her and laid his hand on her arm. "Don't you think—hadn't you better let me go first and see? They told me they'd had a tiring day at the dressmaker's. I dare say they have gone to bed."

"But you said they'd a young man of Charlotte's dining with them. Surely he wouldn't have left by ten? At any rate, I'll go down with you and see. It takes so long if one sends a servant first." She put him gently aside, and then paused as a new thought struck her. "Or wait; my maid's in the next room. I'll tell her to go and ask if Margaret will receive me. Yes, that's much the best way."

She turned back and went toward the door that led to her bedroom; but before she could open it she felt Ide's quick touch again.

"I believe—I remember now—Charlotte's young man was suggesting that they should all go out—to a music hall or something of the sort. I'm sure—I'm positively sure that you won't find them."

Her hand dropped from the door, his dropped from her

281

arm, and as they drew back and faced each other she saw the blood rise slowly through his sallow skin, redden his neck and ears, encroach upon the edges of his beard, and settle in dull patches under his kind troubled eyes. She had seen the same blush on another face, and the same impulse of compassion she had then felt made her turn her gaze away again.

A knock on the door broke the silence, and a porter put his head into the room.

"It's only just to know how many pieces there'll be to go down to the steamer in the morning."

With the words she felt that the veil of painted gauze was torn in tatters, and that she was moving again among the grim edges of reality.

"Oh, dear," she exclaimed, "I never *can* remember! Wait a minute; I shall have to ask my maid."

She opened her bedroom door and called out: "Annette!"

William Trevor

Though English and living in London, the women in William Trevor's "Her Mother's Daughter" seem infused, like all his characters, by what Trevor calls "the Irish circumstance." In this story, the daughter vainly attempts to distance herself from her overbearing mother to define herself by opposition to her mother's rites and manners; instead (and this may be part of what Trevor means by "circumstance"), she runs full circle, finding in her mother's end her own beginning.

"Born Irish," wrote Trevor, "I observe the world through Irish sensibilities, take for granted an Irish way of doing things, am marked by small idiosyncrasies of behaviour and accent, and am reminded of familiarities of early environment when I'm separated from them. The bee-loud glade and the linnet's wings of Yeats's lament, the Mountains of Mourne sweeping down to the sea, are sweet nourishment for the exile. Sweeter still the aeroplane touching down at Dublin or Cork, the car crawling on to the quays at Rosslare. When the green jerseys swarm on to the pitch I will them passionately on. When an atrocity is an Irish one I am ashamed."

HER MOTHER'S DAUGHTER

william trevor

her mother considered it ill-bred to eat sweets on the street, and worse to eat fruit or ice-cream. Her mother was tidy, and required tidiness in others. She peeled an apple in a particular way, keeping the peel in one long piece, as though it were important to do so. Her mother rarely smiled.

Her father, now dead, had been a lexicographer: a small, abstracted man who would not have noticed the eating of food on the street, not even slices of meat or peas from their pods. Most of the time he hadn't noticed Helena either. He died on her eighth birthday.

Her mother had always ruled the household. Tall and neat and greyly dressed, she had achieved her position of command without resort to anger or dictatorial speech; she did not say much, and what she did say she never found necessary to repeat. A look informed the miscreant, indicating a button undone, an unwashed hand. Helena, possessing neither brother nor sister, was the only miscreant.

The house where she and her mother lived was in a southwestern suburb of London. Next door on one side there was a fat widow, Mrs Archingford, who dyed her hair a garish shade of red. On the other an elderly couple were for ever bickering in their garden. Helena's mother did not acknowledge the presence of Mrs Archingford, who arrived at the house next door when Helena was nine; but she had written a note to the elderly man to request him to keep his voice down, a plea that caused him to raise it even more.

Helena played mainly by herself. Beneath the heavy mahogany of the dining-room table she cut the hair of Samson while he slept, then closed her eyes while the table collapsed around her, its great ribbed legs and the polished surface from which all meals were eaten splintering into fragments. The multitude in the temple screamed, their robes wet with blood, Children died, women wept.

'What are you doing, Helena?' her mother questioned her. 'Why are you muttering?'

Helena told a lie, saying she'd been singing, because she felt ashamed: her mother would not easily understand if she mentioned Delilah. She played outside on a narrow concrete path that ran between the rockery and the wooden fence at the bottom of the garden, where no one could see her from the windows. 'Now, here's a book,' her mother said, finding her with snails arranged in a semi-circle. Helena washed her hands, re tied the ribbon in her hair, and sat in the sitting-room to read *Teddy's Button*.

Few people visited the house, for Helena's mother did not go in for friends. But once a year Helena was put in a taxi-cab which drove her to her grandparents on her father's side, the only grandparents she knew about. They were a grinning couple who made a fuss of her, small like her father had been, always jumping up and down at the tea table, passing plates of buttered bread to her and telling her that tea tasted nicer with sugar in it, pressing meringues and cake on her. Helena's mother always put a bowl beside Helena's bed on the nights there'd been a visit to the grandparents.

Her mother was the first teacher Helena had. In the dining-room they would sit together at the table with reading-books and copy-books and history and geography books. When she began to go to school she found herself far in advance of other children of her age, who because of that regarded her with considerable suspicion. 'Our little genius,' Miss Random used to say, meaning it cheerfully but making Helena uncomfortable because she knew she wasn't clever in the least. 'I don't consider that woman can teach at all,' her mother said after Helena had been at the school for six weeks and hadn't learnt anything new. So the dining-room lessons began again, in conjunction with the efforts of Miss Random. 'Pathetic, we have to say': her mother invested this favourite opinion with an importance and a strength, condemning not just Miss Random but also the milkman who whistled while waiting on the doorstep, and Mrs Archingford's attempt at stylish hair. Her mother employed a series of charwomen but was maddened by their chatter and ended by doing the housework herself, even though she found anything like that exceedingly irksome. She far preferred to sit in the dark study, continuing the work that had been cut short by death. In the lifetime of Helena's father her mother had assisted in the study and Helena had imagined her parents endlessly finding words in books and dissecting them on paper. Before the death conversations at mealtimes usually had to do with words. 'Fluxion?' she remembered her father saying, and when she shrugged her mother tightened her lips, her glance lingering on the shrug long after its motion had ceased. 'A most interesting derivation,' her father had supplied, and then went on to speak about the Newtonian calculus. The words he liked to bring up at mealtimes had rare meanings, sometimes five or six, but these, though worthy of record, had often to be dismissed on what he called the journey to the centre of interest. 'Fluxion, Helena, is *the rate at which a flowing motion increases its magnitude.* The Latin *fluxionem.* Now *flux,* Helena, is different. The familiar expression, *to be in a state of flux,* we know of course. But there is interestingly a variation: in mathematical terms, a drawn line is the flux of a point. You understand that, Helena? You place a dot with your pencil in your exercise-book, but you change your mind and continue the dot so that it becomes a line. With *flux* remember our pleasant word, *flow.* Remember our Latin friend, *fluere.* A flowing out, a flowing

in. With *fluxion,* we have the notion of measuring, of calculation.'
Food became cold while he explained, but he did not notice. All
that was her memory of him.

More interesting than Helena's own household were the
households round about. The death that had taken place, the
honouring of the unfinished work, her mother's seriousness, were
far less fascinating than the gaudy hair and dresses of Mrs
Archingford or the arguments of the elderly couple in the garden
of the house next door. Sometimes a son visited this couple, an
unkempt figure who intrigued Helena most of all. Now and again
she noticed him in the neighbourhood, usually carrying a cage
with a bird in it. On one occasion he sat in the garden next door
with a cage on either side of him, and Helena watched from a
window while he pointed out to his mother the features of the
budgerigars these cages contained. His mother poured tea and his
father read a newspaper or protested, in a voice loud enough to
carry to Helena's window, that the conversation about budgerigars
was inane. On another occasion Helena saw the unkempt son
entering Mrs Archingford's house with a cage and later leaving
empty-handed, having presumably made a successful sale. She
would have liked to report these incidents to her mother, but
when once she referred to the elderly couple's son her mother
stared at her in astonishment.

When she was twelve, Helena brought a girl called Judy
Smeeth back to tea. She had asked her mother if she might, since
she had herself been to tea several times with Judy Smeeth, who
was considered at school to be stupid. She was stout, with spectacles, and experienced difficulty in covering her large thighs with her
gymslip. When teachers drew attention to this immodest display
she laughed and said she did the best she could.

Helena's mother looked at Judy Smeeth blankly, and
afterwards said she didn't think she'd ever met a more unattractive
person.

'She's my friend at school,' Helena explained.

'Biscuit after biscuit. No wonder she's the size she is.'

'She invited me to her house five times.'

'You mean by that, do you, Helena, that when she comes here she must make up for all those visits by grabbing as much as she can, by filling herself with biscuits and Swiss roll? Is there not a more attractive girl you could have as a companion?'

'No, there isn't.'

'That was said roughly, Helena.'

'She's my best friend.'

Helena's mother vaguely shook her head. She had never talked about friends, any more than she had talked about her mother or her father. Helena didn't know if she'd had brothers or sisters, and certainly that was not a question she could ask. 'Gosh, *your mother!*' Judy Smeeth said in her amazed way. 'Didn't half give me the jitters, your mother.'

Many months later, in answer to Helena's repeated pleas, Judy Smeeth was permitted to come to the house again. On this occasion they played with a tennis ball in the garden, throwing it to one another. Unfortunately, due to a clumsy delivery of Judy's, it crossed the fence into Mrs Archingford's garden. 'Hey!' Judy cried, having climbed on to a pear tree that grew beside the fence. 'Hey, lady, could we have the ball back?'

Her plump hams, clad only partially in navy-blue school-regulation knickers, were considerably exposed as she balanced herself between the pear tree and the fence. She shouted again, endeavouring to catch the attention of Mrs Archingford, who was reading a magazine beneath her verandah.

'Hey! Yoo-hoo, lady!'

Mrs Archingford looked up and was surprised to see the beaming face of Judy Smeeth bespectacled and crowned with frizzy hair. Hearing the sound, she had expected the tidier and less extrovert presence of the girl next door. She rose and crossed her garden.

'It's only the ball, missus. We knocked the ball a bit hard.'

'Oh, I *see*,' said Mrs Archingford. 'D'you know, dearie, for a minute I thought your appearance had changed most peculiarly.'

'Eh?'

Mrs Archingford smiled at Judy Smeeth, and asked her what her name was. She picked the tennis ball out of her lupins.

'Judy the name is. Smeeth.'

'Mine's Mrs Archingford. Nice to meet you, Judy. Come to tea, have you?'

'That's right. Thanks for the ball.'

'Tell you what, why don't you and what's-her-name climb over that fence and have a glass of orangeade? Like orangeade, do you?'

'Yeah. Sure.'

'Tell you what, I've got a few Danish pastries. Almond and apple. Like Danish pastries, Judy?'

'Hey, Helena, the woman wants us to go over her place.'

'No,' Helena said.

'Why not?'

'Just no.'

'Sorry, missus. Cheerio then.'

Judy descended, having first thrown the ball to Helena.

'Hey, look,' she said when she was standing on the lawn, 'that woman was on about pastries. Why couldn't we?'

'Let's go into the house.'

Her mother would have observed the incident. She would have noticed the flesh of Judy's thighs and Judy's tongue sticking out of the corner of her mouth as she struggled to retain her balance. Two of a kind, she'd probably say when Judy had gone, she and vulgar Mrs Archingford. Her lips would tighten, her whole face would look like iron.

'I don't want that girl here again, Helena,' was what in fact she did say. 'She is far from suitable.'

Helena did not protest, nor attempt to argue. She had long since learnt that you could not win an argument with her mother because her mother refused to engage in arguments. 'Gor, she don't half frighten me,' Judy Smeeth remarked after that second visit to the house. Helena had realised a long time ago that she was frightened of her also.

'The completion of your father's work,' her mother announced one day, 'is taking a great deal longer than I had anticipated, even though he left such clear and copious notes. I am unworthy and ill-equipped, but it is a task that must be undertaken. So much begun, so much advanced. Someone must surely carry it to fruition.'

'Yes,' Helena said.

'I cannot manage you and the work together, child. I do not wish you to go away to school, I prefer to have you by me. But circumstances dictate. I have no choice.'

So Helena went to a boarding-school in Sussex, and it never at that time occurred to her to wonder how the fees at this expensive place were afforded, or indeed to wonder where any money at all came from. She returned at the end of that first term to find her mother more deeply involved in the unfinished work and also somewhat changed in her manner, as if affected by the lack of a companion. Sarcasm snapped more freely from her. Her voice had become like a whip. She hates me, Helena thought, because I am a nuisance.

The house had become even more reclusive than it had been, no friend from school could ever be invited there now. The wireless, which had occasionally been listened to, was silent. The telephone was used only to order food and household goods from Barker's of Kensington. Letters rarely came.

Then one afternoon just after Easter, when Helena was fifteen, a visitor arrived. She heard the doorbell from her bedroom and went to answer it because her mother wouldn't bother to. It would be an onion-seller, she thought, or one of those people who pressed the *Encyclopaedia Britannica* on you.

'Hullo,' a middle-aged man said, smiling at her from a sandy face. His short hair was sandy also. He wore a greenish suit. 'Are you Helena?'

'Yes.'

'Then I am your uncle. One of your mother's brothers. Did you know you had uncles and an aunt?'

She shook her head. He laughed.

'I was the one who made up the games we used to play. Different games for different parts of the garden. Aren't you going to let me in?'

'I'm sorry.'

He stepped into the hall, that awful fusty hall she hated so, its grim brown curtains looping in the archway at the bottom of the stairs, its grim hallstand, the four mezzotints of Australian landscape, the stained ceiling.

She led him into the sitting-room, which was awful also, cluttered with tawdry furniture her mother didn't notice had grown ugly with wear and time, the glass-fronted cabinets full of forgotten objects, the dreary books drearily filling bookcase after bookcase.

'I heard about your father's death, Helena. I'm sorry.'

'It's ages ago now. Seven years actually. He died on my birthday.'

291

'I only met your father once.' He paused. 'We've often wondered about you, you know.'

'Wondered?'

'The family have. We've known of course that your mother wouldn't be short, but even so.'

He smiled his easy smile at her. It was her mother who had supplied the money there had been, Helena intuitively realised. Something about the way he had mentioned the family and had said her mother wouldn't be short had given this clear impression. Not just obsessive in his scholarship, her father had been needy also.

'I thought I'd call,' he said. 'I've written of course, but even so I just thought I'd call one of these days.'

She left him and went to knock on the study door, as her mother liked her to do. There was no reply, and when she knocked a second time her mother called out in irritation.

'An uncle has come,' Helena said.

'Who?'

'Your brother.'

'Is here, you mean?' Her mother, wearing reading glasses on a chain, which she had recently taken to, had a finger marking the point on a page at which she had been interrupted. She was seated at the desk, papers and books all around her, the desk light turned on even though it was the middle of the afternoon.

'He's downstairs.'

Her mother said nothing, nor did she display further surprise, or emotion. She stared at Helena, her scrutiny suggesting that Helena was somehow to blame for the presence of this person, which in a sense Helena was, having opened the hall door to him and permitted his entrance. Her mother drew a piece of paper towards her, at the same time releasing her finger from the place it marked. She picked up a fountain pen and then opened a drawer and found an envelope.

'Give him this,' she said, and returned to her books.

Helena carried the missive to the sitting-room. The man had pulled back an edge of the grubby lace curtain and was gazing out into the empty street. He took the envelope from Helena and opened it.

'Well, there you are,' he said when he had read the message, and sighed. He left the note behind when he went. Her mother had simply ordered him to go away. *Please me by not returning to this house,* her mother had added, signing her full name.

*   *   *

In the dormitory called the Upper Nightingale Helena retailed the excesses of her mother. How the elderly couple in the house next door had been written to and requested to make less noise. How Mrs Archingford had been snubbed. How Judy Smeeth had been forbidden the house, how her mother's sandy-faced brother had been summarily dismissed. She told how her mother had never visited the grinning little grandparents, and how they had never come to the house. She described the house—the Australian mezzotints, the fustiness, the dim lights and curtained windows, the dirtiness that was beginning to gather. In their beds, each with a blue cover, other girls of Upper Nightingale listened with delight. None of them had a mother whose tongue was like a whip. None feared a mother's sarcasm. None dreaded going home.

When she closed her eyes after lights-out Helena saw her mother in the dark study, listing words and derivations, finding new words or words no longer used, all in loving memory. 'Oh God,' pleaded Helena in those moments given up to private prayer at the beginning and end of church. 'Oh God, please make her different.'

Her mother supplied her with money so that at the end of each term she could make her way from the school by train and then across London in a taxi-cab. It was not her mother's way to stand waiting at a railway station; nor, indeed, when Helena did arrive, to answer the doorbell until it had been rung twice or three times. It was not her way to embrace Helena, but instead to frown a little as if she had forgotten that her advent was due on a particular day. 'Ah, Helena,' she would say eventually.

These holiday periods were spent by Helena in reading, cleaning the kitchen, cooking, and walking about the avenues and crescents of the neighborhood. When she painted the shelves in her bedroom, her mother objected to the smell of paint, causing Helena to lose her temper. In awkward adolescent rage, unreasonably passionate, she shouted at her mother. The matter was petty, she was being made petty herself, yet she could not, as she stood there on the landing, bear for a second longer her mother's pretence that the smell of paint could not possibly be coming from within the house since no workman had been employed to paint anything. There was astonishment in her mother's face when Helena said she had been painting her shelves.

'I went out and bought paint,' she cried, red-faced and furious. 'Is there something sinful in that? I went into a shop and bought paint.'

'Of course there's nothing sinful, Helena.'

'Then why are you blaming me? What harm is there in painting the shelves in my bedroom? I'm seventeen. Surely I don't have to ask permission for every single action I take?'

'I merely wondered about the smell, child.'

'You didn't wonder. You knew about the smell.'

'I do not care for that, Helena.'

'Why do you hate me?'

'Now, Helena, please don't be tiresome. Naturally I do not hate you.'

'Everyone knows you hate me. Everyone at school, even Mrs Archingford.'

'Mrs Archingford? What on earth has Mrs Archingford to do with it?'

'She is a human being, that's all.'

'No one denies that Mrs Archingford is a human being.'

'You never think of her like that.'

'You are in a tiresome mood, Helena.'

Her mother turned and went away, descending the stairs to the study. Without a show of emotion, she closed the door behind her, quietly, as if there had not been an angry scene, or as if no importance could possibly attach to anything that had been said.

In her bedroom, that afternoon, Helena wept. She lay on her bed and pressed her face into her pillow, not caring how ugly she was making herself, for who was there to see? In waves of fury that came and calmed, and then came on again, she struck at her thighs with her fists until the repeated impact hurt and she guessed there would be black and blue marks. She wished she had reached out and struck her mother as she stood at the top of the stairs. She wished she had heard the snap of her mother's neck and had seen her body lifeless, empty of venom in the hall.

Twilight was gathering when she got up and washed her face in the bathroom. She held a sponge to each puffed-up eye in turn, and then immersed her whole face in a basin of cold water, holding it there for as long as she could. Her hair was bedraggled as a result, clinging to her damp face. She looked awful, she thought, her mouth pulled down with wretchedness, but she didn't care.

She walked along the crescents and the avenues, and down by the river, finding a common she'd only visited once before.

She wished she could simply go on walking through the evening, and never return to her mother's house. She wished that some young man in a motor-car would call out to her and ask her where she was going and say jump in. She would have, she knew she would have.

Instead she turned around and found her way back to the house, her footsteps dawdling and reluctant the closer she came to it. It was ten past nine by the clock in the sitting-room. Her mother, sitting by the electric fire, did not ask where she'd been.

'He will be forgotten,' she said instead, 'if I cannot complete his work.'

She spoke in a voice so matter-of-fact, so dry and spiritless that she might have been reciting a grocery list. Vaguely, Helena had listened when once she'd been told that the work consisted of the completion of a scholarly book, an investigation into how, over centuries, the meanings of words had altered. 'Difficult as it is,' her mother vowed, still without emotion, 'it shall not go unfinished.'

Helena nodded, for some reason feeling sorry she'd been so cross. There was a silence. Her mother stared without interest at the electric fire.

'When you were little,' Helena dared to begin.

'Little?'

'A child.'

'I didn't much care for being a child.'

'I just wondered if—'

'When you don't much care for something you prefer not to dwell upon it, Helena.'

The conversation ended, as abruptly as other attempts to elicit information always had. 'Of course I shall endeavour,' her mother said. 'I intend to continue to make an effort. He would consider it pusillanimous if I did not.'

Helena tried to imagine her as a child and then as an older girl but in neither of these efforts was she successful. The only photograph in the house was of her mother and her father on their wedding day, standing against an undefined background. Her father was smiling because, Helena has always guessed, the photographer had asked him to. But her mother had not heeded this request.

'I've cooked us moussaka,' Helena said the next day, wanting to make up for her outburst. 'A kind of shepherd's pie.'

'Good heavens, child, how very ambitious of you!'

Her mother left most of it on her plate and went away to find herself a slice of bread. Some time later they spoke again of cooking. Helena said:

'There's a course you can take.'

'A course, Helena?'

She explained, her mother carefully listened. Her mother said:

'But surely you can take a more interesting course? What would be at the end of this, for instance?'

'A job, if I am lucky.'

'You would cook in some kitchen, is that it? Other people's food? Food for mouths in a hotel—or a hospital or a school? Is that it?'

'Well, perhaps.'

'I can only call it pathetic, Helena, to cook food for people in an institution.'

'Cooking is something I like.'

'I do not understand that.'

Genuinely, Helena knew, her mother didn't. The meals they ate—which as a child she had assumed to be as all meals were—had never been prepared with interest. Meat and vegetables arrived from the food department of the Kensington store and had, with as scant attention as possible, found their way on to the mahogany surface of the dining-table.

'The course doesn't cost a lot.'

'Child, it doesn't matter what it costs. Your father would be disappointed is what matters.'

There was resentment in her mother's voice. There was astonished disbelief, as if Helena had confessed to a crime. 'I'm glad he's dead,' her mother said, 'so that he need not suffer to see his only child becoming a cook.'

'I'm sorry it's such a tragedy.'

'It makes no sense, child.'

Her mother turned away, leaving the sitting-room, where the brief conversation had taken place. Helena might have told the truth: that any course, in cooking, in typing and short-hand, in nursery management, in accountancy or gardening, would have fulfilled her need, which was to close the door of the house behind her and never to return.

* * *

She worked in the kitchens of Veitch and Company, paper manufacturers, helping to cook canteen food for two hundred employees. Braised steak, silverside, gammon, beef, roast potatoes or mashed, peas, carrots, Brussels sprouts, broad beans in season, trifle or Black Forest gâteau, stewed plums or custard tart: they were dishes and tastes which represented a world as distant as it could possibly be from her mother's and father's. 'Helena!' a voice shouted in the kitchens one day and there was Mrs Archingford on the telephone, talking about the police and how the name of Veitch and Company had been discovered on a postcard in the dark study, where Helena's mother had been found also. It was Mrs Archingford who had noticed the curtains not drawn back in the sitting-room of her mother's house, who had worried and had finally spoken to a policeman on the beat. Starvation was given as the cause of death on the death certificate: still struggling with the work in the study, Helena's mother had not bothered to eat. Not having visited her for more than three years, Helena had tried not to think about her while that time passed.

'You'll forgive me, dear, if I fail to attend the funeral,' Mrs Archingford requested. 'She didn't care for the look of me and no bones about it. Would be a trifle hypocritical, should we say?'

Helena was the only person who did attend the funeral. While a clergyman who had never known her mother spoke his conventional farewell she kept thinking of the busy kitchens of

Veitch and Company—all that mound of food, while her mother had absentmindedly starved.

She cleared the house, taking a week off from the kitchens. She gathered together her mother's clothes—and her father's, which still remained—and placed them ready in the hall, to be collected by a charitable organisation. She telephoned a firm which a girl in the kitchens had told her about, which purchased the contents of empty houses. She telephoned a house agents' and put the house on the market.

She found nothing, in her mother's bedroom or the study, that belonged to the past, before the time of the marriage. There were no personal letters of any kind, no photographs privately kept, no diaries. There was dust everywhere, some of her mother's clothes were unwashed; the gas cooker in the kitchen, the refrigerator and the kitchen cupboards, were all filthy. But the order which was absent elsewhere dominated the study. The papers and notebooks dealing with lexicographic matters were arranged tidily on the long rectangular table beneath the window, and on the desk itself were two stacks of lined foolscap, one covered with the tiny handwriting of Helena's father, the other with her mother's, larger and firmer. The pages were numbered: there were seven hundred and forty-six of them. *I do not know about a title for the work,* her mother had written in the draft of a letter she had clearly been intending to dispatch to a publisher. *My husband left no instruction, but some phrase may particularly strike you from what he has written himself, and a title thus emanate. The work is now complete, in the form my husband wished it.* Had her mother put aside all other form of life as the final pages were composed, pathetically clinging to the relationship her wealth had bought? Helena wondered if she had bothered to go to bed since she had not bothered with food. She might have died of exhaustion as well as of starvation. She might have lost track of day and night, afraid to leave the study in case the long task should by some awful mischance be lost when the end was so very close. She imagined her mother struggling with sleep, weak in her body, the clarity of her bold handwriting now

298

the most important fragment of her existence. She imagined her blinking away a sudden dizziness, and then moving in the room, one hand still on the desk to balance her progress, another reaching out into the gloom. She imagined her dead, lying on the unclean carpet.

On the foolscap pages there were underlined words, printed in capital letters: *Nympholepsy. Disembogue. Graphotype. Imagist. Macle. Rambunctious.* The precision of alphabetical order, the endlessly repeated reflections of her mother's seriousness, the intensity of her devotion to the subject out of which she and the man she'd married had spun a life together: all that lingered in the study, alive in the conjoined handwriting on the foolscap pages and the notebooks. The explanations of the paragraphs were meaningless to Helena and the burden of reading them caused her head to ache. She didn't know what to do with all the paper and the writing that had been left so purposefully behind. She didn't know what to do about the letter to a publisher, probably the last effort her mother had made. She closed the study door on all of it.

She did not sleep in the house. Each evening she returned to her two-room flat near Shepherd's Bush, where she turned the television on immediately to drive the house out of her thoughts. She sat in front of the bustling little screen with a glass of whisky and water, hoping that it, too, would help to cloud the images of the day. She longed to be back in her noisy kitchens, surrounded by different kinds of food. Sometimes, when she'd had a second and a third glass of whisky, the catalogue of the food which had become her life reminded her in a wry way of the catalogue of words in the study, one so esoteric, one so down-to-earth. Toad-in-the-hole, cabinet pudding, plaice and chips, French onion soup, trifle, jelly surprise.

One morning she arrived at the house with a cardboard carton into which she packed the foolscap pages. She carried it upstairs and placed it in a corner of the bedroom that had been her parents', with a note to the effect that it should not be taken away by the firm she had employed to take everything else. The books in the study would go, of course. In her small flat she could not possibly store them, and since they were of no possible interest to her what was the point?

Mrs Archingford kept ringing the doorbell, to ask if she would like a cup of tea or if she could help with anything. Mrs Archingford was, not unnaturally after the years that had gone by, curious. She told Helena that at Number 10 the elderly couple's son had moved in, to look after them in their now extreme old age. Birds flew about the rooms, so Mrs Archingford reported; the son was odd in the extreme.

'I dare say you'll be relieved to turn your back on the house?' she probed. 'No place for a young person, I shouldn't wonder?'

'Well, I don't want to live here, certainly.'

'My dear, however could you?'

Mrs Archingford's tone implied a most distressful childhood. She wouldn't be surprised to hear, her tone suggested, that Helena had been beaten and locked in cupboards, just to teach her. 'Most severe, your mother was, I always thought.'

'It was her way.'

'Forgive a nosy neighbour, dear, but your mother didn't look happy. Her own worst enemy, as I said one time to the gas man. "Be brisk about it," she ordered him, really sharply, you know, when the poor fellow came to read the meter. Oh, years ago it must have been, but I often remember it. Imagine that said to a meter man, when all the time he has to go careful in case of errors! And of course if he had made an error she'd be the first—'

'Actually, my mother wouldn't have noticed.'

'Why don't you slip in for a Nescafé and a Danish, eh? Smells like a morgue this hall does—oh, there, what a clumsy I am! Now, take that as unsaid, dear!'

Helena replied that it was quite all right, as indeed it was. Mrs Archingford pressed her invitation.

'What about a warming cup, though? D'you know I've never in all my days been inside this house? Not that I expected to, I mean why should I? But really it's interesting to see it.'

Mrs Archingford poked a finger into the dust on the hallstand, and as she did so the doorbell rang. Women from the charitable organisation had come for the clothes, so Helena was saved from having to continue the conversation about Nescafé and Danish pastries. That morning, too, a man arrived to estimate the value of the house and its contents so that death duties might be calculated. Then a man who was to purchase the contents came. He looked them over and suggested a figure far below that of the death duties man, but he pointed out that he was offering a full removal service, that in some unexplained way Helena was saving a fortune. She didn't argue. In the afternoon Mrs Archingford rang the bell again to say the estate agents Helena had chosen were not the best ones, so the woman in the Express Dairy had told her when she'd happened to allude to the matter while buying smoked ham. But Helena replied that the choice had been made.

A few days later she watched the furniture being lifted away, the books and ornaments in tea-chests, the crockery and saucepans and cutlery, even the gas cooker and the refrigerator. When everything was gone she walked about the empty rooms. Why had she not asked the sandy-haired man who had come? Why had she not made tea for him and persuaded him to tell her anything at all? Through a blur of mistiness she saw her mother as a child, playing with her brother in the garden he had mentioned. Helena stood in the centre of the room that had been her mother's bedroom and it seemed to her then that there were other children in the garden also, and voices faintly echoing. Trees and shrubs defined themselves; a house had lawns in front of it. 'Come on!' the children good-naturedly cried, but her mother didn't want to. Her mother hated playing. She hated having to laugh and run about. She hated being exposed to a jolliness that made her feel afraid. She wanted peace, and the serious silence of her room, but they always came in search of her and they always found her. Laughing and shouting, they dragged her into their games, not understanding that she felt afraid. She stammered and her face went white, but still they did not notice. Nobody listened when she tried to explain, nobody bothered.

These shadows filled her mother's bedroom. Helena knew that the playing children were a figment without reality, yet some instinct informed her that such shadows had been her mother's ghosts, that their dreaded world had accompanied her even after she had hidden from them in a suburban house where the intolerable laughter was not allowed. Companions too ordinary to comprehend her mother's different nature had left her afraid of ordinariness, and fear was what she had passed on to an ordinary daughter. Helena knew she would never marry; as long as she lived she would be afraid to bring a child into the world, and reflecting on that now she could feel within her the bitterness that had been her mother's, and even the vengeful urge to destroy that had been hers also.

Curtains had been taken down, light-shades removed. Huge patches glared from ancient wallpaper where furniture had stood or pictures hung. The bare boards echoed with Helena's footsteps. She bolted what it was necessary to bolt and saw that all the windows were secure. She banged the hall-door behind her and for the last time walked through the avenues and crescents she knew so well, on her way to drop the keys through the estate agents' letter-box. The cardboard carton containing her father's work, and her mother's achievement in completing it, remained in a corner of an empty bedroom. When the house was sold and the particulars completed the estate agents would telephone her in the kitchens at Veitch and Company to point out that this carton had been overlooked. Busy with meat or custard tart, she'd say it didn't matter, and give the instruction that it should be thrown away.

302

❁

Katherine Mansfield

As a schoolgirl in New Zealand, Katherine Mansfield was much preoccupied with the question of friendship between women. How deep do such true friendships run? And can they last forever? One day she turned to her best friend and asked, "What would you do if you found out that I had done something really awful, like killing somebody with a hatpin?" The answer was not recorded, but the question stayed with Mansfield all her life. "What was unusual about Katherine Mansfield—genius apart—was the persistence within her of the schoolgirl," wrote Elizabeth Bowen. "Theatrical, passionate in her wishes, surgically inquisitive, ruthlessly self-regarding in her decisions. As against which, reckon her generosities, her tenderness to the weak, and her doughty courage."

She believed in the community of women, but apart from the "social set" of the Edwardian age, in which she found little honesty and less inspiration; her impatience was aggravated by the knowledge of her advancing tuberculosis. Describing a party among the gentry, she wrote, "A silly, unreal evening. Pretty rooms and pretty people, pretty coffee, and cigarettes out of a silver tankard. . . . I was wretched. I have nothing to say to 'charming' women. I feel like a cat among tigers."

THE YOUNG GIRL

katherine mansfield

in her blue dress, with her cheeks lightly flushed, her blue, blue eyes, and her gold curls pinned up as though for the first time—pinned up to be out of the way for her flight—Mrs. Raddick's daughter might have just dropped from this radiant heaven. Mrs. Raddick's timid, faintly astonished, but deeply admiring glance looked as if she believed it, too; but the daughter didn't appear any too pleased—why should she?—to have alighted on the steps of the Casino. Indeed, she was bored—bored as though heaven had been full of casinos with snuffy old saints for *croupiers* and crowns to play with.

"You don't mind taking Hennie?" said Mrs. Raddick. "Sure you don't? There's the car, and you'll have tea and we'll be back here on this step—right here—in an hour. You see, I want her to go in. She'd not been before, and it's worth seeing. I feel it wouldn't be fair to her."

"Oh, shut up, mother," said she wearily. "Come along. Don't talk so much. And your bag's open; you'll be losing all your money again."

"I'm sorry, darling," said Mrs. Raddick.

"Oh, *do* come in! I want to make money," said the impatient voice. "It's all jolly well for you—but I'm broke!"

"Here—take fifty francs, darling, take a hundred!" I saw Mrs. Raddick pressing notes into her hand as they passed through the swing doors.

Hennie and I stood on the steps a minute, watching the people. He had a very broad, delighted smile.

"I say," he cried, "there's an English bulldog. Are they allowed to take dogs in there?"

"No, they're not."

"He's a ripping chap, isn't he? I wish I had one. They're such fun. They frighten people so, and they're never fierce with their—the people they belong to." Suddenly he squeezed my arm. "I say, *do* look at that old woman. Who is she? Why does she look like that? Is she a gambler?"

The ancient, withered creature, wearing a green satin dress, a black velvet cloak and a white hat with purple feathers, jerked slowly, slowly up the steps as though she were being drawn up on wires. She stared in front of her, she was laughing and nodding and cackling to herself; her claws clutched round what looked like a dirty boot-bag.

But just at that moment there was Mrs. Raddick again with—*her*—and another lady hovering in the background. Mrs. Raddick rushed at me. She was brightly flushed, gay, a different creature. She was like a woman who is saying "good-bye" to her friends on the station platform, with not a minute to spare before the train starts.

"Oh, you're here, still. Isn't that lucky! You've not gone. Isn't that fine! I've had the most dreadful time with—her," and she waved to her daughter, who stood absolutely still, disdainful, looking down, twiddling her foot on the step, miles away. "They won't let her in. I swore she was twenty-one. But they won't believe me. I showed the man my purse; I didn't dare do more. But it was no use. He simply scoffed. . . . And now I've just met Mrs. MacEwen from New York, and she just won thirteen thousand in the *Salle Privée*—and she wants me to go back with her while the luck lasts. Of course I can't leave—her. But if you'd—"

At that "she" looked up; she simply withered her mother. "Why can't you leave me?" she said furiously. "What utter rot! How dare you make a scene like this? This is the last time I'll come out with you. You really are too awful for words." She looked her mother up and down. "Calm yourself," she said superbly.

Mrs. Raddick was desperate, just desperate. She was "wild" to go back with Mrs. MacEwen, but at the same time . . .

I seized my courage. "Would you—do you care to come to tea with—us?"

"Yes, yes, she'll be delighted. That's just what I wanted, isn't it, darling? Mrs. MacEwen . . . I'll be back here in an hour . . . or less . . . I'll—"

Mrs. R. dashed up the steps. I saw her bag was open again.

So we three were left. But really it wasn't my fault. Hennie looked crushed to the earth, too. When the car was there she wrapped her dark coat round her—to escape contamination. Even her little feet looked as though they scorned to carry her down the steps to us.

"I am so awfully sorry," I murmured as the car started.

"Oh, I don't *mind*," said she. "I don't *want* to look twenty-one. Who would—if they were seventeen! It's"—and she gave a faint shudder—"the stupidity I loathe, and being stared at by fat old men. Beasts!"

Hennie gave her a quick look and then peered out of the window.

We drew up before an immense palace of pink-and-white marble with orange trees outside the doors in gold-and-black tubs.

"Would you care to go in?" I suggested.

She hesitated, glanced, bit her lip, and resigned herself. "Oh well, there seems nowhere else," said she. "Get out, Hennie."

I went first—to find the table, of course—she followed. But the worst of it was having her little brother, who was only twelve, with us. That was the last, final straw—having that child, trailing at her heels.

There was one table. It had pink carnations and pink plates with little blue tea-napkins for sails.

"Shall we sit here?"

She put her hand wearily on the back of a white wicker chair.

"We may as well. Why not?" said she.

Hennie squeezed past her and wriggled on to a stool at the end. He felt awfully out of it. She didn't even take her gloves off. She lowered her eyes and drummed on the table. When a faint violin sounded she winced and bit her lip again. Silence.

The waitress appeared. I hardly dared to ask her. "Tea—coffee? China tea—or iced tea with lemon?"

Really she didn't mind. It was all the same to her. She didn't really want anything. Hennie whispered, "Chocolate!"

But just as the waitress turned away she cried out carelessly, "Oh, you may as well bring me a chocolate too."

While we waited she took out a little, gold powder-box with a mirror in the lid, shook the poor little puff as though she loathed it, and dabbed her lovely nose.

"Hennie," she said, "take those flowers away." She pointed with her puff to the carnations, and I heard her murmur, "I can't bear flowers on a table." They had evidently been giving her intense pain, for she positively closed her eyes as I moved them away.

The waitress came back with the chocolate and the tea. She put the big, frothing cups before them and pushed across my clear glass. Hennie buried his nose, emerged, with, for one dreadful moment, a little trembling blob of cream on the tip. But he hastily wiped it off like a little gentleman. I wondered if I should dare draw her attention to her cup. She didn't notice it—didn't see it—until suddenly, quite by chance, she took a sip. I watched anxiously; she faintly shuddered.

"Dreadfully sweet!" said she.

A tiny boy with a head like a raisin and a chocolate body came round with a tray of pastries—row upon row of little freaks, little inspirations, little melting dreams. He offered them to her. "Oh, I'm not at all hungry. Take them away."

He offered them to Hennie. Hennie gave me a swift look—it must have been satisfactory—for he took a chocolate cream, a coffee éclair, a meringue stuffed with chestnut and a tiny horn filled with fresh strawberries. She could hardly bear to watch him. But just as the boy swerved away she held up her plate.

"Oh well, give me *one*," said she.

The silver tongs dropped one, two, three—and a cherry tartlet. "I don't know why you're giving me all these," she said, and nearly smiled. "I shan't eat them; I couldn't!"

I felt much more comfortable. I sipped my tea, leaned back, and even asked if I might smoke. At that she paused, the fork in her hand, opened her eyes and really did smile. "Of course," said she. "I always expect people to."

But at that moment a tragedy happened to Hennie. He speared his pastry horn too hard, and it flew in two, and one half spilled on the table. Ghastly affair! He turned crimson. Even his ears flared, and one ashamed hand crept across the table to take what was left of the body away.

"You *utter* little beast!" said she.

Good heavens! I had to fly to the rescue. I cried hastily, "Will you be abroad long?"

But she had already forgotten Hennie. I was forgotten too. She was trying to remember something. . . . She was miles away.

"I—don't—know," she said slowly, from that far place.

"I suppose you prefer it to London. It's more—more—"

When I didn't go on she came back and looked at me, very puzzled. "More—?"

"*Enfin*—gayer," I cried, waving my cigarette.

But that took a whole cake to consider. Even then, "Oh well, that depends!" was all she could safely say.

Hennie had finished. He was still very warm.

I seized the butterfly list off the table. "I say—what about an ice, Hennie? What about tangerine and ginger? No, something cooler. What about a fresh pine-apple cream?"

Hennie strongly approved. The waitress had her eye on us. The order was taken when she looked up from her crumbs.

"Did you say tangerine and ginger? I like ginger. You can bring me one." And then quickly, "I wish that orchestra wouldn't play things from the year One. We were dancing to that all last Christmas. It's too sickening!"

But it was a charming air. Now that I noticed it, it warmed me.

"I think this is rather a nice place, don't you, Hennie?" I said.

Hennie said: "Ripping!" He meant to say it very low but it came out very high in a kind of squeak.

Nice? This place? Nice? For the first time she stared about her, trying to see what there was. . . . She blinked; her lovely eyes wondered. A very good-looking elderly man stared back at her through a monocle on a black ribbon. But him she simply couldn't see. There was a hole in the air where he was. She looked through and through him.

Finally the little flat spoons lay still on the glass plates. Hennie looked rather exhausted, but she pulled on her white gloves again. She had some trouble with her diamond wristwatch; it got in her way. She tugged at it—tried to break the stupid little thing—it wouldn't break. Finally, she had to drag her glove over. I saw, after that, she couldn't stand this place a moment longer, and, indeed, she jumped up and turned away while I went through the vulgar act of paying for the tea.

And then we were outside again. It had grown dusky. The sky was sprinkled with small stars; the big lamps glowed. While we waited for the car to come up she stood on the step, just as before, twiddling her foot, looking down.

Hennie bounded forward to open the door and she got in and sank back with—oh—such a sigh!

"Tell him," she gasped, "to drive as fast as he can."

Hennie grinned at his friend the chauffeur. "Allie veet!" said he. Then he composed himself and sat on the small seat facing us.

The gold powder-box came out again. Again the poor little puff was shaken; again there was that swift, deadly-secret glance between her and the mirror.

We tore through the black-and-gold town like a pair of scissors tearing through brocade. Hennie had great difficulty not to look as though he were hanging on to something.

And when we reached the Casino, of course Mrs. Raddick wasn't there. There wasn't a sign of her on the steps—not a sign.

"Will you stay in the car while I go and look?"

But no—she wouldn't do that. Good heavens, no! Hennie could stay. She couldn't bear sitting in a car. She'd wait on the steps.

"But I scarcely like to leave you," I murmured. "I'd very much rather not leave you here."

At that she threw back her coat; she turned and faced me; her lips parted. "Good heavens—why! I—I don't mind it a bit. I—I like waiting." and suddenly her cheeks crimsoned, her eyes grew dark—for a moment I thought she was going to cry. "L—let me, please," she stammered, in a warm, eager voice. "I like it. I love waiting! Really—really I do! I'm always waiting—in all kinds of places. . . ."

Her dark coat fell open, and her white throat—all her soft young body in the blue dress—was like a flower that is just emerging from its dark bud.

❁

Yūko Tsushima

After the Meiji Restoration of 1868 put an end to Japan's long closure from the West, writers abandoned the form of light entertainment known as *gesaku,* or "playful composition," that had dominated their literary scene for over a century and began imitating popular European models. Among the first books translated from the English was Edward Bulwer-Lyton's dreadful Victorian potboiler, *Ernest Maltravers.* Curiously, however, only the novel's form—neither the style nor the mawkish contents—was carried over into the other culture, and from such an awkward model the Japanese writers carried the genre to extraordinary heights. One of its foremost masters, Shuji Tsushima (who took on the pseudonym Dazai Osamu), a fierce opponent of the militarists, made his reputation with books that combined black humor and social realism. He drowned in 1948, perhaps having committed suicide. His daughter, Yūko Tsushima, born a year before her father's death, is an acknowledged master of the short story and winner of the coveted Kawabata Prize for fiction. "The Silent Traders" makes use of the animal world as a mirror for our own sufferings, the family relationship she describes finding echoes in the simpler, more dignified world of cats and dogs.

THE SILENT TRADERS

yūko tsushima

Translated from the Japanese by Geraldine Harcourt

there was a cat in the wood. Not such an odd thing, really: wildcats, pumas, and lions all come from the same family and even a tabby shouldn't be out of place. But the sight was unsettling. What was the creature doing there? When I say 'wood,' I'm talking about Rikugien, an Edo-period landscape garden in my neighbourhood. Perhaps 'wood' isn't quite the right word, but the old park's trees—relics of the past amid the city's modern buildings—are so overgrown that the pathways skirting its walls are dark and forbidding even by day. It does give the impression of a wood; there's no other word for it. And the cat, I should explain, didn't look wild. It was just a kitten, two or three months old, white with black patches. It didn't look at all ferocious—in fact it was a dear little thing. There was nothing to fear. And yet I was taken aback, and I tensed as the kitten bristled and glared in my direction.

The kitten was hiding in a thicket beside the pond, where my ten-year-old daughter was the first to spot it. By the time I'd made out the elusive shape and exclaimed 'Oh, you're right!' she was off calling at the top of her voice: 'There's another! And here's one over here!' My other child, a boy of five, was still hunting for the first kitten, and as his sister went on making one discovery after another he stamped his feet and wailed 'Where? Where is it!' His sister beckoned him to bend down and showed him triumphantly where to find the first cat. Several passers-by, hearing my daughter's shouts, had also been drawn into the search. There were many strollers in the park that Sunday evening. The cats were everywhere, each concealed in its own clump of bushes. Their eyes followed people's feet on the gravelled walk, and at the slightest move toward a hiding place the cat would scamper away. Looking down from an adult's height it was hard enough to detect them at all, let alone keep count, and this gave the impression of great numbers.

I could hear my younger child crying. He had disappeared while my back was turned. As I looked wildly around, my daughter pointed him out with a chuckle: 'See where he's got to!' There he was, huddled tearfully in the spot where the first kitten had been. He'd burst in eagerly, but succeeded only in driving away the kitten and trapping himself in the thicket.

313

'What do you think you're doing? It'll never let *you* catch it.' Squatting down, my daughter was calling through the bushes. 'Come on out, silly!'

His sister's tone of amusement was no help to the boy at all. He was terrified in his cobwebbed cage of low-hanging branches where no light penetrated.

'That's no use. You go in and fetch him out.' I gave her shoulder a push.

'He got himself in,' she grumbled, 'so why can't he get out?' All the same, she set about searching for an opening. Crouching, I watched the boy through the thick foliage and waited for her to reach him.

'How'd he ever get in there? He's really stuck,' she muttered as she circled the bushes uncertainly, but a moment later she'd broken through to him, forcing a way with both hands.

When they rejoined me, they had dead leaves and twigs snagged all over them.

After an attempt of her own to pick one up, my daughter

understood that life in the park had made these tiny kittens quicker than ordinary strays, and too wary to let anyone pet them. Explaining this to her brother, she looked to me for agreement. 'They were born here, weren't they? They belong here, don't they? Then I wonder if their mother's here too?'

The children scanned the surrounding trees once again.

'She may be,' I said, 'but she'd stay out of sight, wouldn't she? Only the kittens wander about in the open. Their mother's got more sense. I'll bet she's up that tree or somewhere like that where nobody can get at her. She's probably watching us right now.'

I cast an eye at the treetops as I spoke—and the thought of the unseen mother cat gave me an uncomfortable feeling. Whether these were alley cats that had moved into the park or discarded pets that had survived and bred, they could go on multiplying in the wood—which at night was empty of people—and be perfectly at home.

It is exactly twenty-five years since my mother came to live near Rikugien with her three children, of which I, at ten, was the youngest. She told us the park's history, and not long after our arrival we went inside to see the garden. In spite of its being on our doorstep we quickly lost interest, however, since the grounds were surrounded by a six-foot brick wall with a single gate on the far side from our house. A Japanese garden was not much fun for children anyway, and we never went again as a family. I was reminded that we lived near a park, though, because of the many birds—the blue magpies, Eastern turtledoves, and tits—that I would see on rooftops and in trees. And in summer I'd hear the singing of evening cicadas. To a city child like me, evening cicadas and blue magpies were a novelty.

I visited Rikugien with several classmates when we were about to leave elementary school, and someone hit on the idea of making a kind of time capsule. We'd leave it buried for ten years— or was it twenty? I've also forgotten what we wrote on the piece of paper that we stuffed into a small bottle and buried at the foot of a pine on the highest ground in the garden. I expect it's still there as I haven't heard of it since, and now whenever I'm in Rikugien I keep an eye out for the landmark, but I'm only guessing. We were confident of knowing exactly where to look in years to come, and if I can remember that so clearly it's puzzling that I can't recognize the tree. I'm not about to dig any holes to check, however—not with my own children watching. The friends who left this senti-mental reminder were soon to part, bound for different schools. Since then, of course, we've ceased to think of one another, and I'm not so sure now that the bottle episode ever happened.

The following February my brother (who was close to my own age) died quite suddenly of pneumonia. Then in April my sister went to college and, not wanting to be left out, I pursued her new interests myself: I listened to jazz, went to movies, and was friendly toward college and high school students of the oppo-site sex. An older girl introduced me to a boy from senior high and we made up a foursome for an outing to the park—the only time I got all dressed up for Rikugien. I was no beauty, though, nor the popular type, and while the others were having fun I stayed stiff and awkward, and was bored. I would have liked to be as gen-uinely impressed as they were, viewing the landscape garden for the first time, but I couldn't work up an interest after seeing the trees over the brick wall every day. By that time we'd been in the district for three years, and the name 'Rikugien' brought to mind not the tidy, sunlit lawns seen by visitors, but the dark tangles along the walls.

My desire for friends of the opposite sex was short-lived. Boys couldn't provide what I wanted, and what boys wanted had nothing to do with me.

While I was in high school, one day our ancient spitz died. The house remained without a dog for a while, until mother was finally prompted to replace him when my sister's marriage, soon after her graduation, left just the two of us in an unprotected home. She found someone who let her have a terrier puppy. She bought a brush and comb and began rearing the pup with the best

315

of care, explaining that it came from a clever hunting breed. As it
grew, however, it failed to display the expected intelligence and
still behaved like a puppy after six months; and besides, it was
timid. What it did have was energy as, yapping shrilly, it frisked
about the house all day long. It may have been useless but it was a
funny little fellow. Its presence made all the difference to me in
my intense boredom at home. After my brother's death, my mother
(a widow since I was a baby) passed her days as if at a wake. We saw
each other only at mealtimes, and then we seldom spoke. In high
school a fondness for the movies was about the worst I could have
been accused of, but Mother had no patience with such frivolity
and would snap angrily at me from time to time. 'I'm leaving home
as soon as I turn eighteen,' I'd retort. I meant it, too.

It was at that time that we had the very sociable dog. I
suppose I'd spoiled it as a puppy, for now it was always wanting
to be let in, and when I slid open the glass door it would bounce
like a rubber ball right into my arms and lick my face and hands
ecstatically.

Mother, however, was dissatisfied. She'd had enough of
the barking; it got on her nerves. Then came a day when the dog
was missing. I thought it must have got out of the yard. Two or
three days passed and it didn't return—it hadn't the wit to find the
way home once it had strayed. I wondered if I should contact the
pound. Concern finally drove me to break our usual silence and
ask Mother: 'About the dog . . .' 'Oh, the dog?' she replied. 'I
threw it over the wall of Rikugien the other day.'

I was shocked—I'd never heard of disposing of a dog
like that. I wasn't able to protest, though. I didn't rush out to comb
the park, either. She could have had it destroyed, yet instead she'd
taken it to the foot of the brick wall, lifted it in her arms, and
heaved it over. It wasn't large, only about a foot long, and thus not
too much of a handful even for Mother.

Finding itself tossed into the wood, the dog wouldn't
have crept quietly into hiding. It must have raced through the area
barking furiously, only to be caught at once by the caretaker. Would

the next stop be the pound? But there seemed to me just a chance that it hadn't turned out that way. I could imagine the wood by daylight, more or less: there'd be a lot of birds and insects, and little else. The pond would be inhabited by a few carp, turtles, and catfish. But what transformations took place at night? As I didn't dare stay beyond closing time to see for myself, I wondered if anyone could tell of a night spent in the park till the gates opened in the morning. There might be goings-on that by day would be unimaginable. Mightn't a dog entering that world live on, not as a tiny terrier, but as something else?

I had to be thankful that the dog's fate left that much to the imagination.

From then on I turned my back on Rikugien more firmly than ever. I was afraid of the deep wood, so out of keeping with the city: it was the domain of the dog abandoned by my mother.

In due course I left home, a little later than I'd promised. After a good many more years I moved back to Mother's neighbourhood—back to the vicinity of the park—with a little daughter and a baby. Like my own mother, I was one who couldn't give my children the experience of a father. That remained the one thing I regretted.

Living in a cramped apartment, I now appreciated the Rikugien wood for its greenery and open spaces. I began to take the children there occasionally. Several times, too, we released pet turtles or goldfish into the pond. Many nearby families who'd run out of room for aquarium creatures in their overcrowded apartments would slip them into the pond to spend the rest of their lives at liberty.

Rocks rose from the water here and there, and each was studded with turtles sunning themselves. They couldn't have bred naturally in such numbers. They must have been the tiny turtles sold at fairground stalls and pet shops, grown up without a care in the world. More of them lined the water's edge at one's feet. No doubt there were other animals on the increase—goldfish, loaches, and the like. Multi-storeyed apartment buildings were going up around the wood in quick succession, and more living things were brought down from their rooms each year. Cats were one animal I'd overlooked, though. If tossing out turtles was common practice, there was no reason why cats shouldn't be dumped here, and dogs too. No type of pet could be ruled out. But to become established in any numbers they'd have to escape the caretaker's notice and hold their own against the wood's other hardy inhabitants. Thus there'd be a limit to survivors: cats and reptiles, I'd say.

Once I knew about the cat population, I remembered the dog my mother had thrown away, and I also remembered my old fear of the wood. I couldn't help wondering how the cats got by from day to day.

Perhaps they relied on food left behind by visitors—but all of the park's litter baskets were fitted with mesh covers to keep out the crows, whose numbers were also growing. For all their nimbleness, even cats would have trouble picking out the scraps. Lizards and mice were edible enough. But on the other side of the wall lay the city and its garbage. After dark, the cats would go out foraging on the streets.

Then, too, there was the row of apartment towers along one side of the wood, facing the main road. All had balconies that overlooked the park. The climb would be quick work for a cat, and if its favourite food were left outside a door it would soon come back regularly. Something told me there must be people who put out food: there'd be elderly tenants and women living alone. Even children. Children captivated by a secret friendship with a cat.

I don't find such a relationship odd—perhaps because it occurs so often in fairy stories. But to make it worth their while the apartment children would have to receive something from the cat; otherwise they wouldn't keep it up. There are tales of mountain men and villagers who traded a year's haul of linden bark for a gallon and a half of rice in hard cakes. No villager could deal openly with the lone mountain men; so great was their fear of each other, in fact, that they avoided coming face to face. Yet when a bargain was struck, it could not have been done more skillfully. The trading

was over in a flash, before either man had time to catch sight of
the other or hear his voice. I think everyone wishes privately that
bargains could be made like that. Though there would always be
the fear of attack, or discovery by one's own side.

Supposing it were my own children: what could they be
getting in return? They'd have no use for a year's stock of linden
bark. Toys, then, or cakes. I'm sure they want all sorts of things, but
not a means of support like linden bark. What, then? Something
not readily available to them; something the cat has in abundance
and to spare.

The children leave food on the balcony. And in return
the cat provides them with a father. How's that for a bargain?
Once a year, male cats procreate; in other words, they become
fathers. They become fathers ad nauseam. But these fathers don't
care how many children they have—they don't even notice that
they are fathers. Yet the existence of offspring makes them so.
Fathers who don't know their own children. Among humans, it
seems there's an understanding that a man only becomes a father
when he recognises the child as his own; but that's a very narrow
view. Why do we allow the male to divide children arbitrarily into
two kinds, recognised and unrecognised? Wouldn't it be enough
for the child to choose a father when necessary from among suitable males? If the children decide that the tom that climbs up to
their balcony is their father, it shouldn't cause him any inconvenience. A father looks in on two of his children from the balcony
every night. The two human children faithfully leave out food to
make it so. He comes late, when they are fast asleep, and they
never see him or hear his cries. It's enough that they know in the
morning that he's been. In their dreams, the children are hugged
to their cat-father's breast.

We'd seen the children's human father six months earlier,
and together we'd gone to a transport museum they wanted to
visit. This came about only after many appeals from me. If the
man who was their father was alive and well on this earth, I
wanted the children to know what he looked like. To me, the man

319

was unforgettable: I was once preoccupied with him, obsessed with the desire to be where he was; nothing had changed when I tried having a child, and I'd had the second with him cursing me. To the children, however, especially the younger one, he was a mere shadow in a photograph that never moved or spoke. As the younger child turned three, then four, I couldn't help being aware of that fact. This was the same state that I'd known myself, for my own father had died. If he had been dead it couldn't have been helped. But as long as he was alive I wanted them to have a memory of their father as a living, breathing person whose eyes moved, whose mouth moved and spoke.

On the day, he was an hour late for our appointment. The long wait in a coffee shop had made the children tired and cross, but when they saw the man a shy silence came over them. 'Thanks for coming,' I said with a smile. I couldn't think what to say next. He asked 'Where to?' and stood to leave at once. He walked alone, while the children and I looked as though it was all the same to us whether he was there or not. On the train I still hadn't come up with anything to say. The children kept their distance from the man and stared nonchalantly out of the window. We got off the train like that, and again he walked ahead.

The transport museum had an actual bullet-train carriage, steam locomotives, aeroplanes, and giant panoramic layouts. I remembered enjoying a class trip there while at school myself. My children, too, dashed excitedly around the exhibits without a moment's pause for breath. It was 'Next I want to have a go on that train,' 'Now I want to work that model.' They must have had a good two hours of fun. In the meantime we lost sight of the man. Wherever he'd been, he showed up again when we'd finished our tour and arrived back at the entrance. 'What'll we do?' he asked and I suggested giving the children a drink and sitting down somewhere. He nodded and went ahead to look for a place near the museum. The children were clinging to me as before. He entered a coffee shop that had a cake counter and I followed with them. We sat down, the three of us facing the man. Neither child showed the slightest inclination to sit beside him. They had orange drinks.

I was becoming desperate for something to say. And weren't there one or two things he'd like to ask me? Such as how the children had been lately. But to bring that up, unasked, might imply that I wanted him to watch with me as they grew. I'd only been able to ask for this meeting because I'd finally stopped feeling that way. Now it seemed we couldn't even exchange such polite remarks as 'They've grown' or 'I'm glad they're well' without arousing needless suspicions. It wasn't supposed to be like this, I thought in confusion, unable to say a word about the children. He was indeed their father, but not a father who watched over them. As far as he was concerned the only children he had were the two borne by his wife. Agreeing to see mine was simply a favour on his part, for which I could only be grateful.

If we couldn't discuss the children, there was literally nothing left to say. We didn't have the kind of memories we could reminisce over; I wished I could forget the things we'd done as if it had all been a dream, for it was the pain that we remembered. Inquiring after his family would be no better. His work seemed the safest subject, yet if I didn't want to stay in touch I had to think twice about this, too.

The man and I listened absently as the children entertained themselves.

On the way out the man bought a cake which he handed to the older child, and then he was gone. The children appeared relieved, and with the cake to look forward to they were eager to get home. Neither had held the man's hand or spoken to him. I wanted to tell them that there was still time to run after him and touch some part of his body, but of course they wouldn't have done it.

I don't know when there will be another opportunity for the children to see the man. They may never meet him again, or they may have a chance two or three years from now. I do know that the man and I will probably never be completely indifferent to each other. He's still on my mind in some obscure way. Yet

321

there's no point in confirming this feeling in words. Silence is essential. As long as we maintain silence, and thus avoid trespassing, we leave open the possibility of resuming negotiations at any time.

    I believe the system of bartering used by the mountain men and the villagers was called 'silent trade.' I am coming to understand that there was nothing extraordinary in striking such a silent bargain for survival. People trying to survive—myself, my mother, and my children, for example—can take some comfort in living beside a wood. We toss various things in there and tell ourselves that we haven't thrown them away, we've set them free in another world, and then we picture the unknown woodland to ourselves and shudder with fear or sigh fondly. Meanwhile the creatures multiplying there gaze stealthily at the human world outside; at least I've yet to hear of anything attacking from the wood.

322   Some sort of silent trade is taking place between the two sides. Perhaps my children really have begun dealings with a cat who lives in the wood.

❁

Louise Erdrich

"My mother," Louise Erdrich once said, "is a patient woman. For years, she taught knitting to adolescents. That says it all. She had seven children by age thirty, has fourteen grandchildren now, in her mid-fifties. When the noise and the heat of young lives overwhelm her, she still cans tomatoes. When she is frustrated, she used to press the pedal of her sewing machine flat, sending the needle into a manic frenzy. She never lashed out at a child. That lesson is profound."

It is a lesson that many of the women in Erdrich's fiction have had to learn. Their lives, like that of the protagonist's mother in "A Wedge of Shade," are difficult, uncertain; the lesson at the end of the time's chart slow in coming. "In the growth of children, in the aging of beloved parents, time's chart is magnified, shown in its particularity, focused, so that with each celebration of maturity there is also a pang of loss. This is our human problem, one common to parents, sons and daughters, too—how to let go while holding tight, how to simultaneously cherish the closeness and intricacy of the bond while at the same time letting out the raveling string, the red yarn that ties our hearts."

A WEDGE OF SHADE

louise erdrich

every place that I could name you, in the whole world around us, has better things about it than Argus. I just happened to grow up there for eighteen years and the soil got to be part of me, the air has something in it that I breathed. Argus water, fluoridated by an order of the state, doesn't taste as good as water in the cities. Still, the first thing I do, walking back into my mother's house, is stand at the kitchen sink and toss down glass after glass.

"Are you filled up?" My mother stands behind me. "Sit down if you are."

She's tall and broad square with long arms and big knuckles. Her face is rawboned, fierce, and almost masculine in its edges and planes. Several months ago, a beauty operator convinced her that she should feminize her look with curls. Now the permanent, grown out in grizzled streaks, bristles like the coat of a terrier. I don't look like her. Not just the hair, hers is salt and pepper, mine is a reddish brown, but my build. I'm short, boxy, more like my Aunt Mary, although there's not much about me that corresponds even to her, except it's true that I can't seem to shake this town. I keep coming back here.

"There's jobs at the beet plant."

This rumour, probably false as the plant is in a slump, drops into the dim close air of the kitchen. We have the shades drawn because it's a hot June, over a hundred degrees, and we're trying to stay cool. Outside, the water has been sucked from everything. The veins in the leaves are hollow, the ditch grass is crackling. The sky has absorbed every drop. It's a thin whitish blue veil stretched from end to end over us, a flat gauze tarp. From the depot, I've walked here beneath it, dragging my suitcase.

We're sweating like we're in an oven, a big messy one. For a week, it's been too hot to move much or even clean, and the crops are stunted, failing. The farmer next to us just sold his field for a subdivision, but the workers aren't doing much. They're wearing wet rags on their heads, sitting near the house sites in the brilliance of noon. The studs of woods stand uselessly upright over them. Nothing casts a shadow. The sun has dried them up too.

"The beet plant," my mother says again.

"Maybe so," I say, and then, because I've got something bigger on my mind, "maybe I'll go out there and apply."

"Oh?" She is intrigued now.

"God, this is terrible!" I take the glass of water in my hand and tip some on my head. I don't feel cooler though, I just feel the steam rising off me.

"The fan broke down," she states. "Both of them are kaput now. The motors or something. If Mary would get the damn tax refund we'd run out to Pamida, buy a couple more, set up a breeze. Then we'd be cool out here."

"Your garden must be dead," I say, lifting the edge of the pull shade.

"It's sick, but I watered. And I won't mulch, that draws the damn slugs."

"Nothing could live out there, no bug." My eyes smart from even looking at the yard, cleared on the north, almost incandescent.

"You'd be surprised."

I wish I could blurt it out, just tell her. Even now, the words swell in my mouth, the one sentence, but I'm scared and with good reason. There is this about my mother: it is awful to see her angry. Her lips press together and she stiffens herself within, growing wooden, silent. Her features become fixed and remote, she will not speak. It takes a long time, and until she does you are held in suspense. Nothing that she ever says, in the end, is as bad as that feeling of dread. So I wait, half believing that she'll figure out my secret for herself, or drag it out of me, not that she ever tries. If I'm silent, she hardly notices. She's not like Aunt Mary, who forces me to say more than I know is on my mind.

My mother sighs, "It's too hot to bake. It's too hot to cook. But it's too hot to eat, anyway." She's talking to herself, which makes me reckless. Perhaps she is so preoccupied by the heat that I can slip my announcement past her. I should just say it, but I lose nerve, make an introduction that alerts her.

"I have something to tell you."

I've cast my lot, there's no going back unless I think quickly. My thoughts hum.

But she waits, forgetting the heat for a moment.

"Ice," I say, "we have to have ice." I speak intensely, leaning toward her, almost glaring, but she is not fooled.

"Don't make me laugh," she says, "there's not a cube in town. The refrigerators can't keep cold enough."

She eyes me as if I'm an animal about to pop from its den and run.

"Okay." I break down. "I really do have something." I stand, turn my back. In this lightless warmth I'm dizzy, almost sick. Now I've gotten to her and she's frightened to hear, breathless.

"Tell me," she urges. "Go on, get it over with."

And so I say it. "I got married." There is a surge of relief, as if a wind blows through the room, but then it's gone. The curtain flaps and we're caught again, stunned in an even denser heat. It's now my turn to wait, and I whirl around and sit right across from her. But I can't bear the picture she makes, the shock that parts her lips, the stunned shade of hurt in her eyes. I have to convince her, somehow, that it's all right.

"You hate weddings! Just think, just picture it. Me, white net. On a day like this. You, stuffed in your summer wool, and Aunt Mary, God knows . . . and the tux, the rental, the groom . . ."

Her head lowered as my words fell on her, but now her forehead tips up and her eyes come into view, already hardening. My tongue flies back into my mouth.

She mimics, making it a question, "The groom . . ."

I'm caught, my lips half open, a stuttering noise in my throat. How to begin? I have rehearsed this but my lines melt away, my opening, my casual introductions. I can think of nothing that would, even in a small way, convey any part of who he is. There is no picture adequate, no representation that captures him. So I just put my hand across the table, and I touch her hand.

"Mother," I say, like we're in a staged drama, "he'll arrive here shortly."

There is something forming in her, some reaction. I am afraid to let it take complete shape.

"Let's go out and wait on the steps, Mom. Then you'll see him."

"I do not understand," she says in a frighteningly neutral voice. This is what I mean. Everything is suddenly forced, as though we're reading lines.

"He'll approach from a distance." I can't help speaking like a bad actor. "I told him to give me an hour. He'll wait, then he'll come walking down the road."

We rise and unstick our blouses from our stomachs, our skirts from the backs of our legs. Then we walk out front in single file, me behind, and settle ourselves on the middle step. A scrubby box elder tree on one side casts a light shade, and the dusty lilacs seem to catch a little breeze on the other. It's not so bad out here, still hot, but not so dim, contained. It's worse past the trees. The heat shimmers in a band, rising off the fields, out of the spars and bones of houses which will wreck our view. The horizon and the edge of town show through the spacing now, and as we sit we watch the workers move, slowly, almost in a practised recital, back and forth. Their headcloths hang to their shoulders, their hard hats are dabs of yellow, their white T-shirts blend into the fierce air and sky. They don't seem to be doing anything, although we hear faint thuds from their hammers. Otherwise, except for the whistles of a few birds, there is silence. We certainly don't speak.

It is a longer wait than I anticipated, maybe because he wants to give me time. At last the shadows creep out, hard, hot, charred, and the heat begins to lengthen and settle. We are going into the worst of the afternoon, when a dot at the end of the road begins to form.

Mom and I are both watching. We have not moved our eyes around much, and we blink and squint to try and focus. The dot doesn't change, not for a long while. And then it suddenly springs clear in relief, a silhouette, lost a moment in the shimmer, reappearing. In that shining expanse he is a little wedge of moving shade. He continues, growing imperceptibly, until there are variations in the outline, and it can be seen that he is large. As he passes the construction workers, they turn and stop, all alike in their hats, stock-still.

Growing larger yet, as if he has absorbed their stares, he nears us. Now we can see the details. He is dark, the first thing. I have not told my mother, but he's Chippewa, from the same tribe as she. His arms are thick, his chest is huge and the features of his face are wide and open. He carries nothing in his hand. He wears a black T-shirt, the opposite of the construction workers, and soft jogging shoes. His jeans are held under his stomach by a belt with a star beaded on the buckle. His hair is long, in a tail. I am the wrong woman for him. I am paler, shorter, unmagnificent. But I stand up. Mom joins me, and I answer proudly when she asks, "His name?"

"His name is Gerry."

We descend one step, and stop again. It is here we will receive him. Our hands are folded at our waists. We're balanced, composed. He continues to stroll toward us, his white smile widening, his eyes filling with the sight of me as mine are filling with him.

At the end of the road, behind him, another dot has appeared. It is fast-moving and the sun flares off it twice, a vehicle. Now there are two figures. One approaching in a spume of dust from the rear, and Gerry, unmindful, not slackening or quickening his pace, continuing on. It is like a choreography design. They move at parallel speeds, in front of our eyes. At the same moment, at the end of our yard, as if we have concluded a performance now, both of them halt.

Gerry stands, looking toward us, his thumbs in his belt. He nods respectfully to Mom, looks calmly at me, and half smiles. He raises his brows, and we're suspended. Officer Lovchik emerges from the police car, stooped and tired. He walks up behind Gerry and I hear the snap of handcuffs, then I jump. I'm stopped by Gerry's gaze though, as he backs away from me, still smiling tenderly. I am paralysed halfway down the walk. He kisses the air while Lovchik cautiously prods at him, fitting his prize into the car. And then the doors slam, the engine roars and they back out and turn around. As they move away there is no siren. I think I've heard Lovchik mention questioning. I'm sure it is lots of fuss for nothing, a mistake, but it cannot be denied, this is terrible timing.

I shake my shoulders, smooth my skirt and turn to Mother with a look of outrage.

"How do you like that?" I try.

She's got her purse in one hand, her car keys are out.

"Let's go," she says.

"Okay," I answer. "Fine. Where?"

"Aunt Mary's."

"I'd rather go and bail him out, Mom."

"Bail," she says, "*bail?*"

She gives me such a look of cold and furious surprise that I sink immediately into the front seat, lean back against the vinyl. I almost welcome the sting of the heated plastic on my back, thighs, shoulders.

Aunt Mary's dogs are rugs in the dirt, flattened by the heat of the day. Not one of them barks at us to warn her. We step over them and get no more reaction than a whine, the slow beat of a tail. Inside, we get no answers either, although we call Aunt Mary up and down the hall. We enter the kitchen and sit at the table which contains a half-ruined watermelon. By the sink, in a tin box, are cigarettes. My mother takes one and carefully puts the match to it, frowning.

"I know what," she says. "Go check the lockers."

There are two, a big freezer full of labelled meats and rental space, and another, smaller one that is just a side cooler. I notice, walking past the display counter, that the red beacon beside the outside switch of the cooler is glowing. That tells you when the light is on inside.

I pull the long metal handle toward me and the thick door swishes open. I step into the cool, spicy air. She is there, too proud to even register a hint of surprise. Aunt Mary simply nods and looks away, as though I've just gone out for a minute, although we've not seen one another in six months or more. She is relaxing, reading a scientific magazine article. I sit down on a barrel of alum labelled Zanzibar and drop my bomb with no warning. "I'm married." It doesn't matter how I tell it to Aunt Mary, because she won't be, refuses to be, surprised.

"What's he do?" she simply asks, putting aside the sheaf of paper. I thought the first thing she'd do is scold me for fooling my mother. But it's odd. For two women who have lived through boring times and disasters, how rarely one comes to the other's defence, and how often they are willing to take advantage of the other's absence. But I'm benefitting here. It seems that Aunt Mary is truly interested in Gerry. So I'm honest.

"He's something like a political activist. I mean he's been in jail and all. But not for any crime, you see, it's just because of his convictions."

She gives me a long, shrewd stare. Her skin is too tough to wrinkle, but she doesn't look young. All around us hang loops of sausages, every kind you can imagine, every colour from the purple-black of blutwurst to the pale whitish links that my mother likes best. Blocks of butter and headcheese, a can of raw milk, wrapped parcels and cured bacons are stuffed onto the shelves around us. My heart has gone still, and cool inside of me, and I can't stop talking.

"He's the kind of guy it's hard to describe, very different. People call him a free spirit, but that doesn't say it either because he's very disciplined in some ways. He learned to be neat in jail." I pause, she says nothing, so I go on. "I know it's sudden, but who likes weddings? I hate them, all that mess with the bridesmaids' gowns, getting material to match. I don't even have girlfriends, I mean, how embarrassing, right? Who would sing 'Oh Perfect Love?' Carry the ring?"

She isn't really listening.

"What's he do?" she asks again.

Maybe she won't let go of it until I discover the right answer, like a game with nouns and synonyms.

"He, well he agitates," I tell her.

"Is that some kind of factory work?"

"Not exactly, no, it's not a nine-to-five job or anything . . ."

She lets the pages fall, now, cocks her head to the side and stares at me without blinking her cold yellow eyes. She has the look of a hawk, of a person who can see into the future but won't tell you about it. She's lost business for staring at customers, but she doesn't care.

"Are you telling me that he doesn't"—here she shakes her head twice, slowly, from one side to the other without removing me from her stare—"that he doesn't have regular work?"

"Oh, what's the matter anyway," I say roughly. "I'll work. This is the nineteen seventies."

She jumps to her feet, stands over me, a stocky woman with terse features and short, thin points of gray hair. Her earrings tremble and flash, small fiery opals. Her brown plastic glasses hang crooked on a cord around her neck. I have never seen her become quite so instantaneously furious, so disturbed.

"We're going to fix that," she says.

The cooler instantly feels smaller, the sausages knock at my shoulder and the harsh light makes me blink. I am as stubborn as Aunt Mary, however, and she knows that I can go head-to-head with her.

"We're married and that's final." I manage to stamp my foot.

Aunt Mary throws an arm back, blows air through her cheeks and waves away my statement vigorously.

"You're a little girl. How old is he?"

I frown at my lap, trace the threads in my blue cotton skirt and tell her that age is irrelevant.

"Big word," she says sarcastically. "Let me ask you this. He's old enough to get a job?"

"Of course he is, what do you think. Okay, he's older than me. He's in his thirties."

"Aha, I knew it."

"Geez! So what? I mean, haven't you ever been in love, hasn't some one ever gotten you *right here?*" I smash my fist on my chest. We lock eyes, but she doesn't waste a second in feeling hurt.

"Sure, sure I've been in love. You think I haven't? I know what it feels like, you smartass. You'd be surprised. But he was no lazy sonofabitch. Now listen . . ." She stops, draws a breath, and I let her. "Here's what I mean by 'fix.' I'll teach the sausage-making trade to him, you too, and the grocery business. I've about had it anyway, and so's your mother. We'll do the same as my aunt and uncle—leave the shop to you and move to Arizona. I like this place." She looks up at the burning safety bulb, down to me again. Her face drags in the light. "But what the hell. I always wanted to travel."

I'm kind of stunned, a little flattened out, maybe ashamed of myself.

"You hate going anywhere," I say, which is true.

The door swings open and Mom comes in with us. She finds a can and balances herself, sighing at the delicious feeling of the air, absorbing from the silence the fact we have talked. She hasn't anything to add, I guess, and as the coolness hits her eyes fall shut. Aunt Mary too. I can't help it either, and my eyelids drop although my brain is alert and conscious. From the darkness, I can see us in the brilliance. The light rains down on us. We sit the way we have been sitting, on our cans of milk and flour, upright and still. Our hands are curled loosely in our laps. Our faces are blank as the gods. We could be statues in a tomb sunk into the side of a mountain. We could be dreaming the world up in our brains.

It is later and the weather has no mercy. We are drained of everything but simple thoughts. It's too hot for feelings. Driving home, we see how field after field of beets has gone into shock, and even some of the soybeans. The plants splay, limp, burned into the ground. Only the sunflowers continue to struggle upright, bristling but small.

What drove me in the first place to Gerry was the unexpected. I went to hear him talk just after I enrolled at the U of M and then I demonstrated when they came and got him off the stage. He always went so willingly, accommodating everyone. I began to visit him. I sold lunar calendars and posters to raise his bail and eventually free him. One thing led to another and one night we found ourselves alone in a Howard Johnson's where they put him up when his speech was finished. There were more beautiful women after him, he could have had his pick of Swedes or Yankton Sioux girls, who are the best-looking of all. And then there was no going back once it started, no turning, as though it were meant. We had no choice.

I have this intuition as we near the house, in the fateful quality of light, as in the turn of the day the heat continues to press and the blackness, into which the warmth usually lifts, lowers steadily. We must come to the end of something. There must be a close to this day.

As we turn into the yard we see that Gerry is sitting on the stairs. Now it is our turn to be received. I throw the car door open and stumble out before the motor even cuts. I run to him and

hold him, as my mother, pursuing the order of events, parks carefully.
Then she walks over too, holding her purse by the strap. She stands
before him and says no word but simply looks into his face as if
he's cardboard, a man behind glass who cannot see her. I think
she's rude, but then I realize that he is staring back, that they are
the same height. Their eyes are level. He puts his hand out.

"My name is Gerry."

"Gerry what?"

"Nanapush."

She nods, shifts her weight. "You're from that line, old
strain, the ones . . ." She does not finish.

"And my father," Gerry says, "was Old Man Pillager." He
has said this before but I never heard any special meaning in it.

"Kashpaws," she says, "are my branch of course. We're
probably related through my mother's brother." They do not move.
They are like two opponents from the same divided country, staring
across the border. They do not shift or blink and I see that they
are more alike than I am like either one of them, so tall, solid,
dark-haired. She could be the mother, he the son.

"Well, I guess you should come in," she offers, "you are
a distant relative after all." She looks at me. "Distant enough."

Whole swarms of mosquitoes are whining down, discovering us now, so there is no question of staying where we are. And so
we walk into the house, much hotter than outside with the gathered
heat. Instantly the sweat springs from our skin and I can think of
nothing else but cooling off. I try to force the windows higher in
their sashes, but there's no breeze anyway, nothing stirs, no air.

"Are you sure," I gasp, "about those fans?"

"Oh, they're broke," my mother says, distressed. I rarely
hear this in her voice. She switches on the lights, which makes
the room seem hotter, and we lower ourselves into the easy chairs.
Our words echo as if the walls have baked and dried hollow.

"Show me those fans," says Gerry.

My mother points toward the kitchen. "They're sitting
on the table. I've already tinkered with them. See what you can do."

334

And so he does. After a while she hoists herself and walks out back with him. Their voices close together now, absorbed, and their tools clank frantically as if they are fighting a duel. But it is a race with the bell of darkness and their waning energy. I think of ice. I get ice on the brain.

"Be right back," I call out, taking the keys from my mother's purse, "do you need anything?"

There is no answer from the kitchen but a furious sputter of metal, the clatter of nuts and bolts spilling to the floor.

I drive out to the Super Pumper, a big new gas-station complex on the edge of town where my mother most likely has never been. She doesn't know about convenience stores, has no credit cards for groceries, gas, pays only with small bills and change. She never has used an ice machine. It would grate on her that a bag of frozen water costs eighty cents, but it doesn't bother me. I take the Styrofoam cooler and I fill it for a couple dollars. I buy two six-packs of Shasta sodas and I plunge them into the uniform coins of ice. I drink two myself, on the way home, and I manage to lift the whole heavy cooler out of the trunk, carry it to the door.

The fans are whirling, beating the air.

I hear them going in the living room the minute I come in. The only light shines from the kitchen. Gerry and my mother have thrown pillows from the couch onto the living room floor, and they are sitting in the rippling currents of air. I bring the cooler in and put it near us. I have chosen all dark flavours—black cherry, grape, black raspberry, so as we drink it almost seems the darkness swirls inside us with the night air, sweet and sharp, driven by small motors.

I drag more pillows down from the other rooms upstairs. There is no question of attempting the bedrooms, the stifling beds. And so, in the dark, I hold hands with Gerry as he settles down between my mother and me. He is huge as a hill between the two of us, solid in the beating wind.

Liliana Heker

Mothers and daughters are the subject of many of Liliana Heker's stories—their creation of intimate rituals, the small tragedies of betrayal, the comforts of reconciliation. With wry humor, Heker follows their mutual learnings, victories, and failings.

"The Stolen Party" is one of Heker's finest stories. It was included in her first book, which was published in 1966 when Heker was twenty-three, only a few years before the military regime was to plunge Argentina into a bloody civil war that lasted until 1982. During those dreadful years, Heker remained in Argentina writing and editing a literary magazine. With the writer Julio Cortázar, who had lived in Paris since the forties, she maintained a lively correspondence on the subject of exile. Cortázar suggested that a writer best served the cause of justice outside an unjust regime; Heker argued that she worked best helping to bear witness from within. Her fiction is not concerned with political reportage; her latest novel, however, *El final de la historia* ("The end of history"), is a powerful account of how a corrupt system corrupts everything it touches.

THE STOLEN PARTY

liliana heker

as soon as she arrived she went straight to the kitchen to see if the monkey was there. It was. What a relief! She wouldn't have liked to admit that her mother had been right. *Monkeys at a birthday?* her mother had sneered. *Get away with you, believing any nonsense you're told!* She was cross, but not because of the monkey, the girl thought; it's just because of the party.

'I don't like you going,' she told her. 'It's a rich people's party.'

'Rich people go to Heaven too,' said the girl, who studied religion at school.

'Get away with Heaven,' said the mother. 'The problem with you, young lady, is that you like to fart higher than your ass.'

The girl didn't approve of the way her mother spoke. She was barely nine, and one of the best in her class.

'I'm going because I've been invited,' she said. 'And I've been invited because Luciana is my friend. So there.'

'Ah yes, your friend,' her mother grumbled. She paused. 'Listen, Rosaura,' she said at last. 'That one's not your friend. You know what you are to them? The maid's daughter, that's what.'

Rosaura blinked hard: she wasn't going to cry. Then she yelled: 'Shut up! You know nothing about being friends!'

Every afternoon she used to go to Luciana's house and they would both finish their homework while Rosaura's mother did the cleaning. They had their tea in the kitchen, and they told each other secrets. Rosaura loved everything in the big house, and she also loved the people who lived there.

'I'm going because it will be the most lovely party in the whole world, Luciana told me it would. There will be a magician, and he will bring a monkey and everything.'

The mother swung around to take a good look at her child. She put her hands on her hips.

'Monkeys at a birthday?' she said. 'Get away with you, believing any nonsense you're told!'

Rosaura was deeply offended. She thought it unfair of her mother to accuse other people of being liars simply because they were rich. Rosaura wanted to be rich, too, of course. If one day she managed to live in a beautiful palace, would her mother stop loving her? She felt very sad. She wanted to go to that party more than anything else in the world.

'I'll die if I don't go,' she whispered, almost without moving her lips.

She wasn't sure if she had been heard, but on the morning of the party, she discovered that her mother had starched her Christmas dress. And in the afternoon, after washing her hair, her mother rinsed it in apple vinegar so that it would be all nice and shiny. Before going out, Rosaura admired herself in the mirror, with her white dress and glossy hair, and thought she looked terribly pretty.

Señora Ines also seemed to notice. As soon as she saw her, she said, 'How lovely you look today, Rosaura.'

Rosaura gave her starched skirt a slight toss with her hands and walked into the party with a firm step. She said hello to Luciana and asked about the monkey. Luciana put on a secretive look and whispered into Rosaura's ear: 'He's in the kitchen. But don't tell anyone, because it's a surprise.'

Rosaura wanted to make sure. Carefully she entered the kitchen and there she saw it, deep in thought, inside its cage. It

looked so funny that Rosaura stood there for a while, watching it.
Later, every so often, she would slip out of the party unseen and go
and admire it. Rosaura was the only one allowed into the kitchen.
Señora Ines had said, 'You yes, but not the others, they're much
too boisterous, they might break something.' Rosaura had never
broken anything. She even managed the jug of orange juice, carrying it from the kitchen into the dining-room. She held it carefully
and didn't spill a single drop. And Señora Ines had said, 'Are you
sure you can manage a jug as big as that?' Of course she could
manage. She wasn't a butterfingers, like the others. Like that
blonde girl with the bow in her hair. As soon as she saw Rosaura,
the girl with the bow had said, 'And you? Who are you?'

'I'm a friend of Luciana,' said Rosaura.

'No,' said the girl with the bow, 'You are not a friend of
Luciana because I'm her cousin, and I know all her friends. And I
don't know you.'

'So what,' said Rosaura. 'I come here every afternoon
with my mother, and we do our homework together.'

'You and your mother do your homework together?'
asked the girl, laughing.

'I and Luciana do our homework together,' said Rosaura,
very seriously.

The girl with the bow shrugged her shoulders.

'That's not being friends,' she said. 'Do you go to school
together?'

'No.'

'So where do you know her from?' said the girl, getting
impatient.

Rosaura remembered her mother's words perfectly. She
took a deep breath.

'I'm the daughter of the employee,' she said.

Her mother had said very clearly: 'If someone asks, you
say you're the daughter of the employee; that's all.' She also told
her to add: 'And proud of it.' But Rosaura thought that never in
her life would she dare say something of the sort.

'What employee?' said the girl with the bow. 'Employee in a shop?'

'No,' said Rosaura angrily. 'My mother doesn't sell anything in any shop, so there.'

'So how come she's an employee?' said the girl with the bow.

Just then Señora Ines arrived saying *shh shh,* and asked Rosaura if she wouldn't mind helping serve the hot-dogs, as she knew the house so much better than the others.

'See?' said Rosaura to the girl with the bow, and when no one was looking she kicked her in the shin.

Apart from the girl with the bow, all the others were delightful. The one she liked best was Luciana, with her golden birthday crown; and then the boys. Rosaura won the sack race, and nobody managed to catch her when they played tag. When they split into two teams to play charades, all the boys wanted her for their side. Rosaura felt she had never been so happy in all her life.

But the best was still to come. The best came after Luciana blew out the candles. First the cake. Señora Ines had asked her to help pass the cake around, and Rosaura had enjoyed the task immensely, because everyone called out to her, shouting 'Me, me!' Rosaura remembered a story in which there was a queen who had the power of life or death over her subjects. She had always loved that, having the power of life or death. To Luciana and the boys she gave the largest pieces, and to the girl with the bow she gave a slice so thin one could see through it.

After the cake came the magician, tall and bony, with a fine red cape. A true magician, he could untie handkerchiefs by blowing on them and make a chain with links that had no openings. He could guess what cards were pulled out from a pack, and the monkey was his assistant. He called the monkey 'partner.' 'Let's see here, partner,' he would say. 'Turn over a card.' And, 'Don't run away, partner. Time to work now.'

The final trick was wonderful. One of the children had to hold the monkey in his arms, and the magician said he would make him disappear.

'What, the boy?' they all shouted.

'No, the monkey!' shouted back the magician.

Rosaura thought that this was truly the most amusing party in the whole world.

The magician asked a small fat boy to come and help, but the small fat boy got frightened almost at once and dropped the monkey on the floor. The magician picked him up carefully, whispered something in his ear, and the monkey nodded almost as if he understood.

'You mustn't be so unmanly, my friend,' the magician said to the fat boy.

The magician turned around as if to look for spies.

'A sissy,' said the magician. 'Go sit down.'

Then he stared at all the faces, one by one. Rosaura felt her heart tremble.

'You, with the Spanish eyes,' said the magician. And everyone saw that he was pointing at her.

She wasn't afraid. Neither holding the monkey, nor when the magician made him vanish; not even when, at the end, the magician flung his red cape over Rosaura's head and uttered a few magic words . . . and the monkey reappeared, chattering happily, in her arms. The children clapped furiously. And before Rosaura returned to her seat, the magician said, 'Thank you very much, my little countess.'

She was so pleased with the compliment that a while later, when her mother came to fetch her, that was the first thing she told her.

'I helped the magician and he said to me, "Thank you very much, my little countess."'

It was strange because up to then Rosaura had thought that she was angry with her mother. All along Rosaura had imagined that she would say to her, 'See that the monkey wasn't a lie?' But instead she was so thrilled that she told her mother all about the wonderful magician.

Her mother tapped her on the head and said: 'So now we're a countess!'

But one could see that she was beaming.

And now they both stood in the entrance, because a moment ago Señora Ines, smiling, had said, 'Please wait here a second.'

Her mother suddenly seemed worried.

'What is it?' she asked Rosaura.

'What is what?' said Rosaura. 'It's nothing; she just wants to get the presents for those who are leaving, see?'

She pointed at the fat boy and at a girl with pigtails who were also waiting there, next to their mothers. And she explained about the presents. She knew, because she had been watching those who left before her. When one of the girls was about to leave, Señora Ines would give her a bracelet. When a boy left, Señora Ines gave him a yo-yo. Rosaura preferred the yo-yo because it sparkled, but she didn't mention that to her mother. Her mother might have said: 'So why don't you ask for one, you blockhead?' That's what her mother was like. Rosaura didn't feel like explaining that she'd be horribly ashamed to be the odd one out. Instead she said, 'I was the best-behaved at the party.'

And she said no more because Señora Ines came out into the hall with two bags, one pink and one blue.

First she went up to the fat boy, gave him a yo-yo out of the blue bag, and the fat boy left with his mother. Then she went up to the girl and gave her a bracelet out of the pink bag, and the girl with the pigtails left as well.

Finally she came up to Rosaura and her mother. She had a big smile on her face; Rosaura liked that. Señora Ines looked down at her, looked up at her mother, then said something that made Rosaura proud.

'What a marvellous daughter you have, Herminia.'

For an instant, Rosaura thought that she'd give her two presents: the bracelet and the yo-yo. Señora Ines bent down as if about to look for something. Rosaura leaned forward, stretching out her arm. But she never completed the movement.

Señora Ines didn't look in the pink bag. Nor did she look in the blue bag. Instead she rummaged in her purse. In her hand appeared two bills.

'You really and truly earned this,' she said handing them over. 'Thank you for all your help, my pet.'

Rosaura felt her arms stiffen, stick close to her body, and then she noticed her mother's hand on her shoulder. Instinctively she pressed herself against her mother's body. That was all. Except her eyes. Rosaura's eyes had a cold, clear look that fixed itself on Señora Ines' face.

Señora Ines, motionless, stood there with her hand outstretched. As if she didn't dare draw it back. As if the slightest change might shatter an infinitely delicate balance.

❁

Bonnie Burnard

In her seminal 1972 essay *Survival,* Margaret Atwood remarked, "If in England the family is a mansion you live in, and if in America it's a skin you shed, then in Canada it's a trap in which you're caught." For Bonnie Burnard, the escape from the trap comes through learning the lessons of those who have resided in it longer than you have. Her books—two slim collections—record the lives of women in the different stages of such learning. Small girls, sisters, young and old mothers, daughters leaving and returning, lovers and the company of friends—all in some way "women of influence"—attempt different techniques of survival through their apprenticeships; not all succeed.

It may be, as the French psychologist Elizabeth Badinter has suggested, that in our society men define themselves through opposition to their mother, to all women, to their father, and to other men, while a woman has more scope for an alliance with the image of her own mother. For Bonnie Burnard, it is the mother's image that offers the teaching, though the lesson comes at the end, as the mother lies on her death bed; not comforting, but "full of grace."

WOMEN OF INFLUENCE

bonnie burnard

We had a fairly good night. My mother's dying is still following its own steady pace but there was pleasure in being together, pleasure even in silence. Last week, when she acknowledged the approach of her death, simply by saying that she didn't particularly want to be alone, my brothers and I arranged to stay with her in the hospital room, day and night. We take shifts and we cooperate with the staff by keeping out of the way and by accepting, or pretending to accept, their professional judgement. It's good that we are all here now, gathered from our separate parts of the country. The four of us are stronger than any hospital administration. We won't leave her.

She's getting notes and letters with her greeting cards; her friends and relatives offer specific, cherished memories. Odd things. Last night my aunt's letter, written in my uncle's hand, brought full colour scenes to her mind; I could see it in her face as she listened to me reading it. Some of the scenes included me, as a child. Many of them gave off-handed praise for my mother's character, which is her due. As I drive across the city to my aunt's hospital, the red sun is just rising. I notice kitchen lights coming on. There have been no other cars, only a snow-plough, gathering the filthy February build up.

My mother's ward is not one of the new ones wherein family responsibility is acknowledged; many of the other patients, who are also dying, see no-one but uniformed staff from one Sunday to the next. Sunday's a big day, containing, as only Sunday could, a compression of anger and guilt and grief and compassion, as if the visitors cannot deny the day its rights. Through the week there are no flower deliveries; night tables hold Bibles and Testaments and discarded reading glasses and pictures of children, some dated, some very recent. The day nurses do not come bustling down the hall with news of the world. The world doesn't exist. Each day is twenty-four hours of bits of sleep and bits of talk and bits of pain.

The cries and moans come at any time though they are harder to ignore in the night. There is no place to look in the night for distraction, no bright roof-tops in the window. Albert, down the hall, is the best we can hope for at night; of all his loud contributions, we favour the scotch-enema story. Before he was admitted, his wife had had to go to an all-night drugstore for an enema kit, her last valiant effort. It cost her nineteen dollars. He said if he'd known, he would have sent her out for scotch. This in a bellowing voice to the young night nurse and down the hall to us. Maybe my mother's last good laugh. She's made me repeat it twice.

There is no spiritual unease in my mother's room and I am immensely grateful. She has always had at her disposal the God she first decided she believed in. I can lift her and turn her, can feed her as patiently as I have fed my babies. I can reach my arms through the steel bars of her bed to rub her small aching legs. I can jump with her to any time she remembers, lying when I have to, but I can do no more. I could not possibly pray.

There is a staffroom down the hall from my mother's and the nurses encourage me to have a cup of tea while they are with her, changing the catheter or checking the intravenous or shooting the pain-killer into her bruised hip. It's easy to tell when the pain is edging back now; I can get her a shot of codeine and have it working before the grimace comes to her face. One of the nurses told us that we are alike, my mother and I, in the face. I squared my shoulders and stuck my nose into the air. My mother lit up a little, not at my acceptance of the flattery, as the nurse might have thought; we are not good-looking women. She brightened at my urge to be an ass, even at her deathbed. It was a little joke.

The morning is coming brighter now. There are cars at intersections, waiting alone against red lights. I can see the silhouette of the other hospital ahead, looming confidently over the wartime houses which surround it. The sun looks strangely red for winter.

There is an old picture with my aunt's letter. They stand together; my mother, twelve or thirteen in a modest dark dress, holds the hand of the brilliantly beautiful younger sister. I have seen the picture before and I've always imagined that my mother had set my aunt's golden ringlets patiently in preparation for the day of visiting and picture-taking. Her own hair is short and dark, a bob, I think. Her face speaks to the camera with the recent acceptance of her fate as a woman: I know I'm plain, it says, but I'm good, just the same. In her letter my aunt speaks of their young sisterhood on the farm, of harvesting crews and eager young men, as if the men were eager for both of them. In the final paragraph, she comes close to what she wants to say: "You always took such care with my clothes and hair. You taught me to be proud of myself."

I wonder if she's pretty in her hospital bed. She is six years younger than my mother, the fact of their ages is mentioned a lot now, but her prognosis is the same.

She had an early influence on me, the result of my frequent summer stays with her on the farm. My parents took motor trips in the summer, to the coast or to Lake Louise and my aunt always asked if she could have me. I went eagerly because I thought I should.

She would have been younger then than I am now. She was tall and forceful, square-shouldered, competent even in bone structure. She taught school; troublesome kids were saved by a year of her care. The men loved her; she was funny and often

347

quoted, and always quoting others, sharing absurdities and telling stories which made other people look good and worth knowing. If things got too settled at a family gathering she would start something or encourage someone else to. "Ray," she'd say. "Tell the kids about Stew Gault and that mare." If she was met with reticence she would start the story herself, with just a few words, tempting the one whose story it was until he could no longer resist and we'd have it. She was a singer of first bars, reminding the singers, setting them off. She wore bright wool dresses with just the right amount of jewellery and sometimes slacks, creased like a man's, like Lauren Bacall's. She wore make-up daily, flaunting dark eyes and bright lips.

She talked to me when I stayed with her and smiled a lot. She had ideas for my hair, would comb through the curly mess over and over and try with pins and ribbons to expose what she said could be a pretty little face. She nagged me to shed the ten extra pounds I carried, fixed me lots of fruit. But I ran whenever I could to my uncle in the fields, carrying cold water and matrimonial squares wrapped carefully in waxed paper. And I cruised the ditches with the Labs, their muscled black bodies eager to help me find whatever it was I hunted. I remember her disappointed face at the table when I asked my uncle for more potatoes and he scooped whatever was left evenly between his plate and mine. She didn't yet have her own daughter.

My mother has been a quieter kind of woman, short and solid, raising her kids in town, away from the dirt and strain of the farm. She did not finish high school, she stayed on the farm to help with the younger half of the family until she married the serious young man one stile away. I do not remember her ever telling a story. She has always been audience, pure audience. The storytellers, her brothers and friends, measured their skill on her face, working toward the slow sure smile. A very few times, when things were really rolling, a laugh would burst aloud from her and she'd say, "I'd forgotten. Oh, I'd forgotten." When she was made to smile it seemed she had been given something that would stay with her.

She refinished furniture: chairs and trunks and beds. Men from Toronto sniffed her out, offered what she called big prices for the pieces she had stashed all over the basement but she just laughed and gave them coffee and pie, then a motherly pat as she put them out the door. She designed quilts and worked on them in the winter evenings as she watched her hockey games, cheered her Frenchmen down the ice. I have a dozen of her quilts and they are beautiful; my daughters have their own, which I am not to use. She served the people she loved what they craved: hickory nuts in the tarts for John, a good whitefish dinner for Gordon, garden corn for Emily's kids. In her fully modern town kitchen she had bins built for sugar and flour.

In a family crisis, and I mean the big family here, not just us, she would gather people to talk, to see if something couldn't be done. She didn't sit at the table with them, she stood at the counter buttering raisin bread or slicing cake and she didn't offer suggestions, as my aunt did, but it was her table.

When my first university calendar arrived she said, "None of it will do you any harm." The only suggestion I remember, other than the long ago wash your hair kind of suggestion, was when my own first child was born. In a small correct script, on blue scented paper, "Your place is at home with your baby. Don't rush away." This when feminism was already old news. I have followed her advice. My degree is an obscure memory and my kids are solid, though not exceptional in any way. She would think me foolish if I expected them to be.

I blamed her for a time, wished she had come down hard on me, made me into something extreme and wonderful, as my aunt would have. A girl whose mother thinks hair should be nothing more than clean is at a tremendous disadvantage.

The lot here is half empty, parking will not be a problem. I'll sit for a minute and finish my cigarette; there will be oxygen in this room too.

When my brother came into the room this morning, my

mother was still holding my aunt's letter, staring carefully at her own thoughts. She didn't acknowledge him. He had taken his boots off at the door and padded around to the other side of the bed, pulling a chair up close to ask what she wanted for breakfast. He always takes the early morning shift and has developed a system to get her what she thinks she might try to eat. The trolley in the hall holds the trays and he lifts each lid silently, switching things as necessary to make her a perfect breakfast. She rarely eats more than half a bite and that only to please him but it's the way their time begins. He is telling her that he would commit grand larceny on her behalf as he sneaks around the grey hospital hallway in his socks.

My mother gave him her just-a-minute face and spoke to me. "I've wasted a lot of time believing that her beautiful face made mine uglier. Now I'm thinking what a pleasure it was to have her all those years. I should have taken her just the way I took a sunset, or a lace tablecloth."

My brother busied himself by rolling up his sleeves, wanting no explanation.

My mother cleared her throat. "Freshen yourself a little," she said. "You look tired."

I walked to the spotless old bathroom and saw in the mirror a tired middle-aged face that did indeed need freshening. I scrubbed my face hard. My brother came in with my purse. "Mom says your make-up is likely in here," he said, shrugging his shoulders. There was make-up in it all right, enough to transform me, blue and red and pink and brown, each in its respective little case, each with its respective little job. I didn't stop at daytime subtlety, I applied and reapplied. I brushed my hair a hundred strokes, watching it snap back as always to disorder. When I presented myself at my mother's bedside, she grinned. Her teeth were dark and her mouth sore from the dryness. "From the day you were born," she said, "I've loved your hair best." She hesitated, then "I'll see you tonight." I kissed her forehead, leaving a bright red lip print. My brother sat stirring her orange juice with a straw.

The corridors in this hospital are wider, brighter. The

rugs continue beyond the first floor. I see my uncle sitting alone at the end of a long hall, in front of a window. I approach him, careful not to look into the rooms I am passing. A nurse stops to ask if she can help and I say no. My uncle hasn't heard me so I sit down close to him, wishing I could offer cold water and matrimonial squares, wishing he was young and brown. He looks up with bleary eyes and smiles.

"How is your mother this morning?" he asks. I think this is too much for one man.

"Dan's with her," I tell him. "She's talking a bit."

He shakes his head. It is too much. He clears his throat. "Jo-Anne is coming from Ottawa. She left last night, driving."

Jo-Anne is the daughter who was proper raw material. Even when half-grown she was sociable and elegant, capable. She studied dance at the conservatory in Toronto, was driven hundreds of miles for her lessons. My mother has a picture of her at home; she sits in front of a fire at a cottage in a blue angora sweater, her hand caught in the act of lifting her pale blonde hair away from her face. She studied in France where she met and married a French Canadian composer. I suspect she has magnificent children. I can see that my uncle has been following her in his mind all night, knows within a half-hour what her safe arrival time should be.

"Your aunt has had a bit to eat," he says. "If she's sleeping, you just nudge her a little, she'll want to see you."

I stand up and move into the room. My aunt lies flat out, stiff. Her eyes are closed. Her pain has been more sudden and mysterious than my mother's; it's a different kind of thing. She is controlling herself with the force of her will and I hesitate to touch her. She has not wasted away to seventy pounds as my mother has; she still looks beautiful and almost healthy. A cold compress rests on her forehead. One of her hands is flat on her stomach and the other clutches the sheet. I reach for the hand that isn't clutching. She opens her eyes, perhaps expecting her daughter. When she sees it's me she says my name and closes her hand over mine, sliding them together up to her chest.

"How is your mother?" she asks.

"She's comfortable," I answer, angry. "Can't they give you something?"

She ignores my question. "Is she afraid?"

"I don't think so," I tell her.

"Good," she says, moving her head, with a slow effort, toward me. "Did you read her my letter? I said at the top that someone was to read it to her."

"Yes I did," I tell her. "Twice. She remembers it all."

"Your mother was wonderful to me," she says. "I've been such a vain brat, all my life. And all that time I didn't know she was plain. I really didn't. When you look at her you don't see a face, you see someone who loves you, no matter what."

Her grip becomes a little tighter, is, I think, as tight as she can make it. She leaves me to go back to fighting the pain.

I realize I have not been asked to bring my mother's forgiveness here. Or have I? Is my mother counting on me to pass it on or to live with it? I don't want her compromised. I don't want her apologizing for an attitude she was entitled to. But she has recanted, to herself, to the air in her hospital room, to me. I have to say the words here, in this room, whether or not I want to.

"She said you gave pleasure the way a sunset does, or a lace tablecloth."

For an instant the tension on my aunt's face relaxes and I want her to sit up and hold me. I think how proud I will be if this face reappears to me in a grandchild. I must carry the gene, somewhere; I hope I have passed it on unharmed.

I hear someone come into the room. Jo-Anne moves around the bed to the other side and she is lovely. I slip my hand out from under my aunt's to make room for hers. My aunt opens her eyes at the movement of hands and sees us both.

"Tell your mother that I think we've done a bang-up job, both of us. Tell her I'll see her in the line-up for rewards." This is not the mockery it would have been another time.

I kiss her lightly on the cheek. My lips leave a faint red print so I take a tissue from the box on her night table, sure she will not want to be left smudged. "Don't touch that," she says.

In a matter of days these two women will be gone; I can already see the world without them. Beyond my cousin's head, the red sun is fully risen now, a gaudy disrespectful whore of a sun, shining down on children in their beds, warming them.

I can feel in the palms of my hands what passed from sister to sister when they posed for the picture on that shared summer day. It is not unlike the grace I have carried from one to the other this dismal winter morning. And still there is no comfort. There is only the sun, and the steady wet snow.

Good women, full of grace. Stay with me.

❁

ACKNOWLEDGEMENTS

Allison, Dorothy, "Mama," from *Trash,* published by Firebrand Books, Ithaca, New York. Copyright © 1988 by Dorothy Allison.

Ai Bei, "Green Earth Mother," from *Red Ivy, Green Earth Mother,* translated by Howard Goldblatt, published by Gibbs Smith Publishing. Translation copyright © 1990 by Howard Goldblatt.

Burnard, Bonnie, "Women of Influence," from *Women of Influence: Stories,* published by Coteau Books. Copyright © 1988 by Bonnie Burnard. Reprinted by permission of Westwood Creative Artists Ltd.

Carter, Angela, "Ashputtle: or, the Mother's Ghost," from *Burning Your Boats,* published by Chatto & Windus/Vintage. Copyright © 1995 by the Estate of Angela Carter. Reproduced by permission of Rogers, Coleridge & White Ltd, 20 Powis Mews, London W11 1JN.

du Maurier, Daphne, "Split Second," from *Kiss Me Again Stranger.* Copyright © 1952 by Daphne du Maurier. Used by permission of Doubleday, a division of Bantam Doubleday Dell Publishing Group, Inc. (U.S. only) and Curtis Brown Ltd. (Canada only).

Erdrich, Louise, "A Wedge of Shade," from *Louder than Words,* edited by William Shore, 1989. Copyright © 1989 by Louise Erdrich. Used by permission of Rembar & Curtis.

Frame, Janet, "The Pictures" from *The Lagoon and Other Stories.* Copyright © 1945 by Janet Frame. Used by permission of Brandt and Brandt Literary Agents, Inc.

Heker, Liliana, "The Stolen Party," from *The Stolen Party and Other Stories,* translated by Alberto Manguel. Published by Coach House Press. Copyright © 1982 by Liliana Heker. Translation copyright © 1985 by Alberto Manguel. Reprinted by permission of Westwood Creative Artists Ltd.

Jolley, Elizabeth, "The Last Crop," from *Woman in a Lampshade,* published by Penguin Australia. Copyright © 1983 by Elizabeth Jolley. Reprinted with permission of Goodman Associates.

McCullers, Carson, "Breath from the Sky," from *The Mortgaged Heart.* Copyright © 1940, 1941, 1942, 1945, 1949, 1953, 1956, 1959, 1963, 1967, 1971 by Floria V. Lasky, Executrix of the Estate of Carson McCullers. Reprinted by permission of Houghton Mifflin Co. All rights reserved.

Meinkema, Hannes, "My Mother's Name," translated by James Brockway, from *Real Life by Writers from Nine Countries.* Copyright © 1980 by Elsevier Nederland B.V., Amsterdam/Brussels. Translation copyright © 1981 by Doubleday, a division of Bantam Doubleday Dell Publishing Group, Inc. Used by permission of Doubleday, a division of Bantam Doubleday Dell Publishing Group, Inc.

Ortese, Anna Maria, "A Pair of Glasses," translated by Kathrine Jason. Copyright © 1987 by Anna Maria Ortese. Translation copyright © 1990 by Kathrine Jason.

Purdy, James, "Mrs. Benson," from *63: Dream Palace. Selected Stories 1956–1987,* published by Black Sparrow Press, Santa Rosa. Copyright © 1991 by James Purdy. Reprinted by permission of the author.

Tsushima, Yūko, "The Silent Traders," from *The Shooting Gallery,* translated by Geraldine Harcourt, Pantheon Books, 1988.

Trevor, William, "Her Mother's Daughter," from *The Collected Stories.* Reprinted by permission of the Peters Fraser & Dunlop Group Ltd.

AUTHOR BIOGRAPHIES

Dorothy Allison (USA, b. 1949) Allison has published one novel, *Bastard Out of Carolina* (1992), one collection of short fiction, *Trash* (1988), one volume of poetry, *The Women Who Hate Me* (1983), one book of essays, *Skin* (1993), and one memoir, *Two or Three Things I Know for Sure* (1995).

Ai Bei (China, b. 1949) Only one of Ai Bei's books is available in English, a collection of four short pieces translated by Harold Goldblatt, *Red Ivy, Green Earth Mother* (1990).

Bonnie Burnard (Canada) Burnard has published only two collections of short stories, *Women of Influence* (1988) and *Casino and Other Stories* (1994).

Angela Carter (England, 1940–1992) A novelist, essayist, and short-story writer, Carter's books include *Shadow Dance* (1966), *The Magic Toyshop* (1967), *Several Perceptions* (1969), *The Passion of the New Eve* (1977), *The Bloody Chamber* (1979), *The Sadeian Woman: An Exercise in Cultural History* (1979), and *Wise Children* (1991).

Daphne du Maurier (England, 1907–1989) Among du Maurier's more famous novels are *Jamaica Inn* (1936), *Rebecca* (1938), and *My Cousin Rachel* (1951). She also published several collections of short stories and memoirs.

Sara Jeannette Duncan (Canada, 1861–1922) Duncan wrote over twenty novels, of which the best known are *An American Girl in London* (1891), *The Imperialist* (1904), and *Cousin Cinderella: A Canadian Girl in London* (1908).

Louise Erdrich (USA, b. 1954) Among Erdrich's books are *Love Medicine* (1984), *The Beet Queen* (1986), *Tracks* (1988), *Baptism of Desire* (1989), and *The Bingo Palace* (1994). With her husband, Michael Dorris, she wrote *The Crown of Columbus* (1991) and *Route Two* (1991).

Janet Frame (New Zealand, b. 1924) Frame has written many novels, including *Owls Do Cry* (1957), *Faces in the Water* (1961), *The Edge of the Alphabet* (1962), *Scented Gardens for the Blind* (1963), *The Rainbirds* (1968), and *Intensive Care* (1970). Her autobiographical books include *To the Island* (1982) and *An Angel at My Table* (1984).

Liliana Heker (Argentina, b. 1943) Heker is the author of three collections of short stories and three novels: *Un resplandor que se apagó en el mundo* (1977), *Zona de clivaje* (1988), and *El fin de la historia* (1994). A selection of her short fiction was published in English under the title *The Stolen Party and Other Stories* (1996).

Elizabeth Jolley (England/Australia b. 1923) Jolley is the author of the novels *Palomino* (1980), *Mr. Scobie's Riddle* (1982), *Miss Peabody's Inheritance* (1983), and of the volumes of short stories *Five Acre Virgin* (1976), *The Travelling Entertainer* (1979), and *Woman in a Lampshade* (1983).

Katherine Mansfield (New Zealand, 1888–1923) Mansfield's brilliant short stories were collected in *In a German Pension* (1911), *Bliss and Other Stories* (1919), *The Garden Party and Other Stories* (1920), and two posthumous collections, *Something Childish and Other Stories* (1924) and *A Fairy Story* (1932).

Carson McCullers (USA, 1917–1967) McCullers is the author of five novels: *The Heart Is a Lonely Hunter* (1940), *Reflections in a Golden Eye* (1941), *The Ballad of the Sad Café* (1951), *The Member of the Wedding* (1946), and *Clock without Hands* (1961). *The Mortgaged Heart* (1971) is a posthumous collection of short stories.

Hannes Meinkema (Holland, b. 1943) Meinkema's novels include *The Mooneater* (1974), *And Then There'll Be Coffee* (1976), and *The Inner Egg* (1979). Her short stories have been collected in *Summer Is a Long Time in Coming* (1975), *The Green Widow and Other Stories* (1977), and *My Mother's Name* (1980).

Frances Newman (USA, 1883–1928) Newman was the author of two novels, *The Hard-Boiled Virgin* (1926) and *Dead Lovers Are Faithful Lovers* (1928). Her short stories have never been collected.

Anna Maria Ortese (Italy, b. 1915) Ortese's books include *L'iguana* (1986), *In sonno e in veglia* (1987), *Il cardillo addolorato* (1993), *Il mare non bagna Napoli* (1994), *Alonso e i visionari* (1996), and *Corpo celeste* (1997). *The Iguana* and *The Lament of the Linnet* have been translated into English.

Dorothy Parker (USA, 1893–1967) A poet, short-story writer, and critic, Parker was one of the stars of *The New Yorker* magazine. Her books of poems include *Enough Rope* (1926), *Sunset Gun* (1928), and *Death and Taxes* (1931). Her collections of short fiction are *Laments for the Living* (1930) and *After Such Pleasure* (1933).

James Purdy (USA, b. 1923) Purdy's first published book was *Color of Darkness* (1957). His novels include *Malcolm* (1959), *The Nephew* (1960), *Cabot Wright Begins* (1964), *Eustace Chisholm and the Works* (1967), and *In the Hollow of His Hand* (1986). He is the author of several plays and collections of short stories.

William Trevor (Ireland, b. 1928) Trevor's novels include *The Old Boys* (1964), *Mrs. Eckdorf in O'Neill's Hotel* (1969), *Elizabeth Alone* (1973), *The Children of Dynmouth* (1976), *Fools of Fortune* (1983), and *Felicia's Journey* (1994). His short stories were collected in one volume in 1983.

Yūko Tsushima (Japan, b. 1947) Twelve collections of Tsushima's short stories have been published, of which only one, *The Shooting Gallery* (1988), is available in English.

Edith Wharton (USA, 1862–1937). Among Wharton's best-known novels are *The House of Mirth* (1905), *Ethan Frome* (1911), *The Reef* (1912), *The Custom of the Country* (1913), *The Age of Innocence* (1920), and *The World Over* (1936). Her autobiography was published in 1934 under the title *A Backward Glance*.